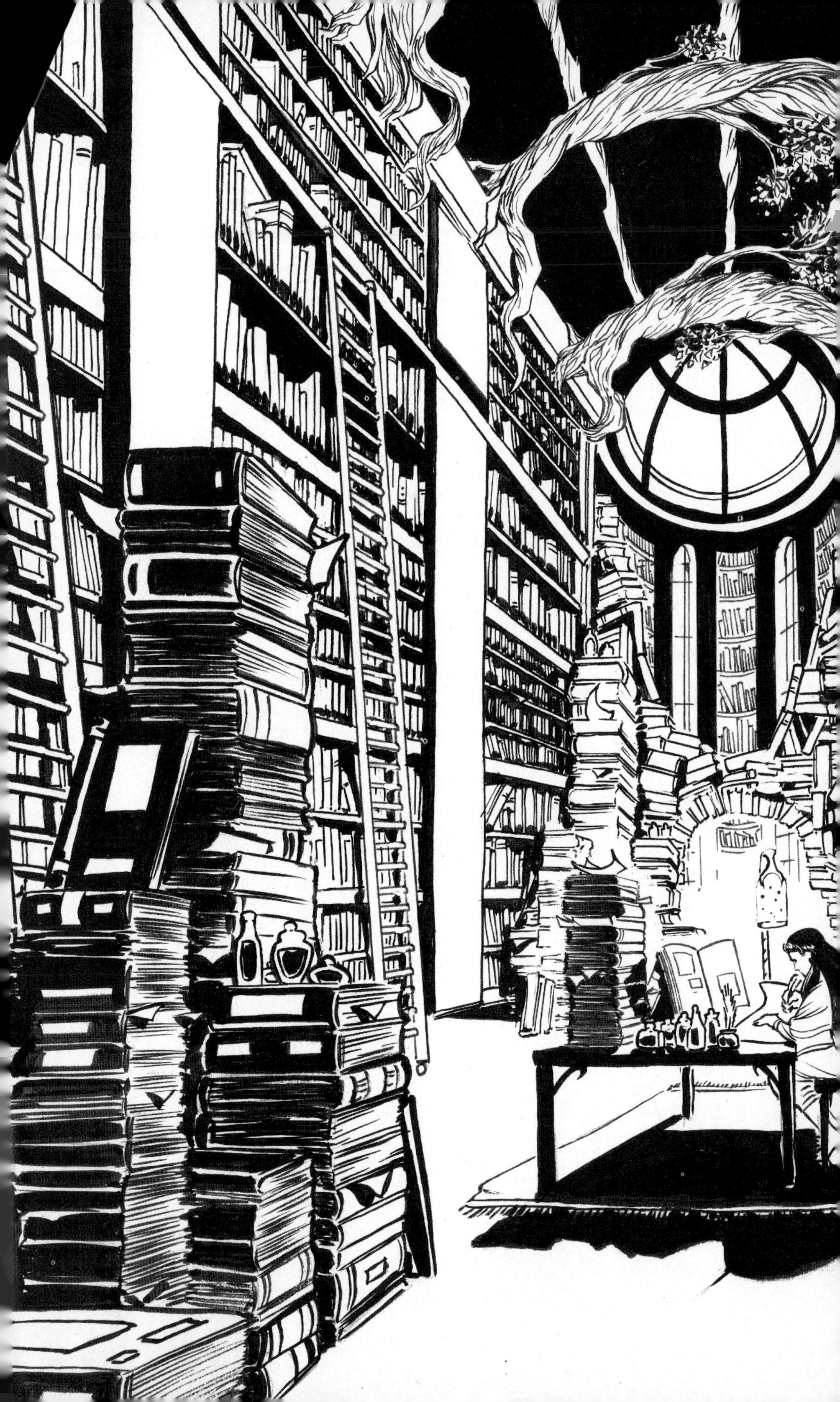

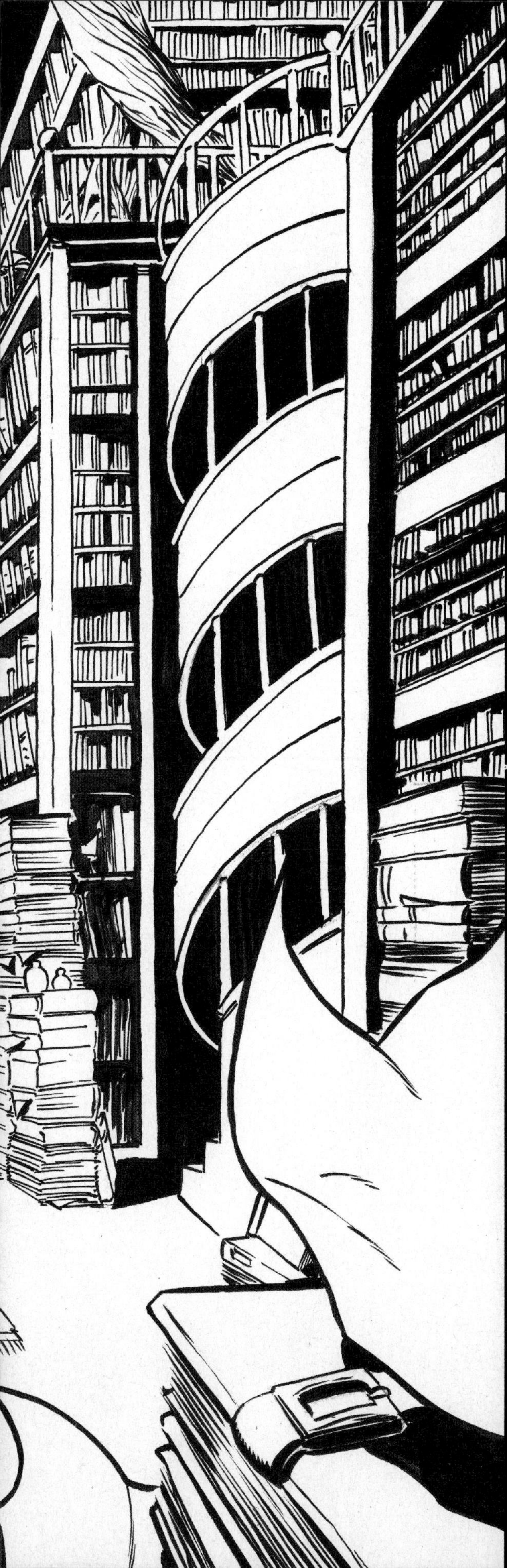

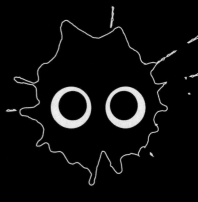

Inkblot.

Created By

Emma Kubert

&

Rusty Gladd

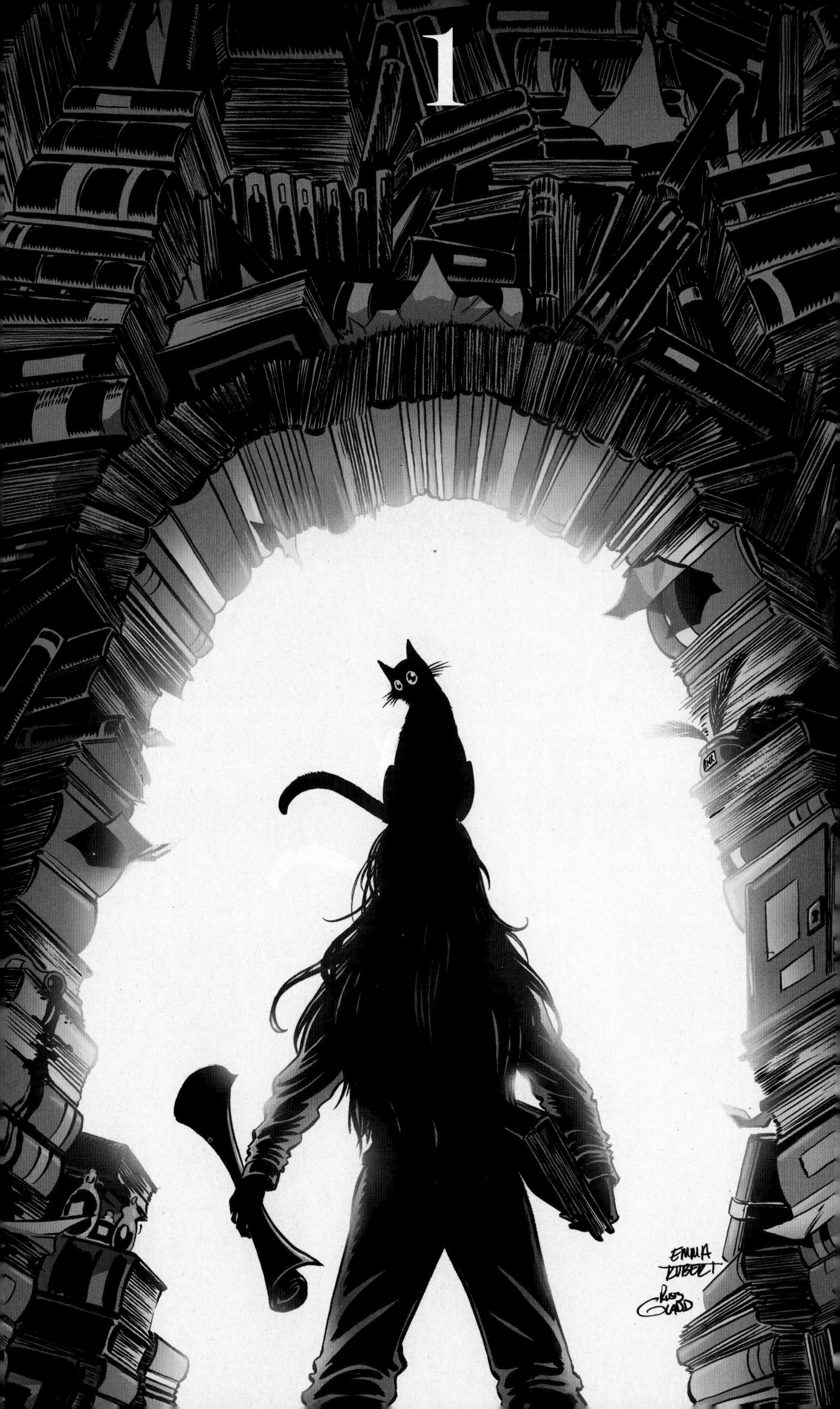
1

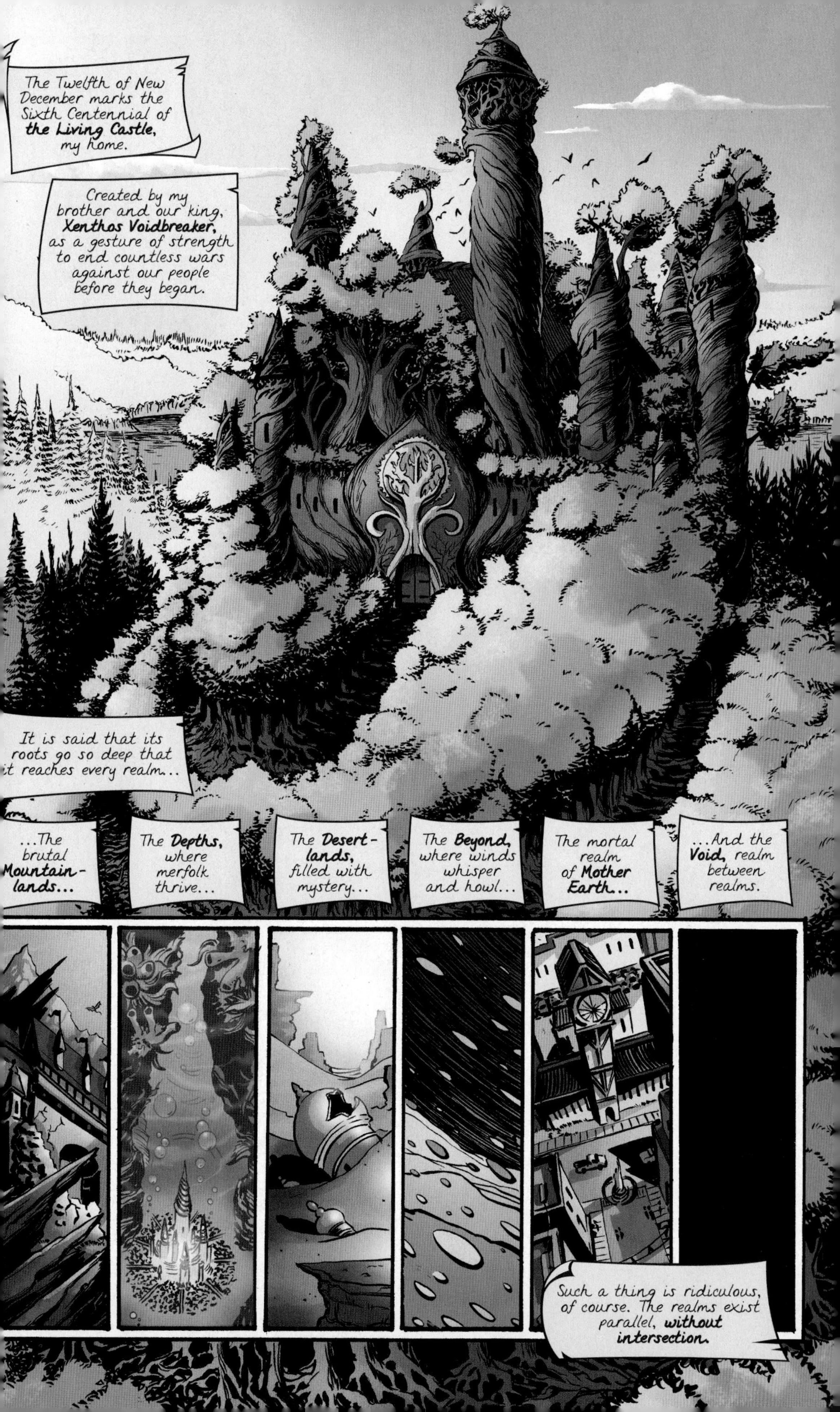
The Twelfth of New December marks the Sixth Centennial of **the Living Castle,** my home.
Created by my brother and our king, **Xenthos Voidbreaker,** as a gesture of strength to end countless wars against our people before they began.
It is said that its roots go so deep that it reaches every realm...
...The brutal **Mountain-lands...**
The **Depths,** where merfolk thrive...
The **Desert-lands,** filled with mystery...
The **Beyond,** where winds whisper and howl...
The mortal realm of **Mother Earth...**
...And the **Void,** realm between realms.
Such a thing is ridiculous, of course. The realms exist parallel, **without intersection.**

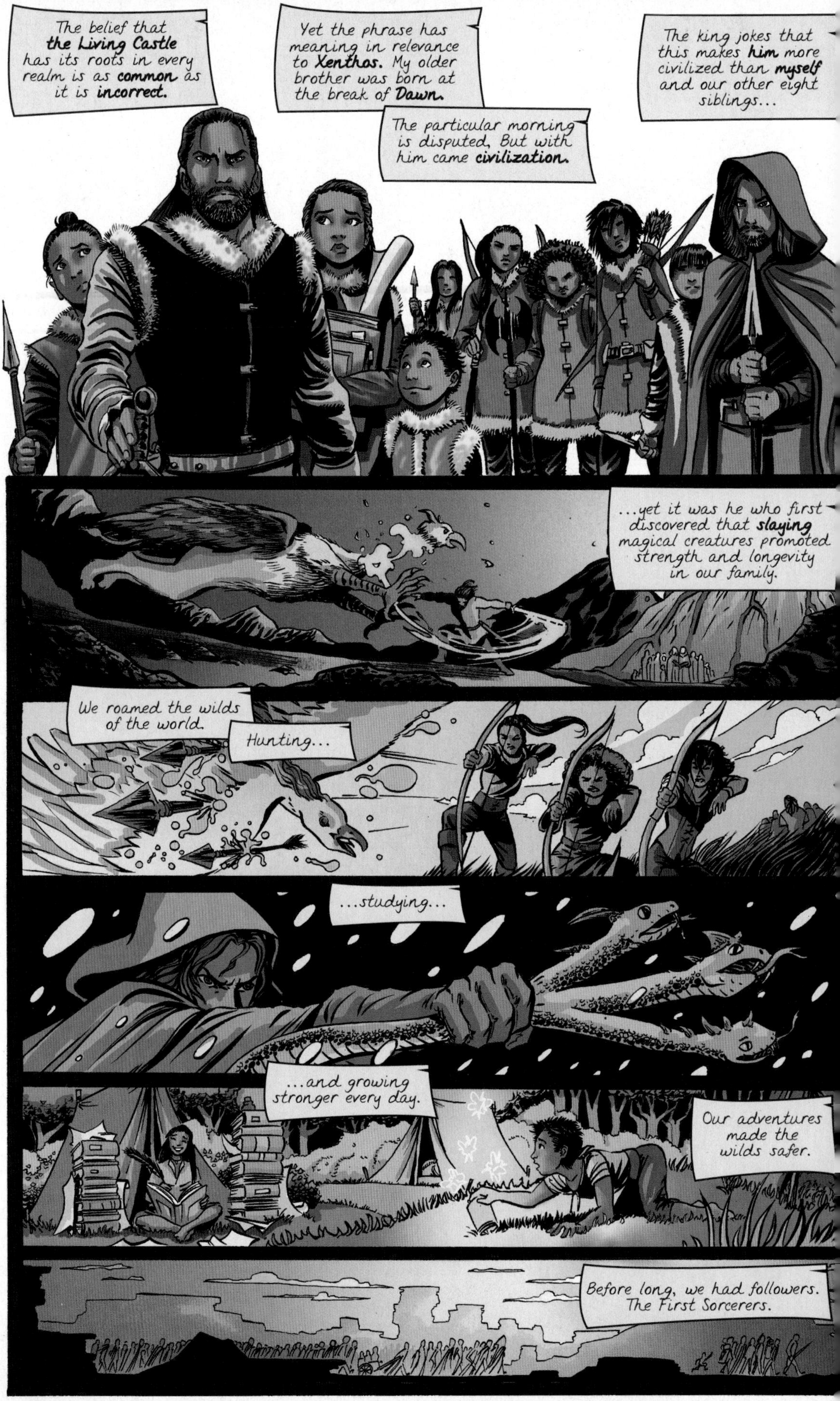
The belief that the Living Castle has its roots in every realm is as common as it is incorrect.
Yet the phrase has meaning in relevance to Xenthos. My older brother was born at the break of Dawn.
The particular morning is disputed, But with him came civilization.
The king jokes that this makes him more civilized than myself and our other eight siblings...
...yet it was he who first discovered that slaying magical creatures promoted strength and longevity in our family.
We roamed the wilds of the world.
Hunting...
...studying...
...and growing stronger every day.
Our adventures made the wilds safer.
Before long, we had followers. The First Sorcerers.

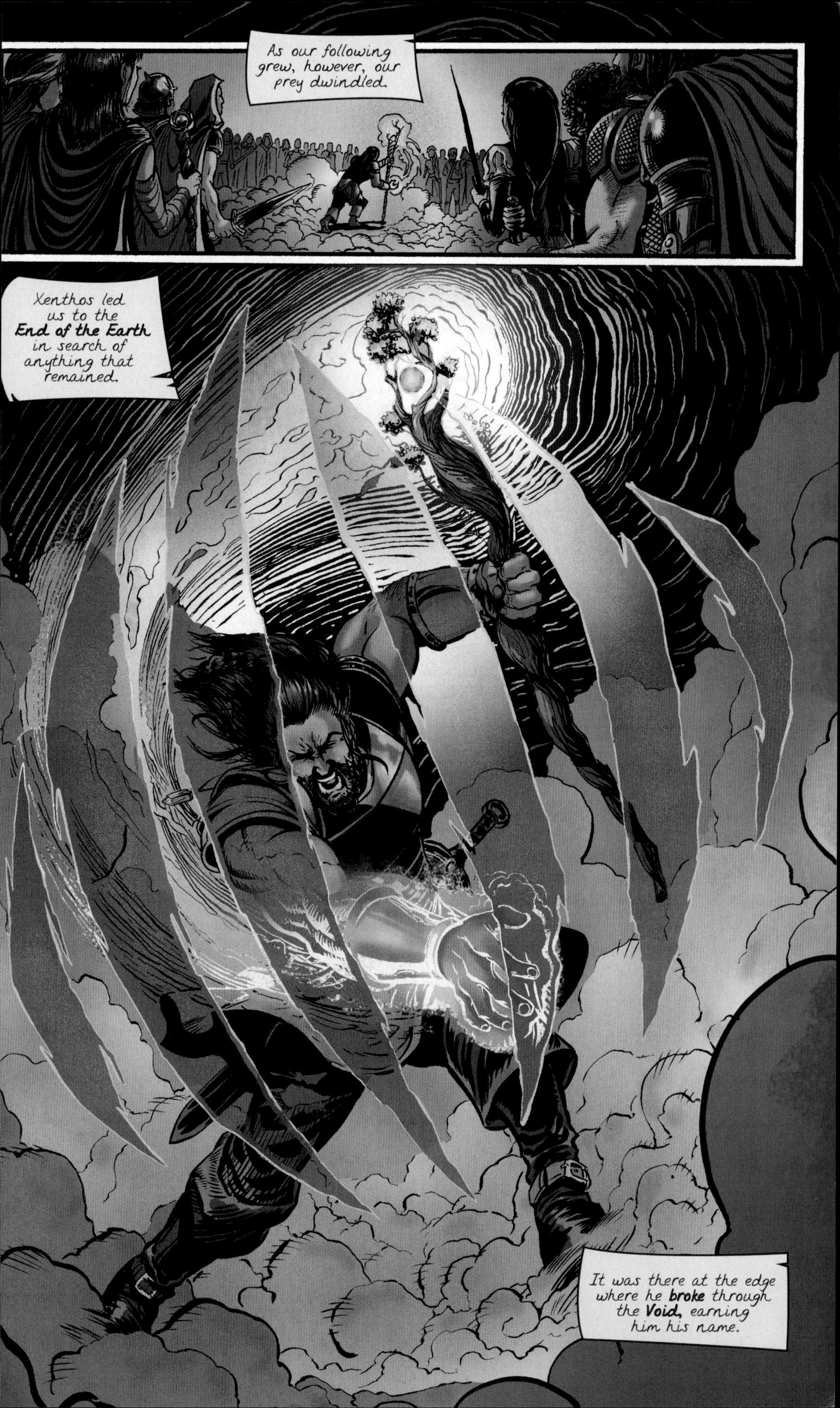
As our following grew, however, our prey dwindled.
Xenthos led us to the End of the Earth in search of anything that remained.
It was there at the edge where he broke through the Void, earning him his name.

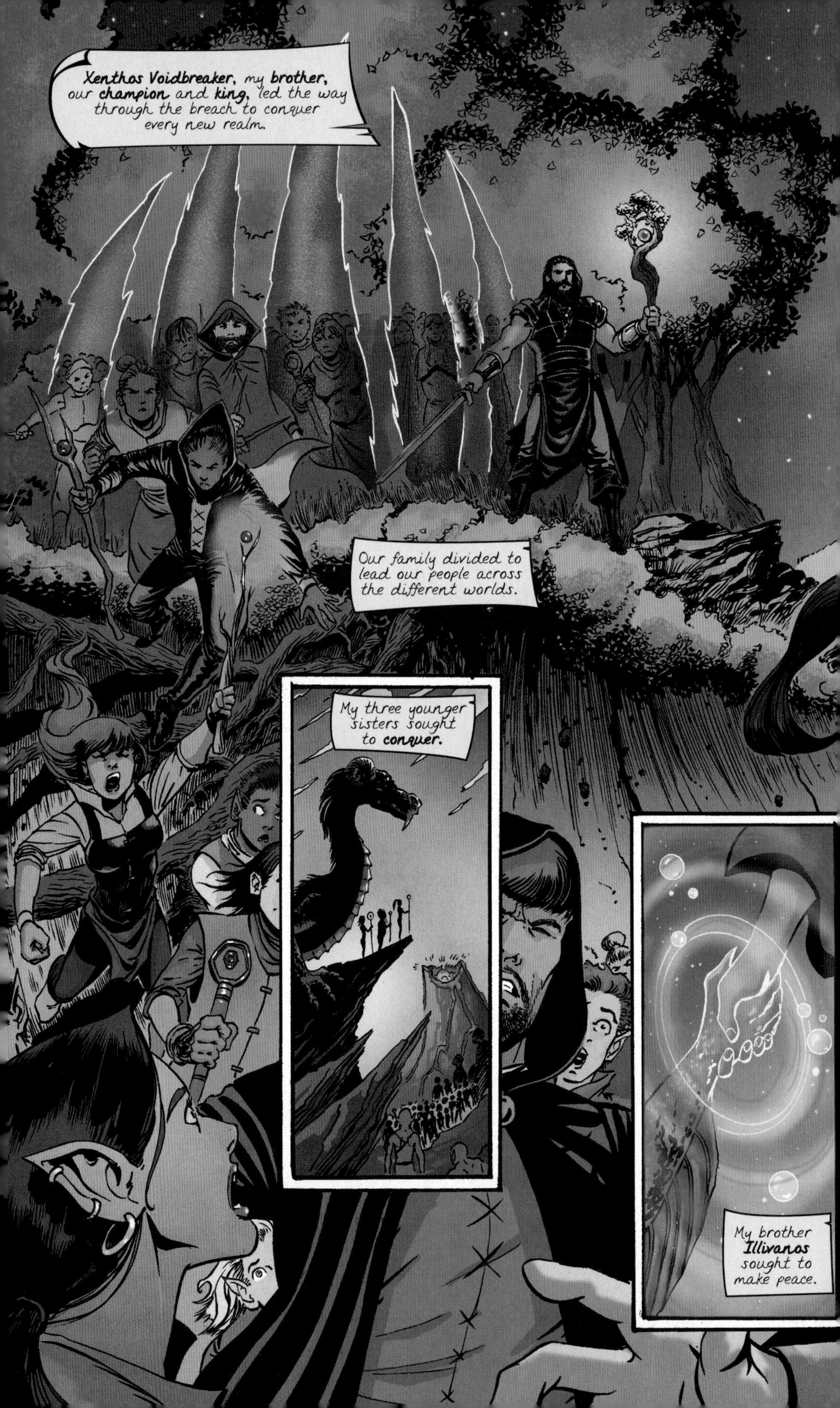
Xenthos Voidbreaker, my **brother**, our **champion** and **king**, led the way through the breach to conquer every new realm.
Our family divided to lead our people across the different worlds.
My three younger sisters sought to **conquer**.
My brother **Illivanos** sought to make peace.

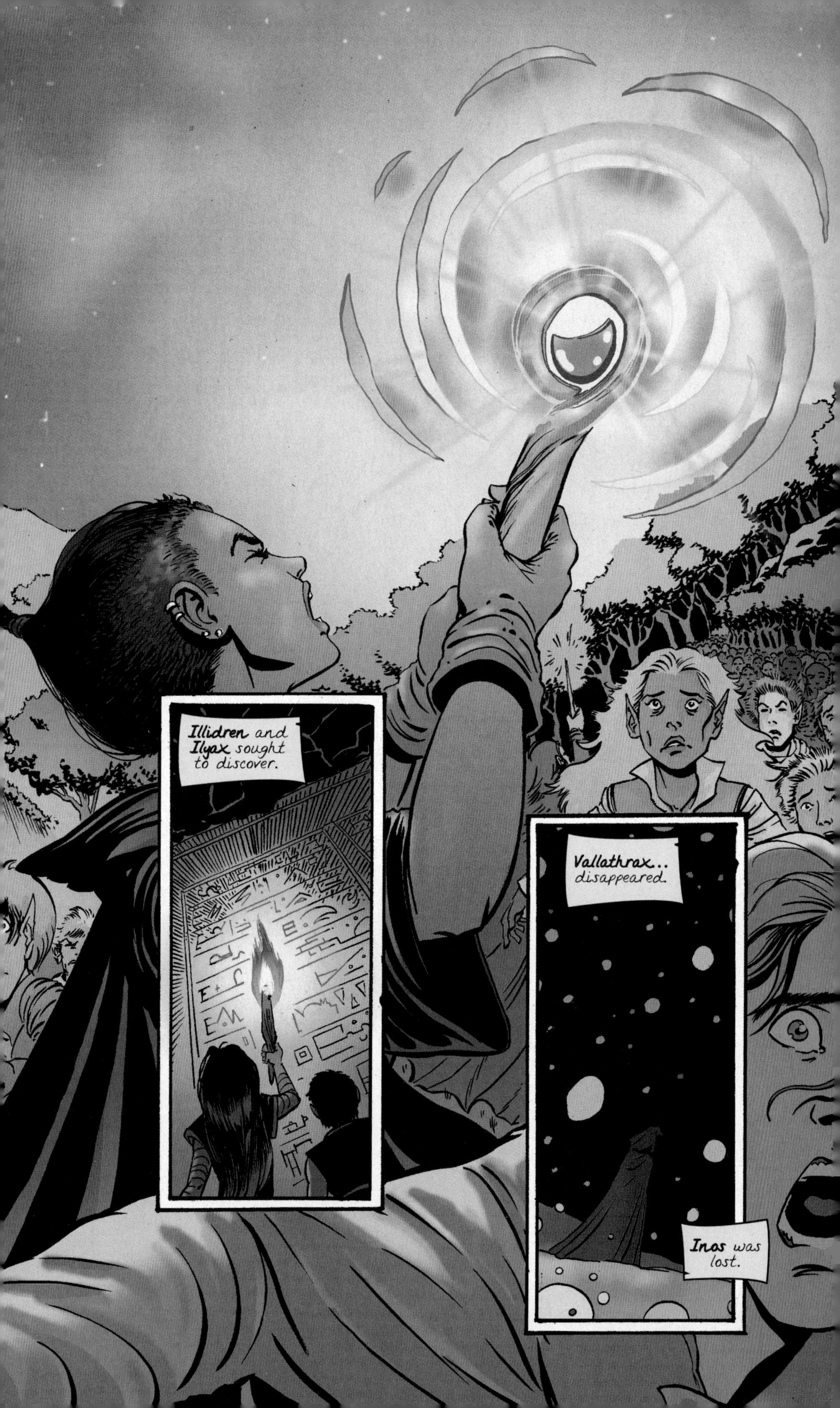
Illidren and Ilyax sought to discover.
Vallathrax... disappeared.
Inos was lost.

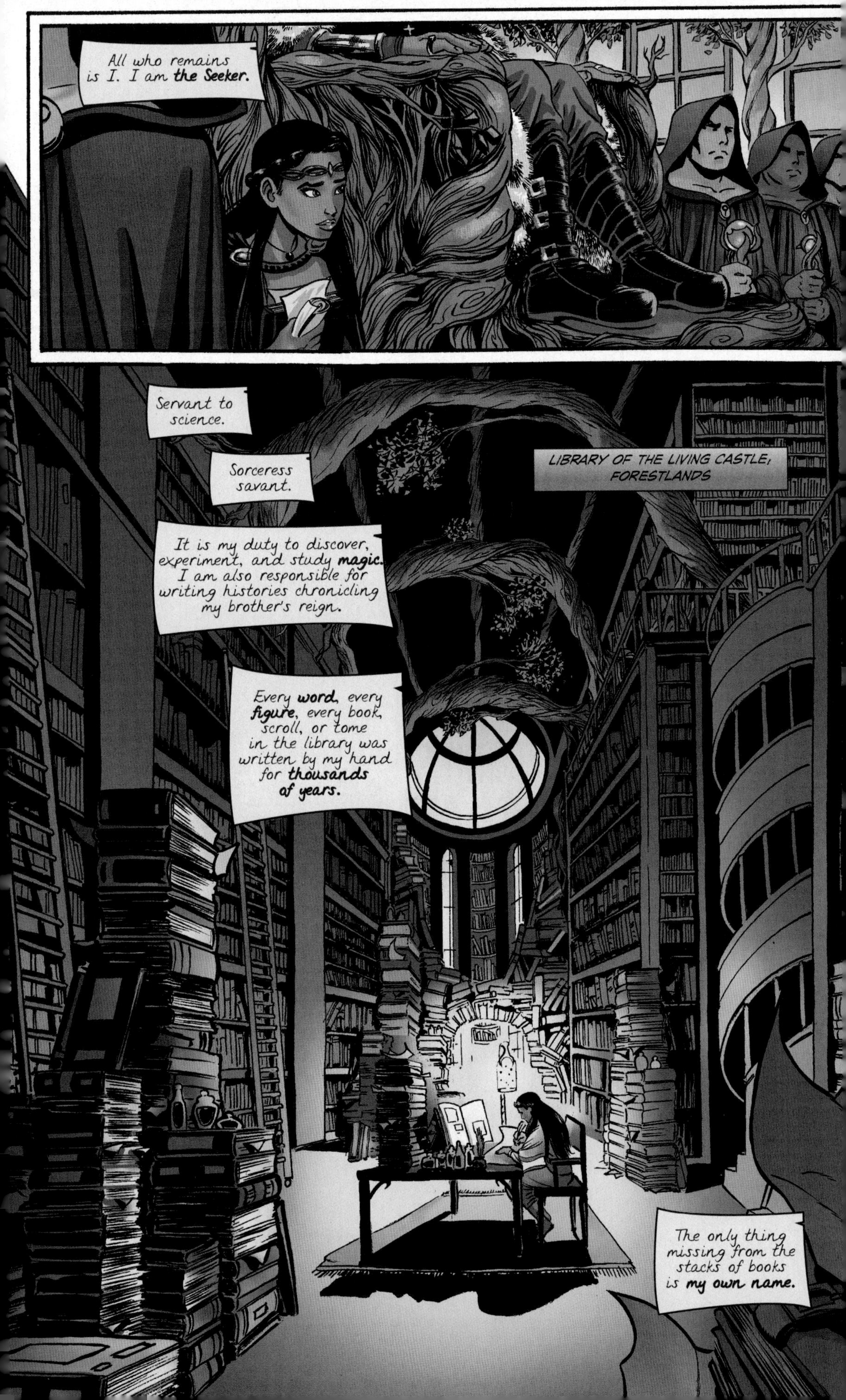

All who remains is I. I am **the Seeker.**
Servant to science.
Sorceress savant.
LIBRARY OF THE LIVING CASTLE, FORESTLANDS
It is my duty to discover, experiment, and study **magic.** I am also responsible for writing histories chronicling my brother's reign.
Every **word**, every **figure**, every book, scroll, or tome in the library was written by my hand for **thousands of years.**
The only thing missing from the stacks of books is **my own name.**

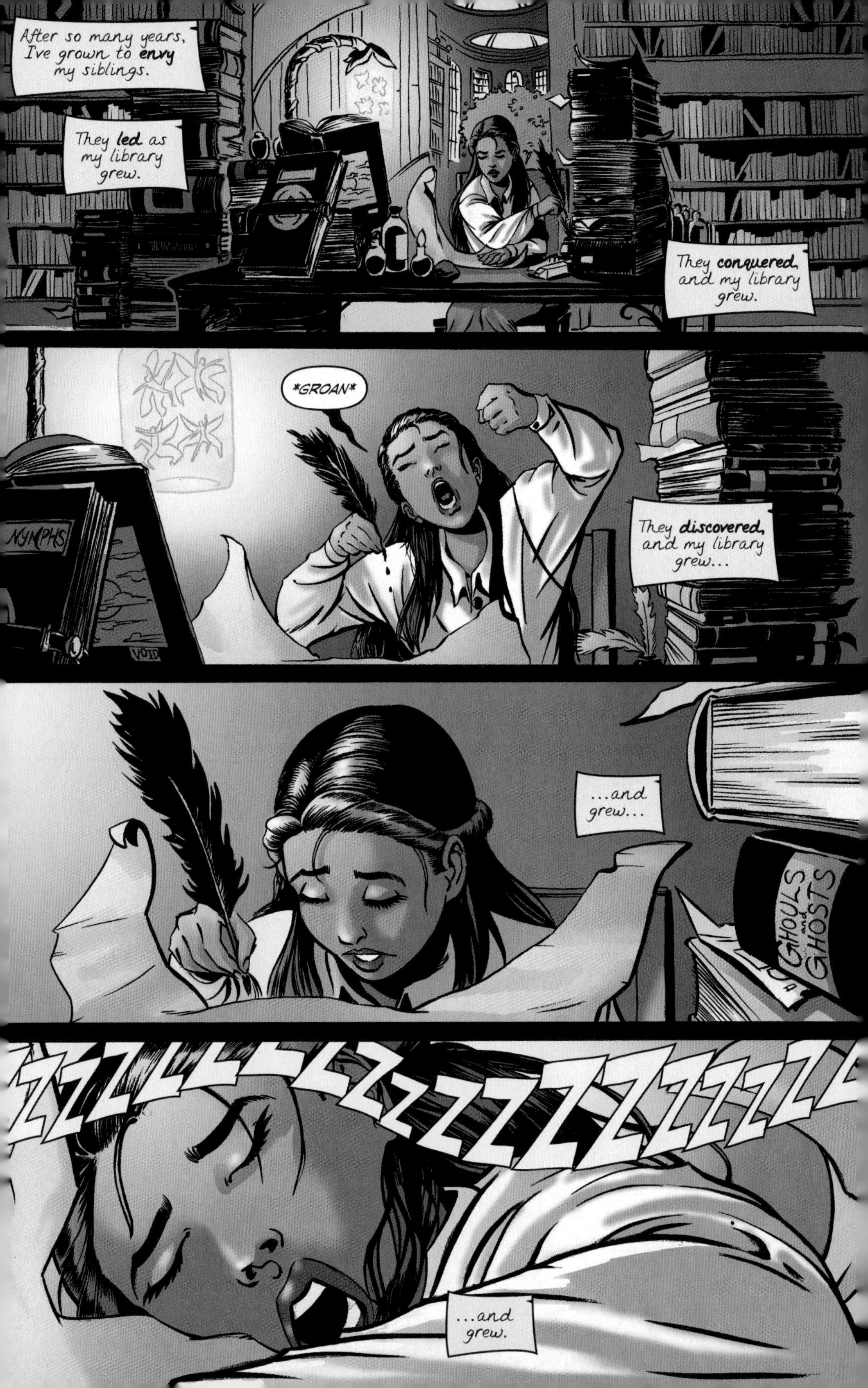
After so many years, I've grown to envy my siblings.
They led as my library grew.
They conquered, and my library grew.
GROAN
NYMPHS
VOID
They discovered, and my library grew...
...and grew...
GHOULS and GHOSTS
ZZZZZZZZZZZZZZZZZZZZZ
...and grew.

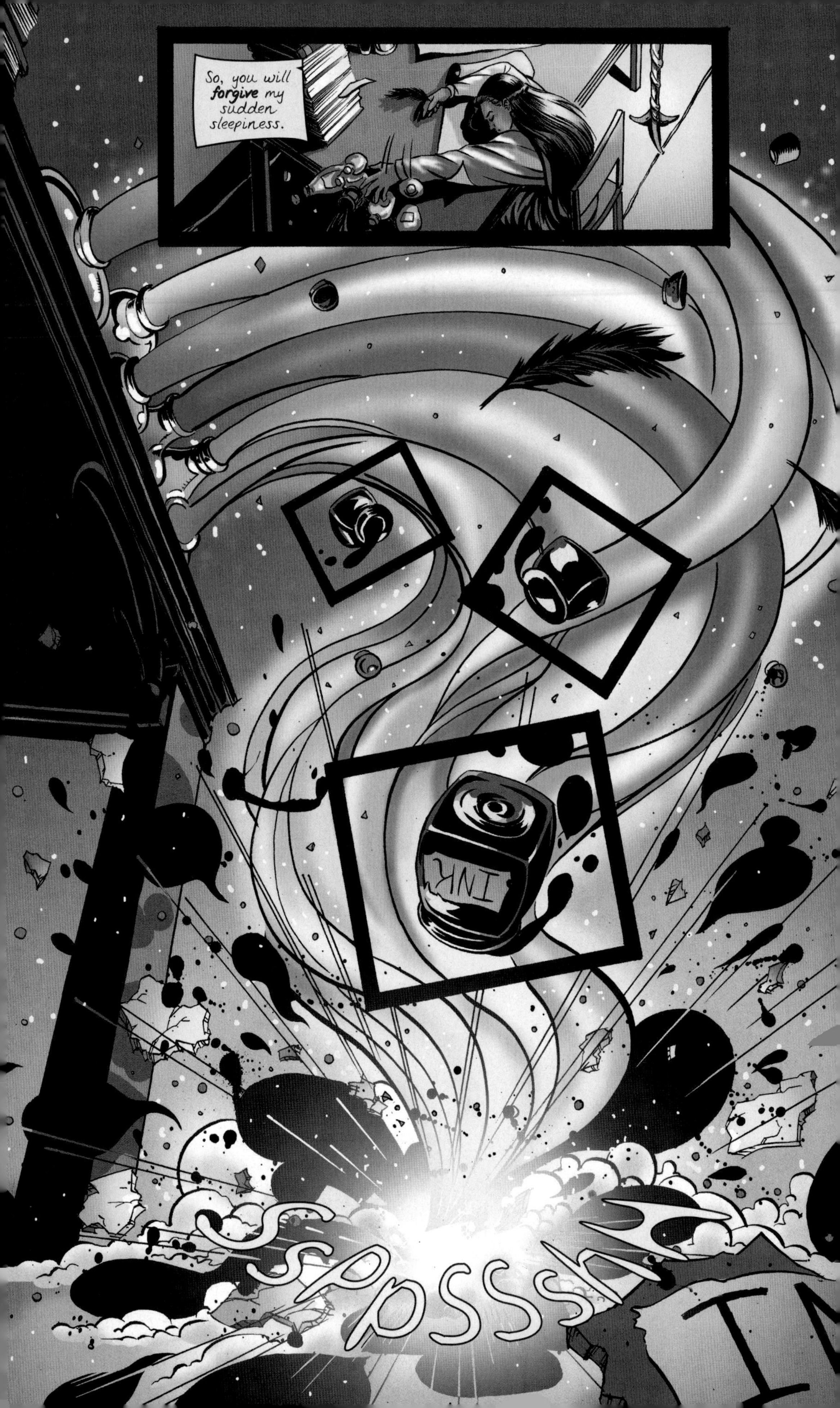
So, you will **forgive** my sudden sleepiness.
INK
SPSSSH

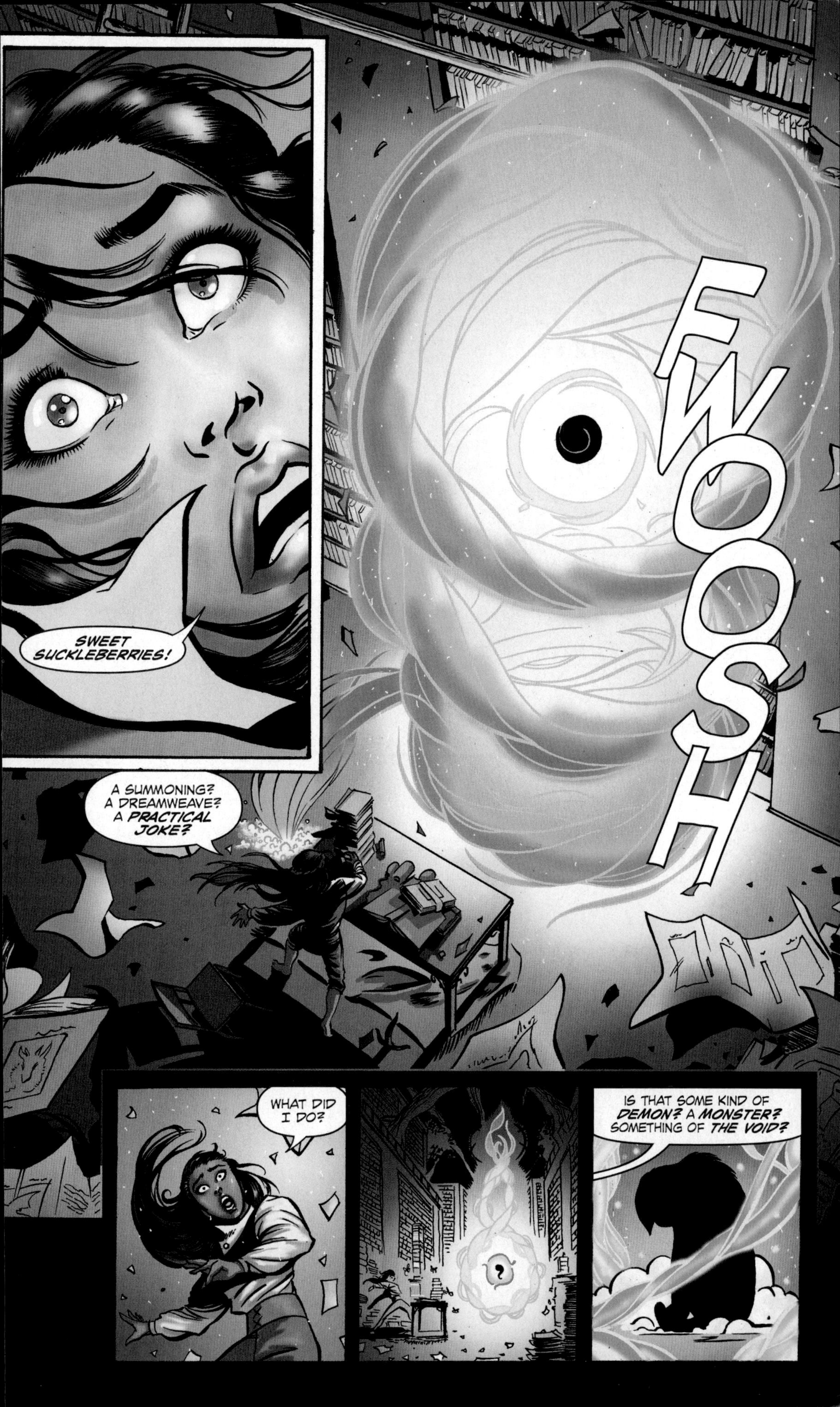
SWEET SUCKLEBERRIES!
A SUMMONING? A DREAMWEAVE? A PRACTICAL JOKE?
FWOOSH
WHAT DID I DO?
IS THAT SOME KIND OF DEMON? A MONSTER? SOMETHING OF THE VOID?

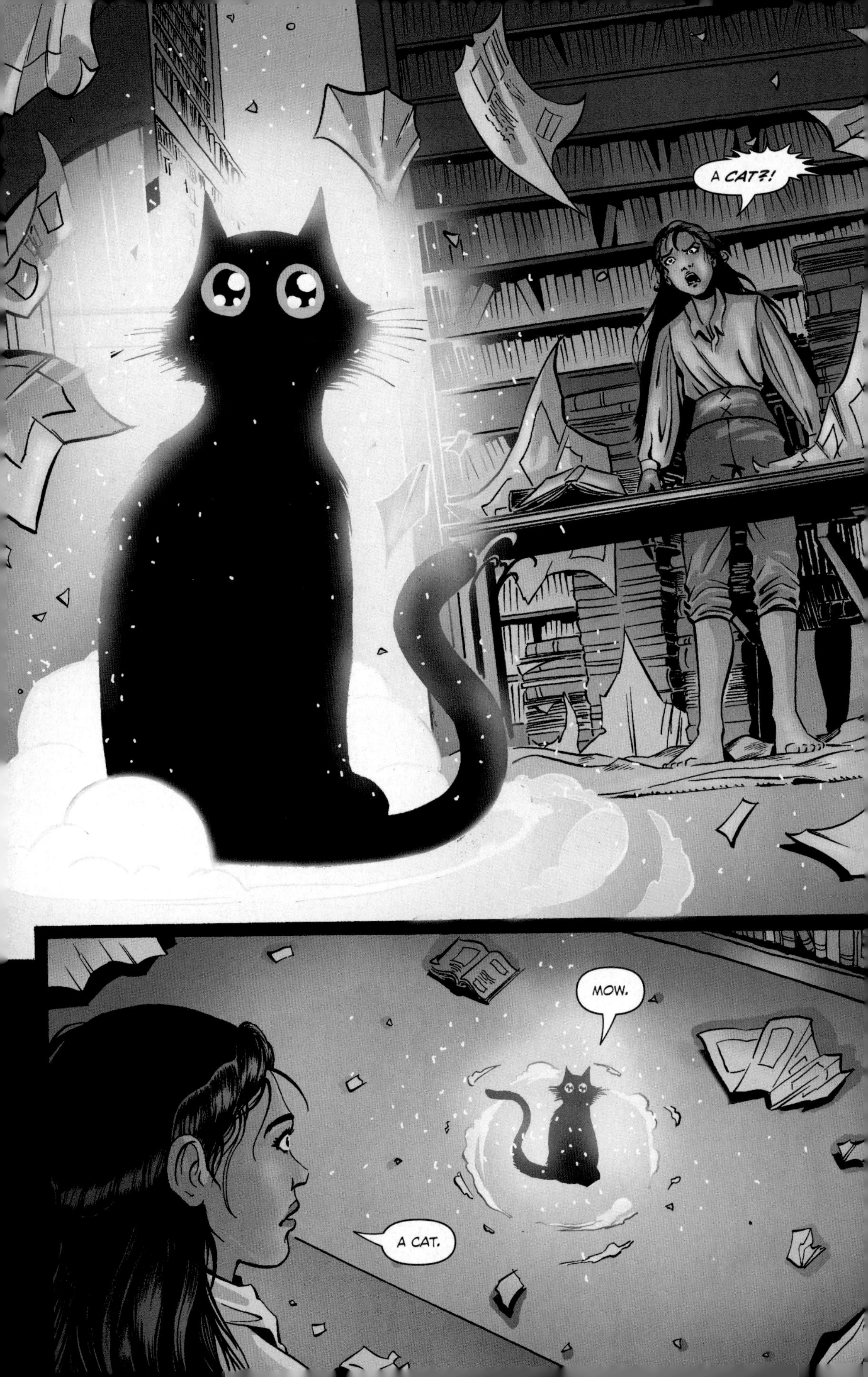
A CAT?!
MOW.
A CAT.

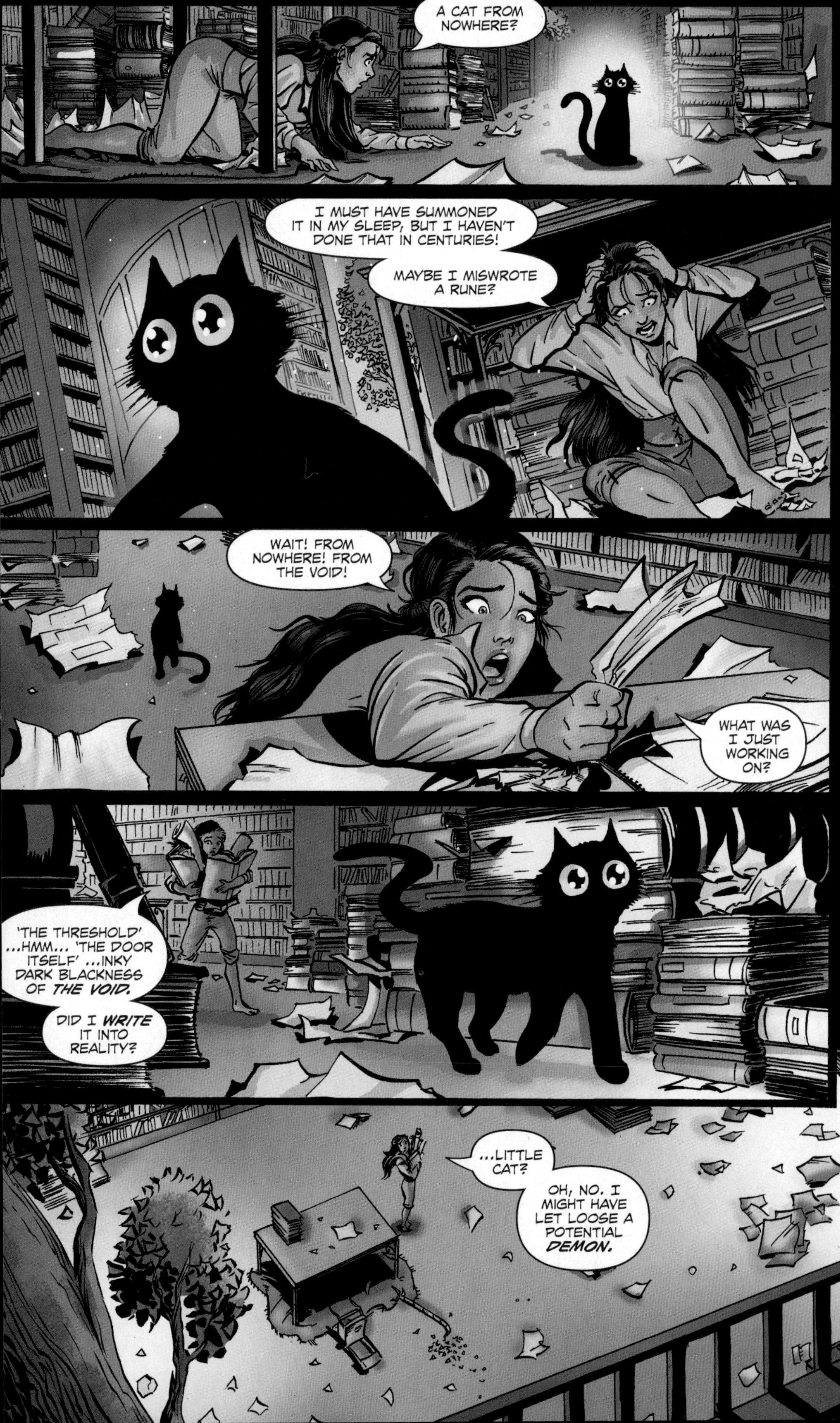
A CAT FROM NOWHERE?
I MUST HAVE SUMMONED IT IN MY SLEEP, BUT I HAVEN'T DONE THAT IN CENTURIES!
MAYBE I MISWROTE A RUNE?
WAIT! FROM NOWHERE! FROM THE VOID!
WHAT WAS I JUST WORKING ON?
'THE THRESHOLD' ...HMM... 'THE DOOR ITSELF' ...INKY DARK BLACKNESS OF *THE VOID.*
DID I *WRITE* IT INTO REALITY?
...LITTLE CAT?
OH, NO. I MIGHT HAVE LET LOOSE A POTENTIAL *DEMON.*

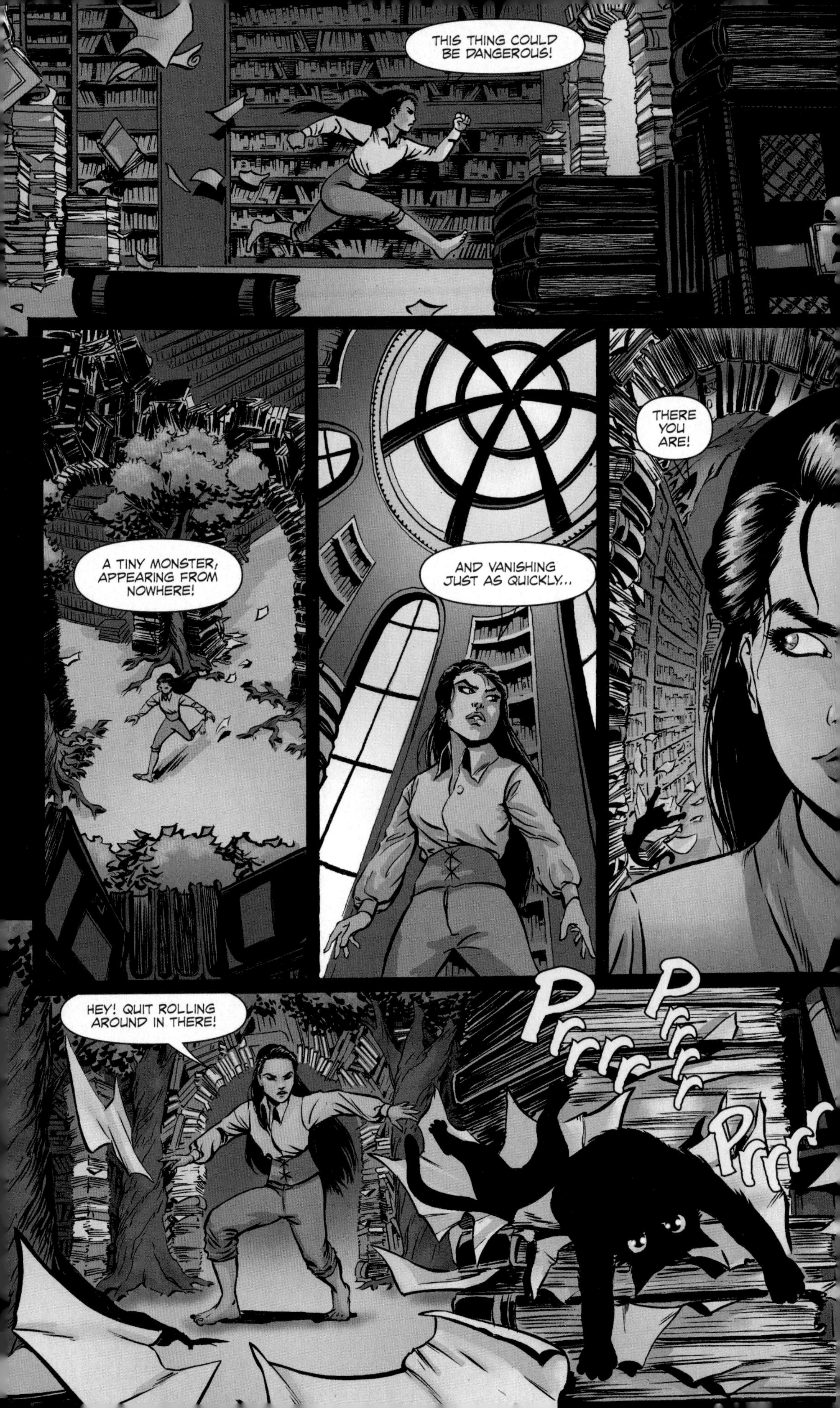
THIS THING COULD BE DANGEROUS!
A TINY MONSTER, APPEARING FROM NOWHERE!
AND VANISHING JUST AS QUICKLY...
THERE YOU ARE!
HEY! QUIT ROLLING AROUND IN THERE!
Prrrr
Prrrr
Prrrr

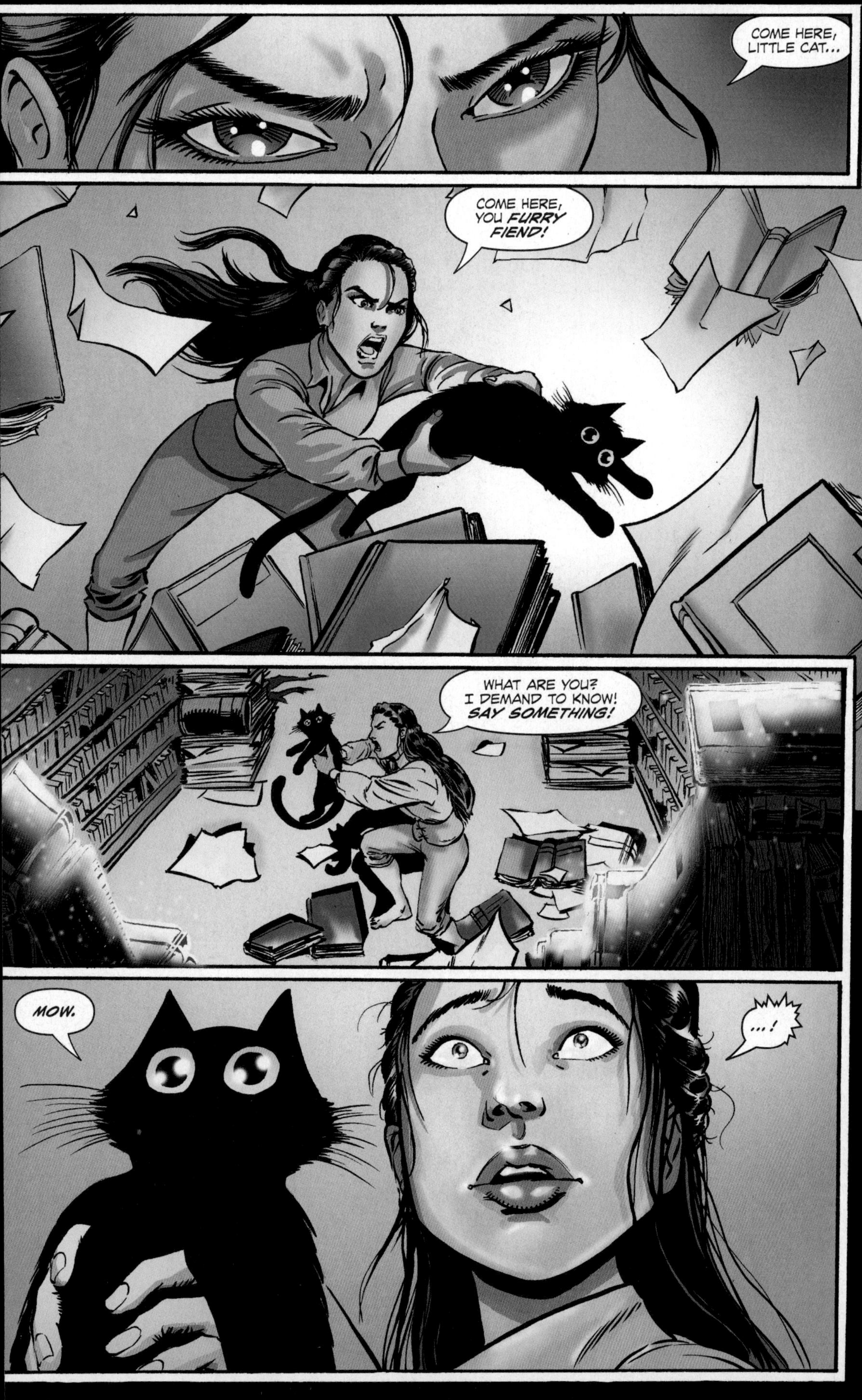
COME HERE, LITTLE CAT...
COME HERE, YOU *FURRY FIEND!*
WHAT ARE YOU? I DEMAND TO KNOW! *SAY SOMETHING!*
MOW.
...!

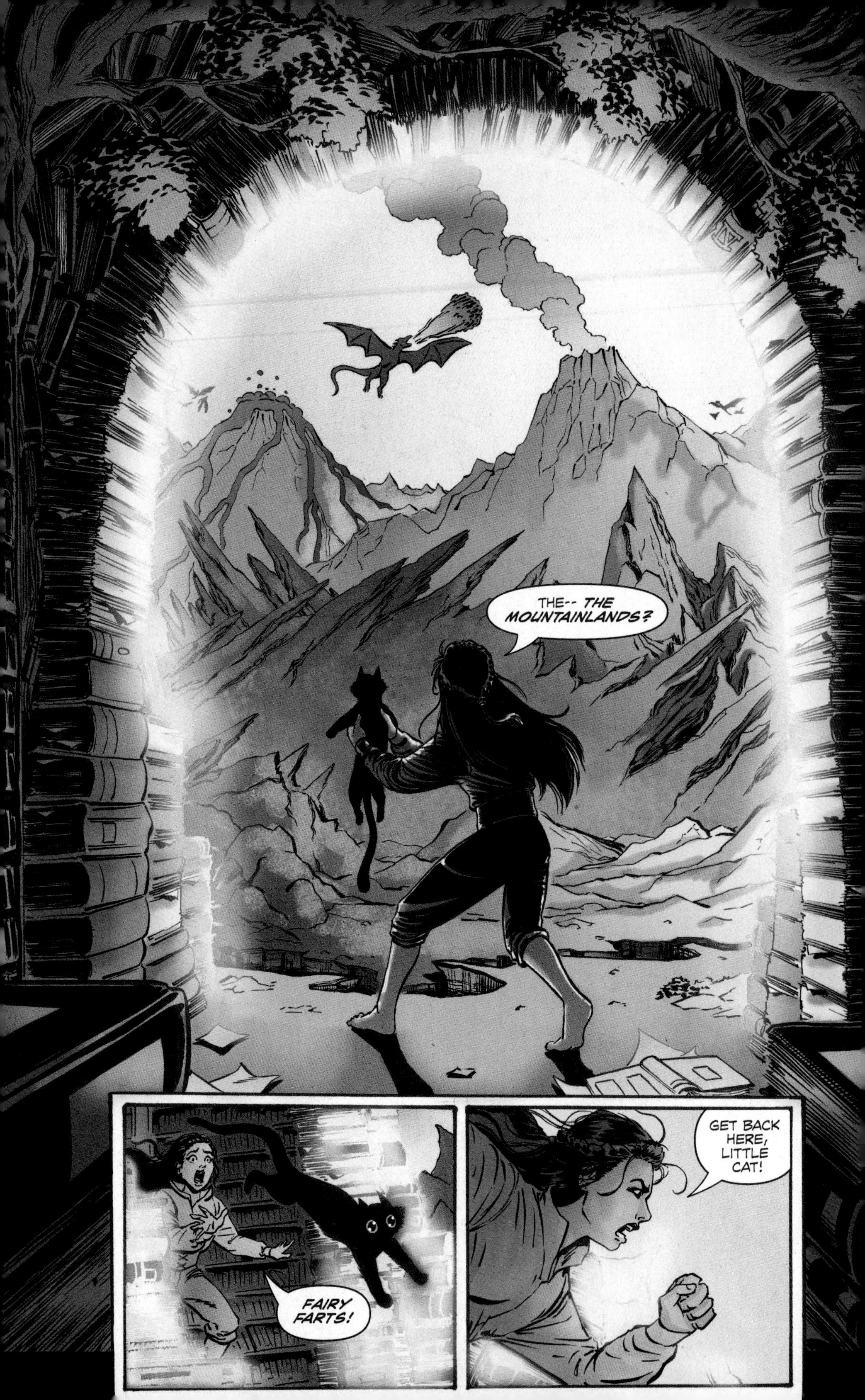
THE-- THE MOUNTAINLANDS?
FAIRY FARTS!
GET BACK HERE, LITTLE CAT!

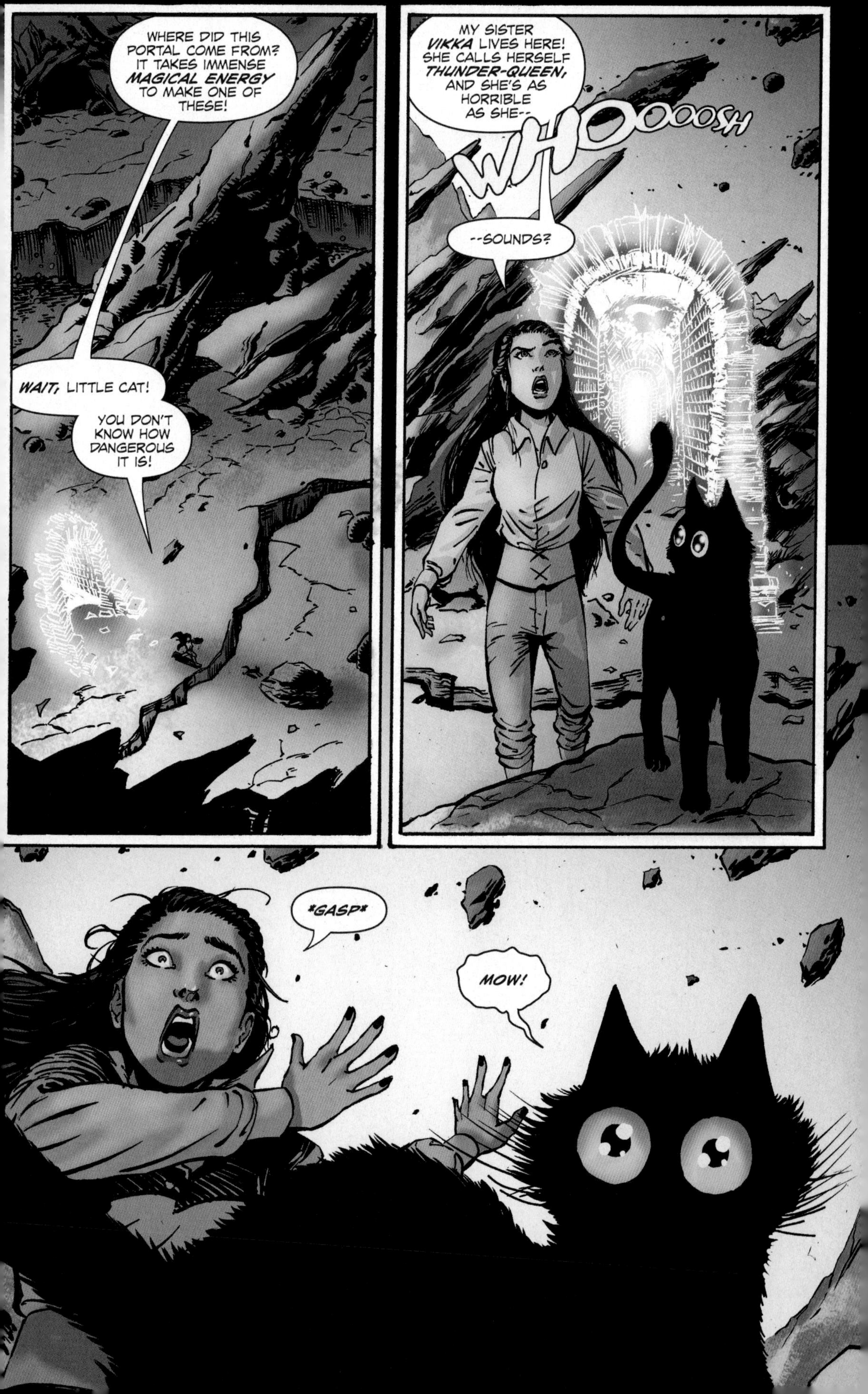
WHERE DID THIS PORTAL COME FROM? IT TAKES IMMENSE MAGICAL ENERGY TO MAKE ONE OF THESE!
WAIT, LITTLE CAT!
YOU DON'T KNOW HOW DANGEROUS IT IS!
MY SISTER VIKKA LIVES HERE! SHE CALLS HERSELF THUNDER-QUEEN, AND SHE'S AS HORRIBLE AS SHE--
WHOOOOOSH
--SOUNDS?
GASP
MOW!

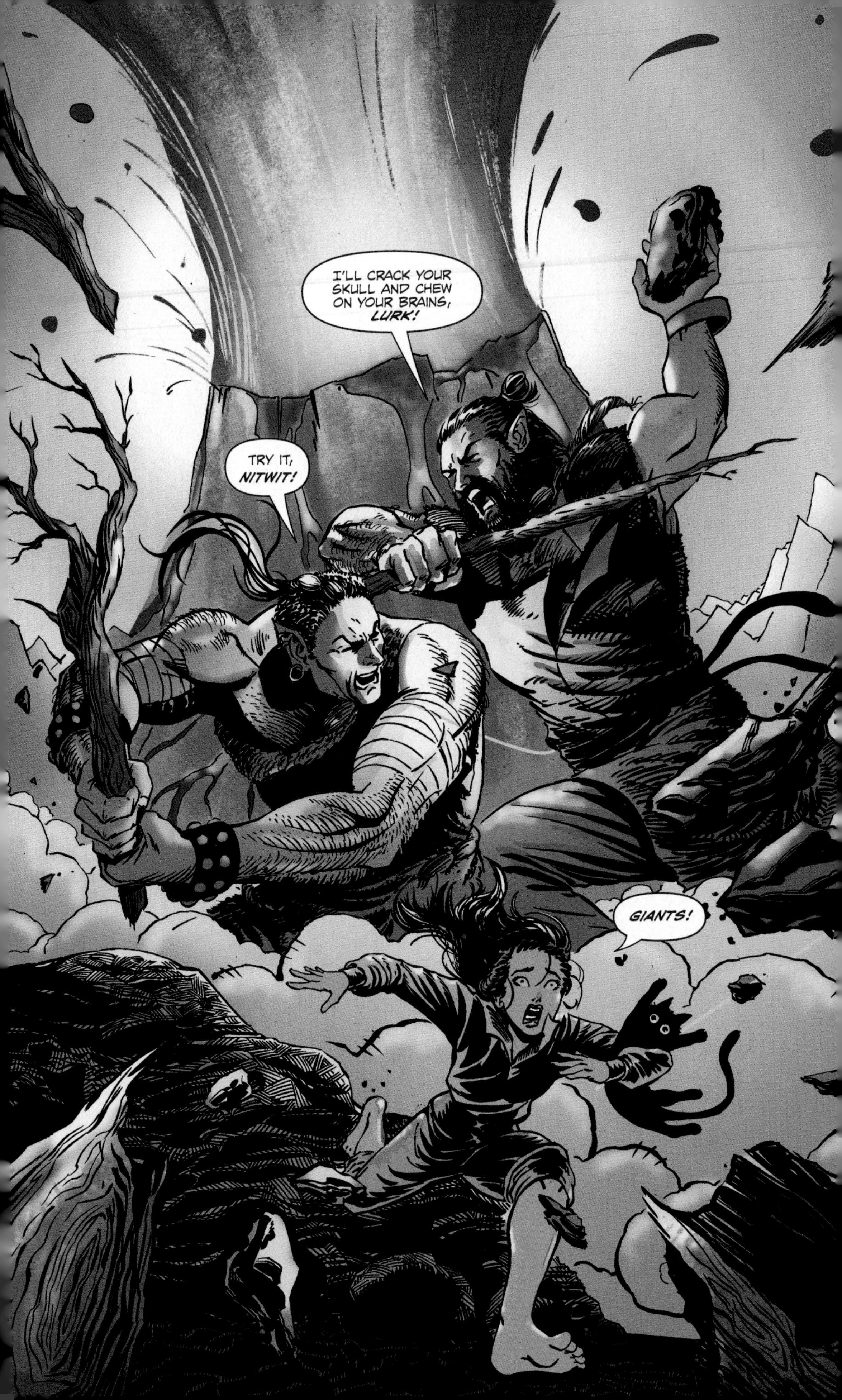
I'LL CRACK YOUR SKULL AND CHEW ON YOUR BRAINS, LURK!
TRY IT, NITWIT!
GIANTS!

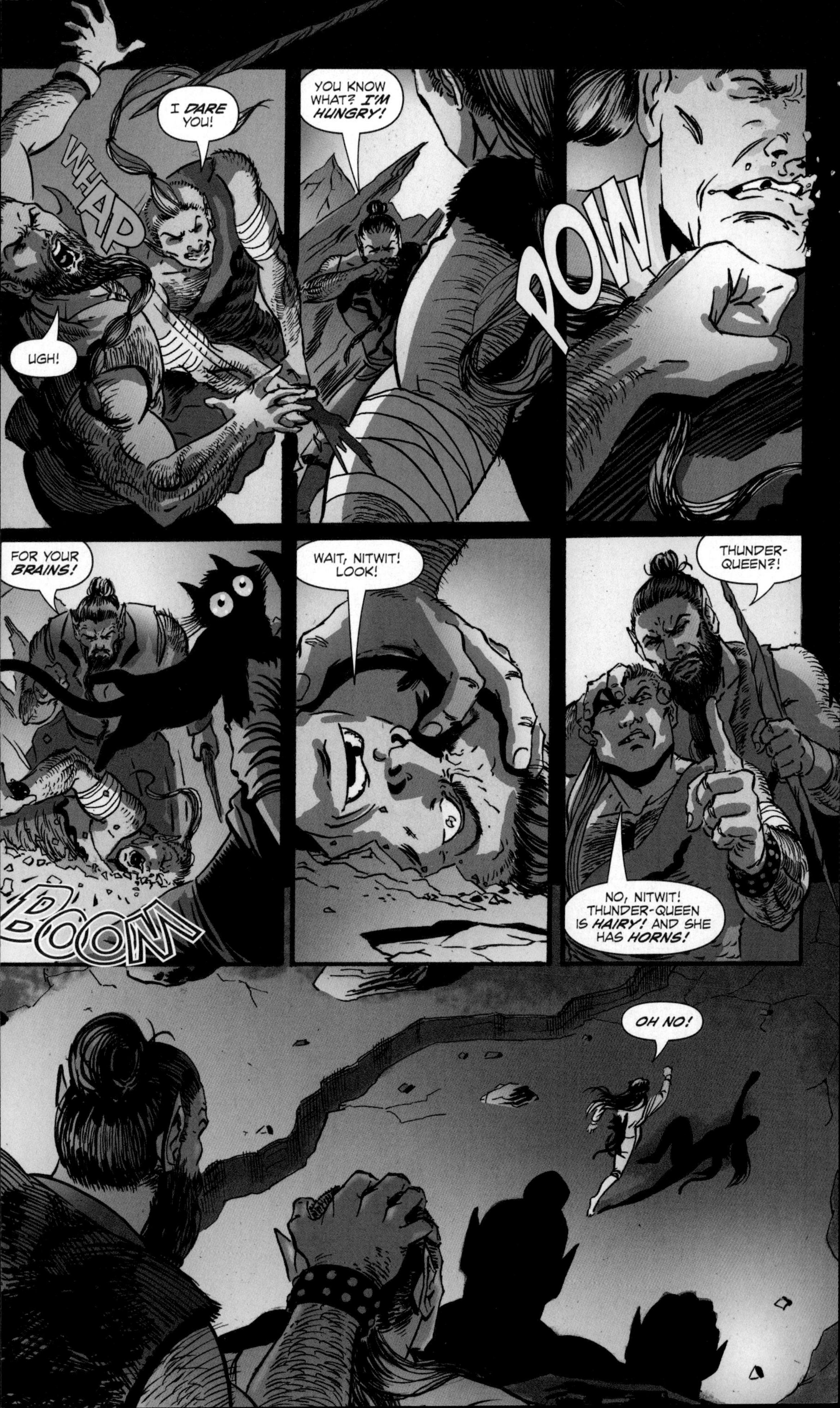
I DARE YOU!
WHAP
UGH!
YOU KNOW WHAT? I'M HUNGRY!
POW
FOR YOUR BRAINS!
BOOM
WAIT, NITWIT! LOOK!
THUNDER-QUEEN?!
NO, NITWIT! THUNDER-QUEEN IS HAIRY! AND SHE HAS HORNS!
OH NO!

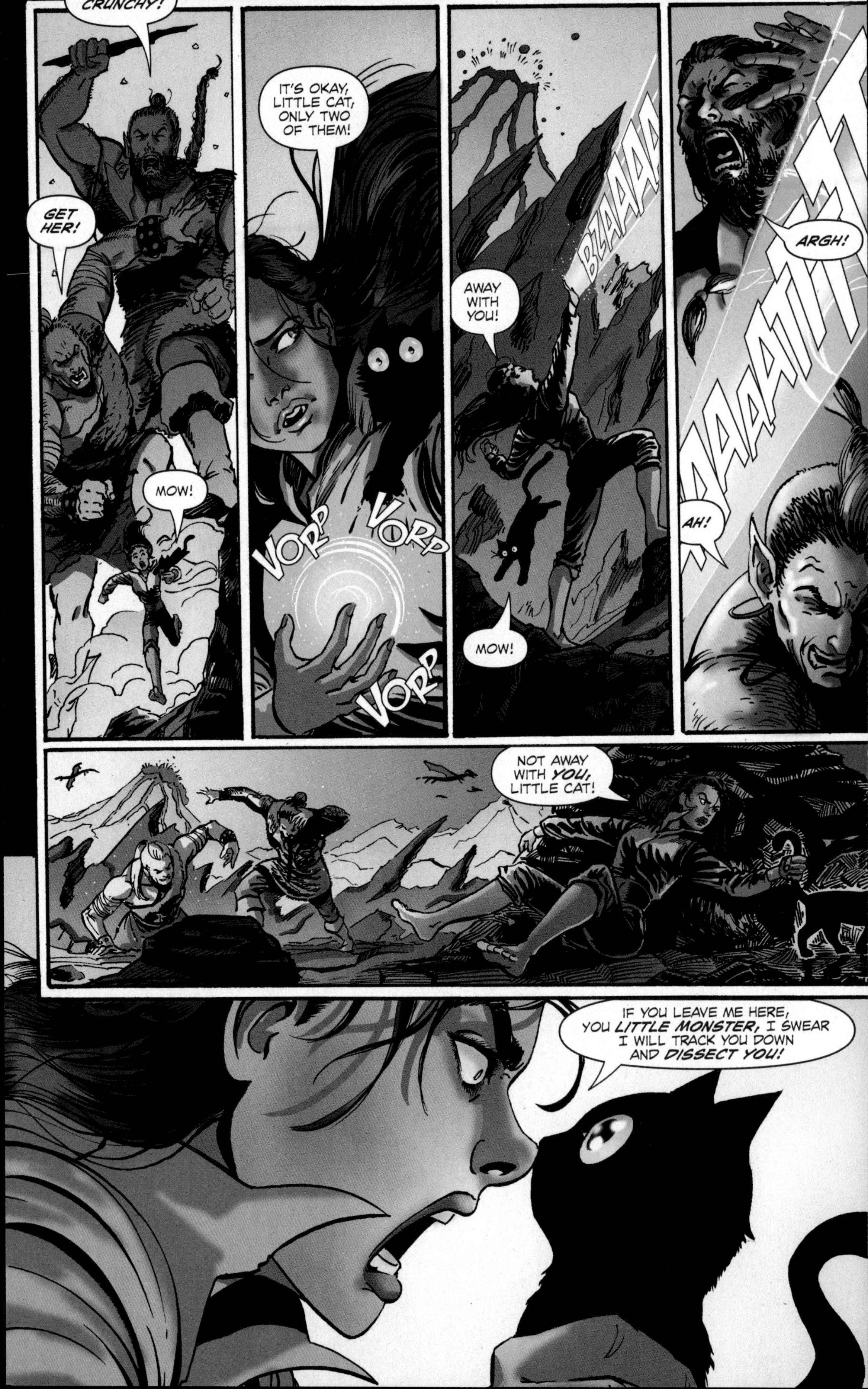
SHE LOOKS CRUNCHY!
GET HER!
MOW!
IT'S OKAY, LITTLE CAT, ONLY TWO OF THEM!
VORP
VORP
VORP
AWAY WITH YOU!
BZAAAAAA
MOW!
ARGH!
AAAAAAAATTTT
AH!
NOT AWAY WITH YOU, LITTLE CAT!
IF YOU LEAVE ME HERE, YOU LITTLE MONSTER, I SWEAR I WILL TRACK YOU DOWN AND DISSECT YOU!

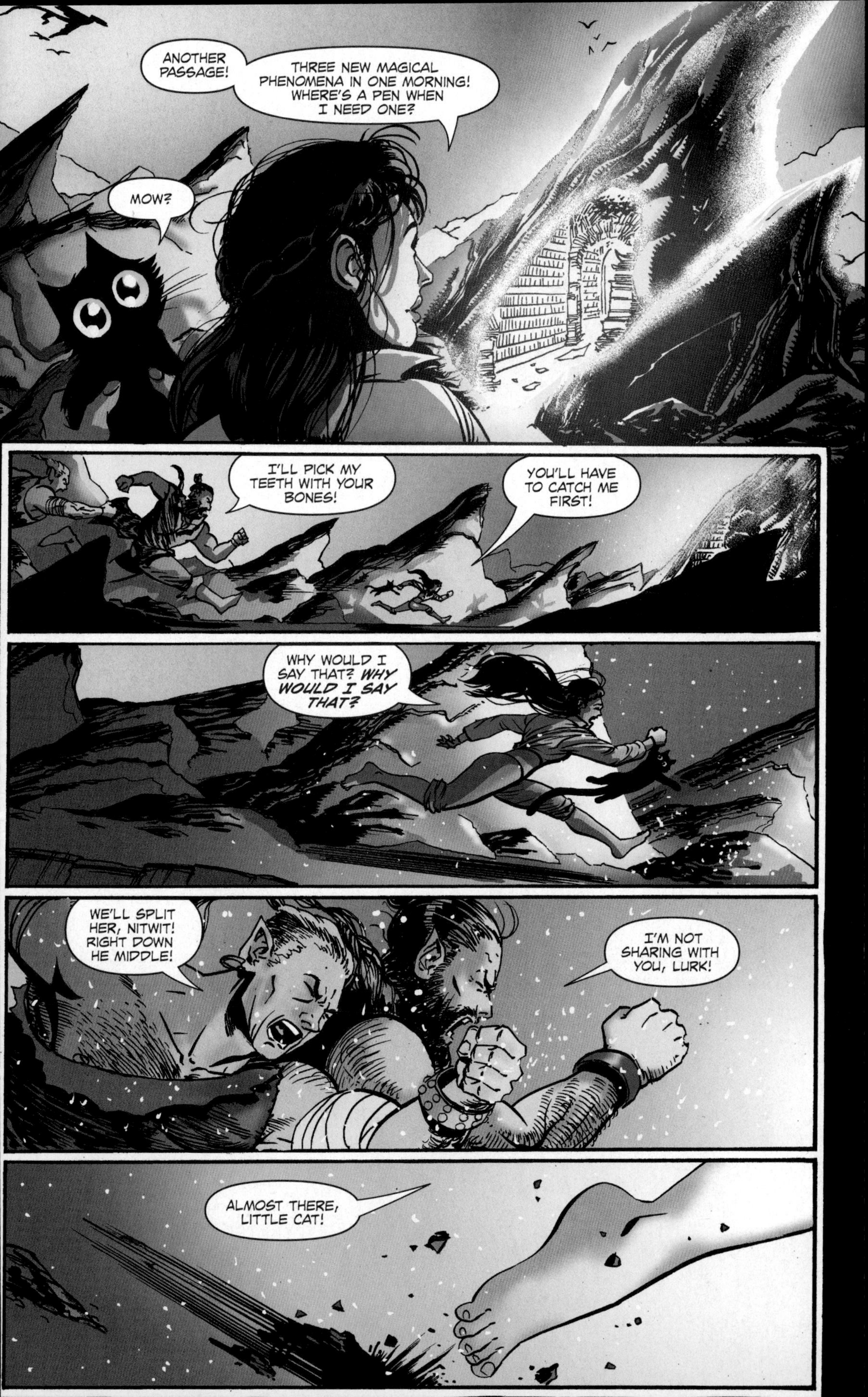

ANOTHER PASSAGE!
THREE NEW MAGICAL PHENOMENA IN ONE MORNING! WHERE'S A PEN WHEN I NEED ONE?
MOW?
I'LL PICK MY TEETH WITH YOUR BONES!
YOU'LL HAVE TO CATCH ME FIRST!
WHY WOULD I SAY THAT? *WHY WOULD I SAY THAT?*
WE'LL SPLIT HER, NITWIT! RIGHT DOWN HE MIDDLE!
I'M NOT SHARING WITH YOU, LURK!
ALMOST THERE, LITTLE CAT!

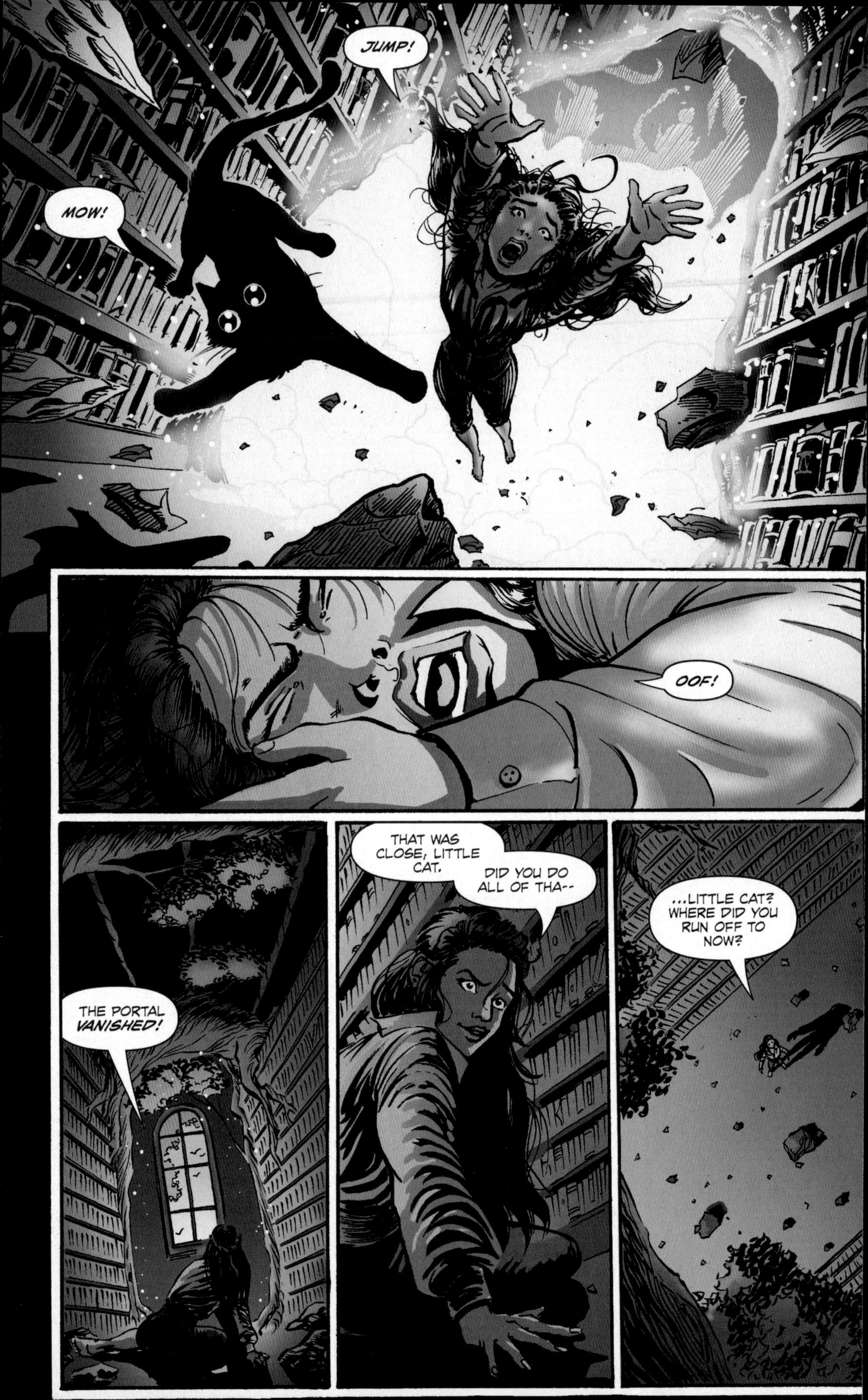
JUMP!
MOW!
OOF!
THE PORTAL VANISHED!
THAT WAS CLOSE, LITTLE CAT.
DID YOU DO ALL OF THA--
...LITTLE CAT? WHERE DID YOU RUN OFF TO NOW?

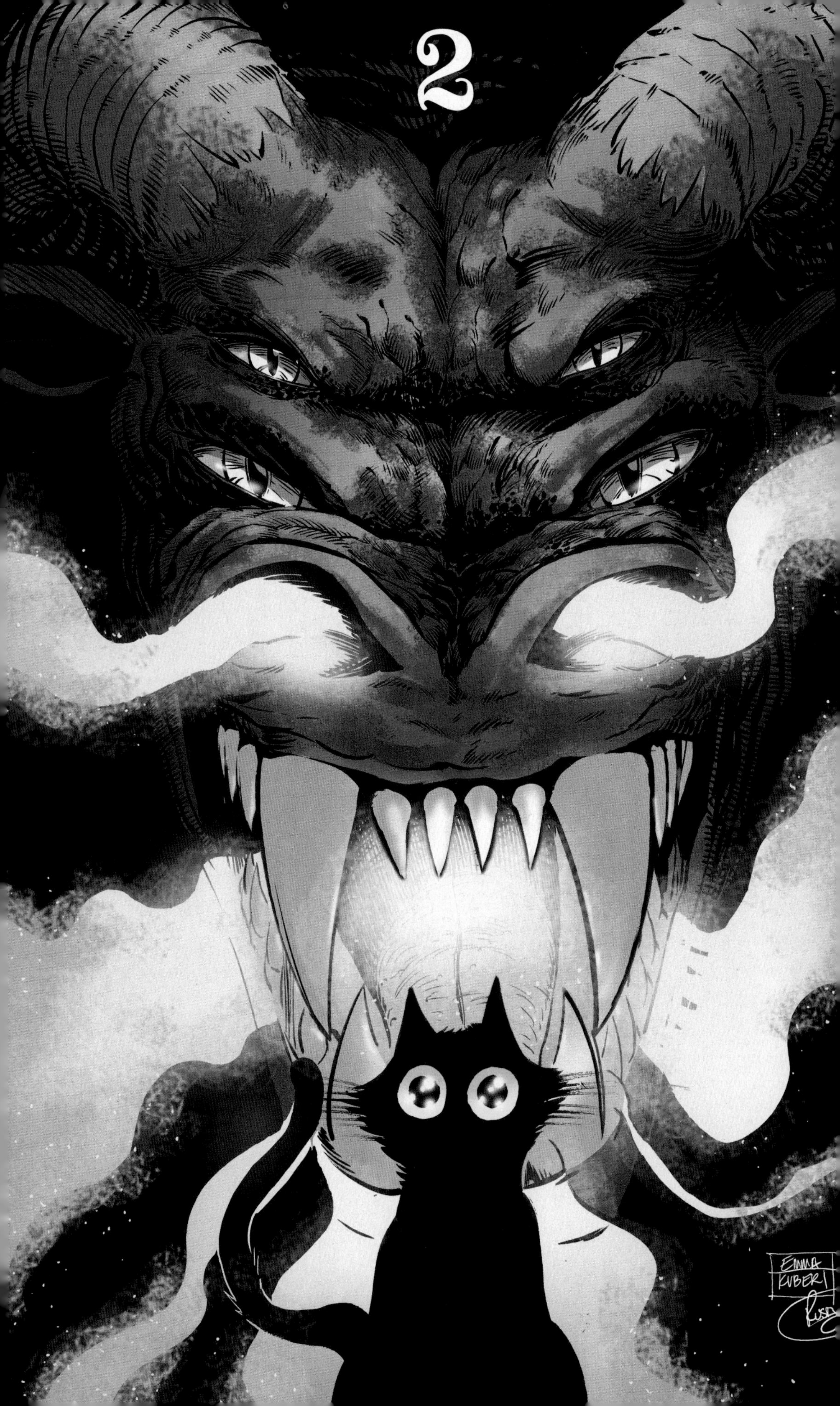
2
EMMA KUBERT

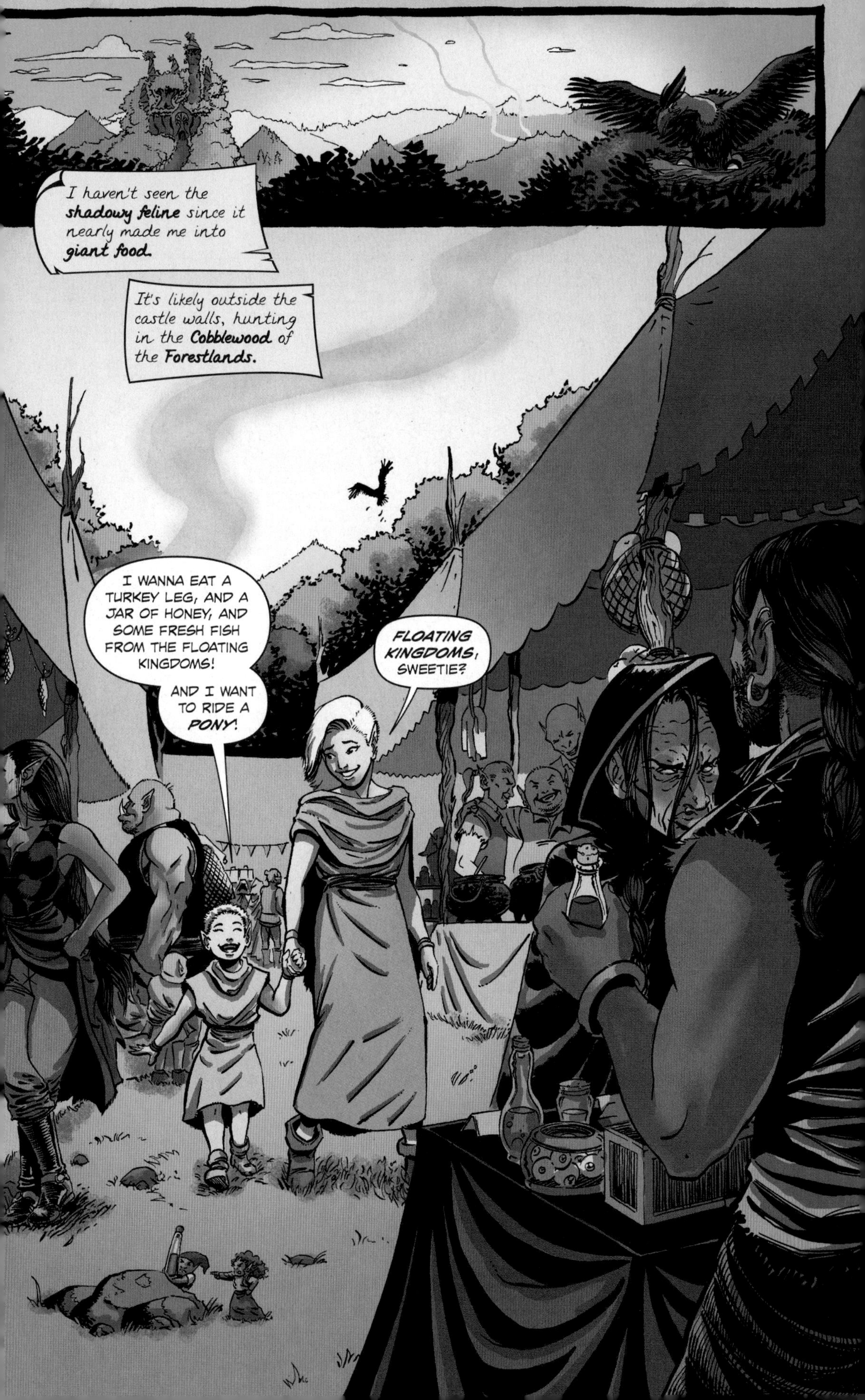
I haven't seen the shadowy feline since it nearly made me into giant food.
It's likely outside the castle walls, hunting in the Cobblewood of the Forestlands.
I WANNA EAT A TURKEY LEG, AND A JAR OF HONEY, AND SOME FRESH FISH FROM THE FLOATING KINGDOMS!
AND I WANT TO RIDE A PONY!
FLOATING KINGDOMS, SWEETIE?

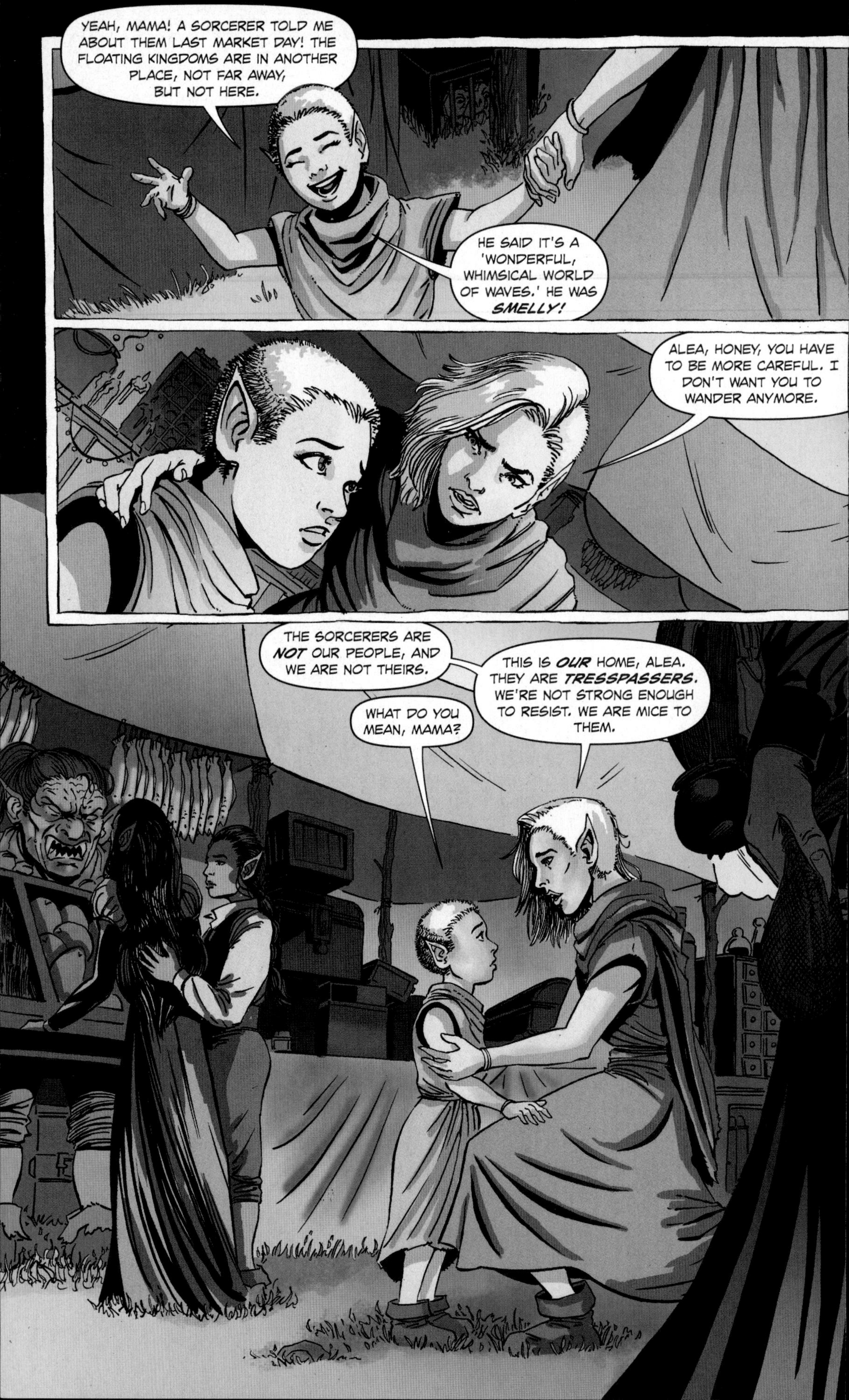
YEAH, MAMA! A SORCERER TOLD ME ABOUT THEM LAST MARKET DAY! THE FLOATING KINGDOMS ARE IN ANOTHER PLACE, NOT FAR AWAY, BUT NOT HERE.
HE SAID IT'S A 'WONDERFUL, WHIMSICAL WORLD OF WAVES.' HE WAS *SMELLY!*
ALEA, HONEY, YOU HAVE TO BE MORE CAREFUL. I DON'T WANT YOU TO WANDER ANYMORE.
THE SORCERERS ARE *NOT* OUR PEOPLE, AND WE ARE NOT THEIRS.
THIS IS *OUR* HOME, ALEA. THEY ARE *TRESSPASSERS.* WE'RE NOT STRONG ENOUGH TO RESIST. WE ARE MICE TO THEM.
WHAT DO YOU MEAN, MAMA?

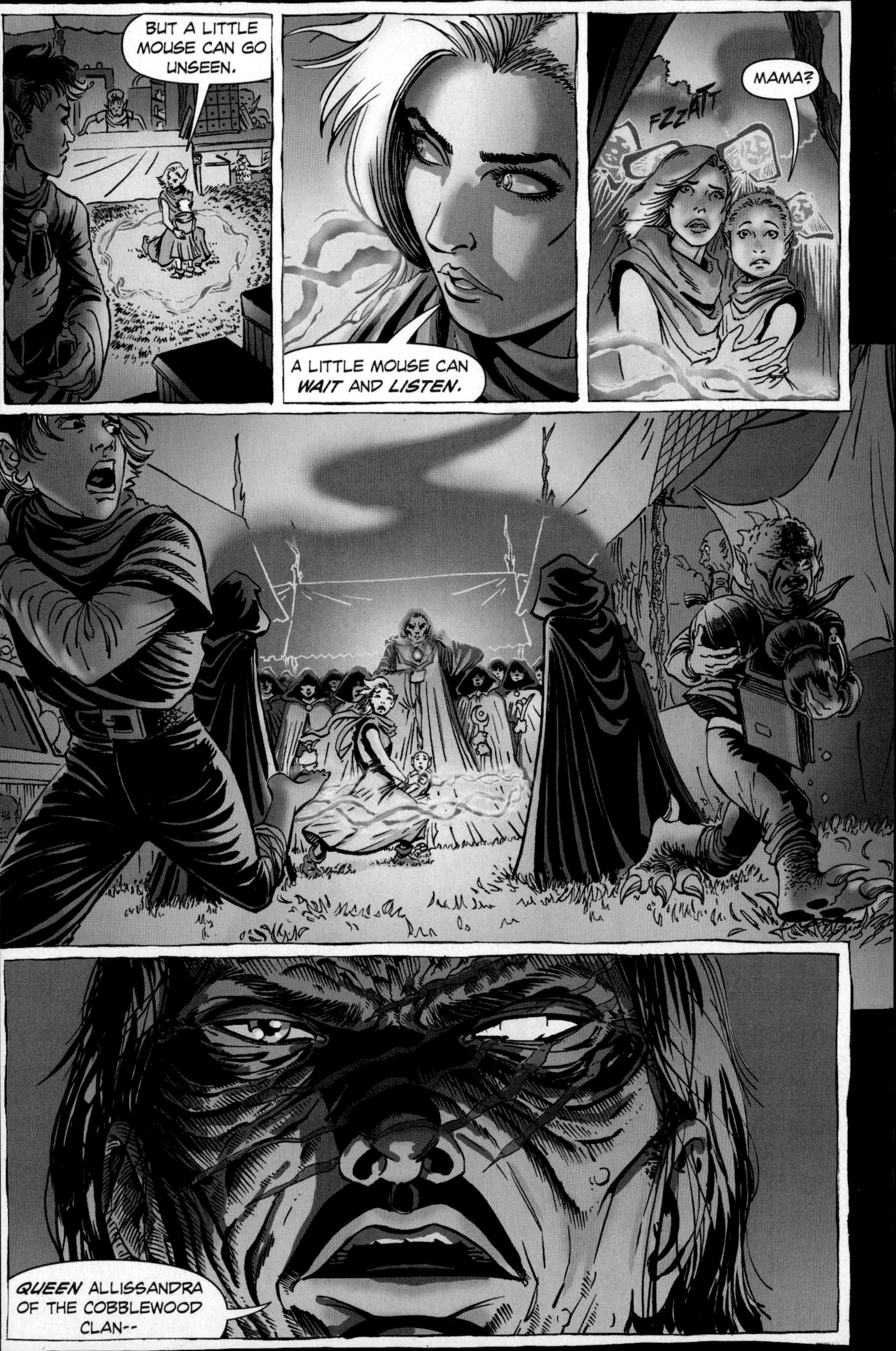
BUT A LITTLE MOUSE CAN GO UNSEEN.
A LITTLE MOUSE CAN *WAIT* AND *LISTEN*.
FZZATT
MAMA?
QUEEN ALLISSANDRA OF THE COBBLEWOOD CLAN--

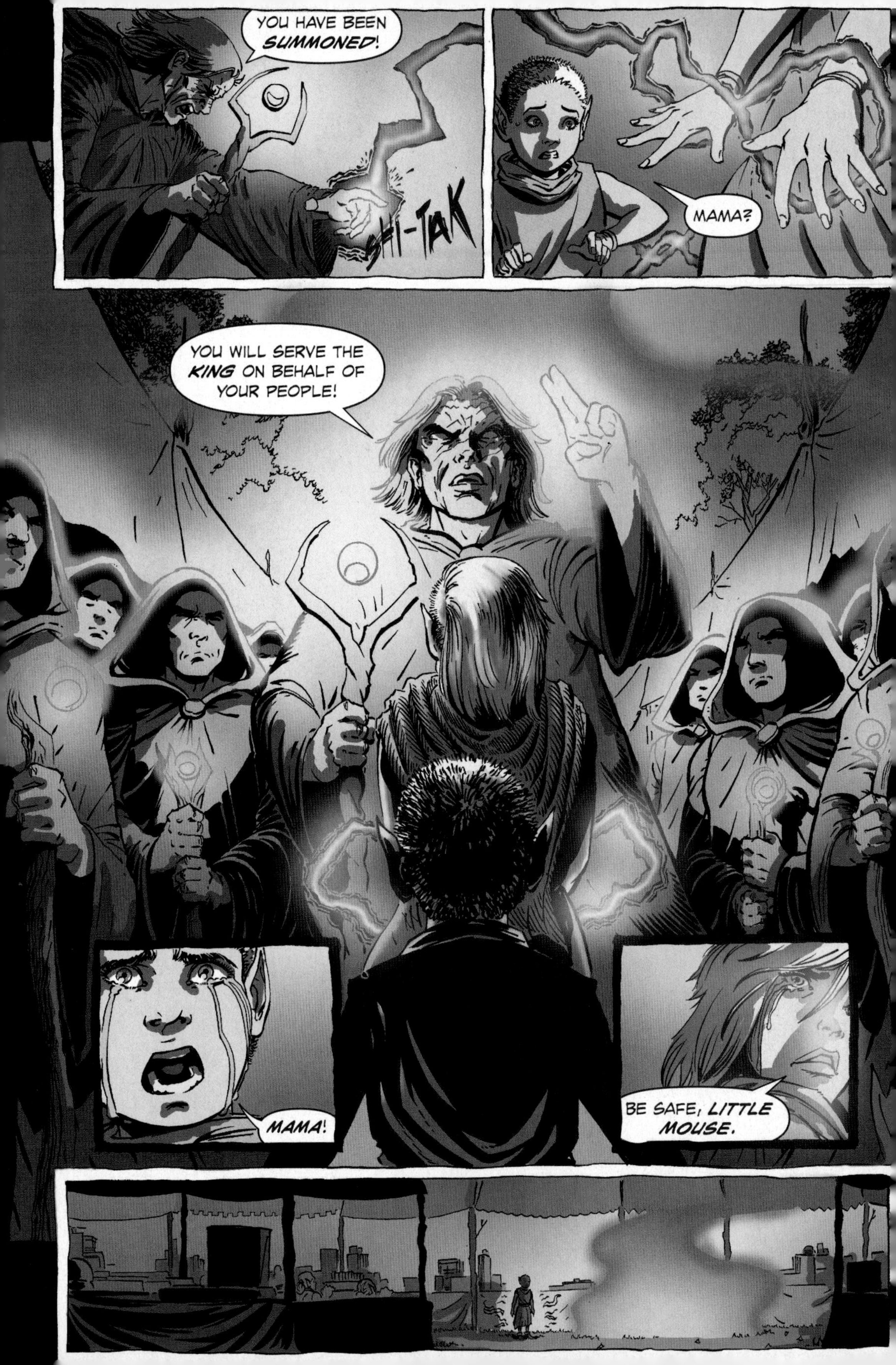
YOU HAVE BEEN SUMMONED!
SHI-TAK
MAMA?
YOU WILL SERVE THE KING ON BEHALF OF YOUR PEOPLE!
MAMA!
BE SAFE, LITTLE MOUSE.

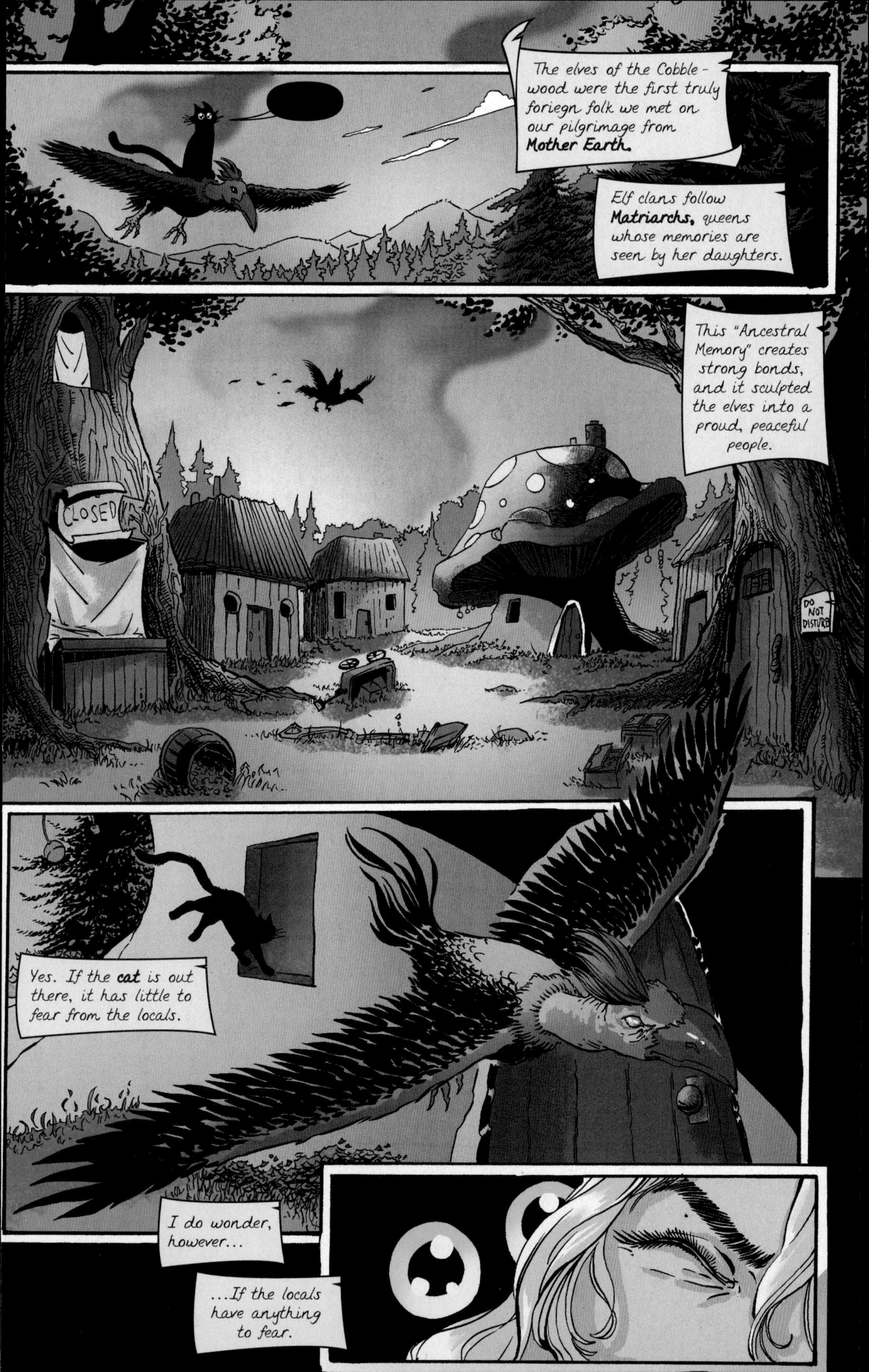

The elves of the Cobble-wood were the first truly foriegn folk we met on our pilgrimage from **Mother Earth.**
Elf clans follow **Matriarchs,** queens whose memories are seen by her daughters.
This "Ancestral Memory" creates strong bonds, and it sculpted the elves into a proud, peaceful people.
CLOSED
DO NOT DISTURB
Yes. If the **cat** is out there, it has little to fear from the locals.
I do wonder, however...
...If the locals have anything to fear.

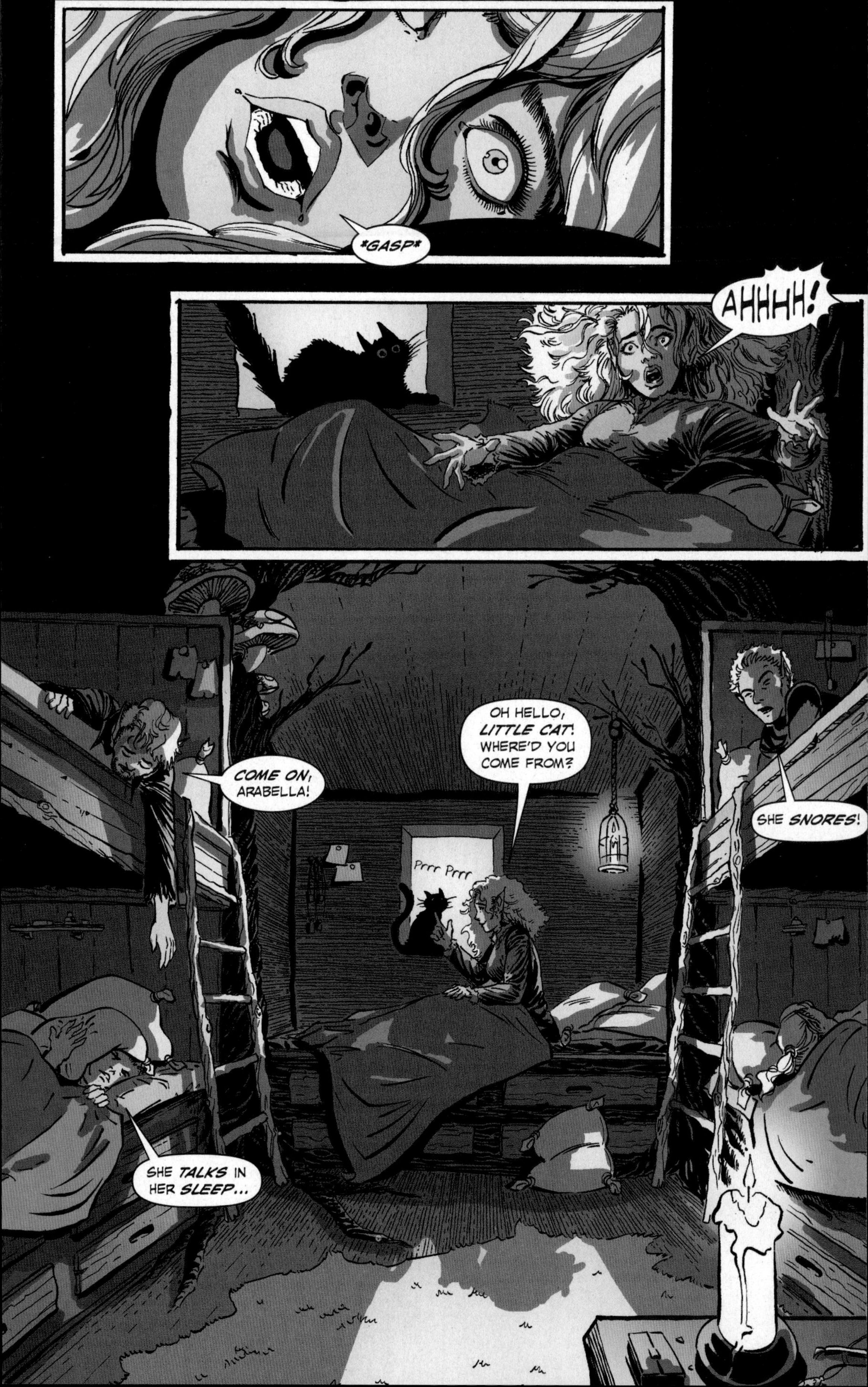
GASP
AHHHH!
COME ON, ARABELLA!
OH HELLO, LITTLE CAT! WHERE'D YOU COME FROM?
Prrr Prrr
SHE SNORES!
SHE TALKS IN HER SLEEP...

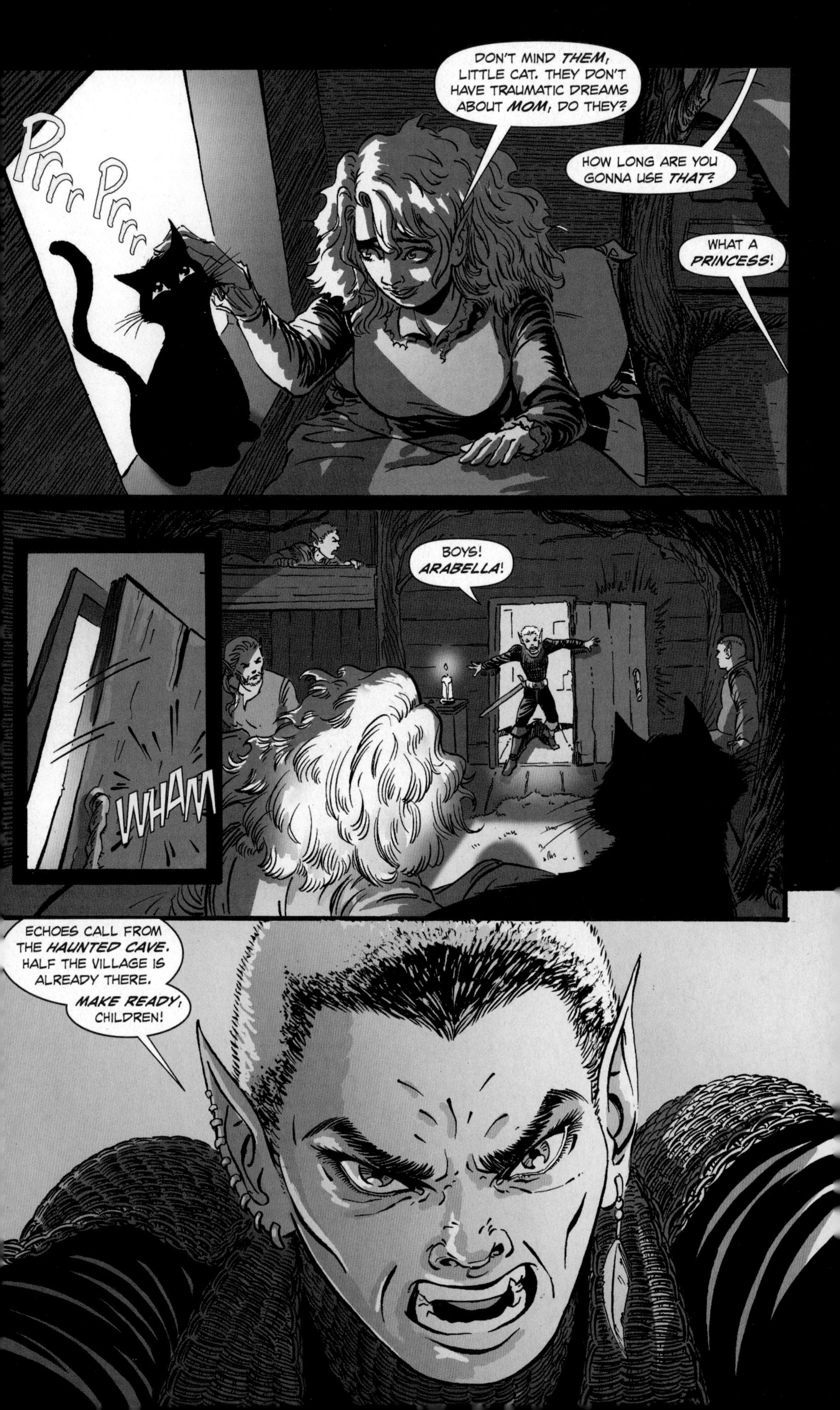
Prrrr Prrrr
DON'T MIND THEM, LITTLE CAT. THEY DON'T HAVE TRAUMATIC DREAMS ABOUT MOM, DO THEY?
HOW LONG ARE YOU GONNA USE THAT?
WHAT A PRINCESS!
WHAM
BOYS! ARABELLA!
ECHOES CALL FROM THE HAUNTED CAVE. HALF THE VILLAGE IS ALREADY THERE.
MAKE READY, CHILDREN!

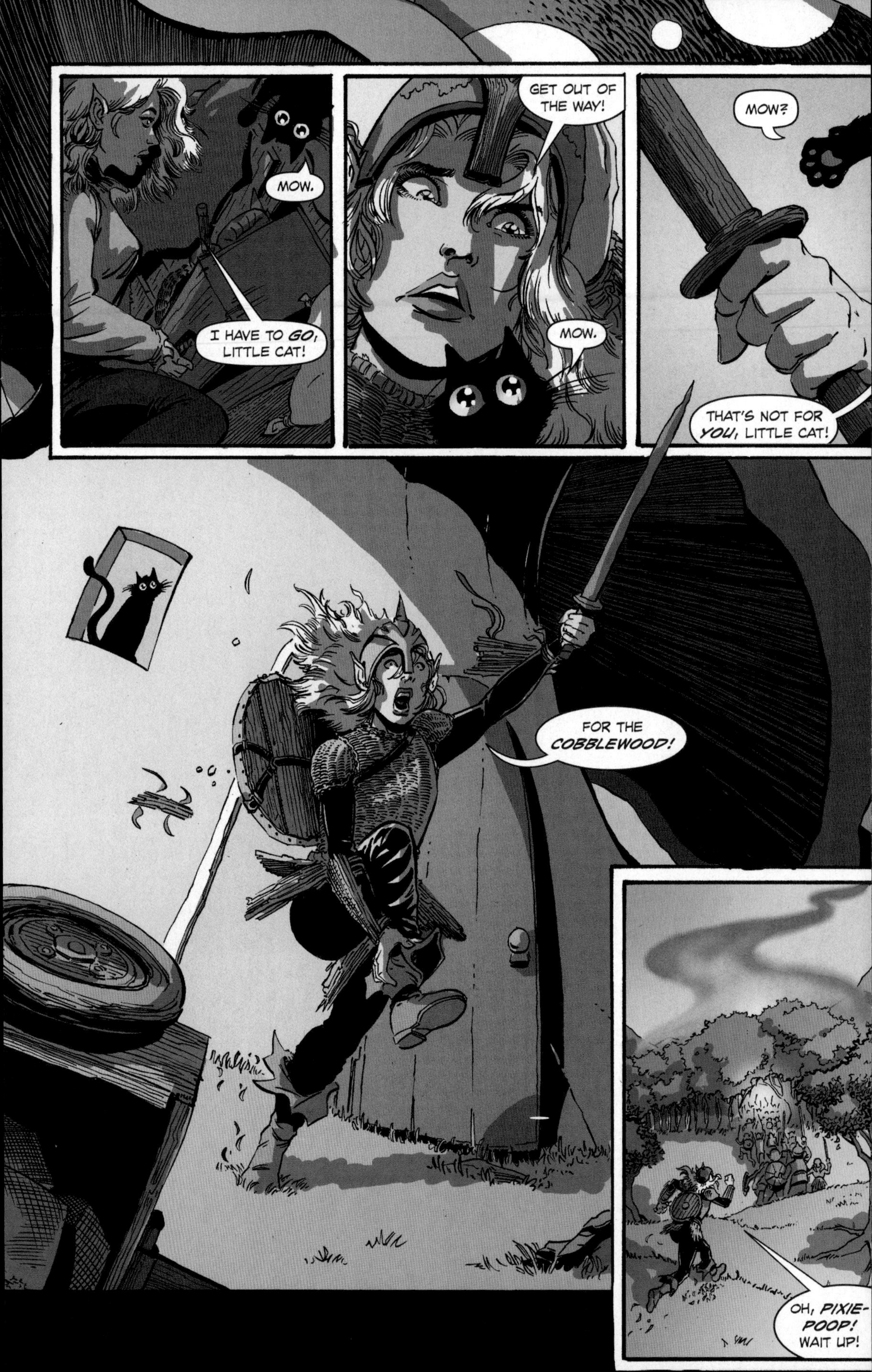
MOW.
I HAVE TO GO, LITTLE CAT!
GET OUT OF THE WAY!
MOW.
MOW?
THAT'S NOT FOR YOU, LITTLE CAT!
FOR THE COBBLEWOOD!
OH, PIXIE-POOP! WAIT UP!

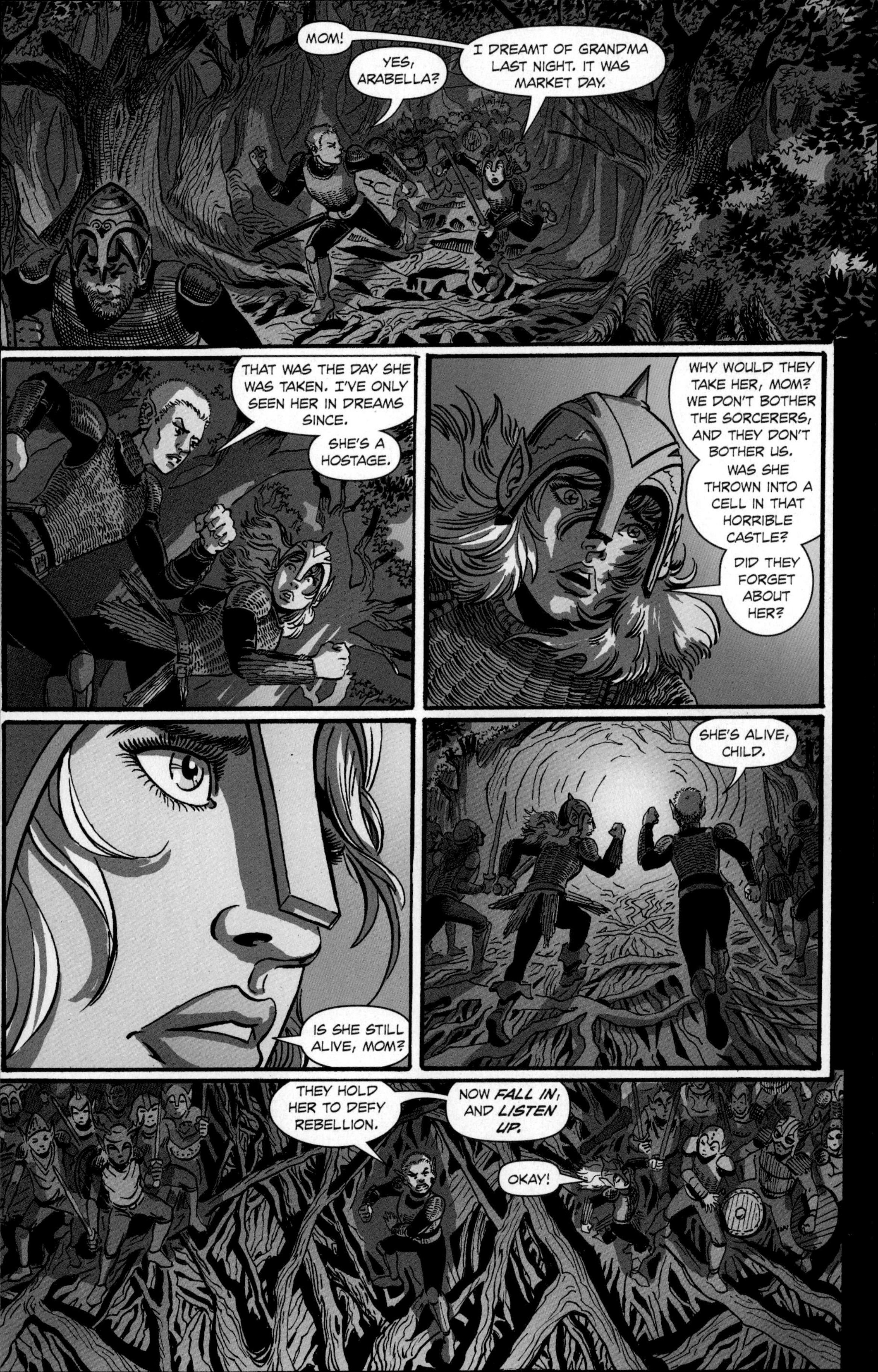
MOM!
YES, ARABELLA?
I DREAMT OF GRANDMA LAST NIGHT. IT WAS MARKET DAY.
THAT WAS THE DAY SHE WAS TAKEN. I'VE ONLY SEEN HER IN DREAMS SINCE.
SHE'S A HOSTAGE.
WHY WOULD THEY TAKE HER, MOM? WE DON'T BOTHER THE SORCERERS, AND THEY DON'T BOTHER US.
WAS SHE THROWN INTO A CELL IN THAT HORRIBLE CASTLE?
DID THEY FORGET ABOUT HER?
IS SHE STILL ALIVE, MOM?
SHE'S ALIVE, CHILD.
THEY HOLD HER TO DEFY REBELLION.
NOW *FALL IN*, AND *LISTEN UP*.
OKAY!

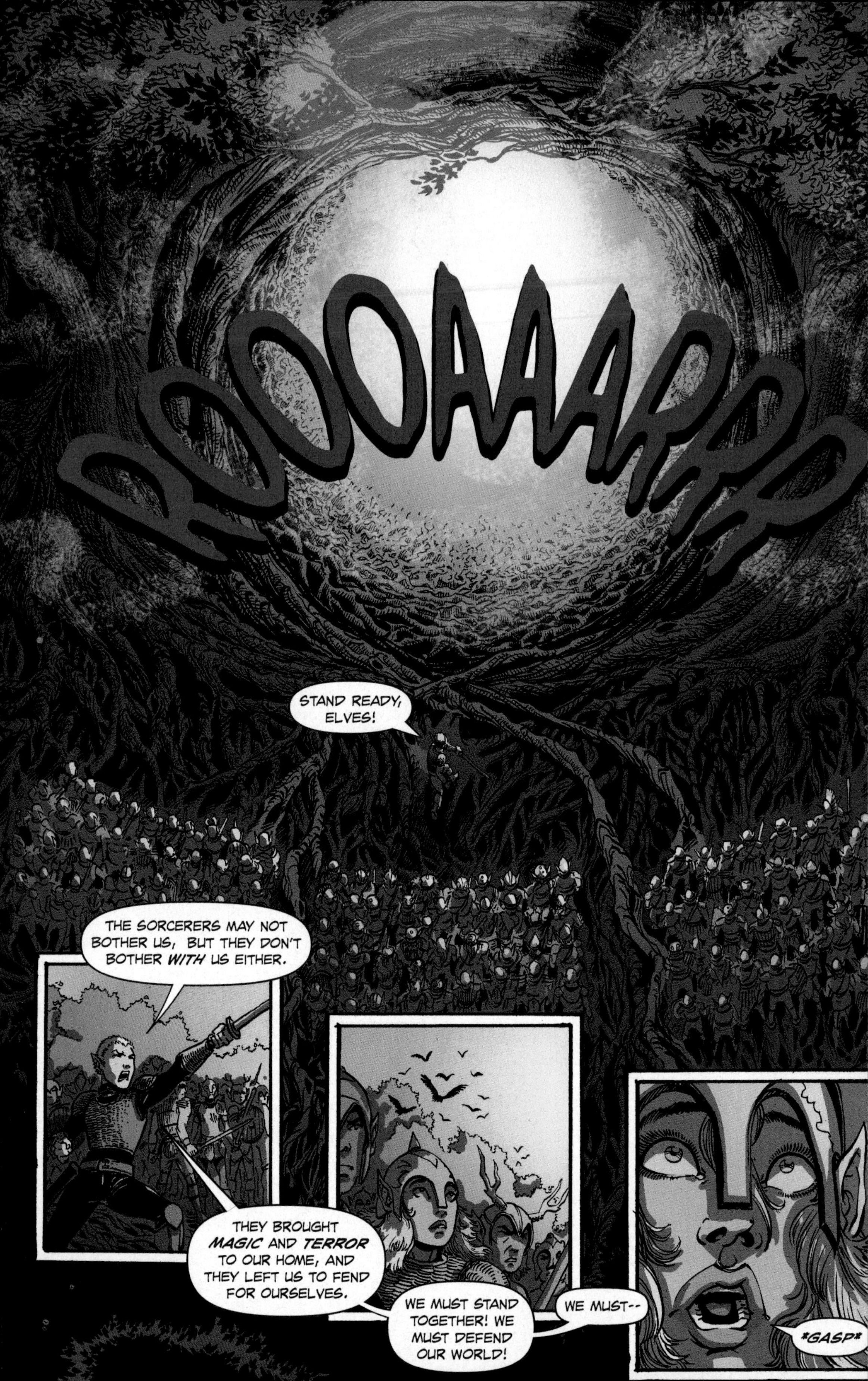
ROOOAAARRR
STAND READY, ELVES!
THE SORCERERS MAY NOT BOTHER US, BUT THEY DON'T BOTHER WITH US EITHER.
THEY BROUGHT MAGIC AND TERROR TO OUR HOME, AND THEY LEFT US TO FEND FOR OURSELVES.
WE MUST STAND TOGETHER! WE MUST DEFEND OUR WORLD!
WE MUST--
GASP

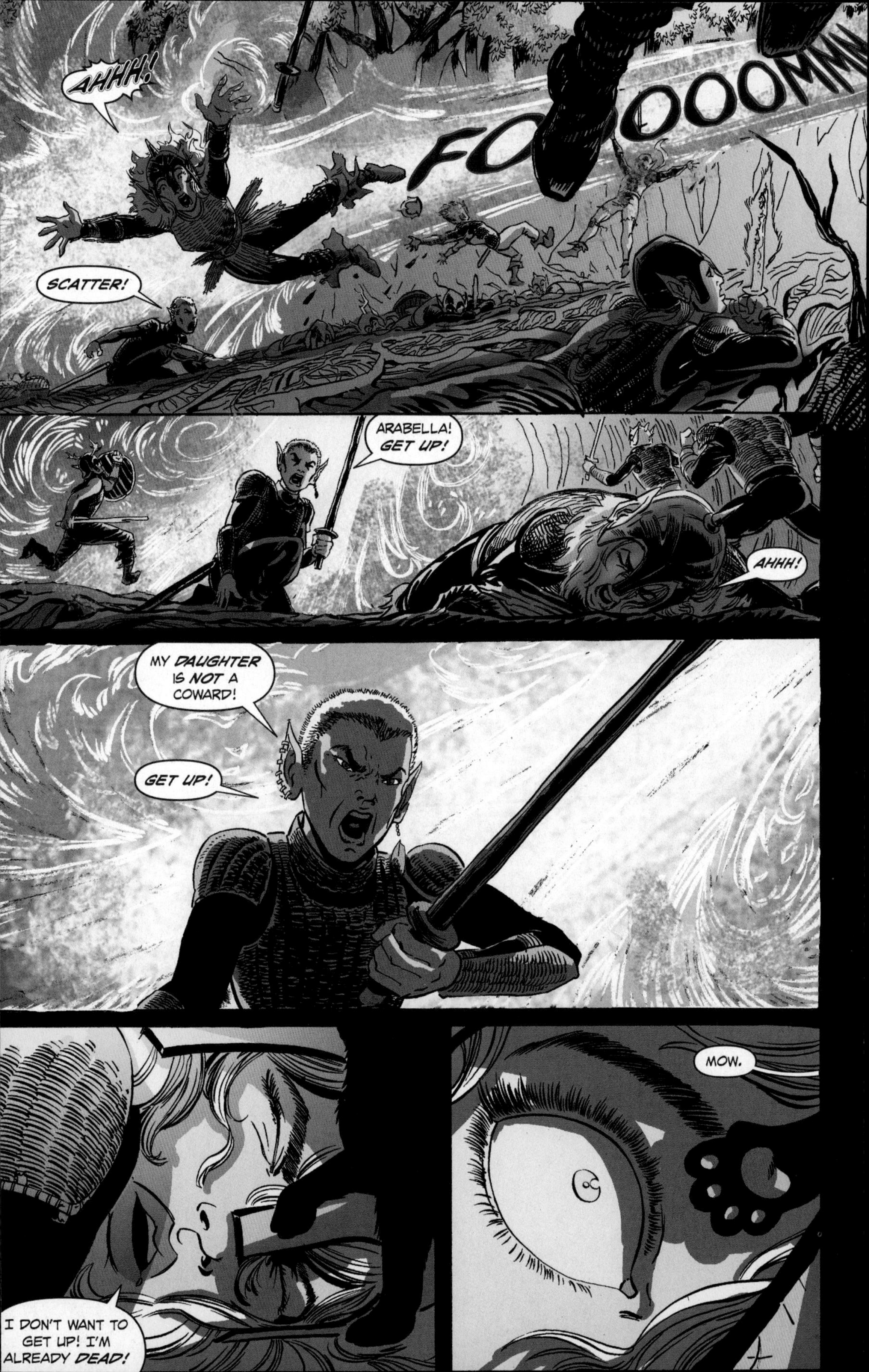
AHHH!
FOOOOOMM
SCATTER!
ARABELLA! GET UP!
AHHH!
MY DAUGHTER IS NOT A COWARD!
GET UP!
I DON'T WANT TO GET UP! I'M ALREADY DEAD!
MOW.

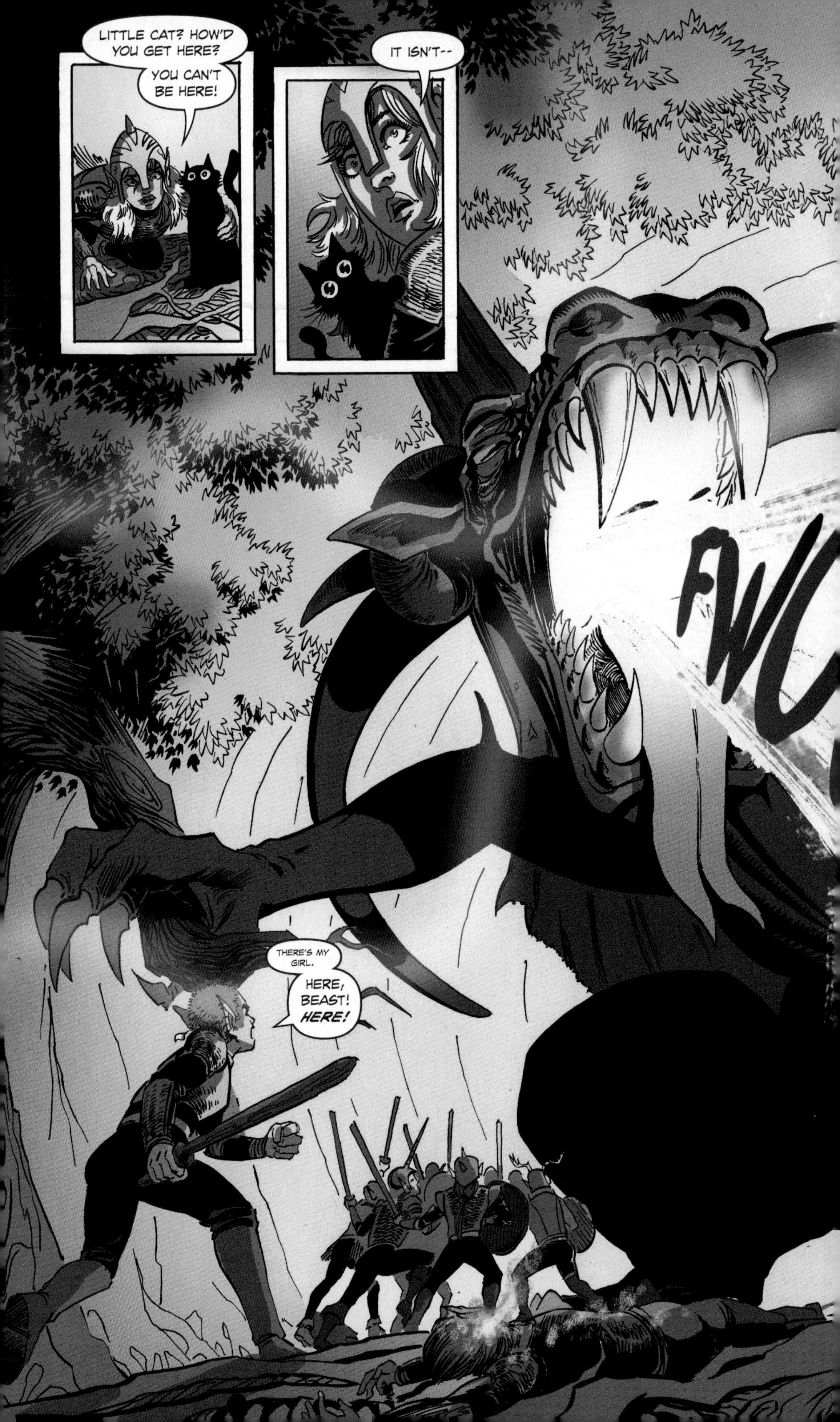
LITTLE CAT? HOW'D YOU GET HERE?
YOU CAN'T BE HERE!
IT ISN'T--
FWC
THERE'S MY GIRL.
HERE, BEAST! HERE!

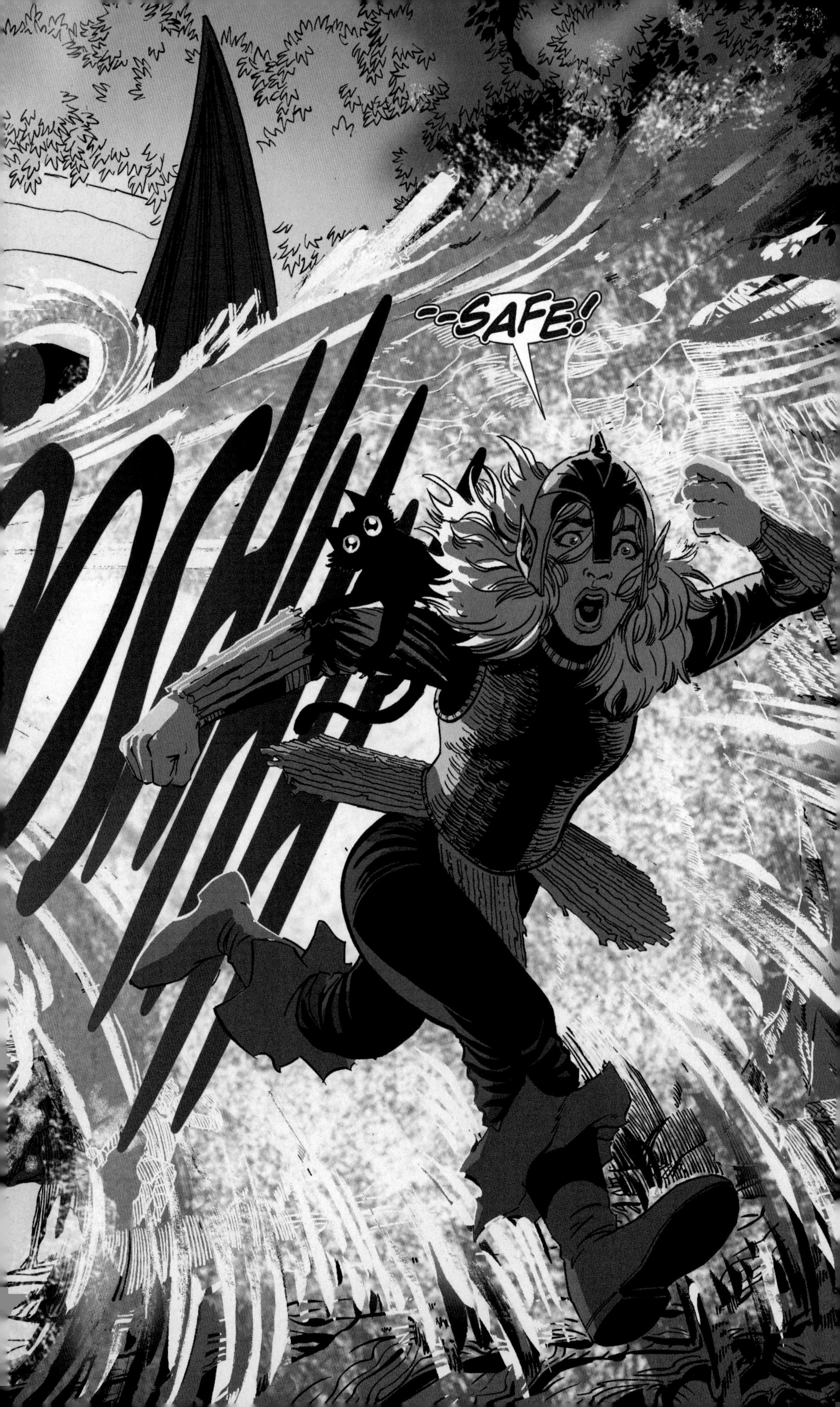
--SAFE!

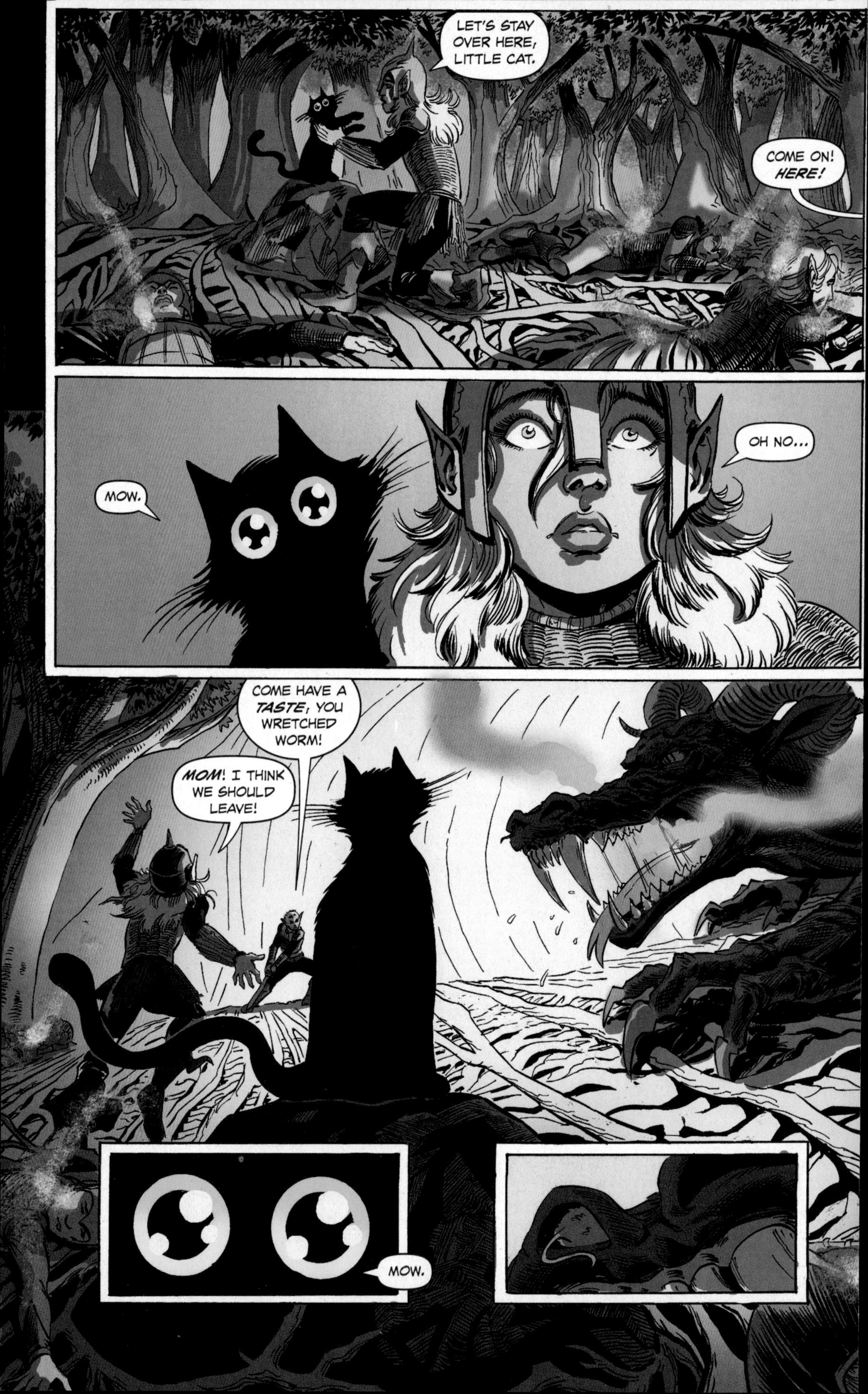
LET'S STAY OVER HERE, LITTLE CAT.
COME ON! *HERE!*
MOW.
OH NO...
COME HAVE A *TASTE*, YOU WRETCHED WORM!
MOM! I THINK WE SHOULD LEAVE!
MOW.

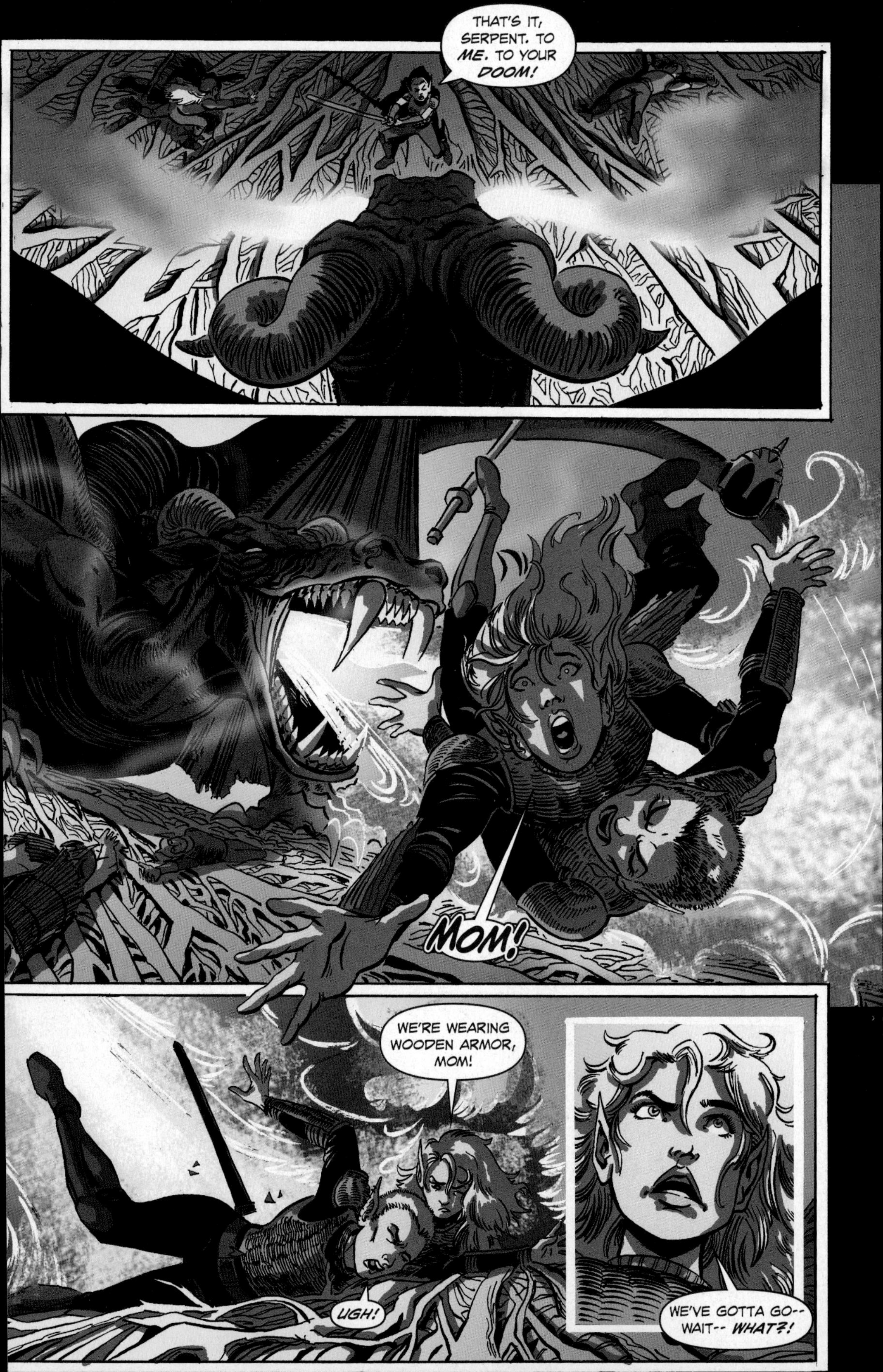
THAT'S IT, SERPENT. TO ME. TO YOUR DOOM!
MOM!
WE'RE WEARING WOODEN ARMOR, MOM!
UGH!
WE'VE GOTTA GO-- WAIT-- WHAT?!

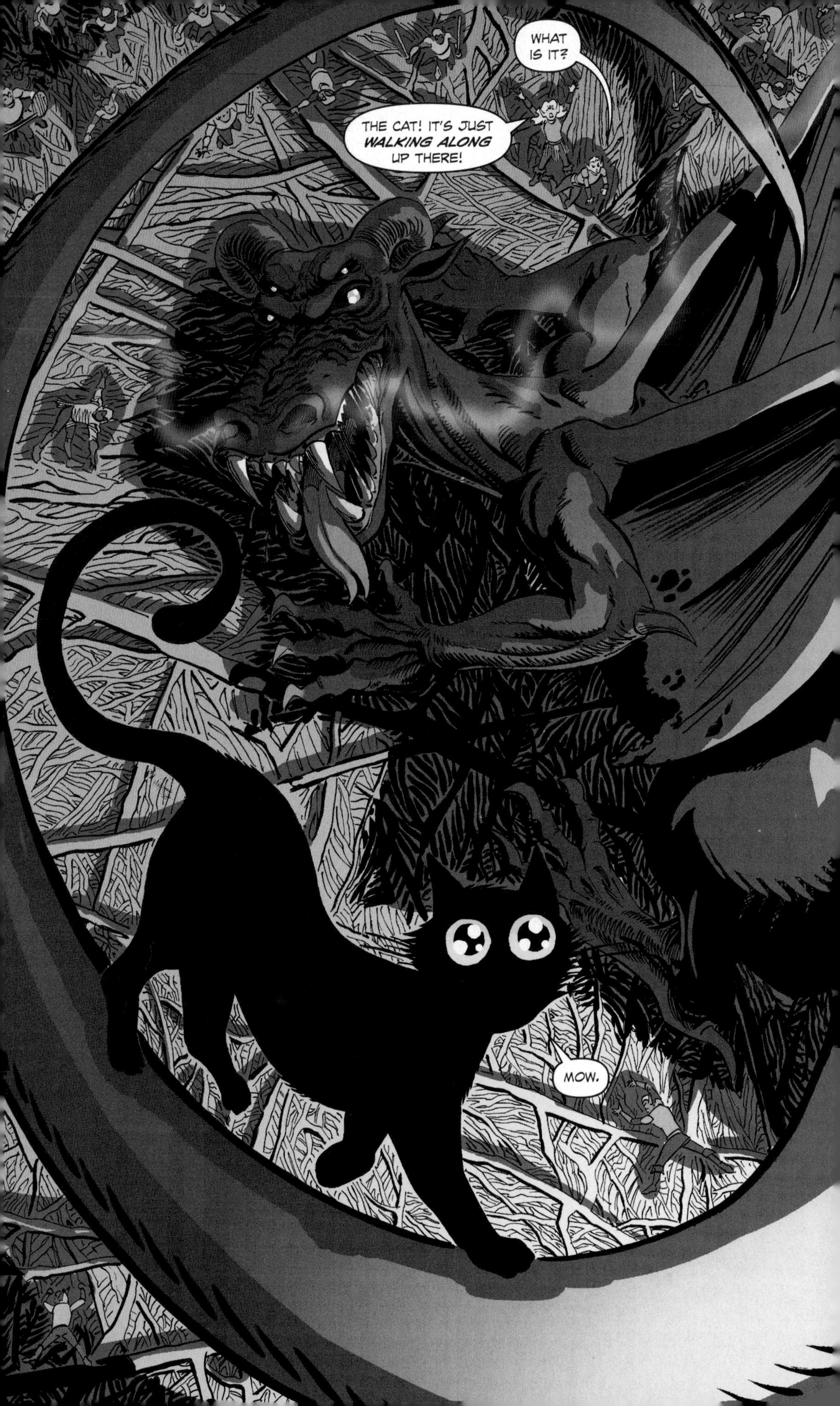

WHAT IS IT?
THE CAT! IT'S JUST *WALKING ALONG* UP THERE!
MOW.

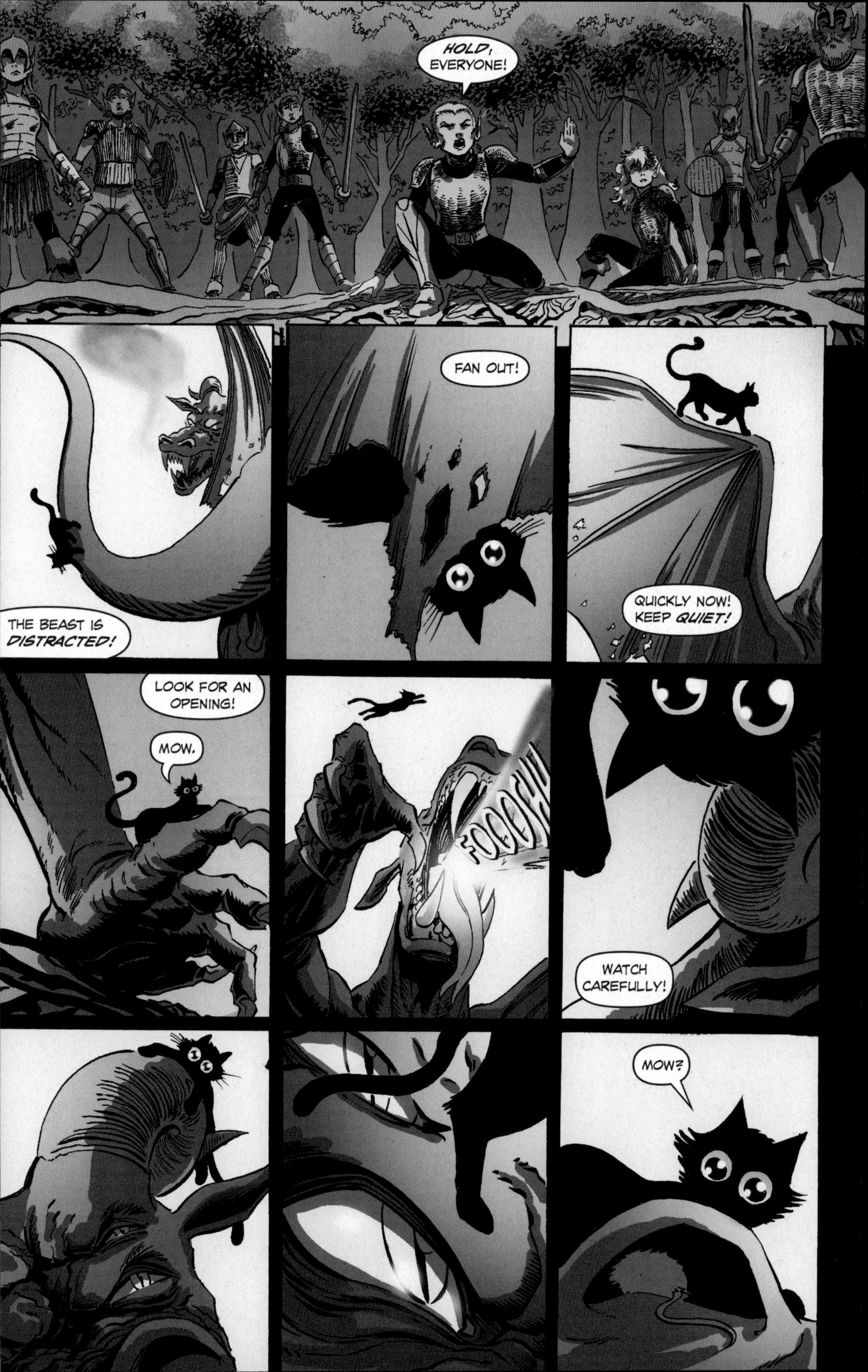
HOLD, EVERYONE!
THE BEAST IS DISTRACTED!
FAN OUT!
QUICKLY NOW! KEEP QUIET!
LOOK FOR AN OPENING!
MOW.
FOOOSH
WATCH CAREFULLY!
MOW?

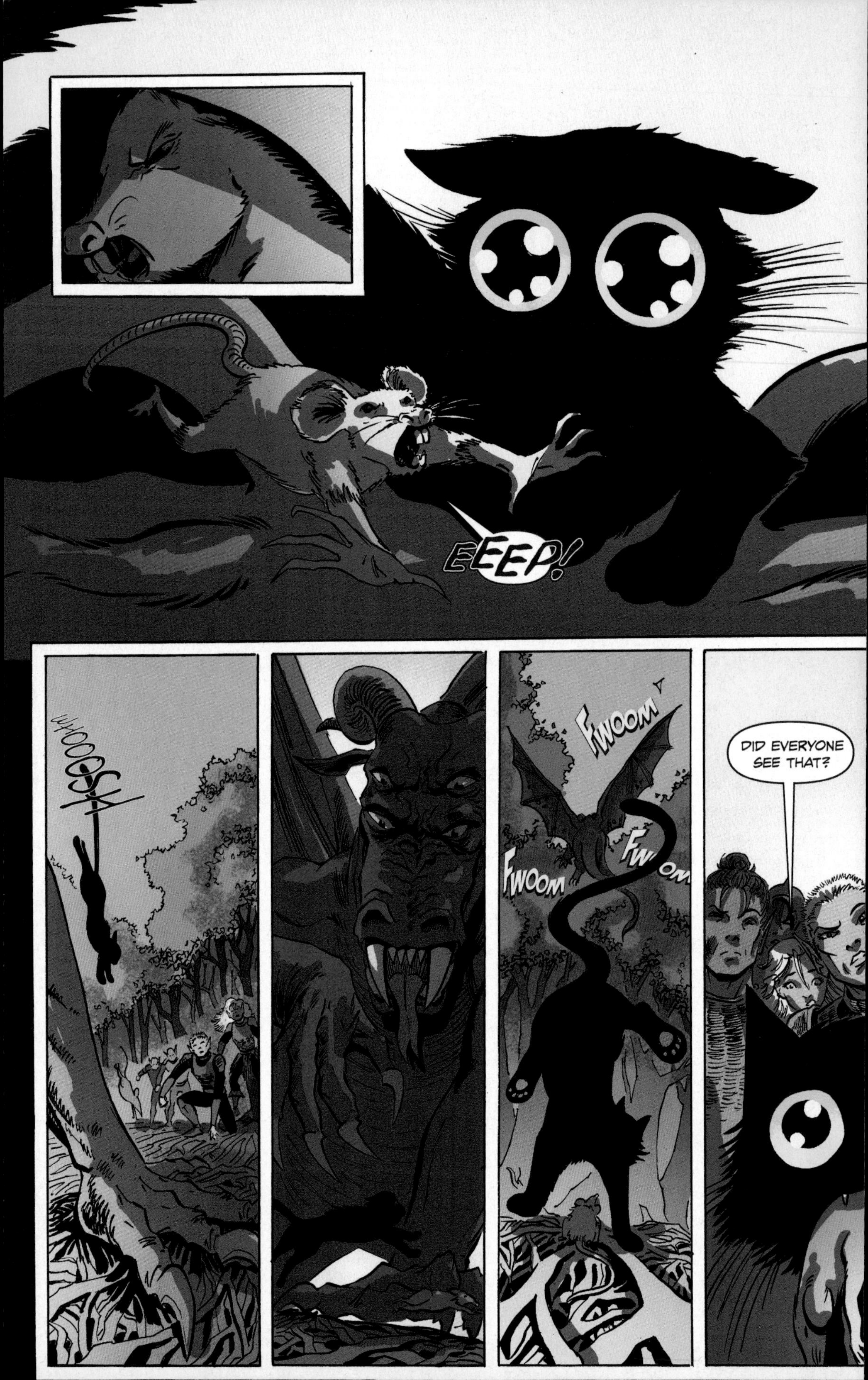
EEEP!
WHOOOSH
FWOOM
FWOOM
FWOOM
DID EVERYONE SEE THAT?

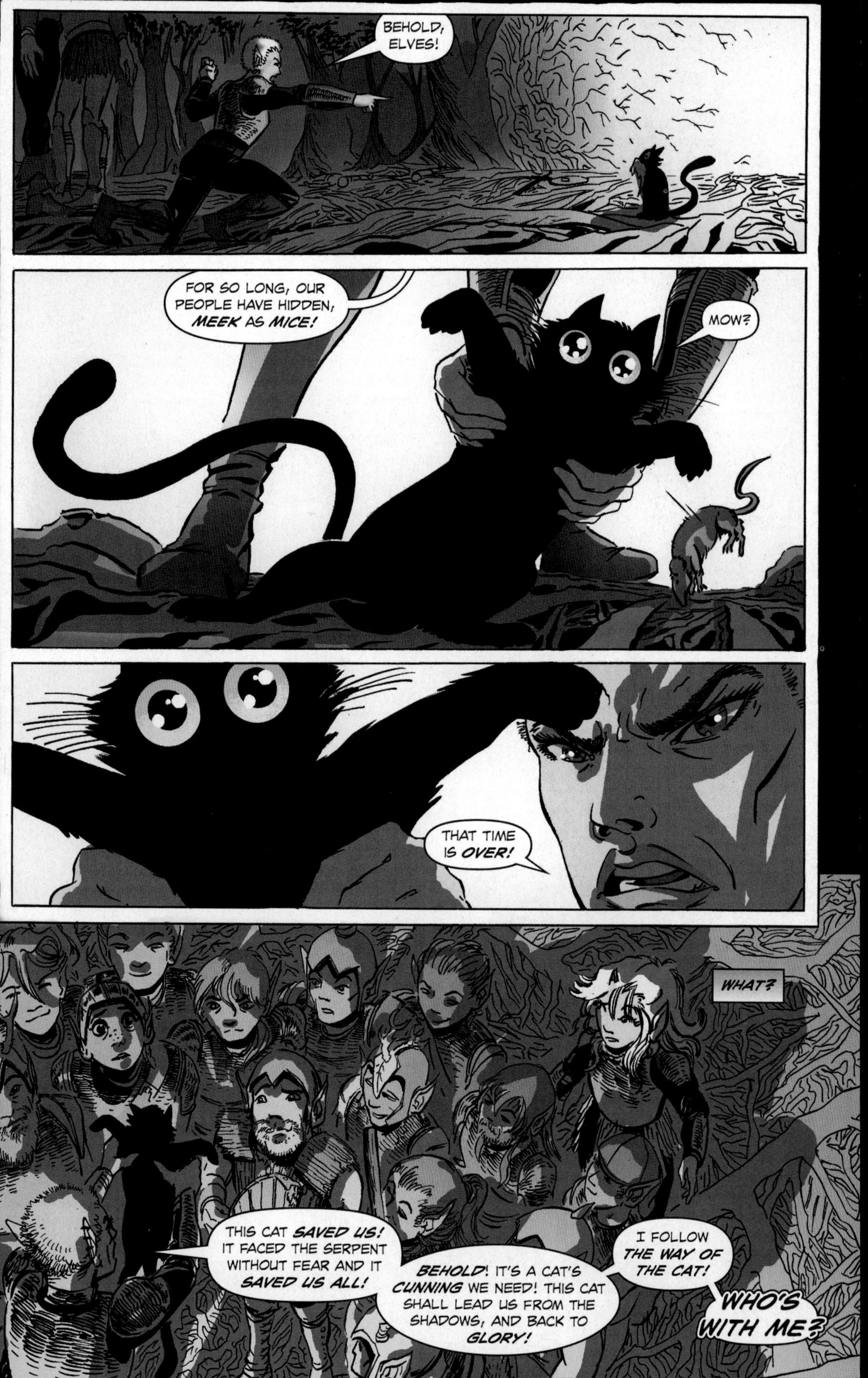
BEHOLD, ELVES!
FOR SO LONG, OUR PEOPLE HAVE HIDDEN, MEEK AS MICE!
MOW?
THAT TIME IS OVER!
WHAT?
THIS CAT SAVED US! IT FACED THE SERPENT WITHOUT FEAR AND IT SAVED US ALL!
BEHOLD! IT'S A CAT'S CUNNING WE NEED! THIS CAT SHALL LEAD US FROM THE SHADOWS, AND BACK TO GLORY!
I FOLLOW THE WAY OF THE CAT!
WHO'S WITH ME?

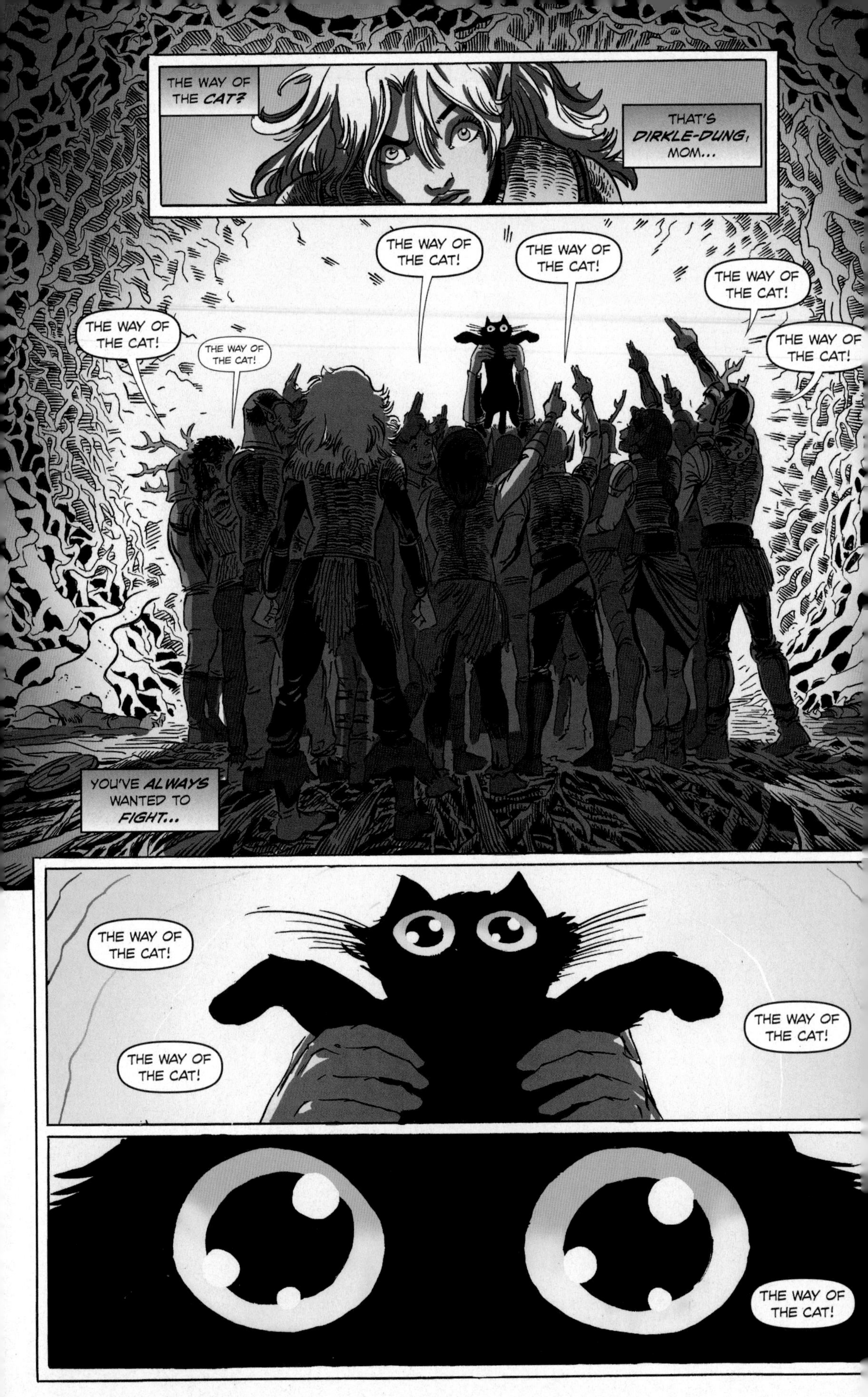
THE WAY OF THE CAT?
THAT'S DIRKLE-DUNG, MOM...
THE WAY OF THE CAT!
THE WAY OF THE CAT!
THE WAY OF THE CAT!
THE WAY OF THE CAT!
THE WAY OF THE CAT!
THE WAY OF THE CAT!
YOU'VE ALWAYS WANTED TO FIGHT...
THE WAY OF THE CAT!
THE WAY OF THE CAT!
THE WAY OF THE CAT!
THE WAY OF THE CAT!

3

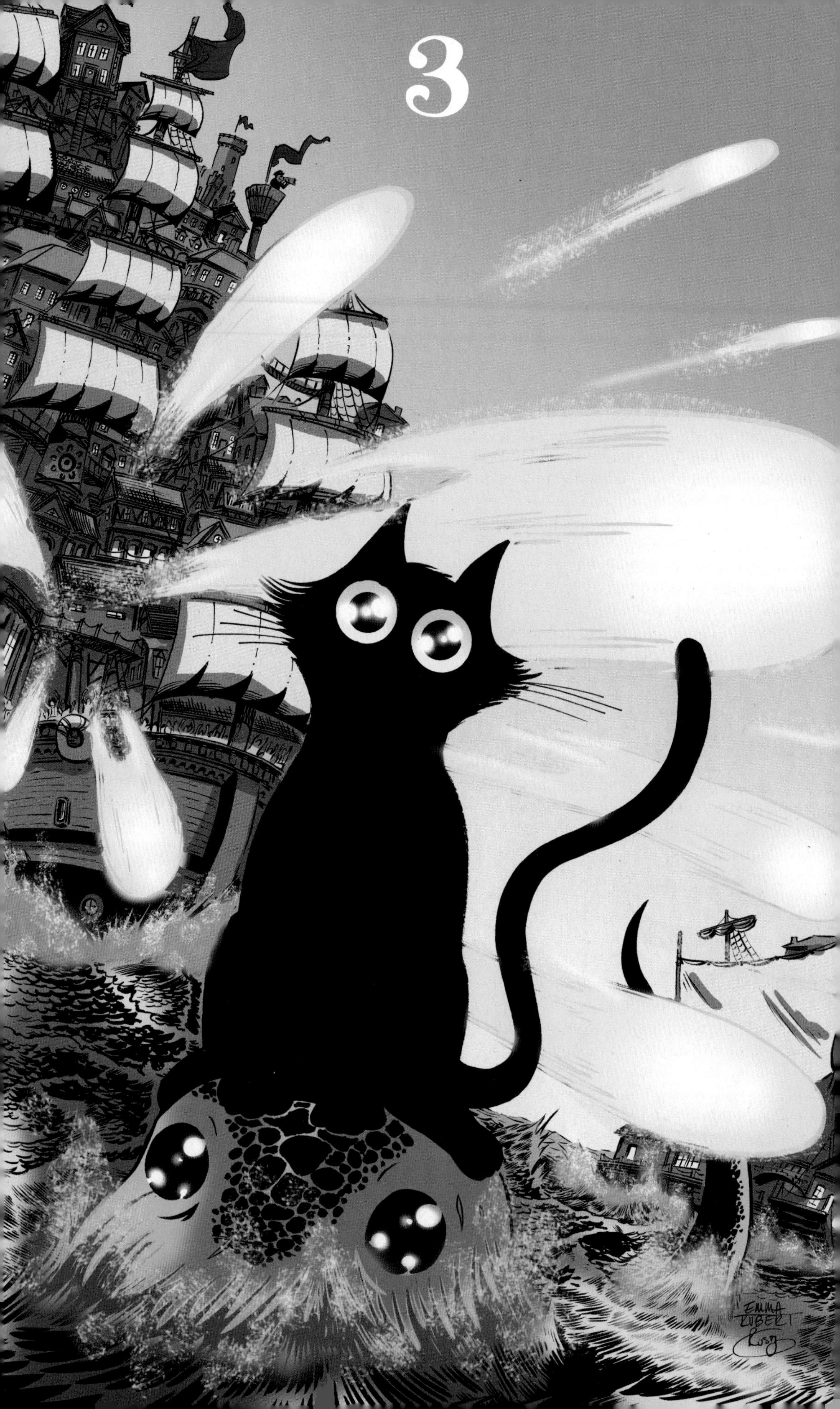
EMMA KUBERT

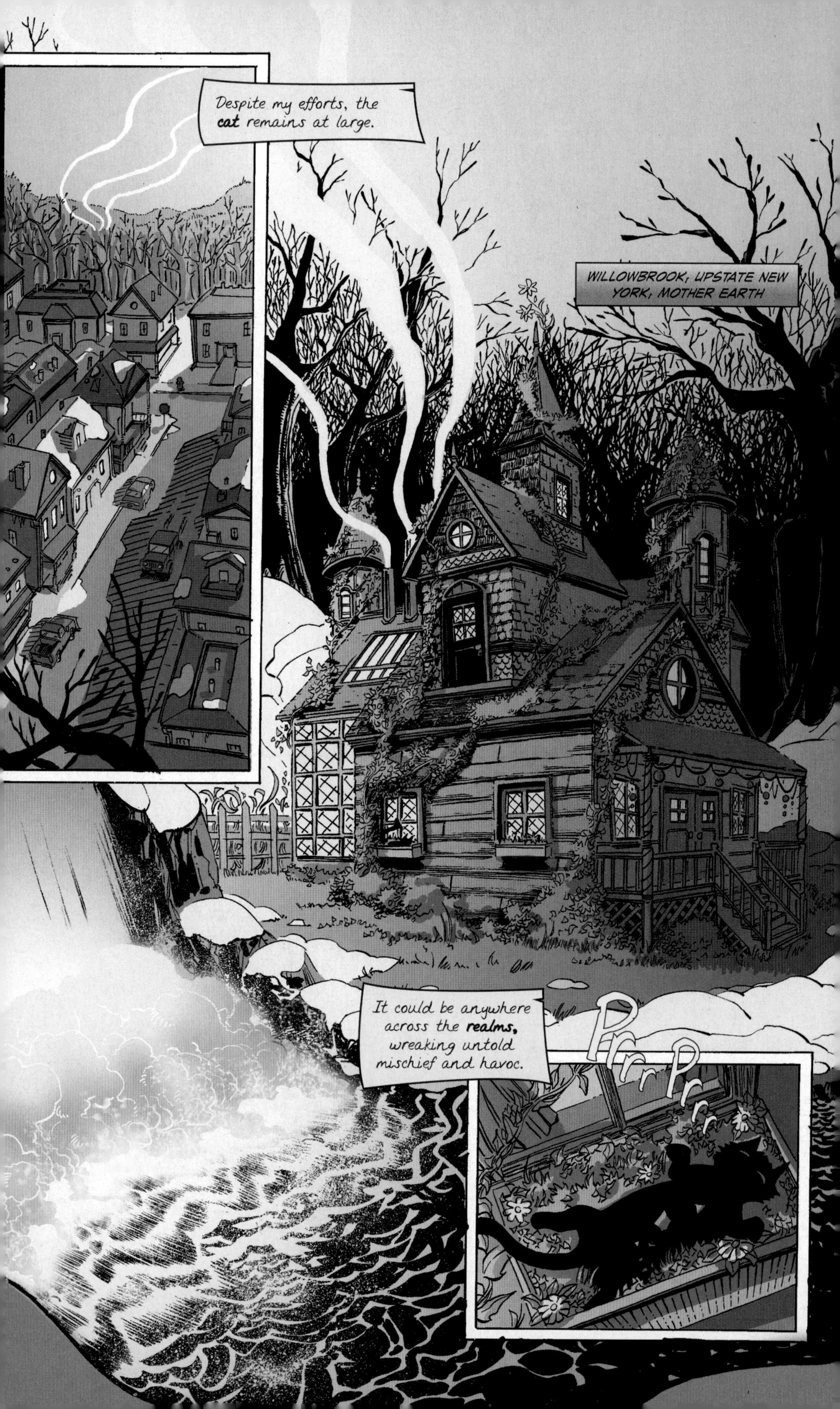

Despite my efforts, the **cat** remains at large.
WILLOWBROOK, UPSTATE NEW YORK, MOTHER EARTH
It could be anywhere across the **realms,** wreaking untold mischief and havoc.
Prrr Prrr

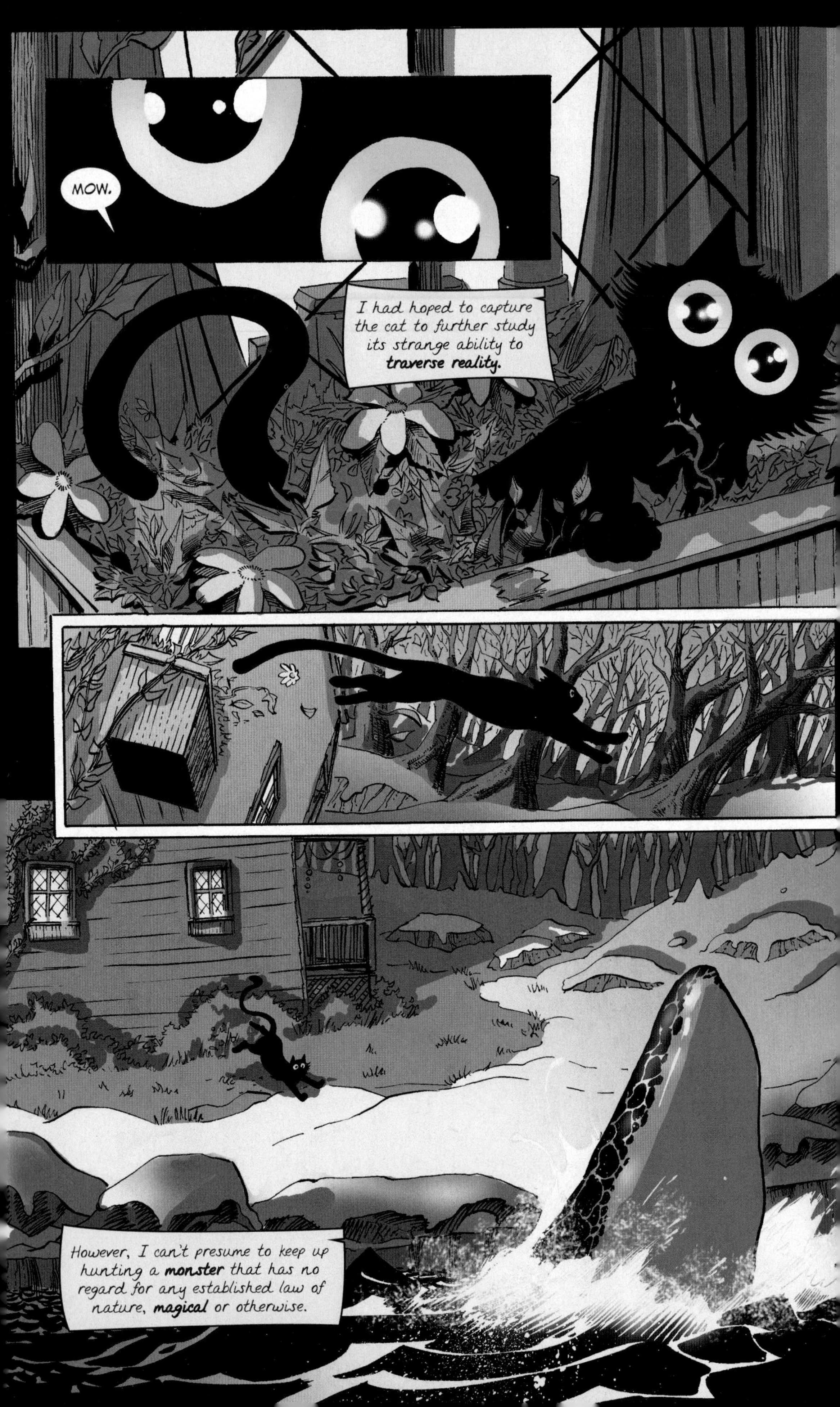
MOW.
I had hoped to capture the cat to further study its strange ability to **traverse reality.**
However, I can't presume to keep up hunting a **monster** that has no regard for any established law of nature, **magical** or otherwise.

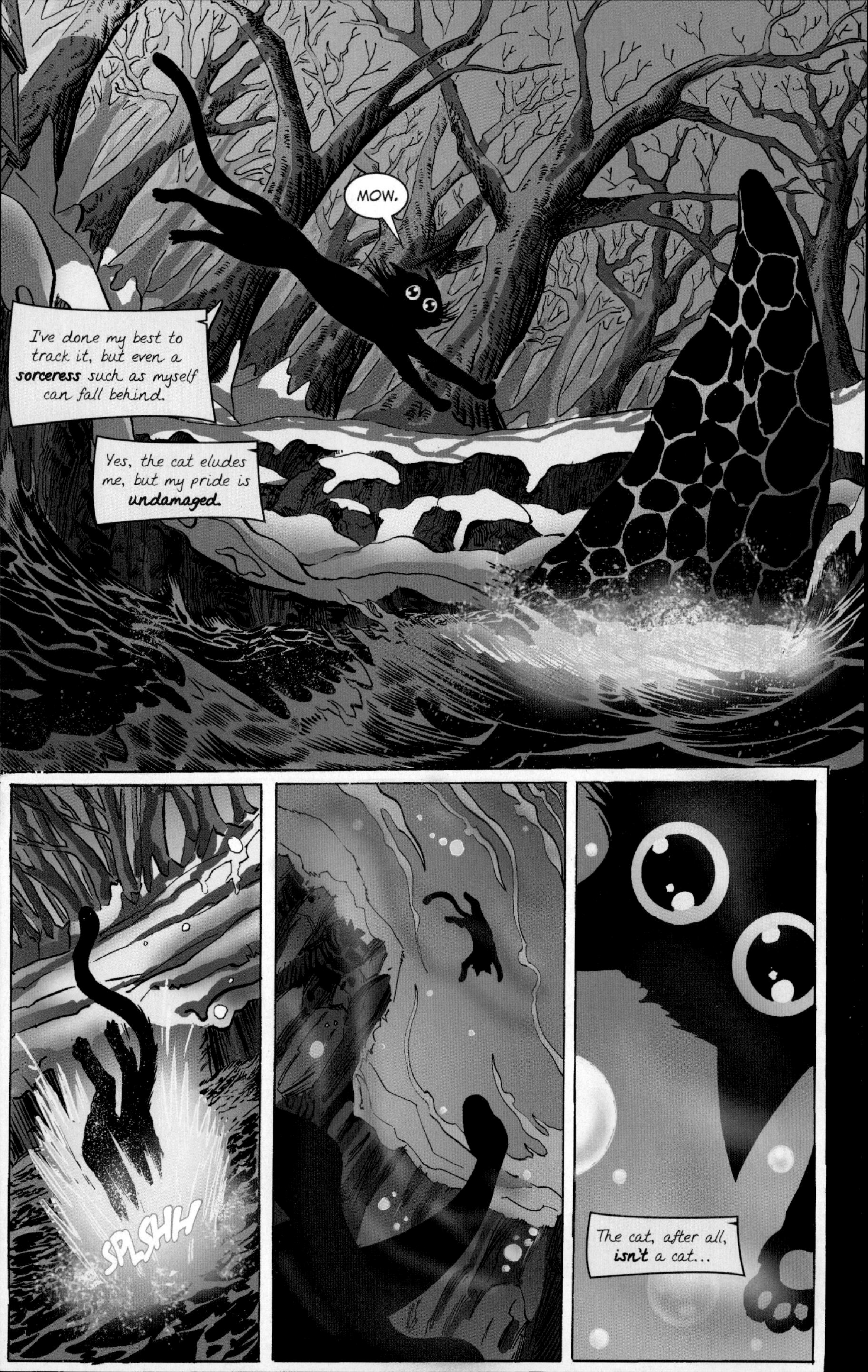
MOW.
I've done my best to track it, but even a **sorceress** such as myself can fall behind.
Yes, the cat eludes me, but my pride is **undamaged.**
SPLSHH
The cat, after all, **isn't** a cat...

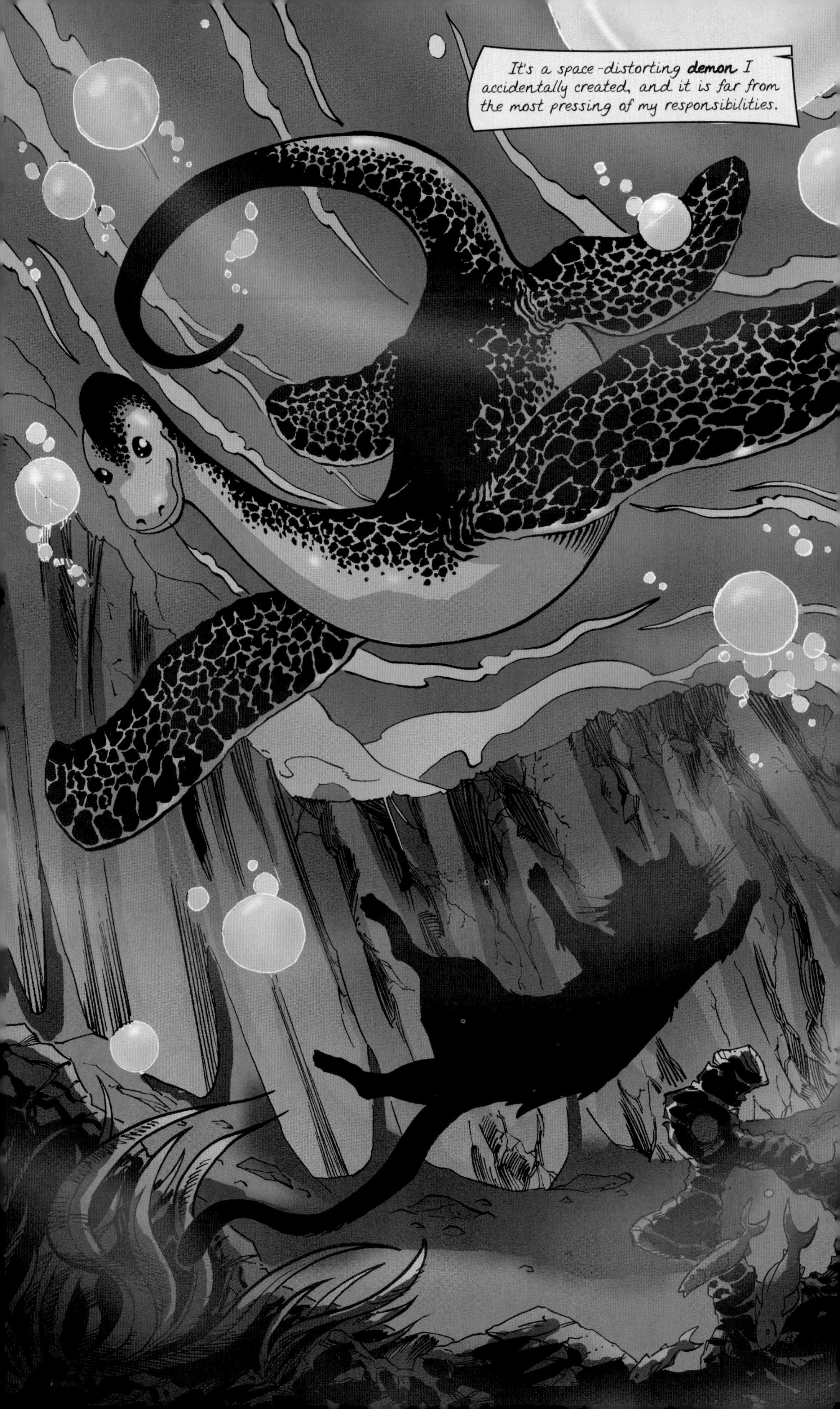
It's a space-distorting **demon** I accidentally created, and it is far from the most pressing of my responsibilities.

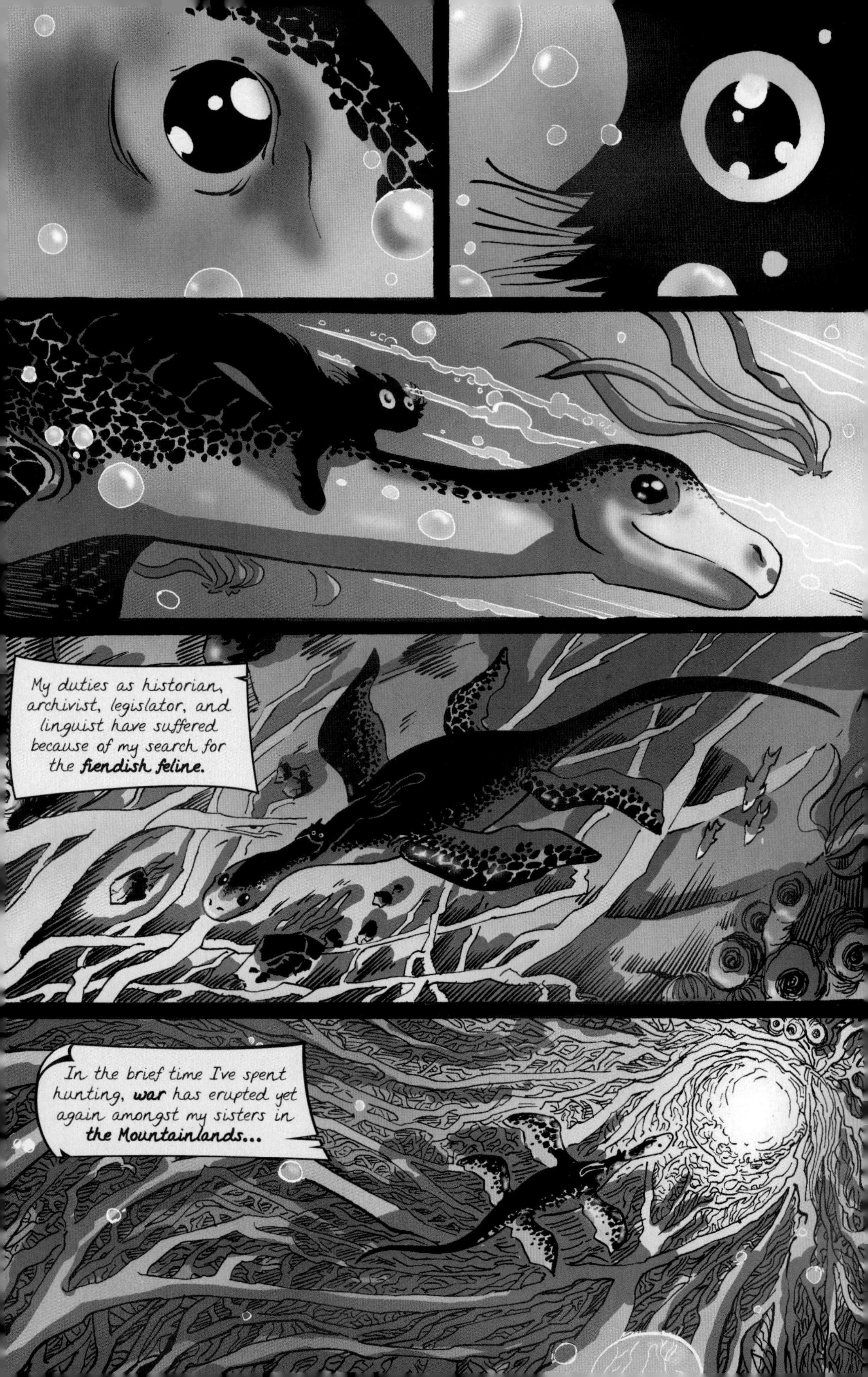
My duties as historian, archivist, legislator, and linguist have suffered because of my search for the **fiendish feline.**
In the brief time I've spent hunting, **war** has erupted yet again amongst my sisters in **the Mountainlands...**

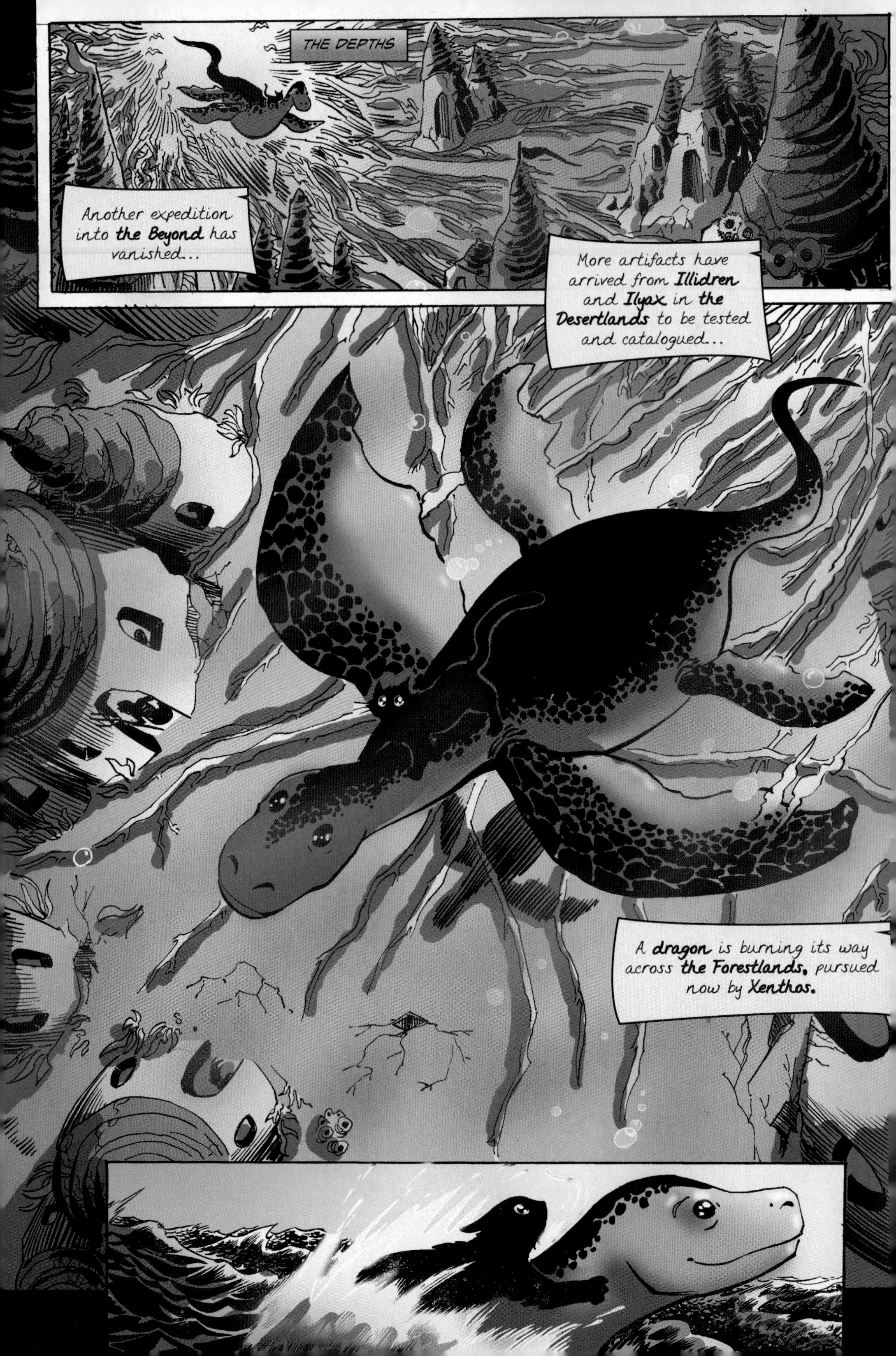
THE DEPTHS
Another expedition into the Beyond has vanished...
More artifacts have arrived from Illidren and Ilyax in the Desertlands to be tested and catalogued...
A dragon is burning its way across the Forestlands, pursued now by Xenthos.

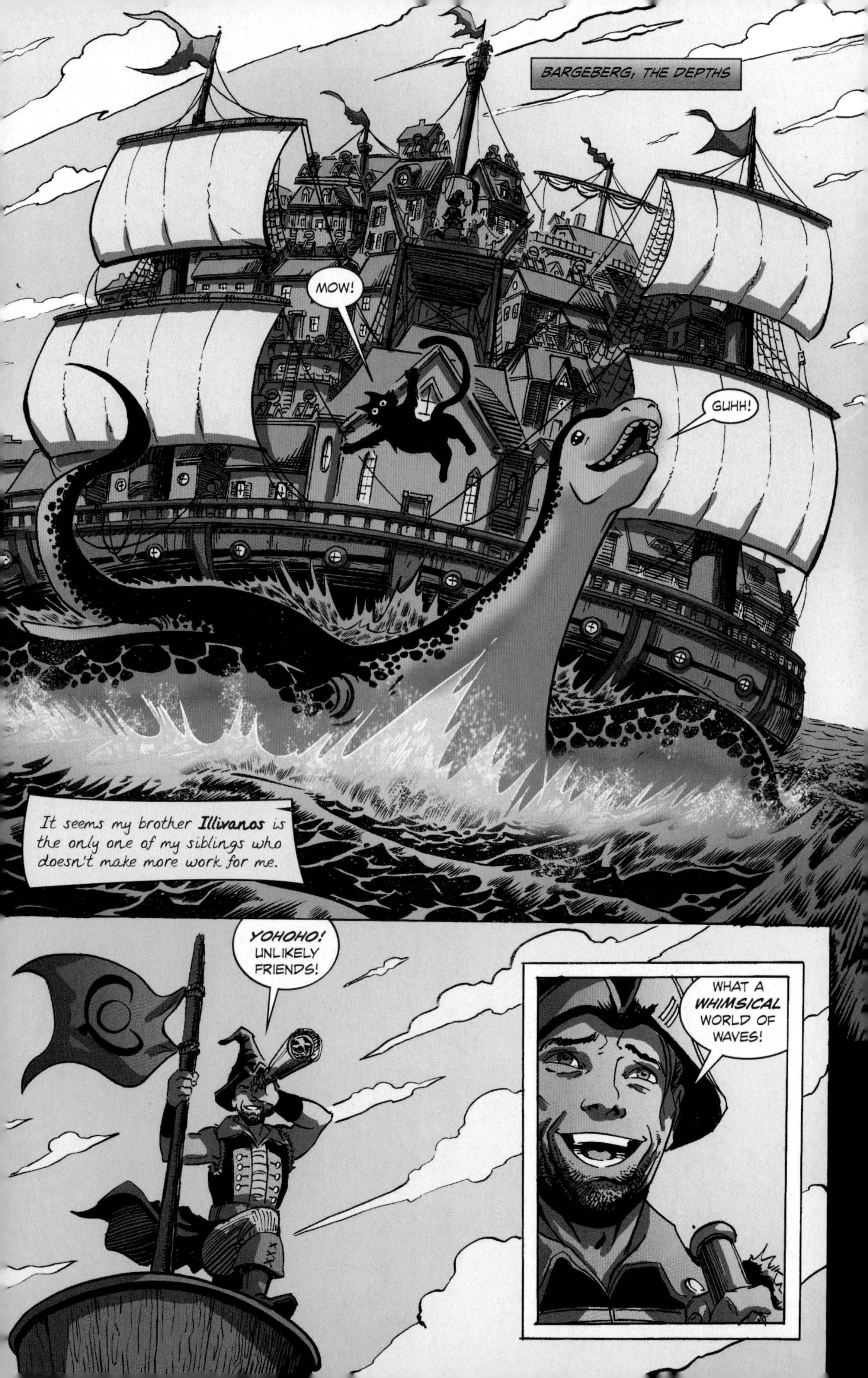
BARGEBERG, THE DEPTHS
MOW!
GUHH!
It seems my brother **Illivanos** is the only one of my siblings who doesn't make more work for me.
YOHOHO! UNLIKELY FRIENDS!
WHAT A WHIMSICAL WORLD OF WAVES!

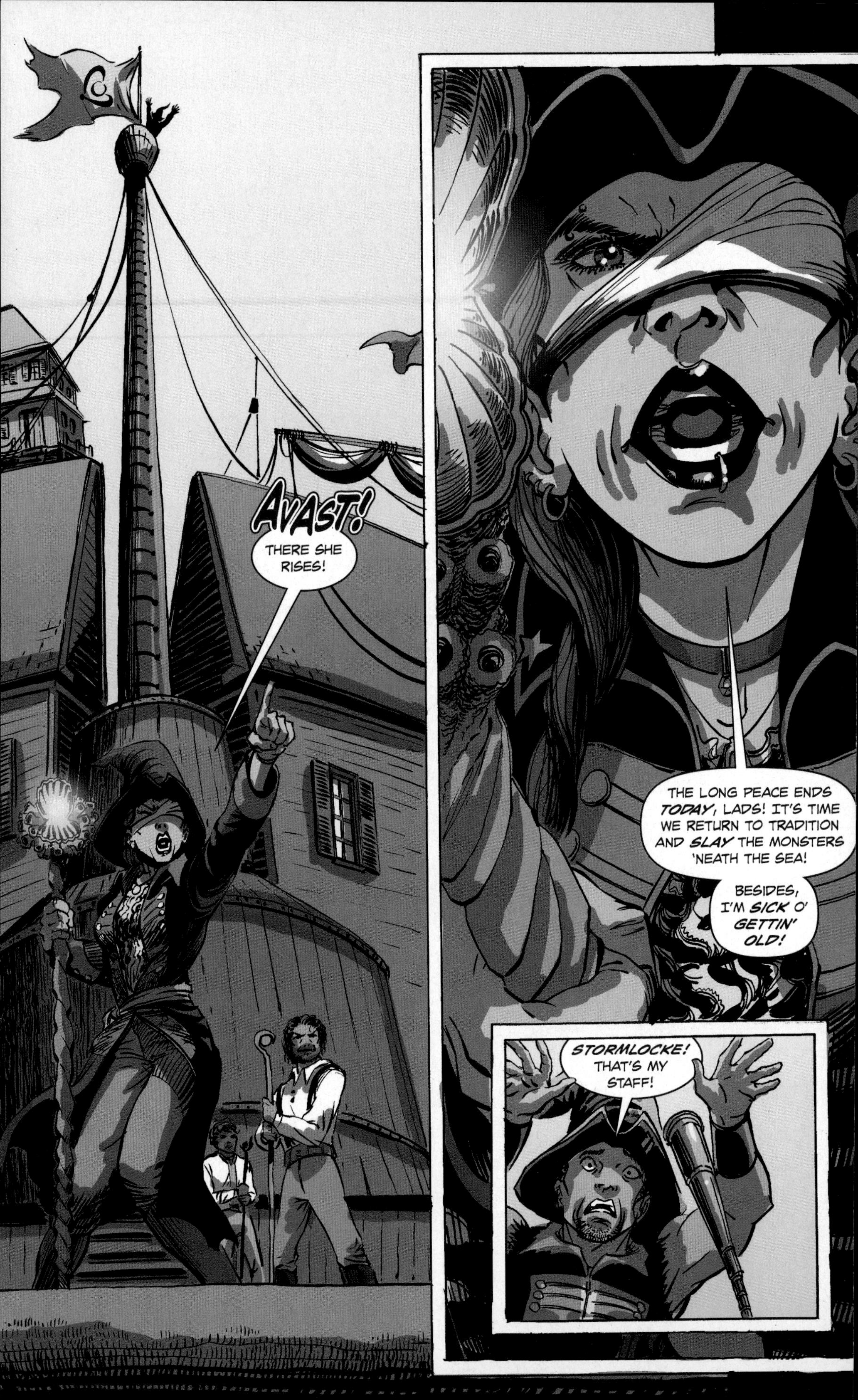
AVAST!
THERE SHE RISES!
THE LONG PEACE ENDS TODAY, LADS! IT'S TIME WE RETURN TO TRADITION AND SLAY THE MONSTERS 'NEATH THE SEA!
BESIDES, I'M SICK O' GETTIN' OLD!
STORMLOCKE! THAT'S MY STAFF!

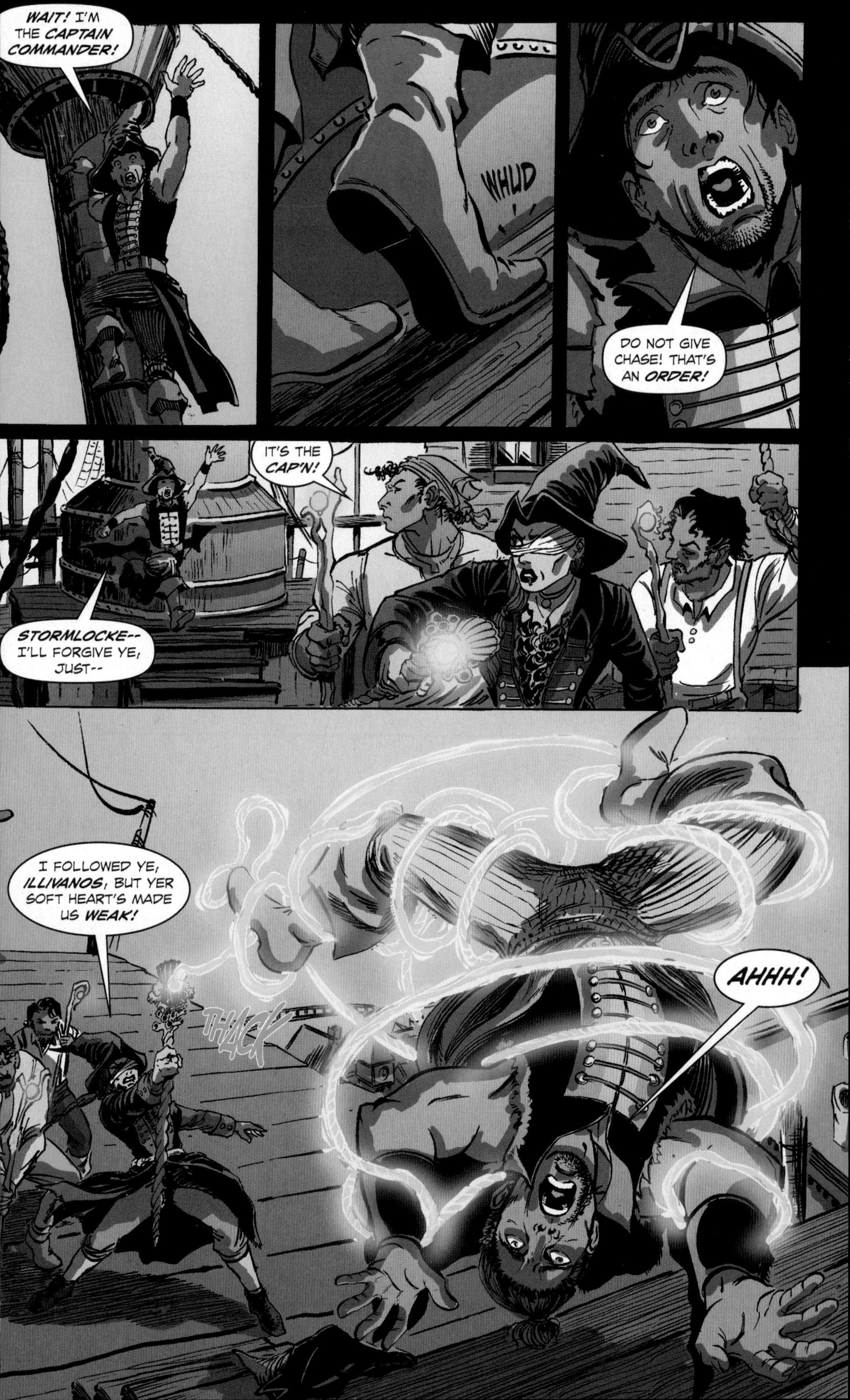
WAIT! I'M THE CAPTAIN COMMANDER!
WHUD
DO NOT GIVE CHASE! THAT'S AN ORDER!
IT'S THE CAP'N!
STORMLOCKE-- I'LL FORGIVE YE, JUST--
I FOLLOWED YE, ILLIVANOS, BUT YER SOFT HEART'S MADE US WEAK!
THACK
AHHH!

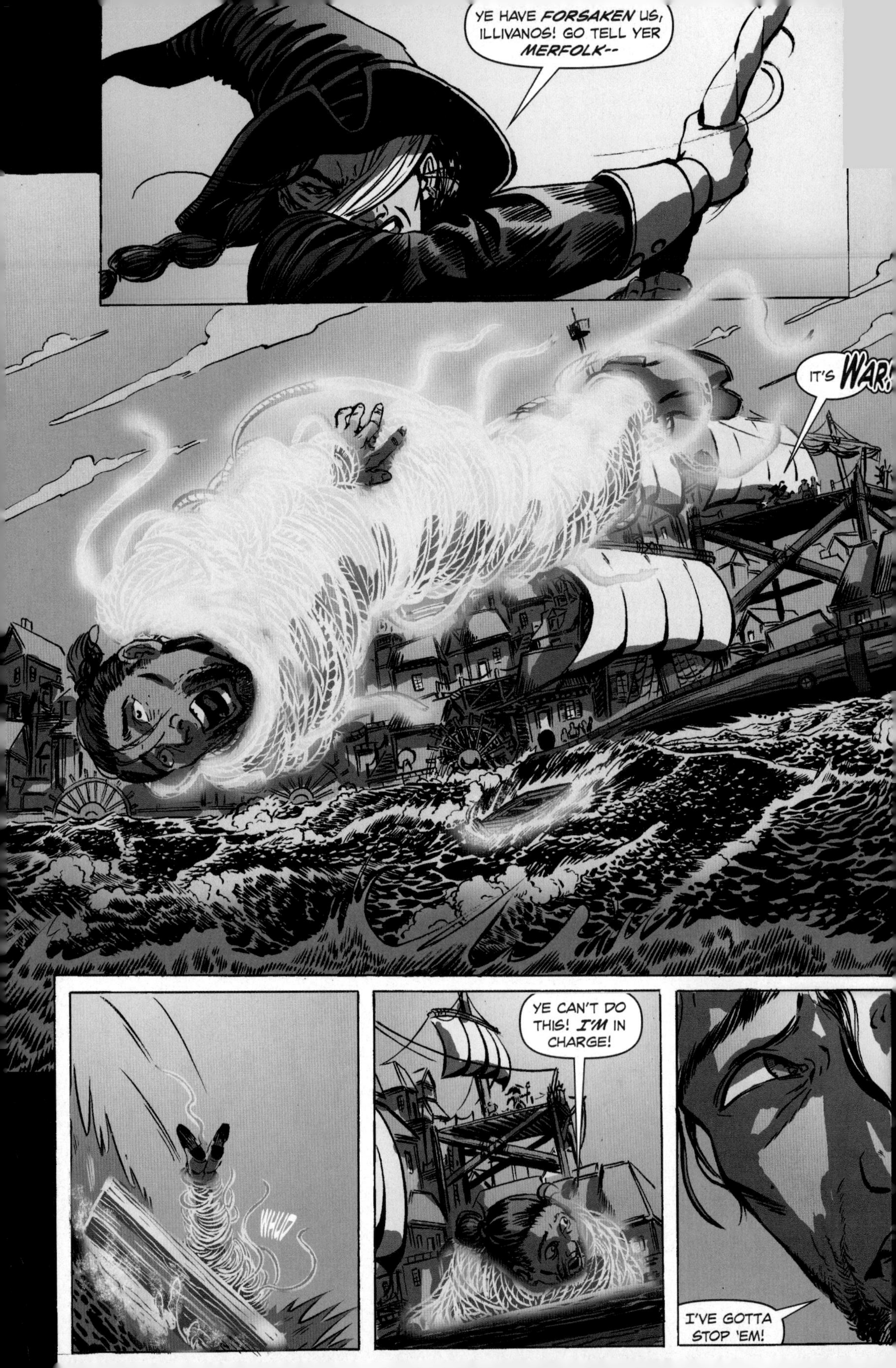
YE HAVE FORSAKEN US, ILLIVANOS! GO TELL YER MERFOLK--
IT'S WAR!
WHUD
YE CAN'T DO THIS! I'M IN CHARGE!
I'VE GOTTA STOP 'EM!

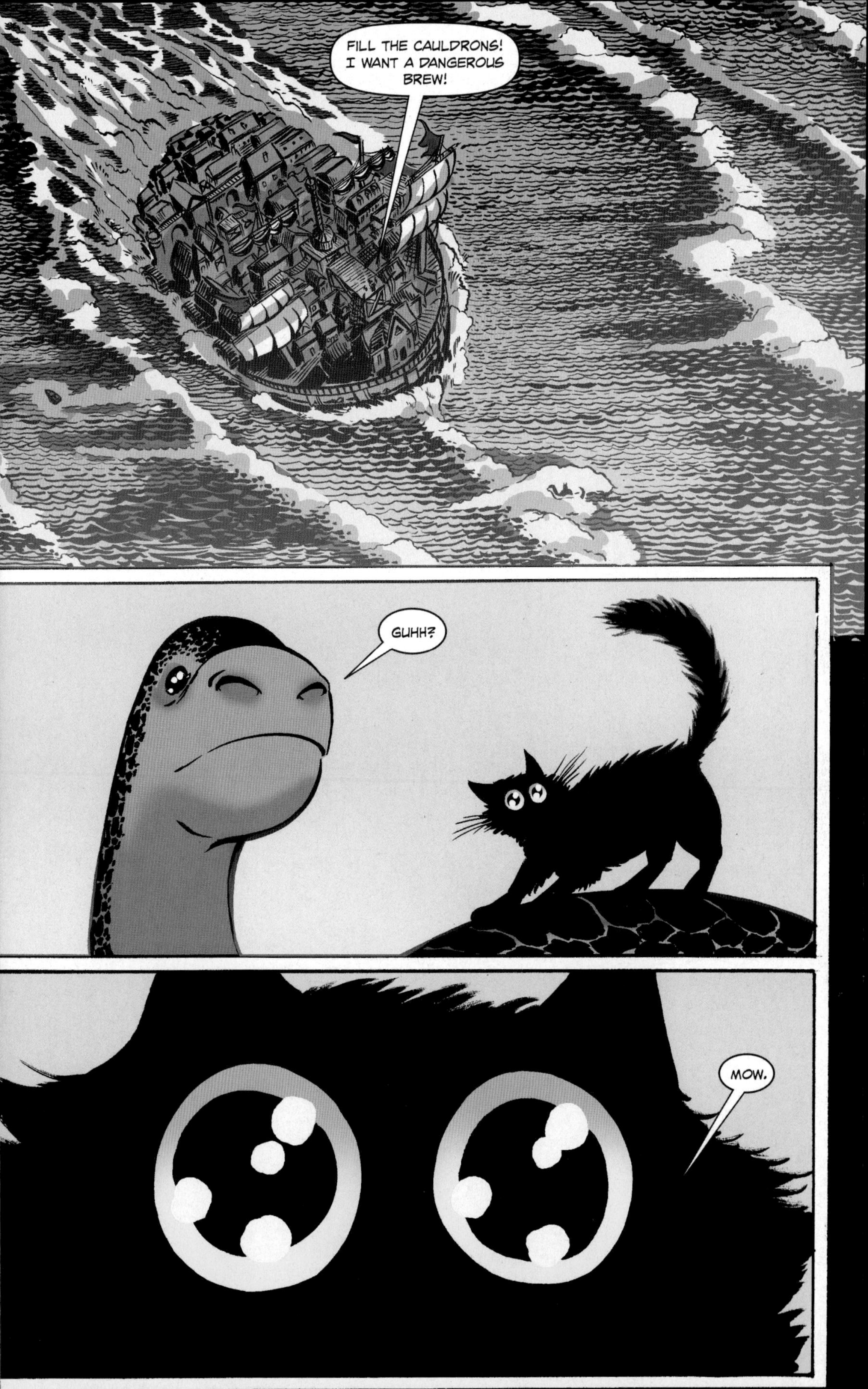
FILL THE CAULDRONS! I WANT A DANGEROUS BREW!
GUHH?
MOW.

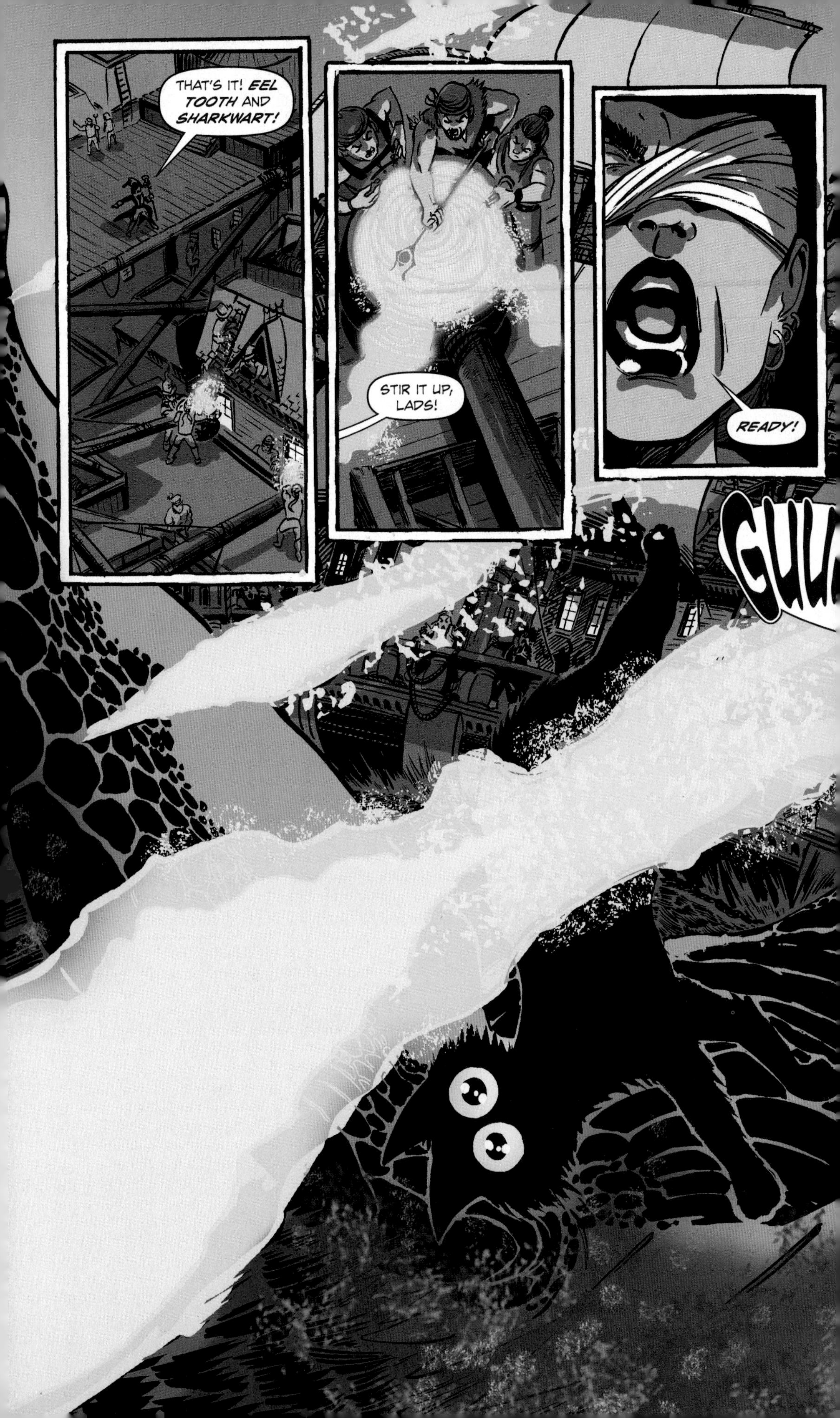
THAT'S IT! EEL TOOTH AND SHARKWART!
STIR IT UP, LADS!
READY!
GULL

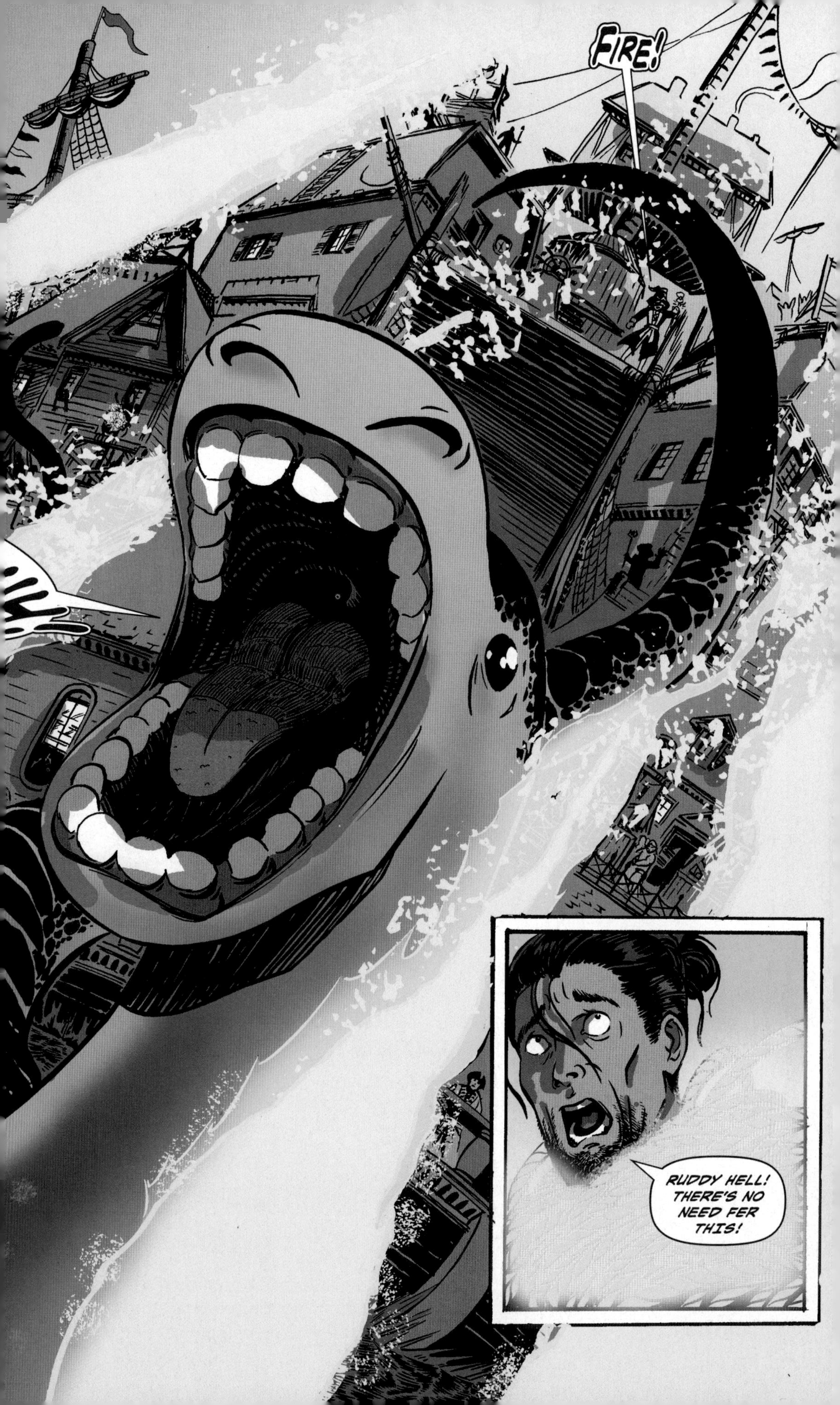
FIRE!
RUDDY HELL! THERE'S NO NEED FER THIS!

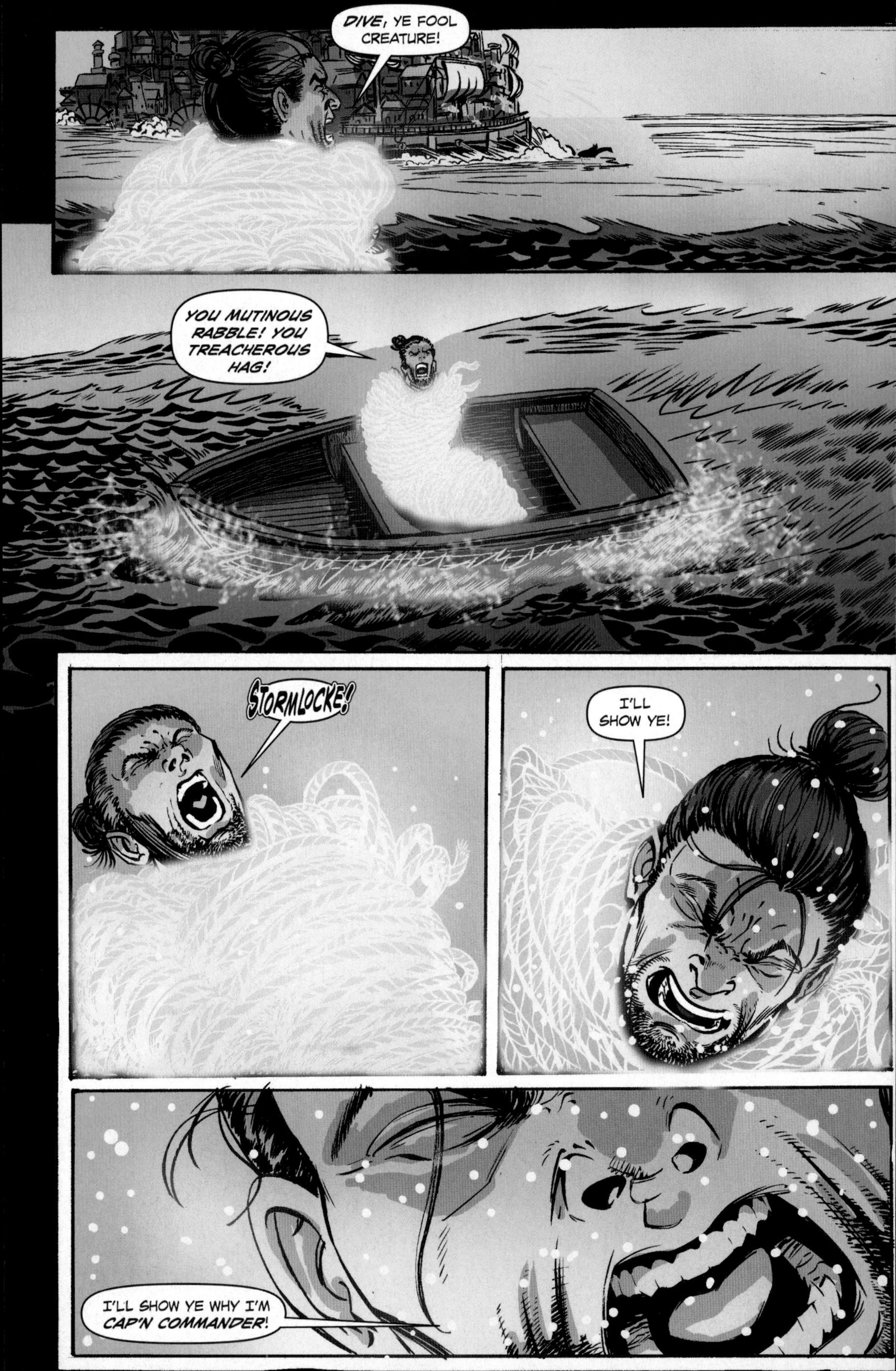
DIVE, YE FOOL CREATURE!
YOU MUTINOUS RABBLE! YOU TREACHEROUS HAG!
STORMLOCKE!
I'LL SHOW YE!
I'LL SHOW YE WHY I'M CAP'N COMMANDER!

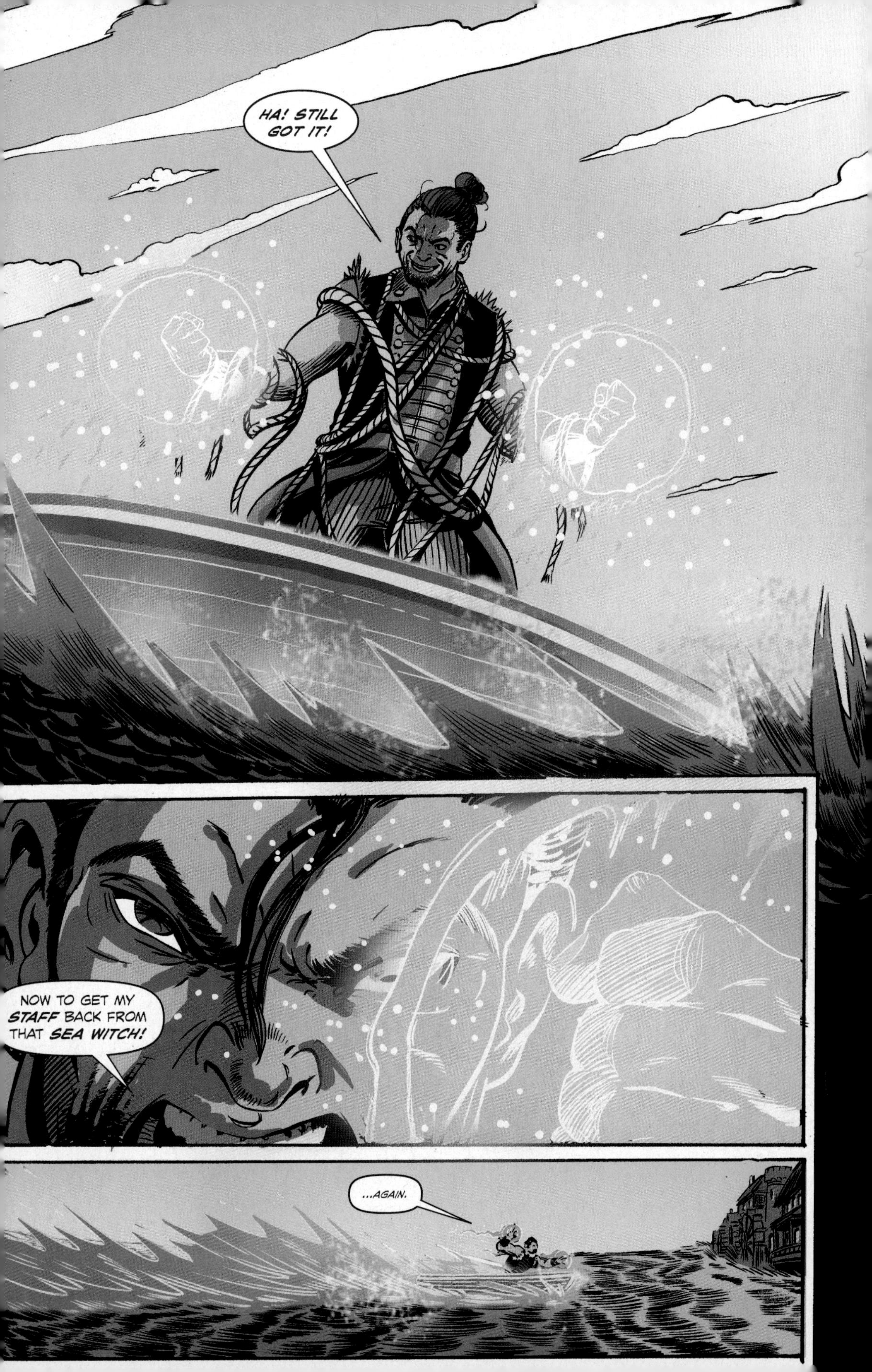
HA! STILL GOT IT!
NOW TO GET MY STAFF BACK FROM THAT SEA WITCH!
...AGAIN.

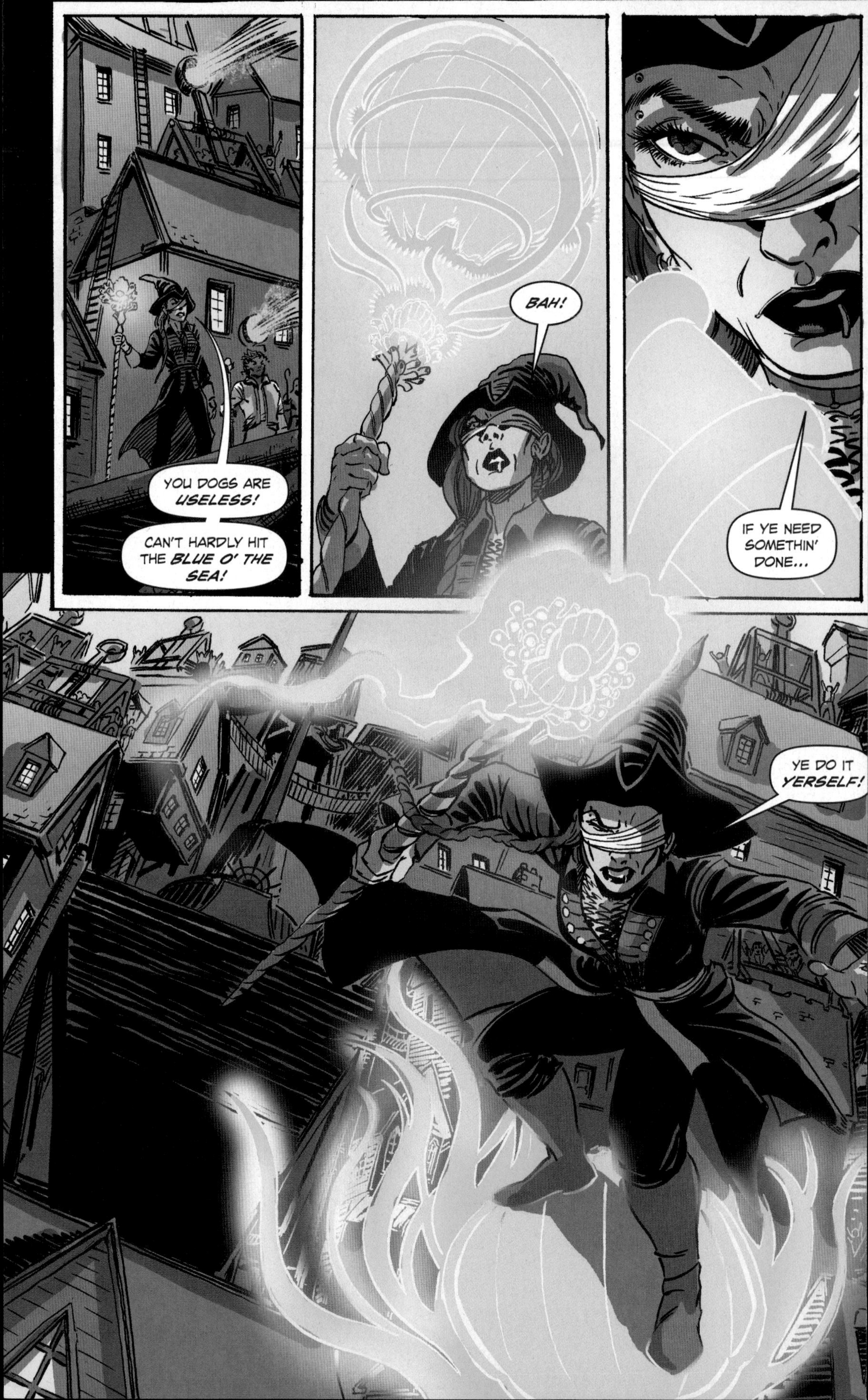
YOU DOGS ARE USELESS!
CAN'T HARDLY HIT THE BLUE O' THE SEA!
BAH!
IF YE NEED SOMETHIN' DONE...
YE DO IT YERSELF!

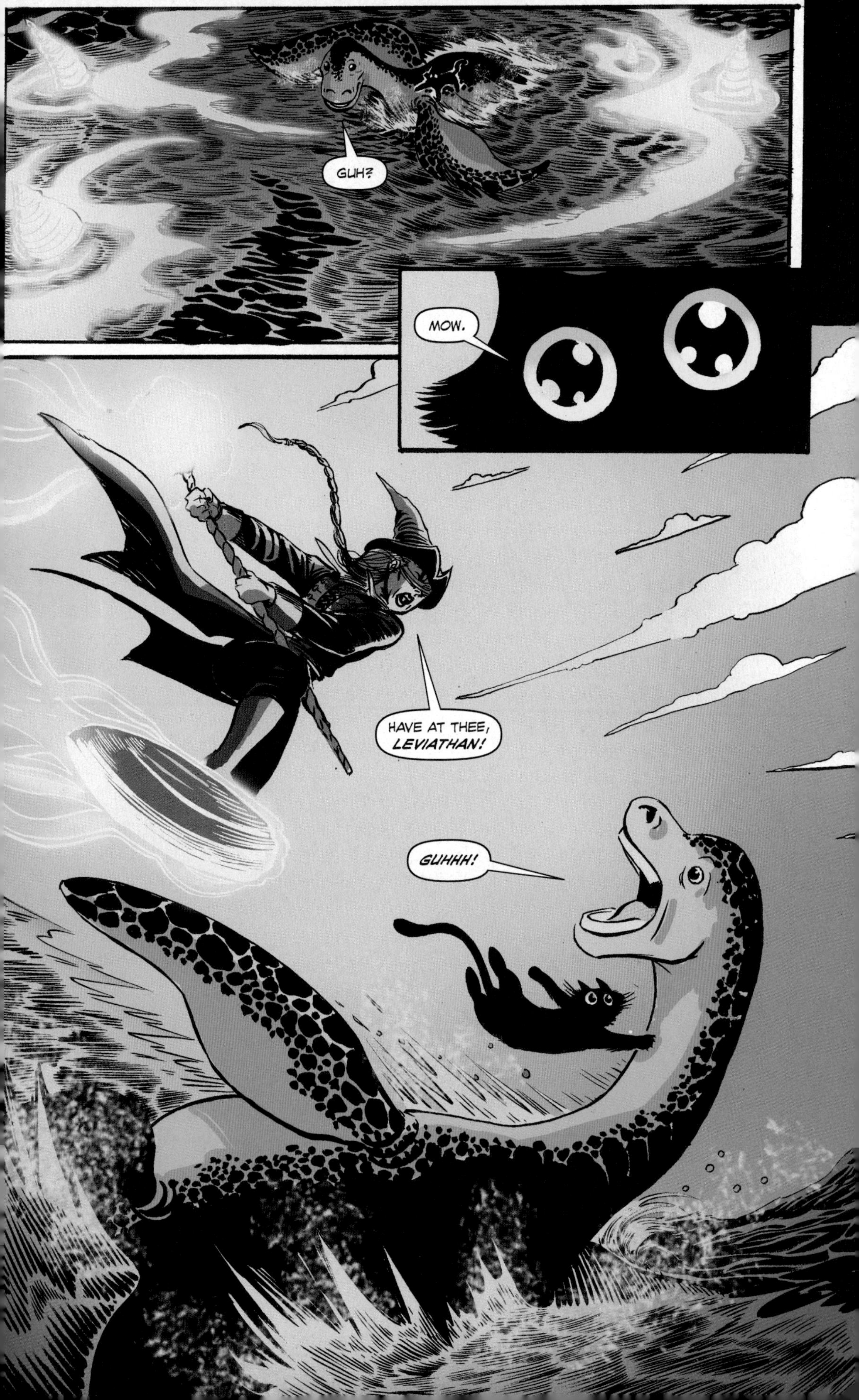
GUH?
MOW.
HAVE AT THEE, *LEVIATHAN!*
GUHHH!

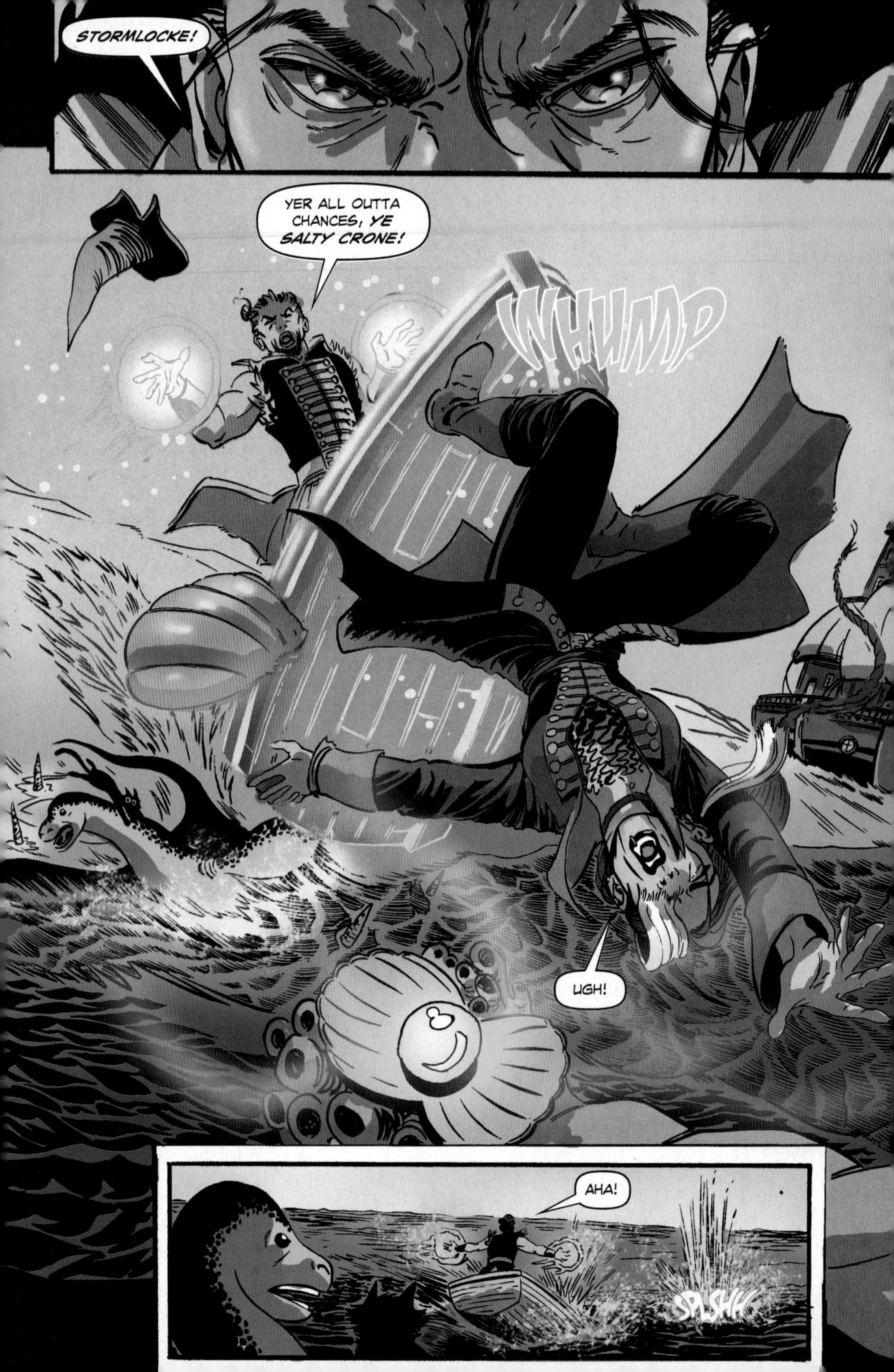
STORMLOCKE!
YER ALL OUTTA CHANCES, YE SALTY CRONE!
WHUMP
UGH!
AHA!
SPLSHH

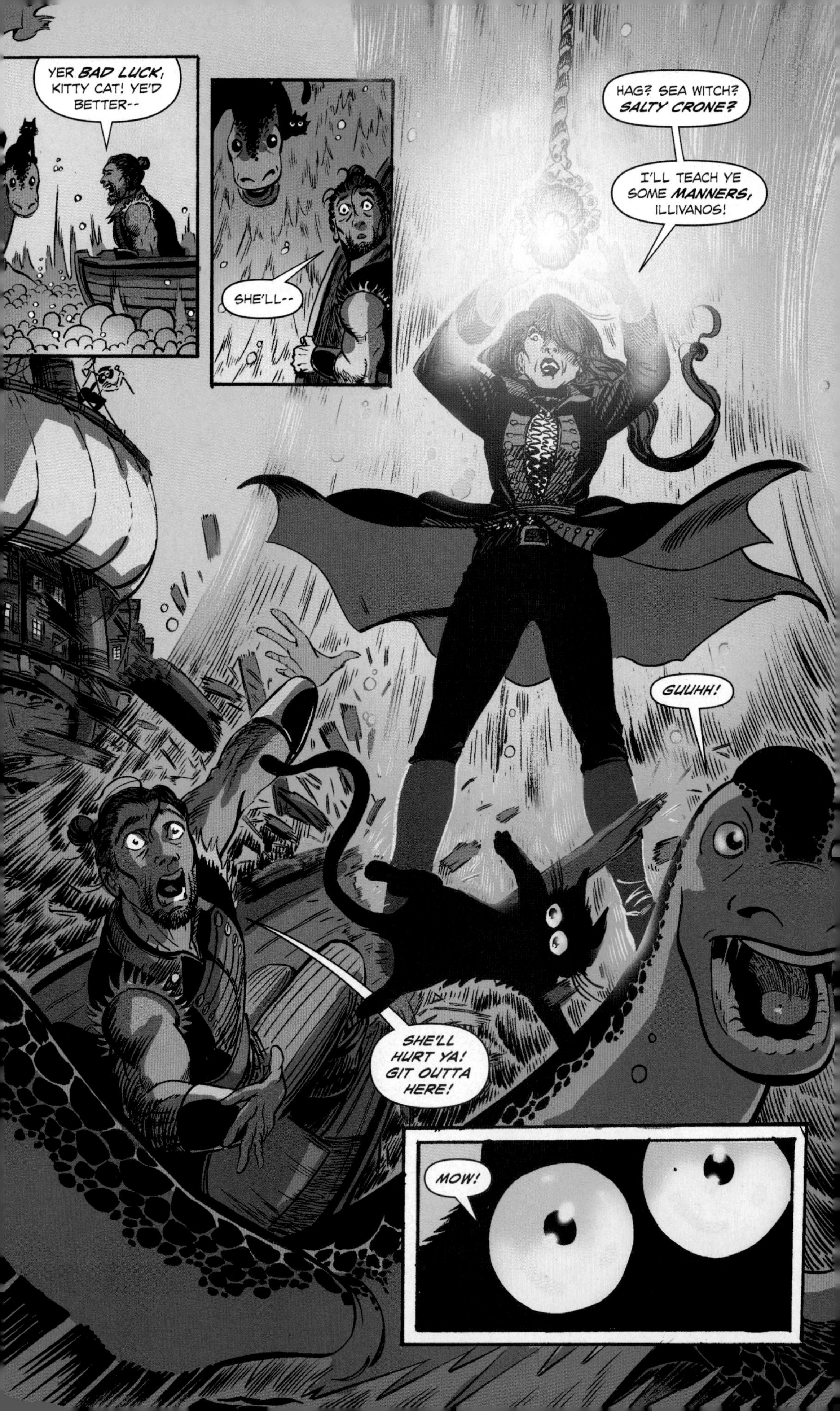
YER BAD LUCK, KITTY CAT! YE'D BETTER--
SHE'LL--
HAG? SEA WITCH? SALTY CRONE?
I'LL TEACH YE SOME MANNERS, ILLIVANOS!
GUUHH!
SHE'LL HURT YA! GIT OUTTA HERE!
MOW!

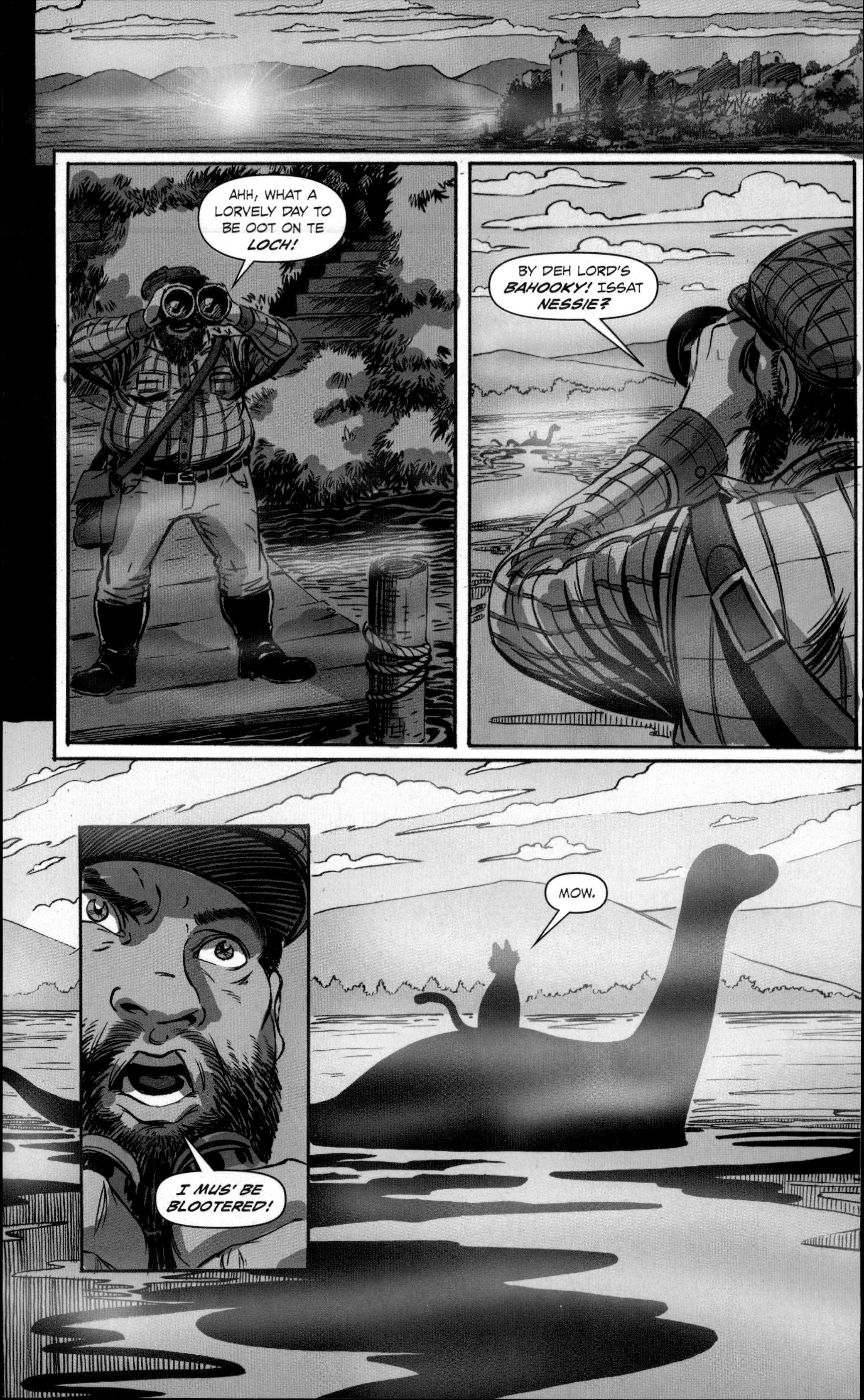
AHH, WHAT A LORVELY DAY TO BE OOT ON TE LOCH!
BY DEH LORD'S BAHOOKY! ISSAT NESSIE?
MOW.
I MUS' BE BLOOTERED!

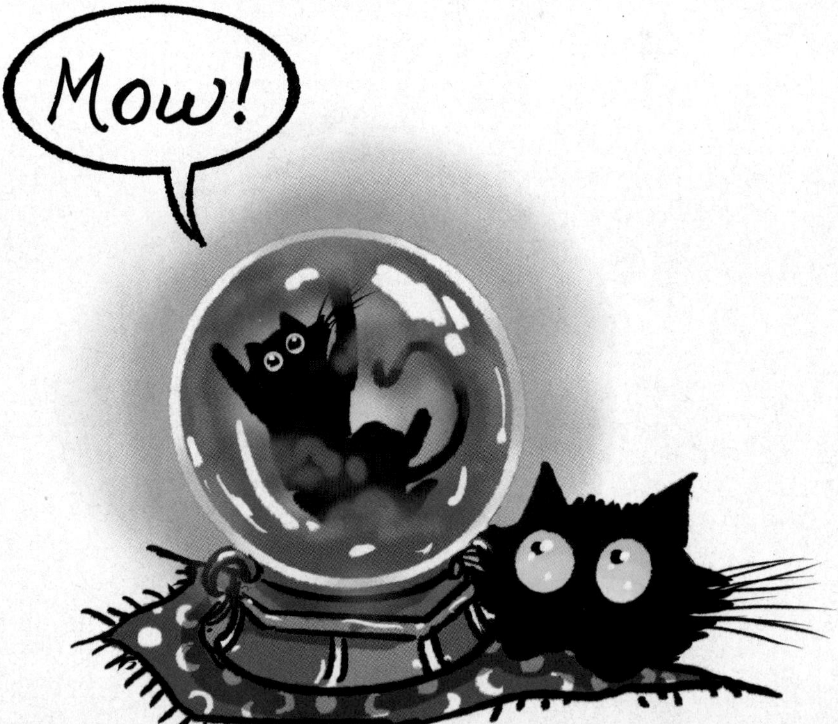
Mow!

4

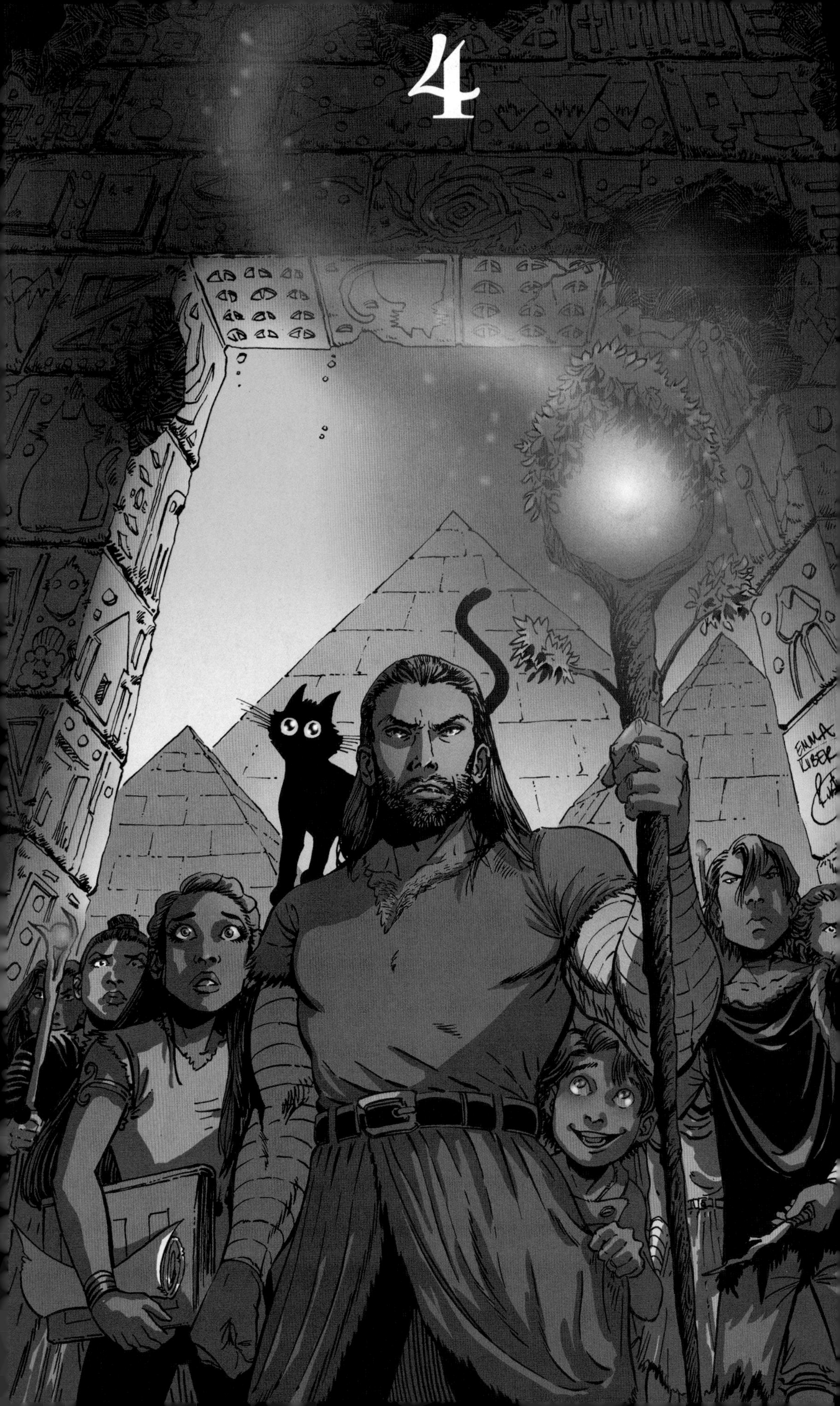

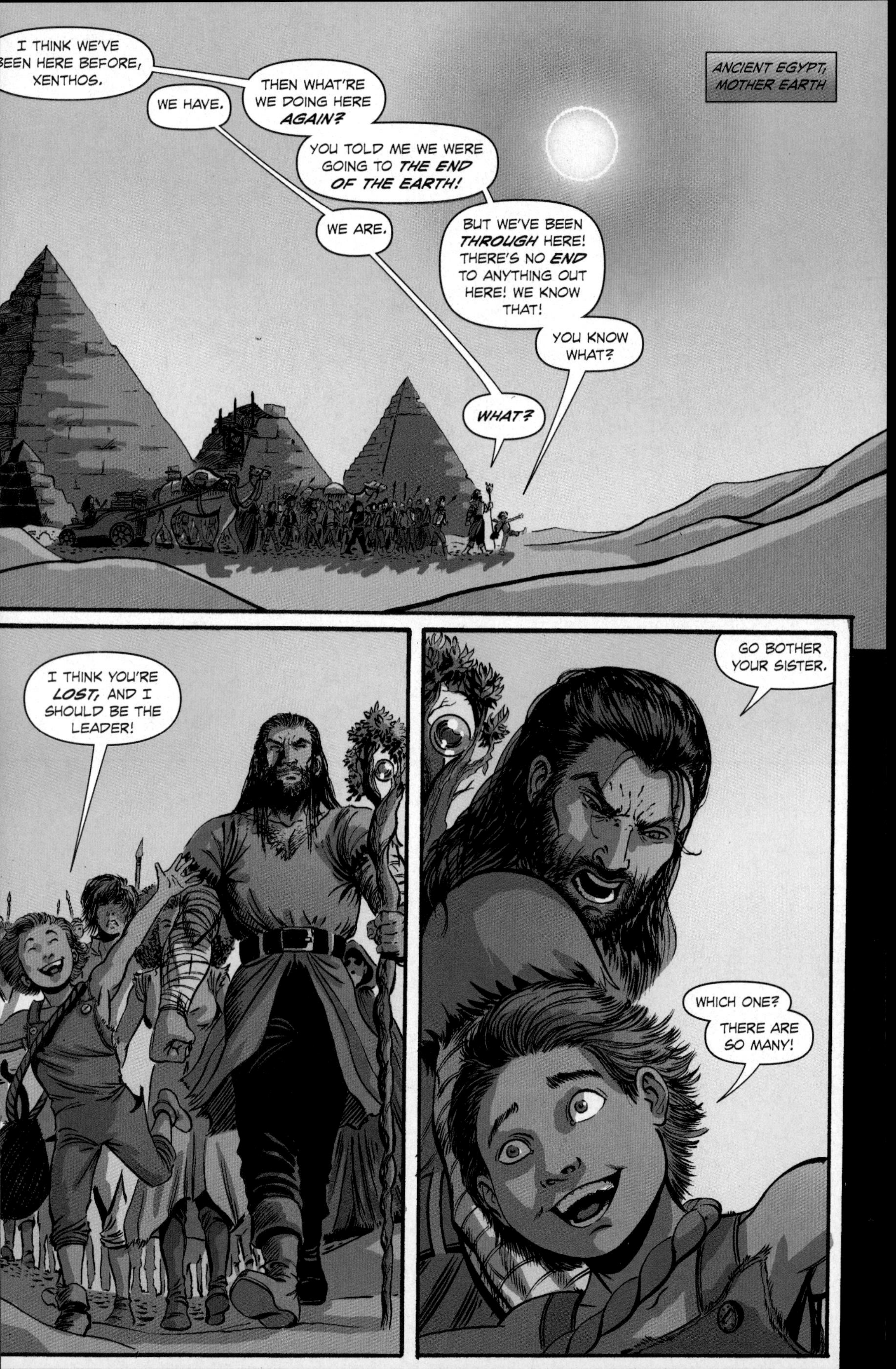
ANCIENT EGYPT, MOTHER EARTH
I THINK WE'VE BEEN HERE BEFORE, XENTHOS.
WE HAVE.
THEN WHAT'RE WE DOING HERE AGAIN?
YOU TOLD ME WE WERE GOING TO THE END OF THE EARTH!
WE ARE.
BUT WE'VE BEEN THROUGH HERE! THERE'S NO END TO ANYTHING OUT HERE! WE KNOW THAT!
YOU KNOW WHAT?
WHAT?
I THINK YOU'RE LOST, AND I SHOULD BE THE LEADER!
GO BOTHER YOUR SISTER.
WHICH ONE?
THERE ARE SO MANY!

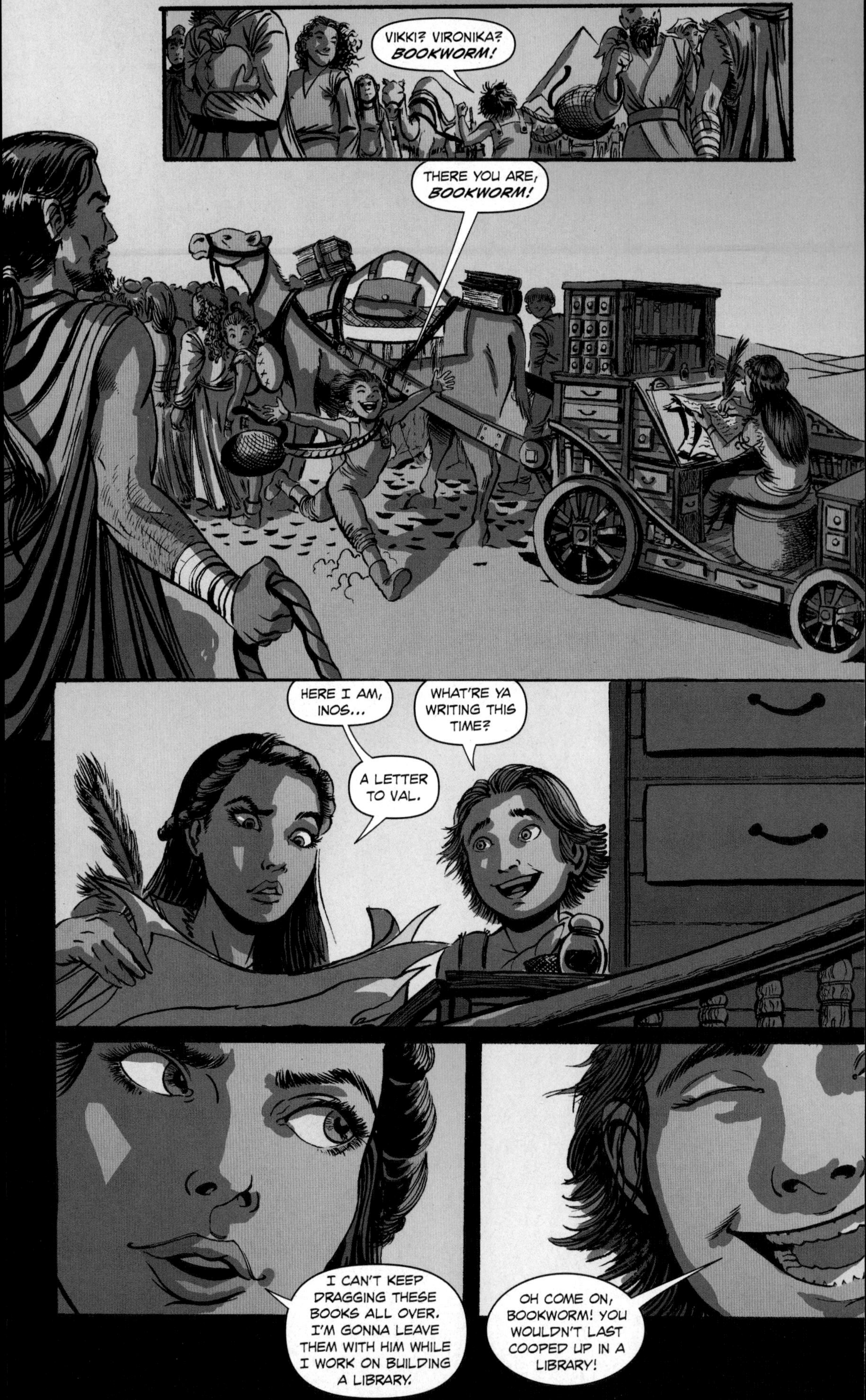
VIKKI? VIRONIKA? BOOKWORM!
THERE YOU ARE, BOOKWORM!
HERE I AM, INOS...
WHAT'RE YA WRITING THIS TIME?
A LETTER TO VAL.
I CAN'T KEEP DRAGGING THESE BOOKS ALL OVER. I'M GONNA LEAVE THEM WITH HIM WHILE I WORK ON BUILDING A LIBRARY.
OH COME ON, BOOKWORM! YOU WOULDN'T LAST COOPED UP IN A LIBRARY!

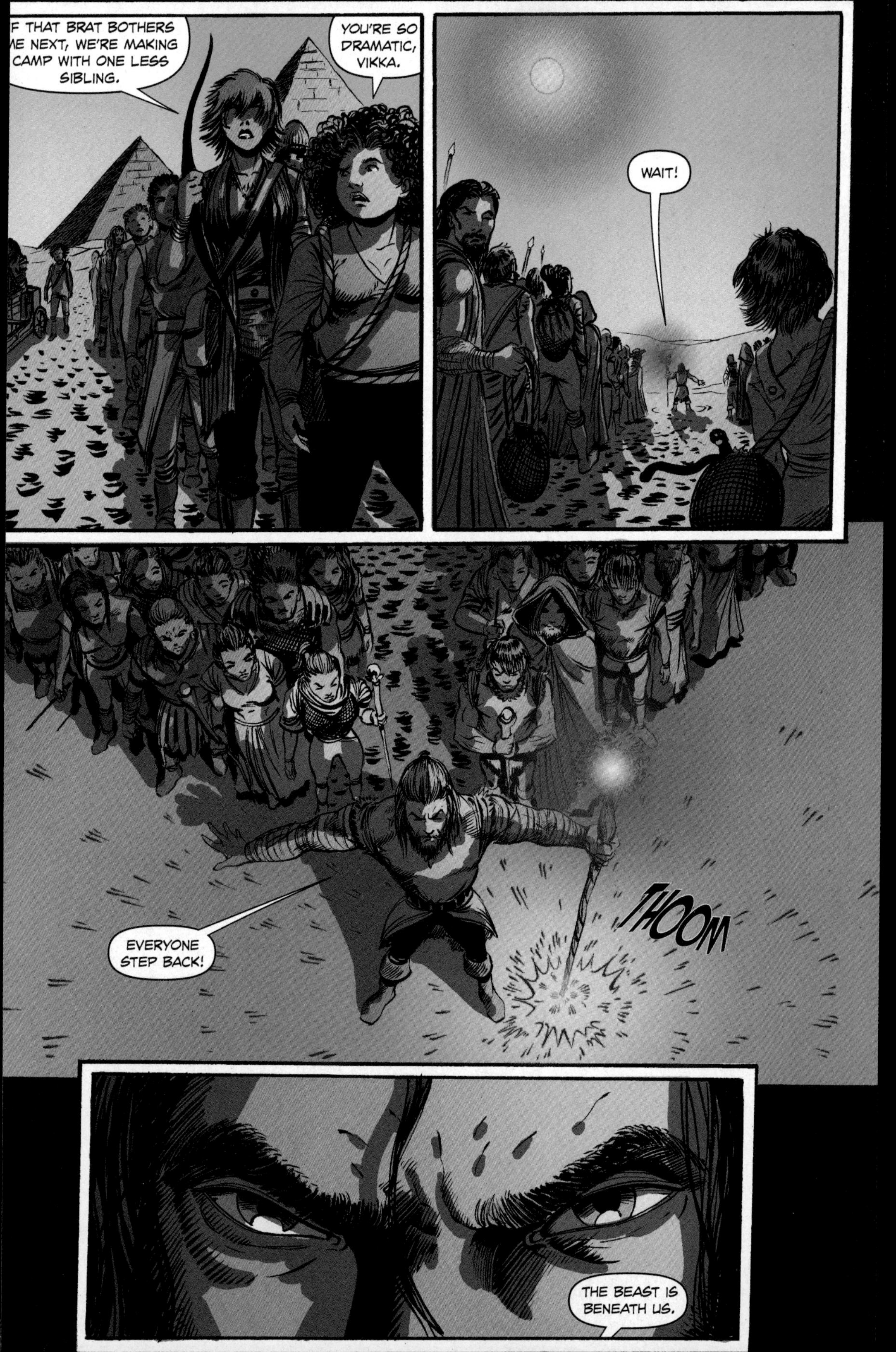
F THAT BRAT BOTHERS
ME NEXT, WE'RE MAKING
CAMP WITH ONE LESS
SIBLING.
YOU'RE SO DRAMATIC, VIKKA.
WAIT!
EVERYONE STEP BACK!
THOOM
THE BEAST IS BENEATH US.

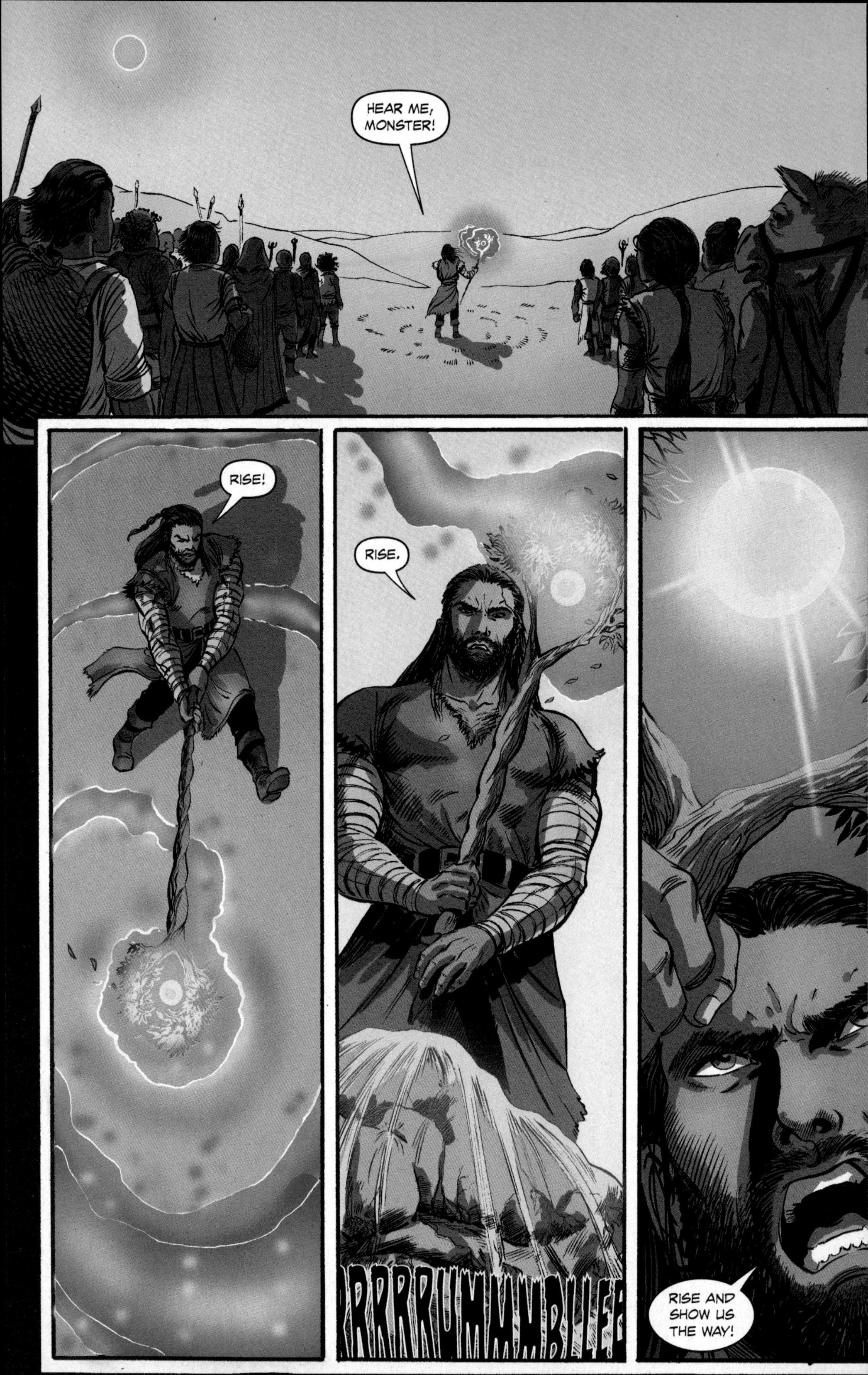
HEAR ME, MONSTER!
RISE!
RISE.
RRRRUMMMBLLE
RISE AND SHOW US THE WAY!

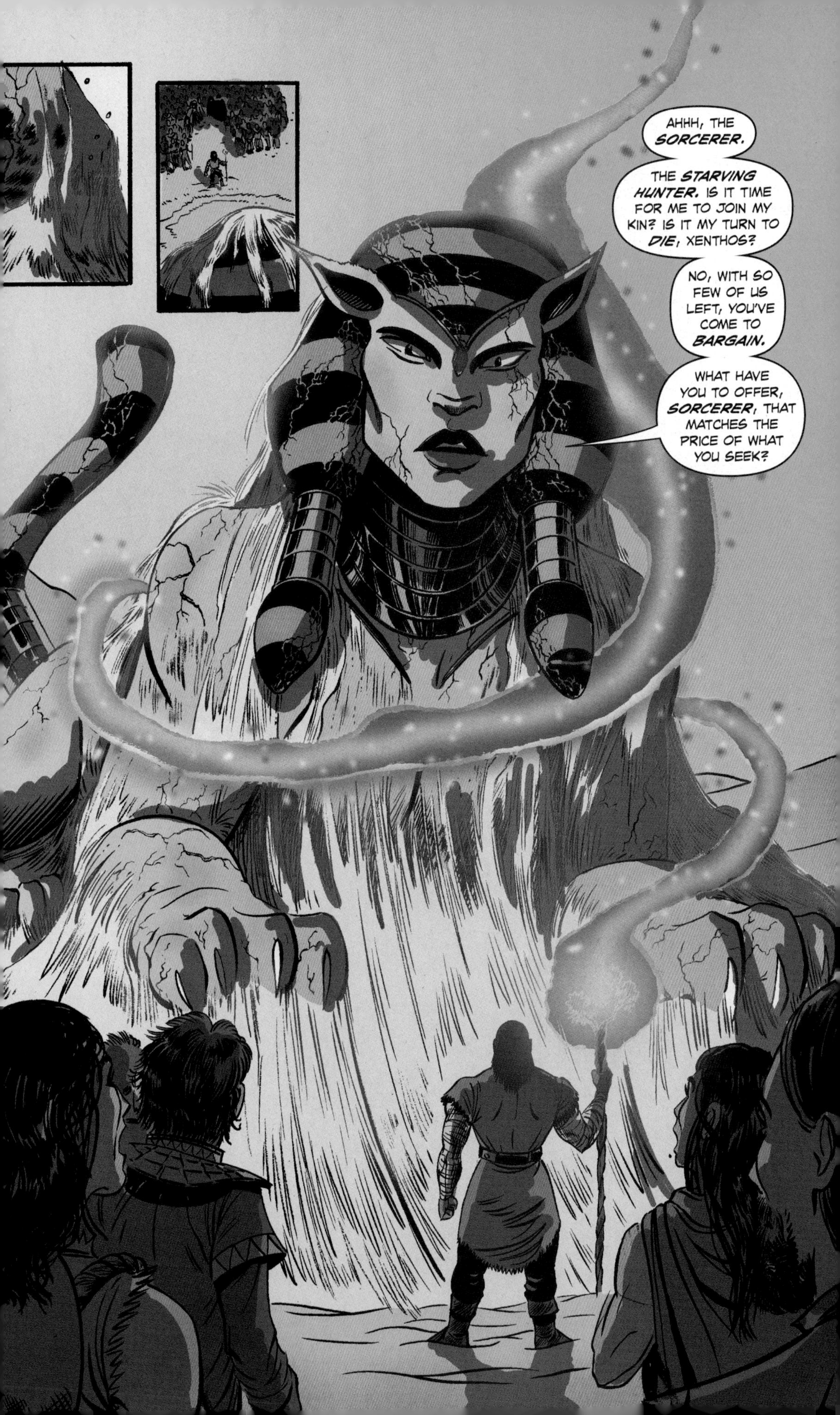
AHHH, THE *SORCERER.*
THE *STARVING HUNTER.* IS IT TIME FOR ME TO JOIN MY KIN? IS IT MY TURN TO *DIE*, XENTHOS?
NO, WITH SO FEW OF US LEFT, YOU'VE COME TO *BARGAIN.*
WHAT HAVE YOU TO OFFER, *SORCERER*, THAT MATCHES THE PRICE OF WHAT YOU SEEK?

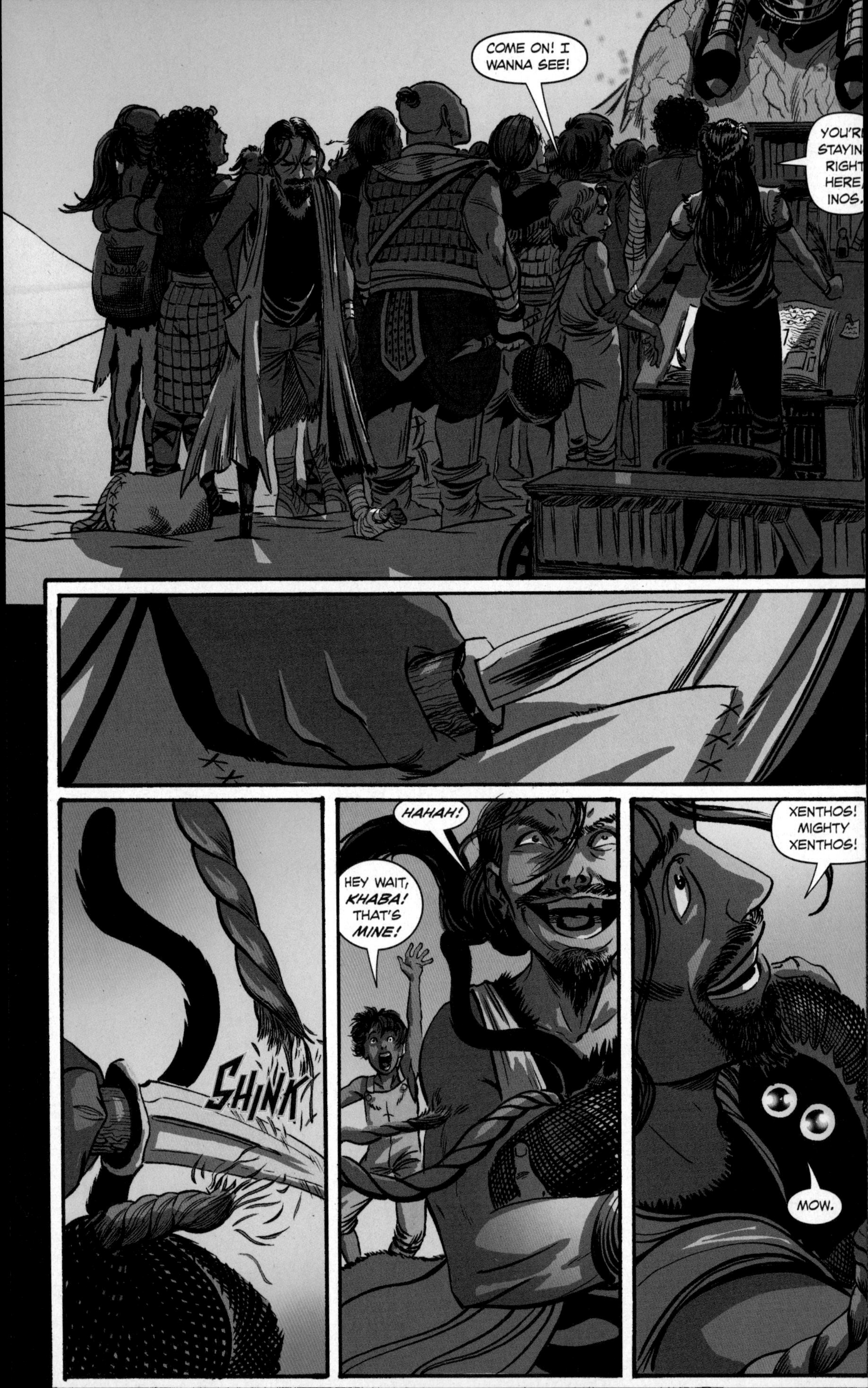
COME ON! I WANNA SEE!
YOU'R STAYIN RIGHT HERE, INOS.
SHINK
HAHAH!
HEY WAIT, KHABA! THAT'S MINE!
XENTHOS! MIGHTY XENTHOS!
MOW.

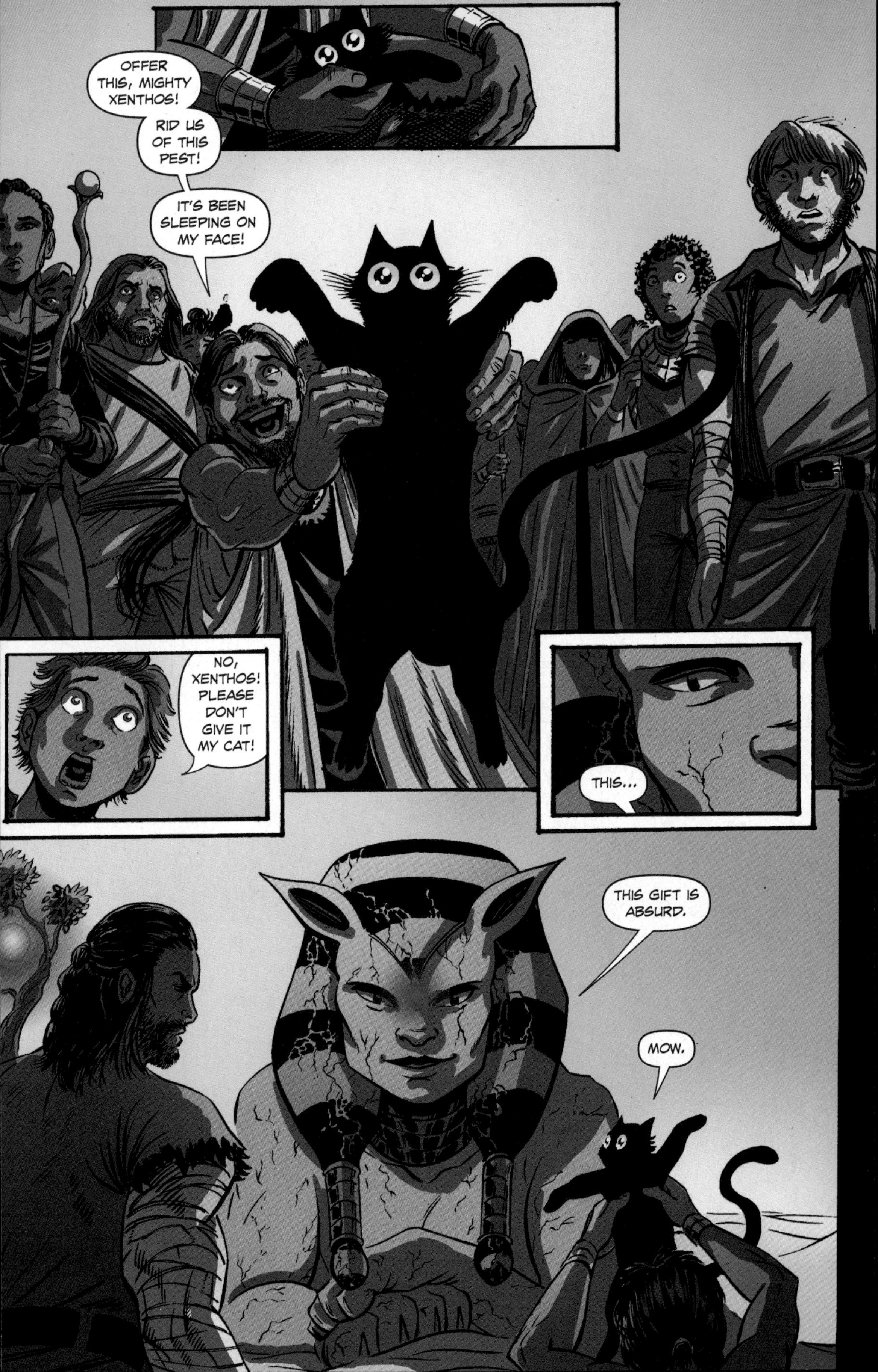
OFFER THIS, MIGHTY XENTHOS!
RID US OF THIS PEST!
IT'S BEEN SLEEPING ON MY FACE!
NO, XENTHOS! PLEASE DON'T GIVE IT MY CAT!
THIS...
THIS GIFT IS ABSURD.
MOW.

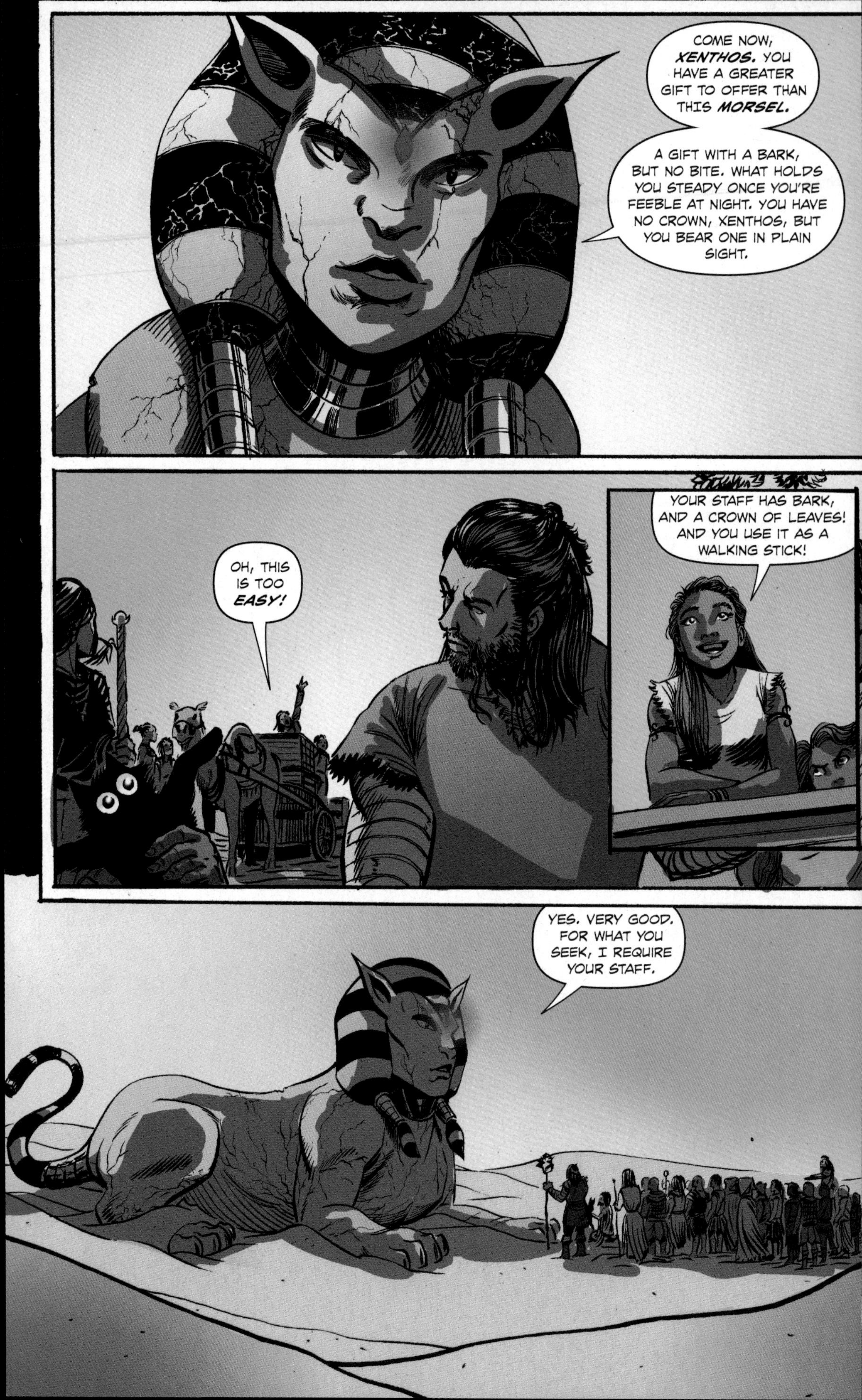
COME NOW, XENTHOS. YOU HAVE A GREATER GIFT TO OFFER THAN THIS MORSEL.
A GIFT WITH A BARK, BUT NO BITE. WHAT HOLDS YOU STEADY ONCE YOU'RE FEEBLE AT NIGHT. YOU HAVE NO CROWN, XENTHOS, BUT YOU BEAR ONE IN PLAIN SIGHT.
YOUR STAFF HAS BARK, AND A CROWN OF LEAVES! AND YOU USE IT AS A WALKING STICK!
OH, THIS IS TOO EASY!
YES. VERY GOOD. FOR WHAT YOU SEEK, I REQUIRE YOUR STAFF.

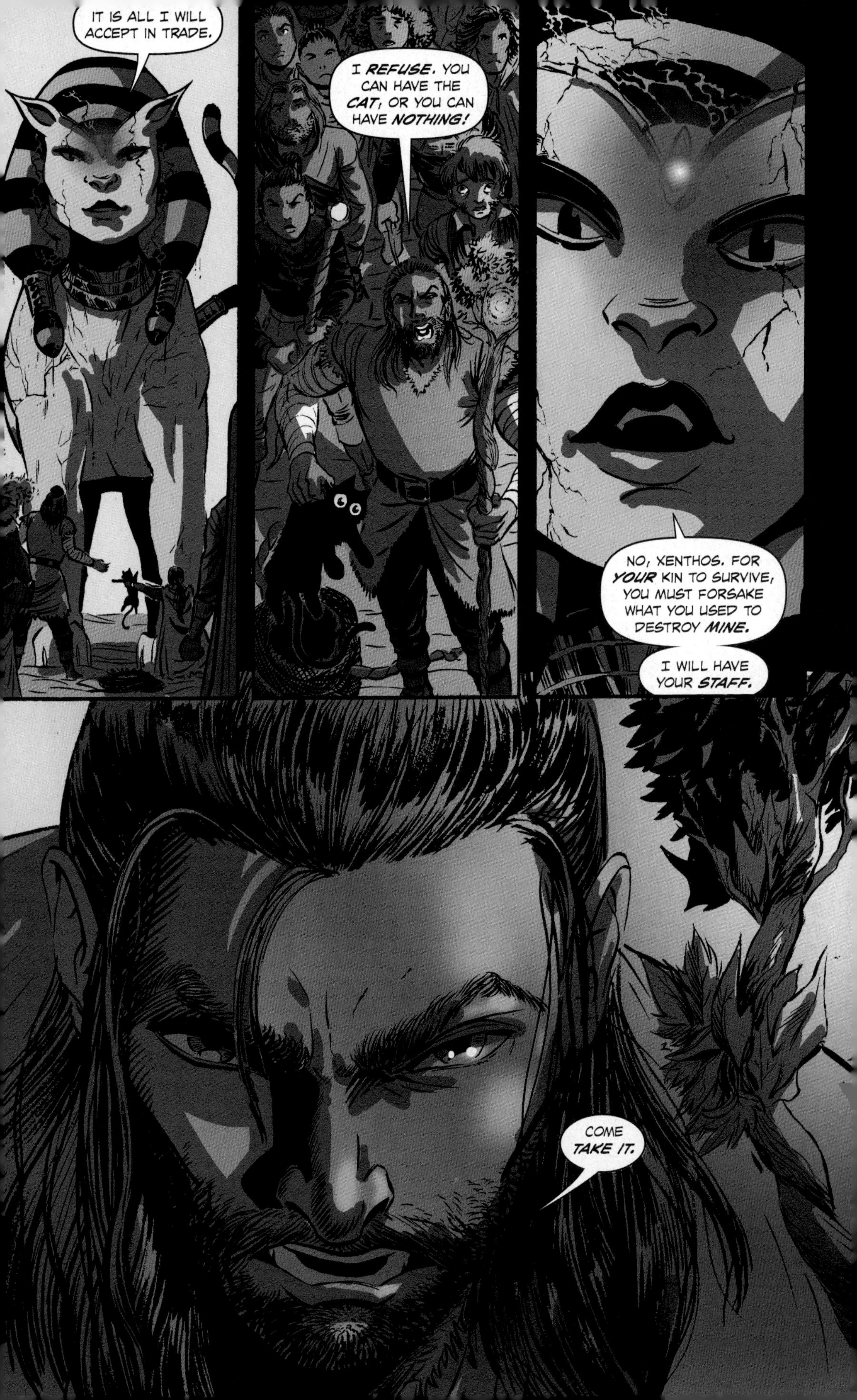
IT IS ALL I WILL ACCEPT IN TRADE.
I REFUSE. YOU CAN HAVE THE CAT; OR YOU CAN HAVE NOTHING!
NO, XENTHOS. FOR YOUR KIN TO SURVIVE, YOU MUST FORSAKE WHAT YOU USED TO DESTROY MINE.
I WILL HAVE YOUR STAFF.
COME TAKE IT.

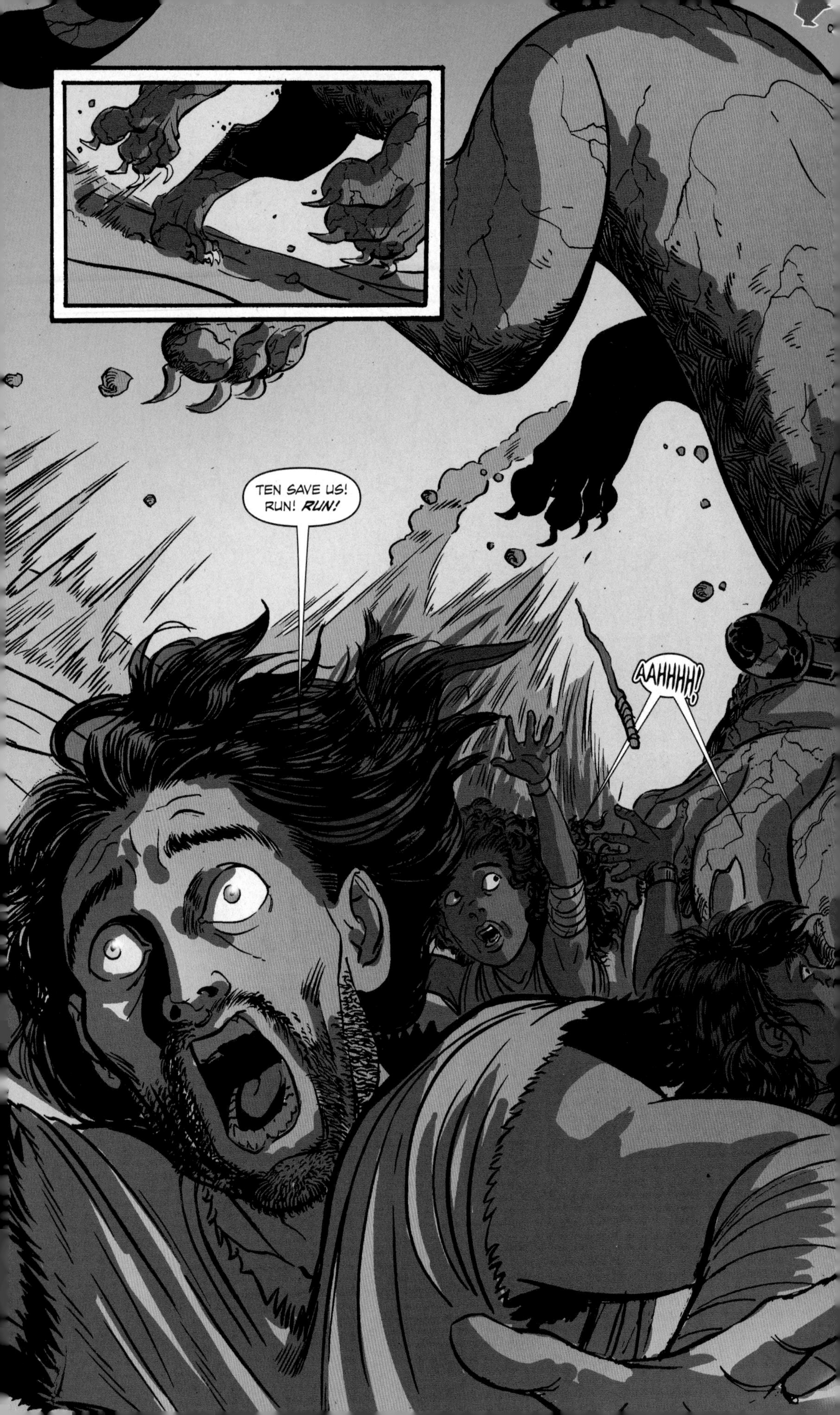
TEN SAVE US!
RUN! RUN!
AAHHHH!

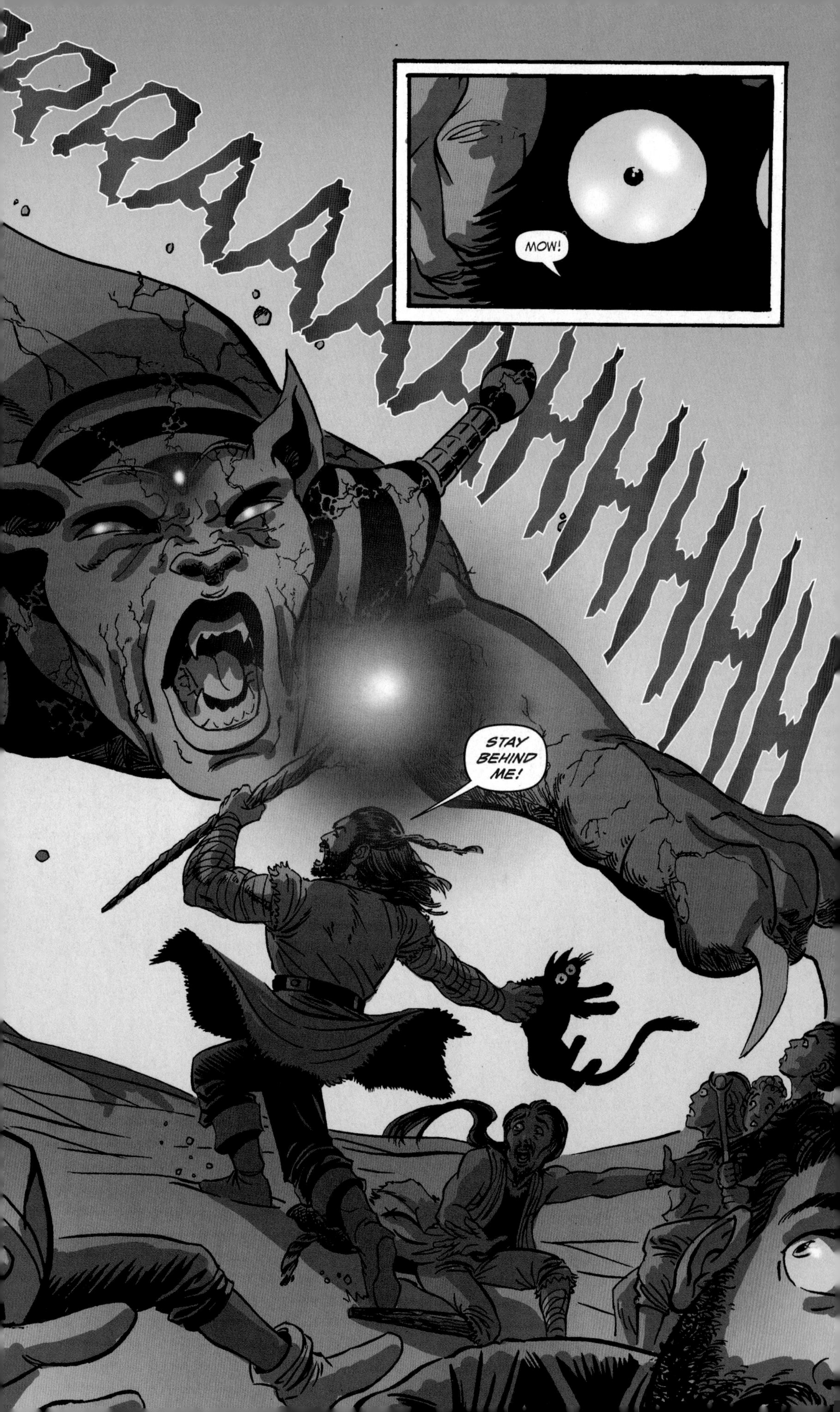
RRAAAAHHHHHHHH
MOW!
STAY BEHIND ME!

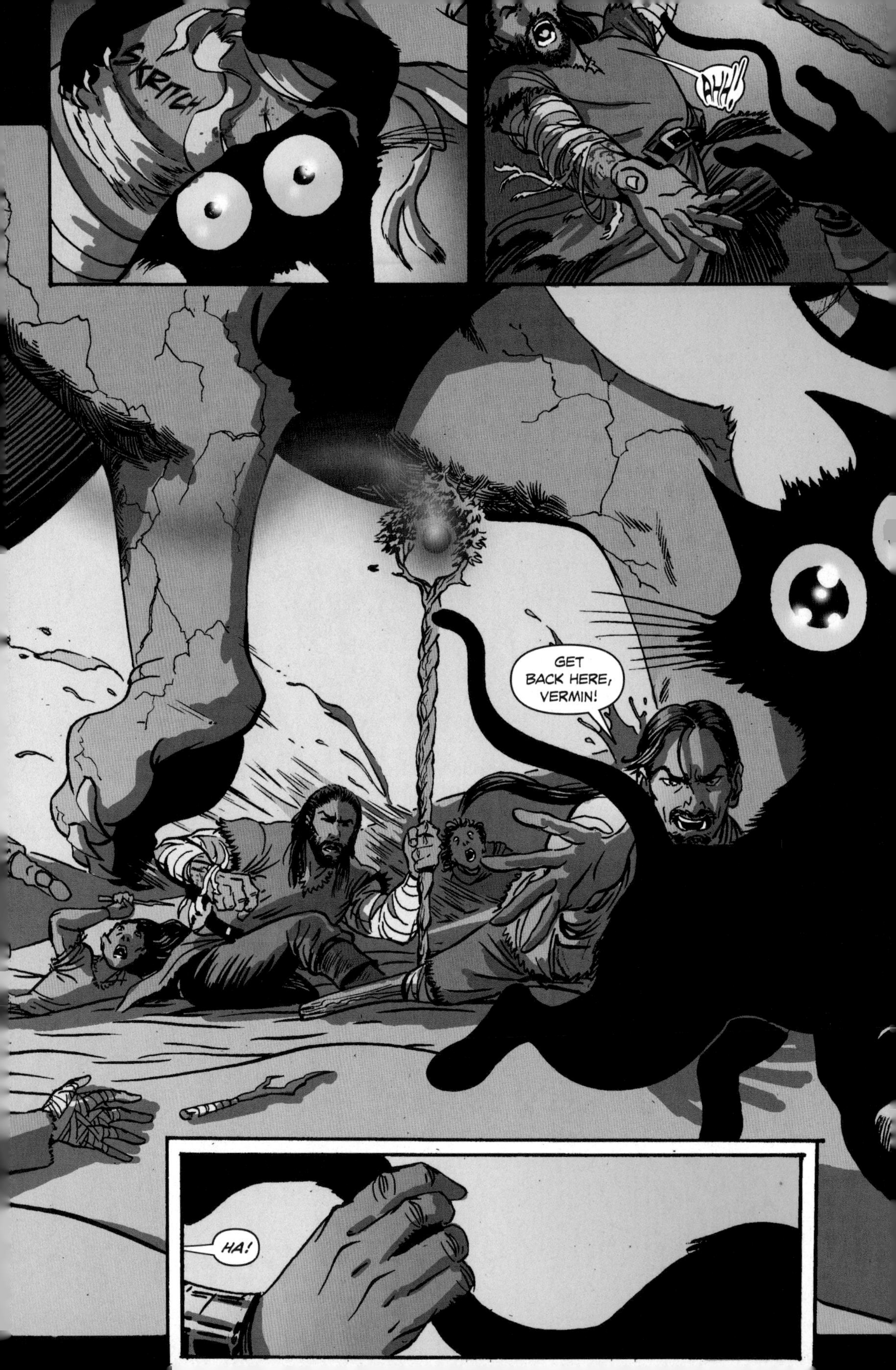
SKRITCH
AHH!
GET BACK HERE, VERMIN!
HA!

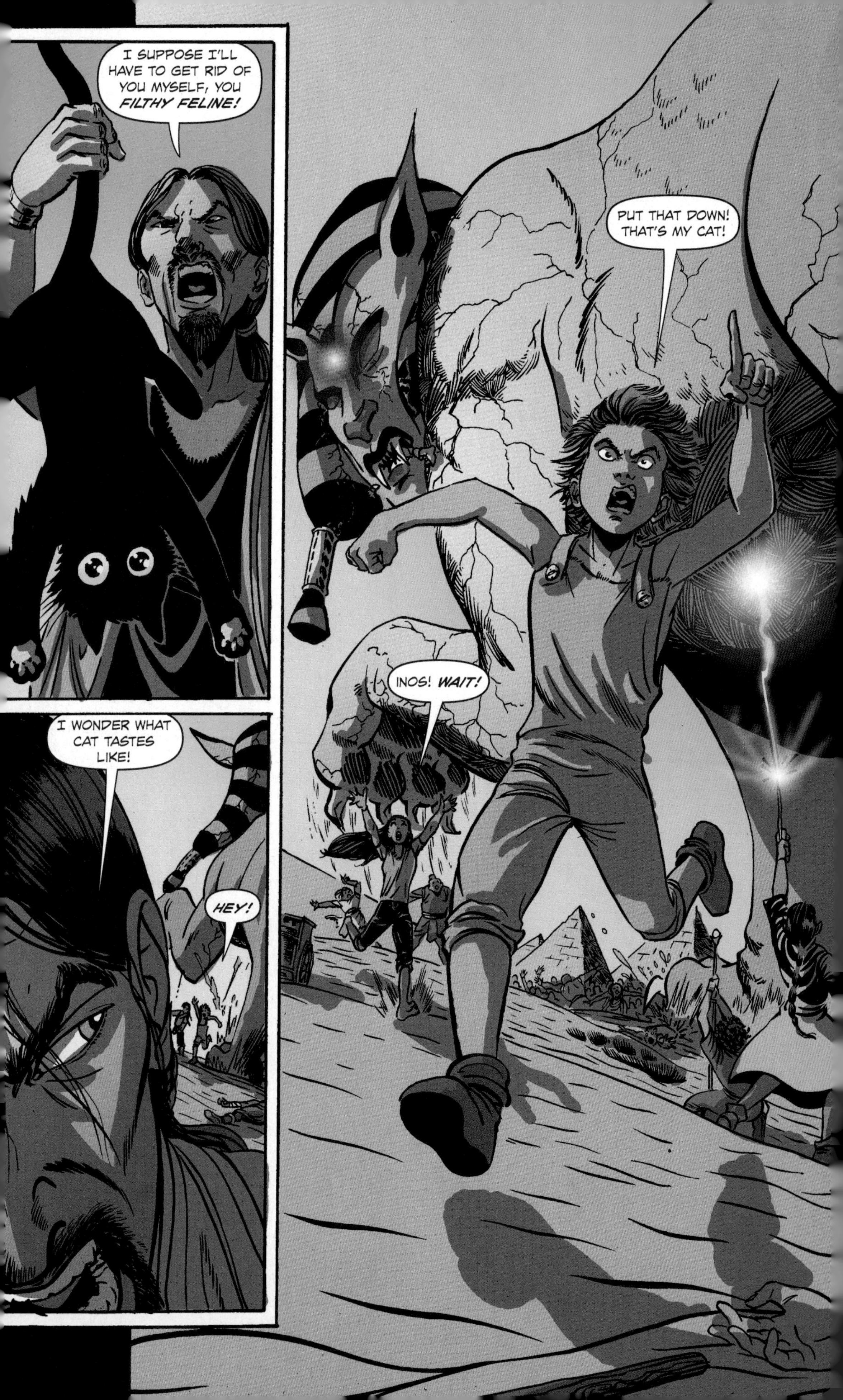

I SUPPOSE I'LL HAVE TO GET RID OF YOU MYSELF, YOU *FILTHY FELINE!*
I WONDER WHAT CAT TASTES LIKE!
HEY!
PUT THAT DOWN! THAT'S MY CAT!
INOS! *WAIT!*

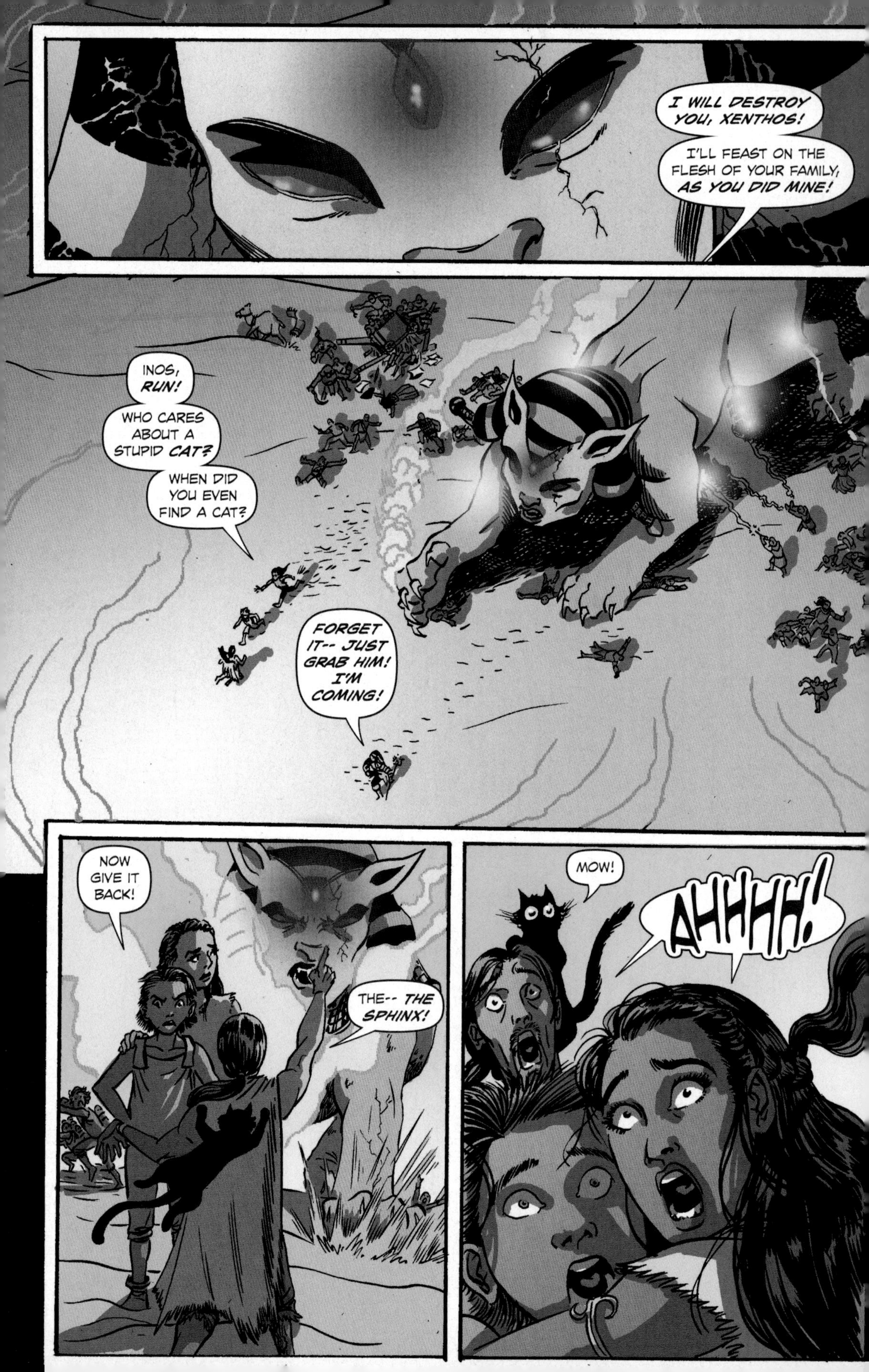
I WILL DESTROY YOU, XENTHOS!
I'LL FEAST ON THE FLESH OF YOUR FAMILY, AS YOU DID MINE!
INOS, RUN!
WHO CARES ABOUT A STUPID CAT?
WHEN DID YOU EVEN FIND A CAT?
FORGET IT-- JUST GRAB HIM! I'M COMING!
NOW GIVE IT BACK!
THE-- THE SPHINX!
MOW!
AHHHH!

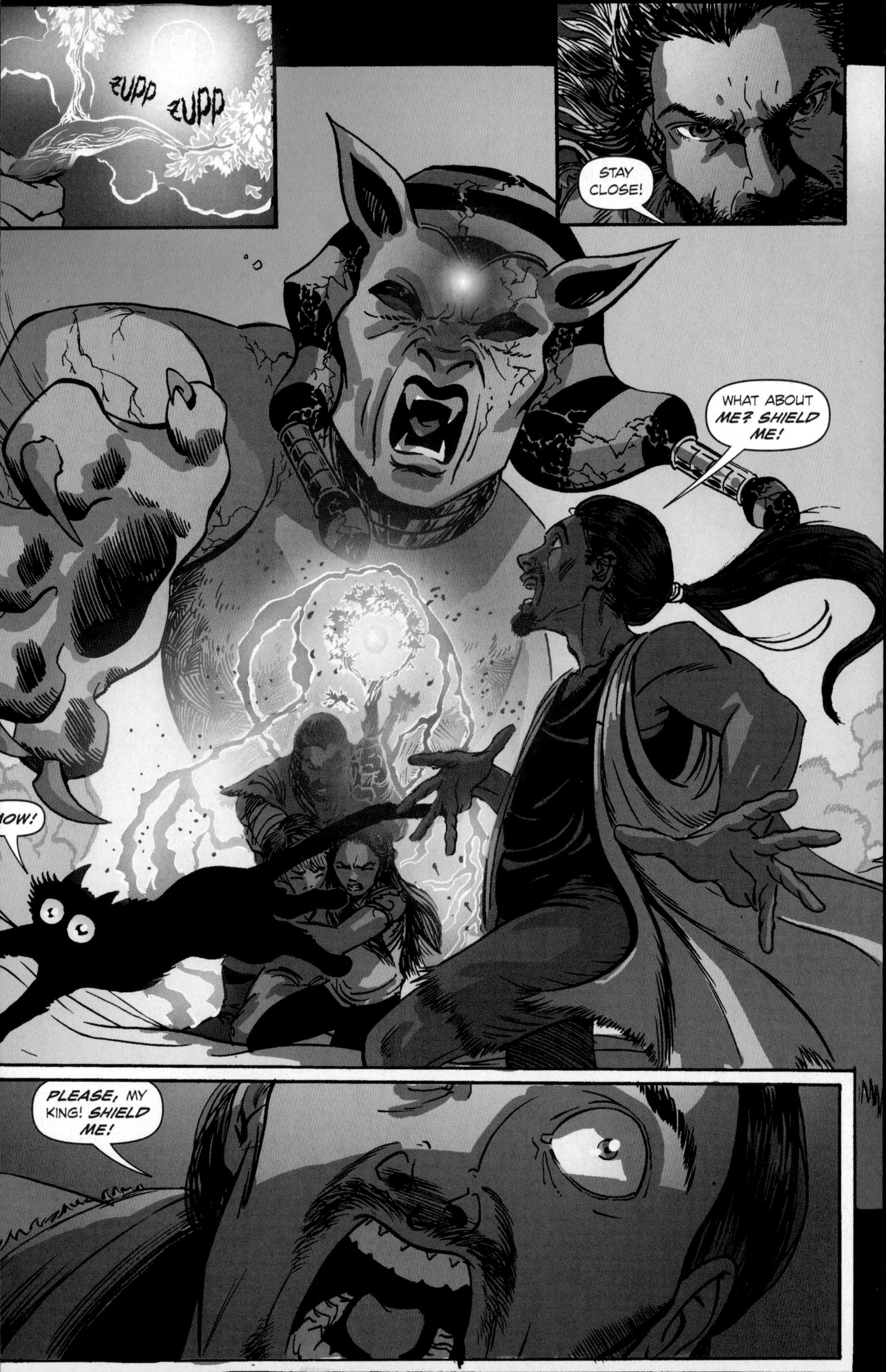
ZUPP ZUPP
STAY CLOSE!
WHAT ABOUT ME? SHIELD ME!
OW!
PLEASE, MY KING! SHIELD ME!

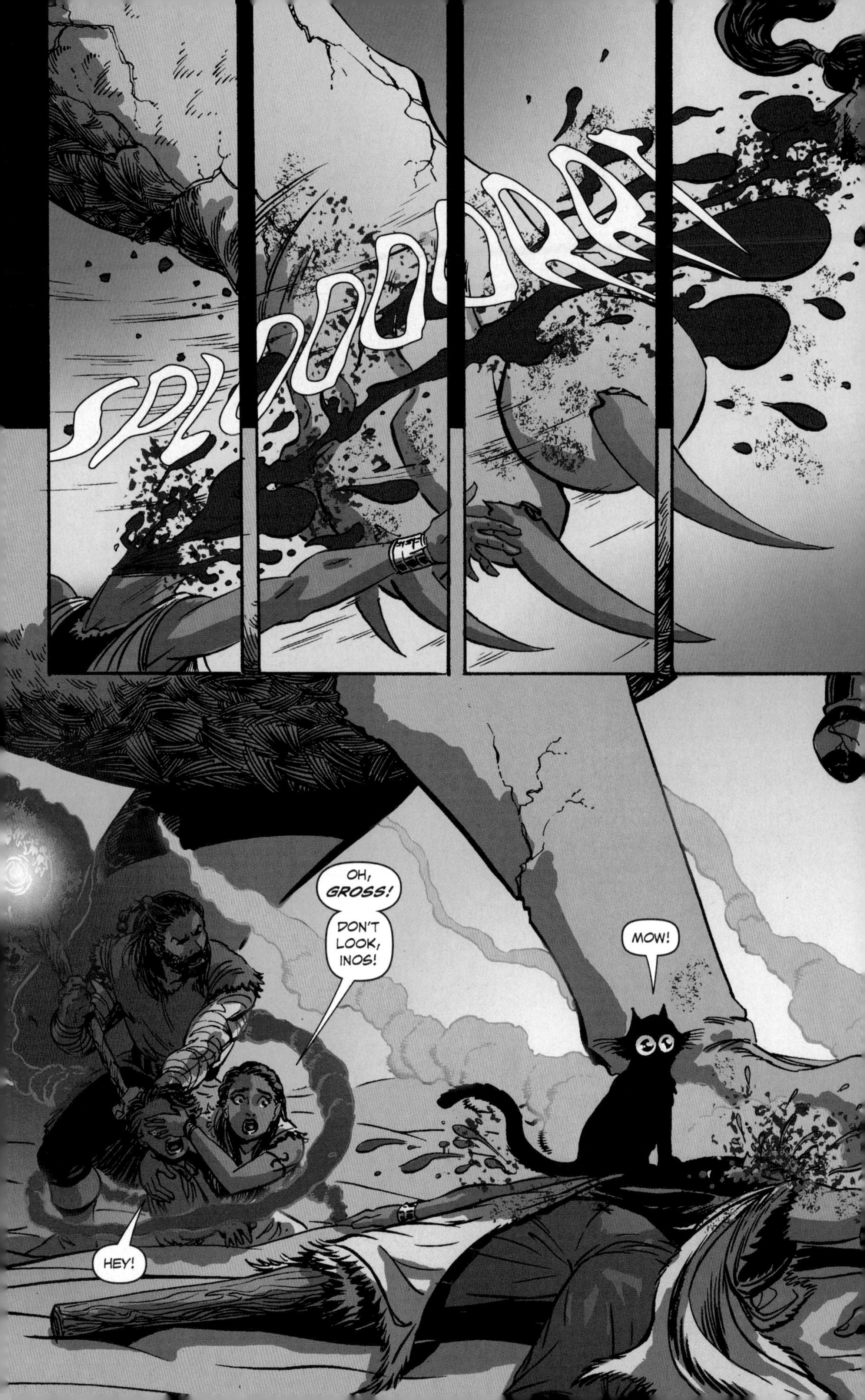
OH, GROSS!
DON'T LOOK, INOS!
MOW!
HEY!

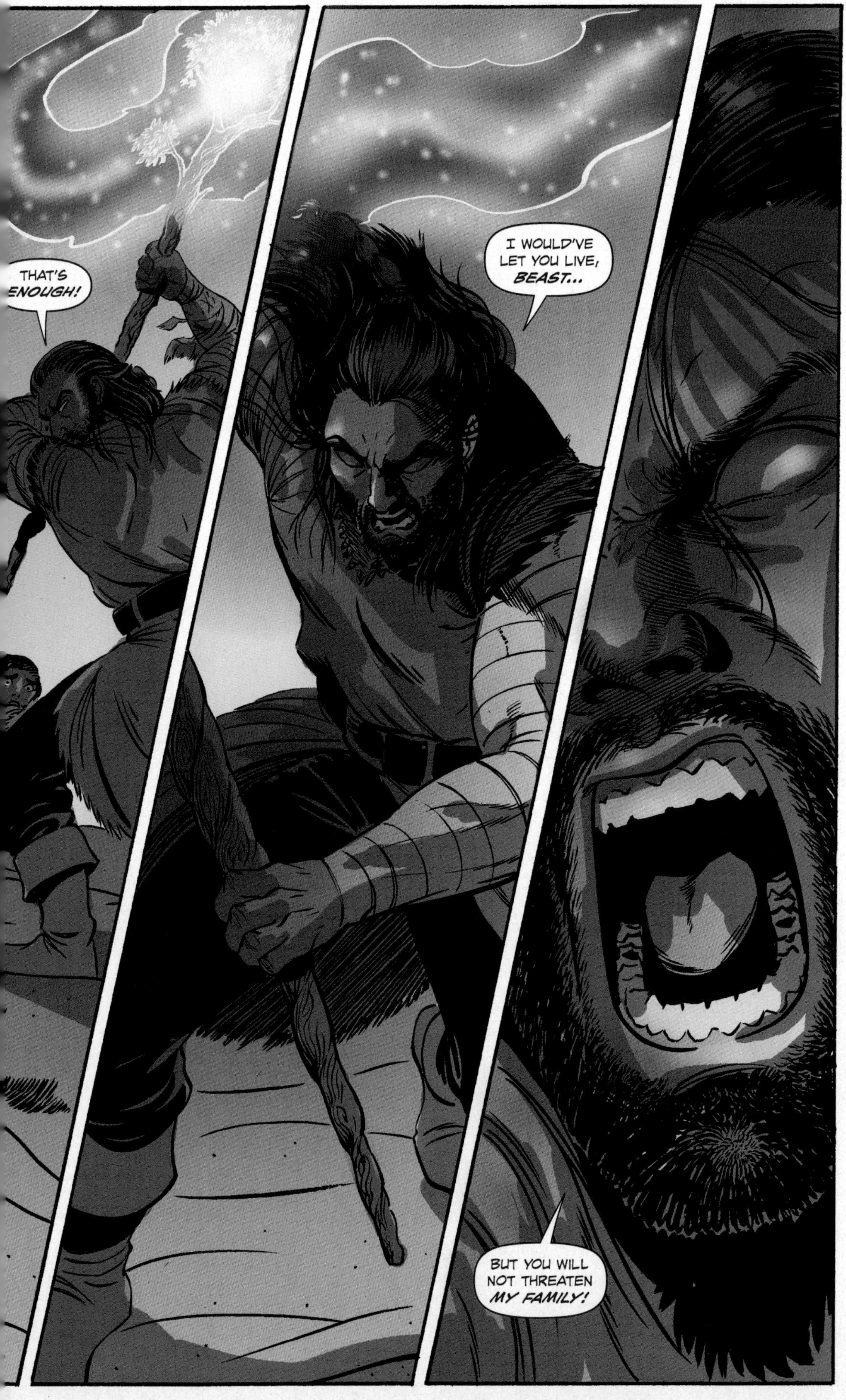
THAT'S ENOUGH!
I WOULD'VE LET YOU LIVE, BEAST...
BUT YOU WILL NOT THREATEN MY FAMILY!

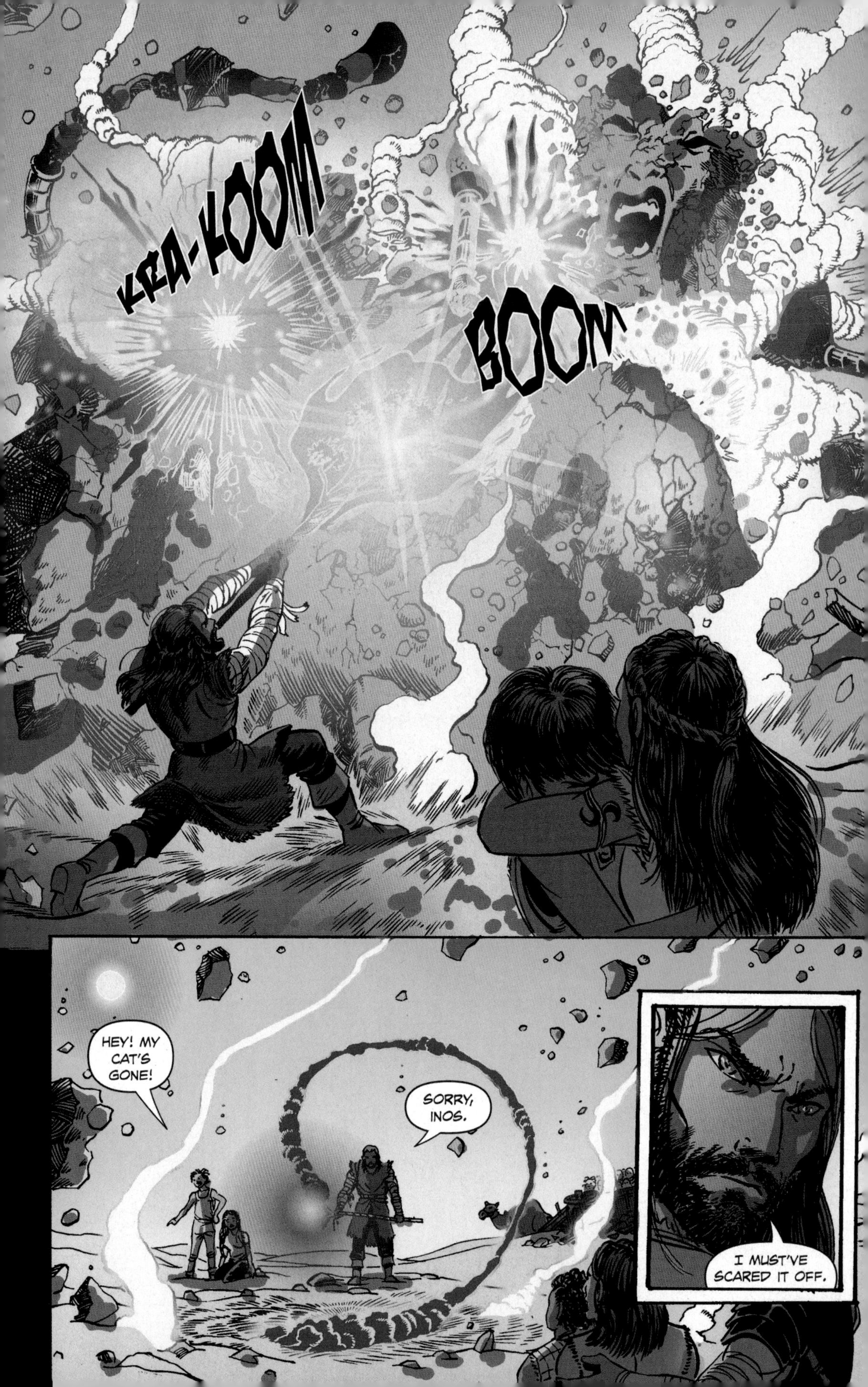
KRA-KOOM
BOOM
HEY! MY CAT'S GONE!
SORRY, INOS.
I MUST'VE SCARED IT OFF.

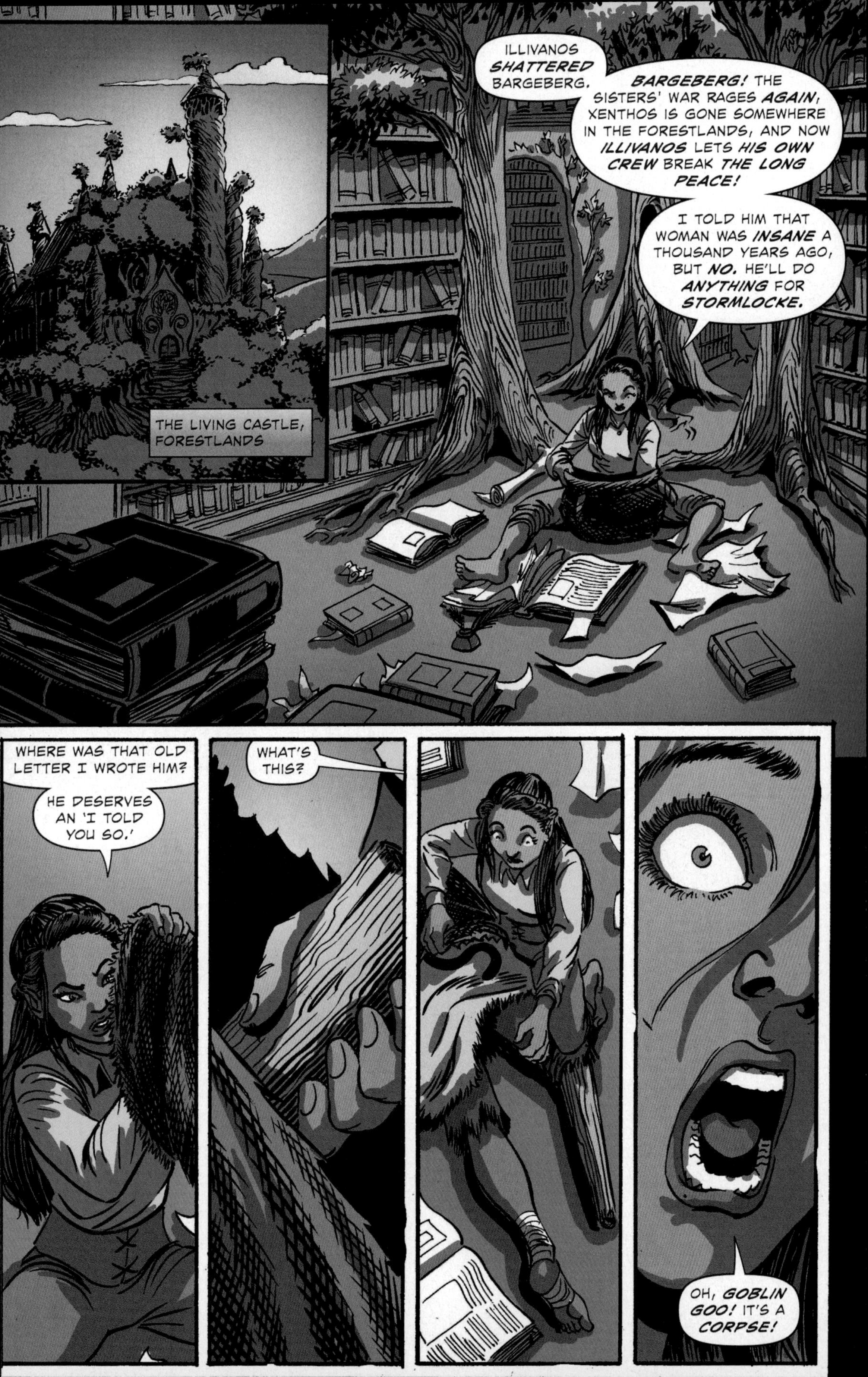
THE LIVING CASTLE, FORESTLANDS
ILLIVANOS SHATTERED BARGEBERG.
BARGEBERG! THE SISTERS' WAR RAGES AGAIN, XENTHOS IS GONE SOMEWHERE IN THE FORESTLANDS, AND NOW ILLIVANOS LETS HIS OWN CREW BREAK THE LONG PEACE!
I TOLD HIM THAT WOMAN WAS INSANE A THOUSAND YEARS AGO, BUT NO. HE'LL DO ANYTHING FOR STORMLOCKE.
WHERE WAS THAT OLD LETTER I WROTE HIM?
HE DESERVES AN 'I TOLD YOU SO.'
WHAT'S THIS?
OH, GOBLIN GOO! IT'S A CORPSE!

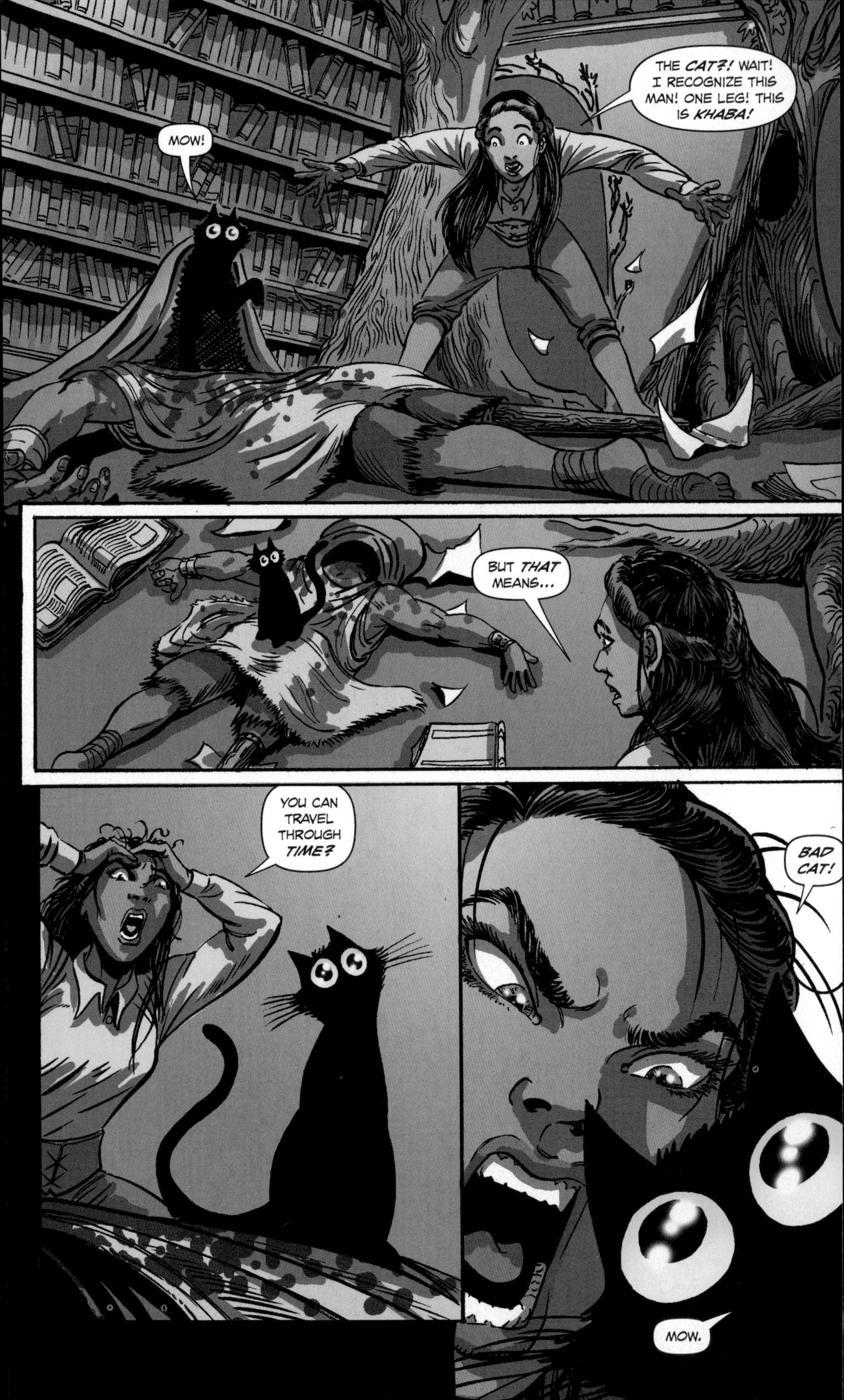
THE CAT?! WAIT! I RECOGNIZE THIS MAN! ONE LEG! THIS IS KHABA!
MOW!
BUT THAT MEANS...
YOU CAN TRAVEL THROUGH TIME?
BAD CAT!
MOW.

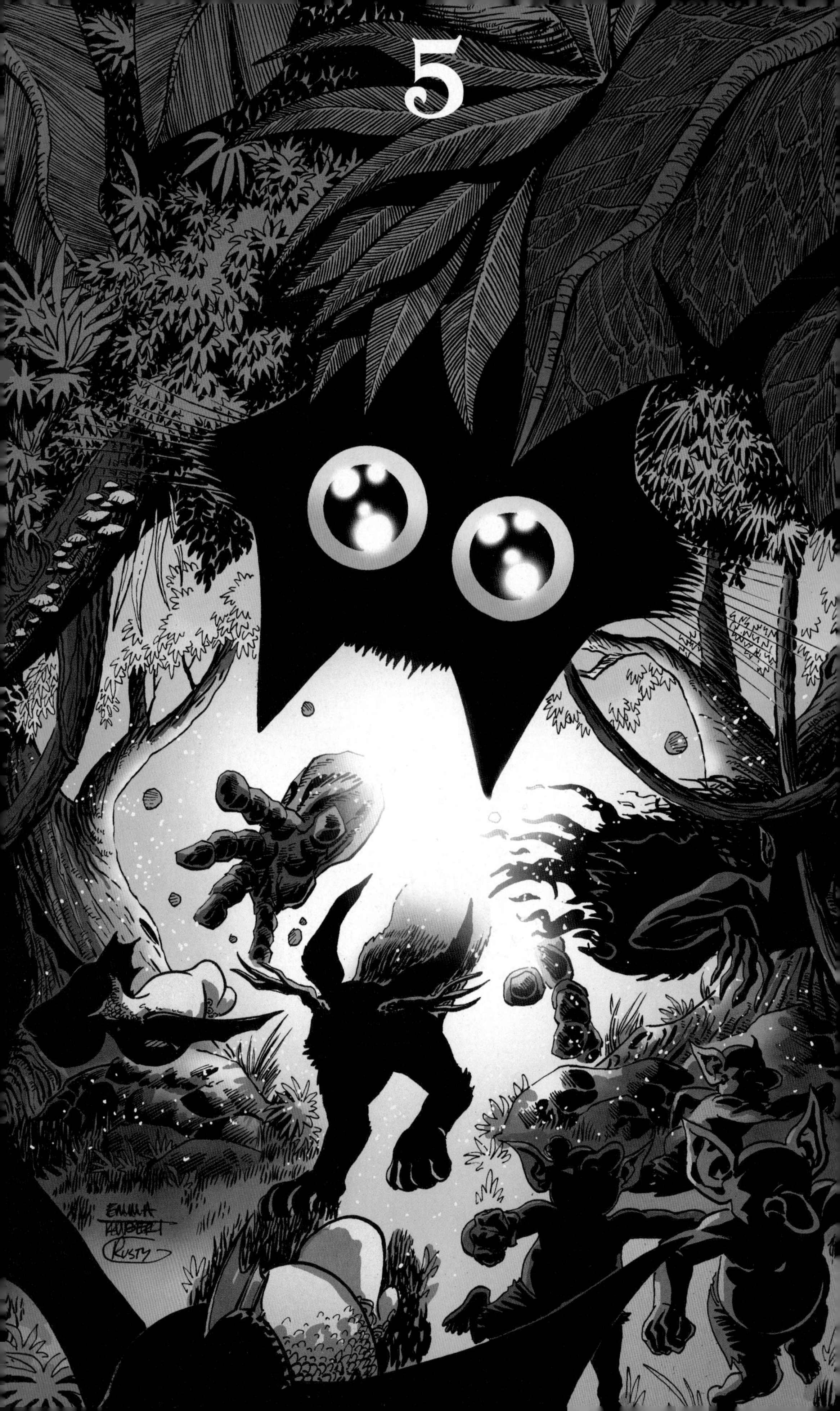
5

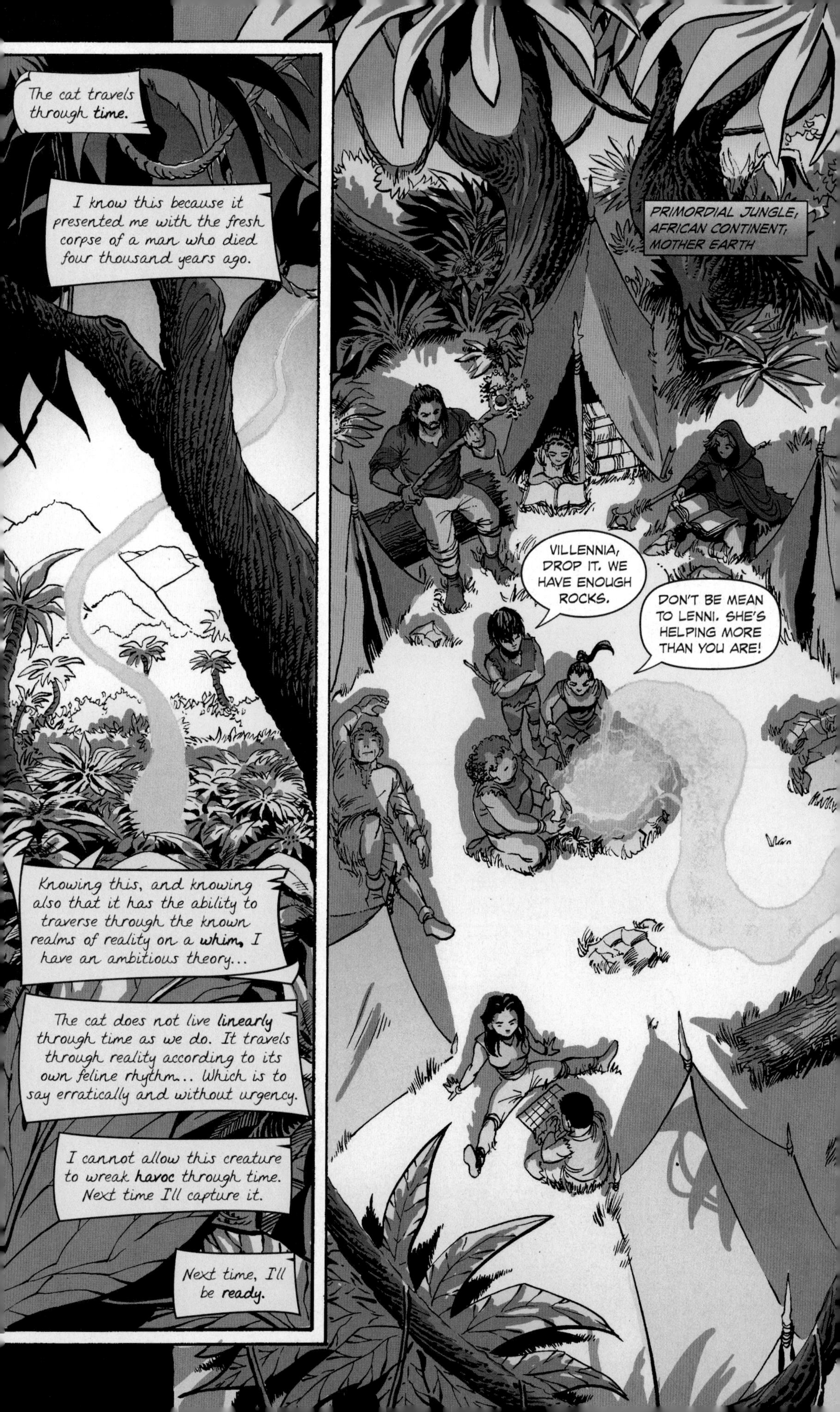

The cat travels through time.
I know this because it presented me with the fresh corpse of a man who died four thousand years ago.
Knowing this, and knowing also that it has the ability to traverse through the known realms of reality on a whim, I have an ambitious theory...
The cat does not live linearly through time as we do. It travels through reality according to its own feline rhythm... Which is to say erratically and without urgency.
I cannot allow this creature to wreak havoc through time. Next time I'll capture it.
Next time, I'll be ready.
PRIMORDIAL JUNGLE, AFRICAN CONTINENT, MOTHER EARTH
VILLENNIA, DROP IT. WE HAVE ENOUGH ROCKS.
DON'T BE MEAN TO LENNI. SHE'S HELPING MORE THAN YOU ARE!

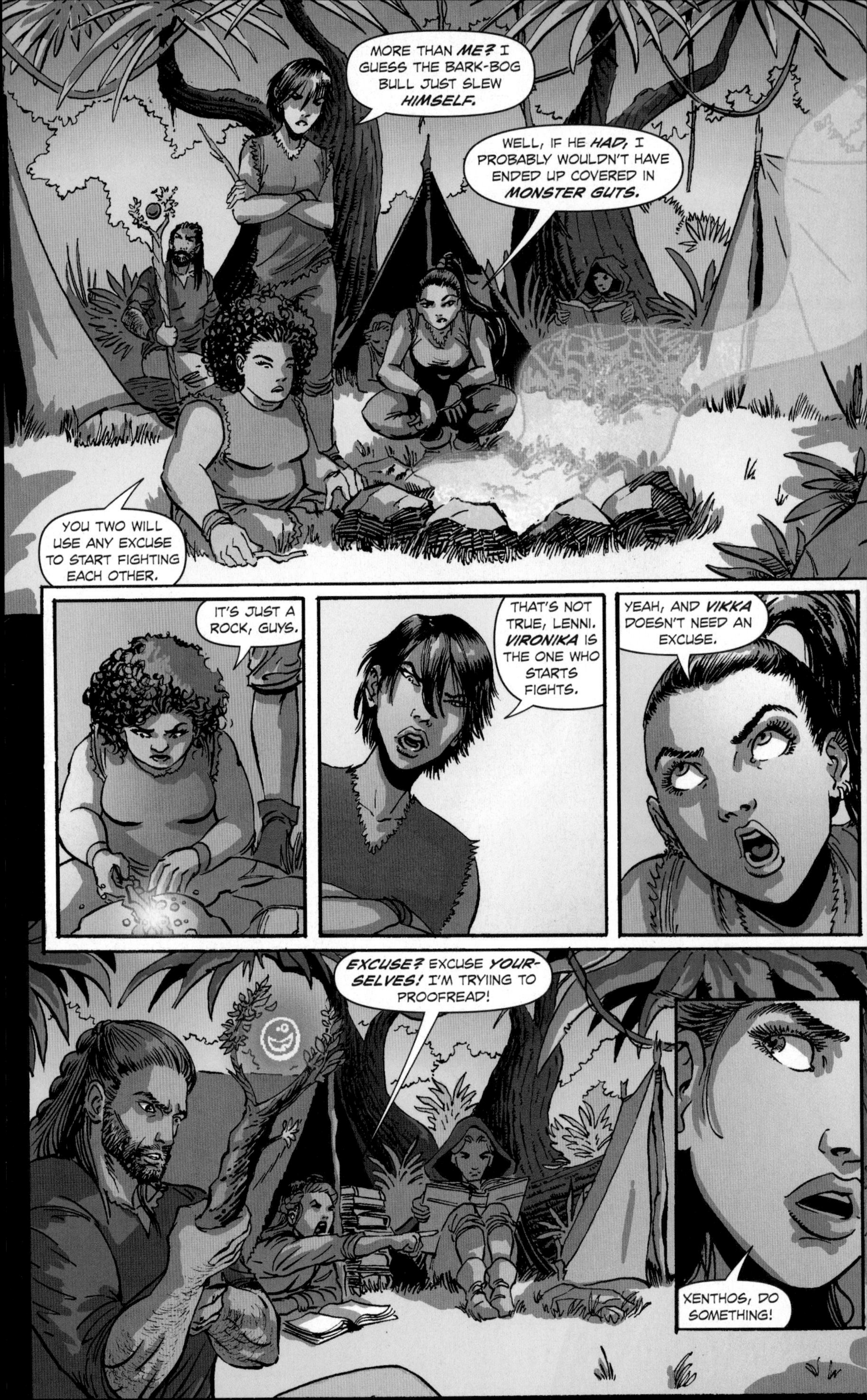
MORE THAN ***ME?*** I GUESS THE BARK-BOG BULL JUST SLEW ***HIMSELF.***
WELL, IF HE ***HAD,*** I PROBABLY WOULDN'T HAVE ENDED UP COVERED IN ***MONSTER GUTS.***
YOU TWO WILL USE ANY EXCUSE TO START FIGHTING EACH OTHER.
IT'S JUST A ROCK, GUYS.
THAT'S NOT TRUE, LENNI. ***VIRONIKA*** IS THE ONE WHO STARTS FIGHTS.
YEAH, AND ***VIKKA*** DOESN'T NEED AN EXCUSE.
EXCUSE? EXCUSE ***YOUR-SELVES!*** I'M TRYIING TO PROOFREAD!
XENTHOS, DO SOMETHING!

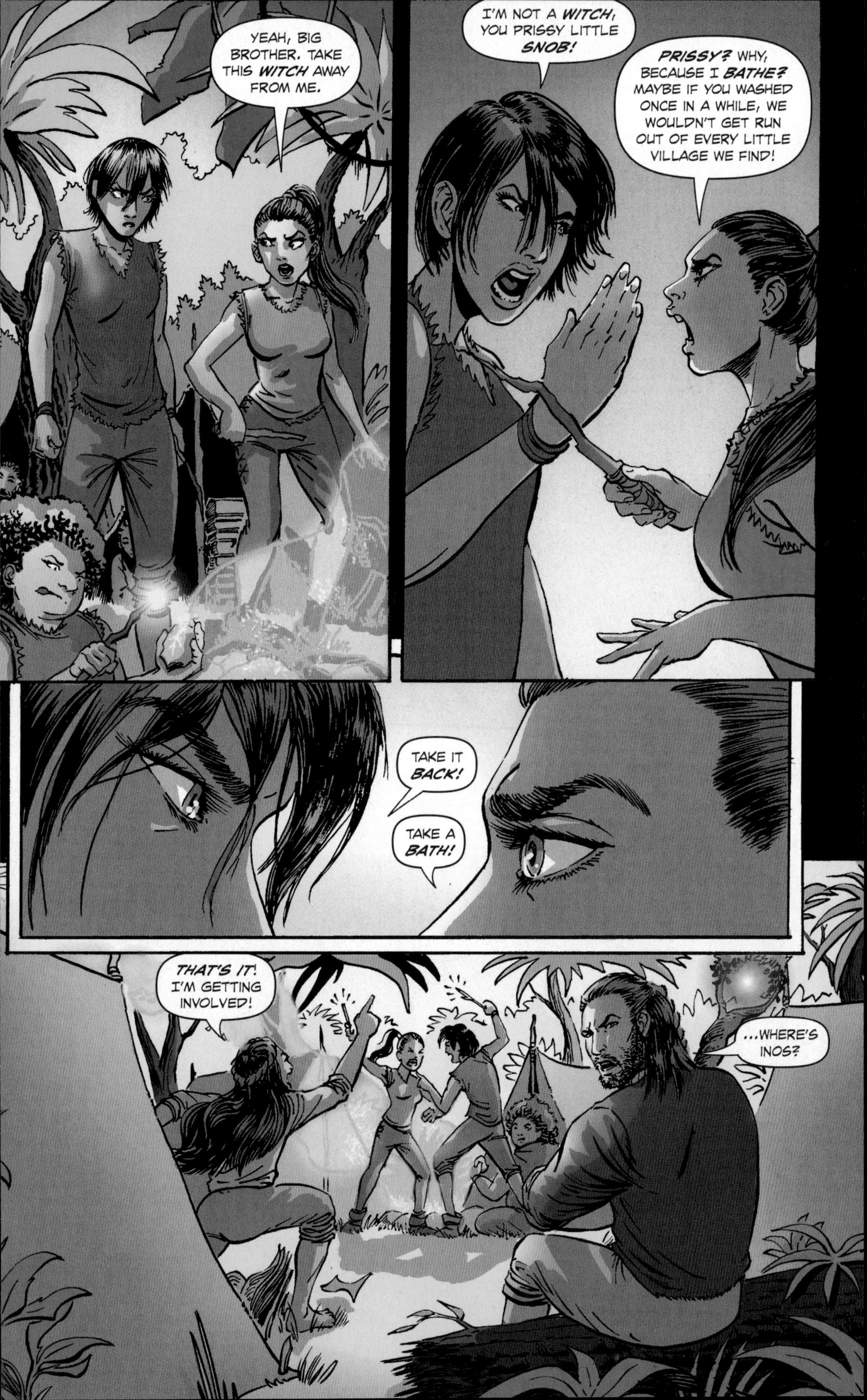
YEAH, BIG BROTHER. TAKE THIS WITCH AWAY FROM ME.
I'M NOT A WITCH, YOU PRISSY LITTLE SNOB!
PRISSY? WHY, BECAUSE I BATHE? MAYBE IF YOU WASHED ONCE IN A WHILE, WE WOULDN'T GET RUN OUT OF EVERY LITTLE VILLAGE WE FIND!
TAKE IT BACK!
TAKE A BATH!
THAT'S IT! I'M GETTING INVOLVED!
...WHERE'S INOS?

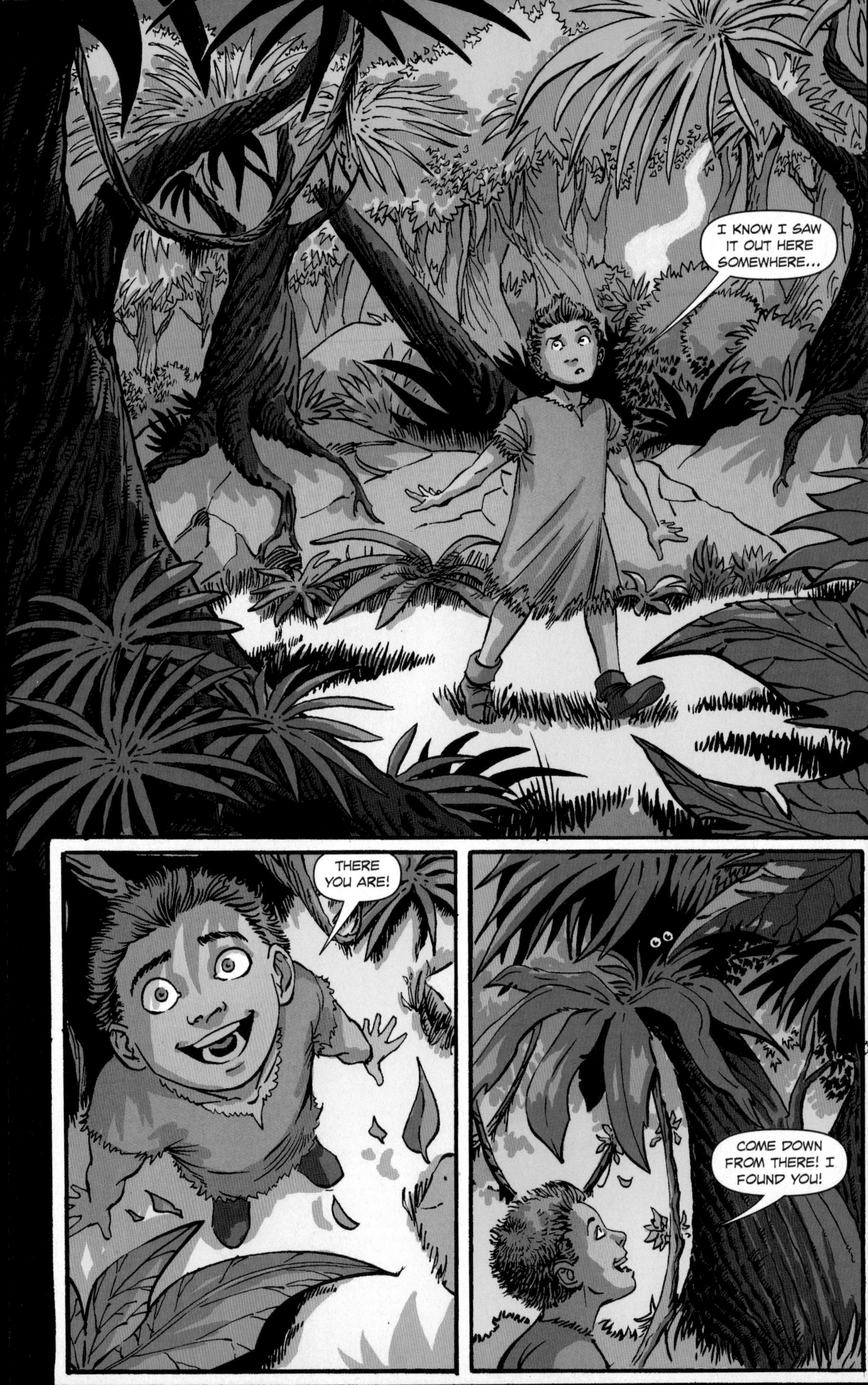
I KNOW I SAW IT OUT HERE SOMEWHERE...
THERE YOU ARE!
COME DOWN FROM THERE! I FOUND YOU!

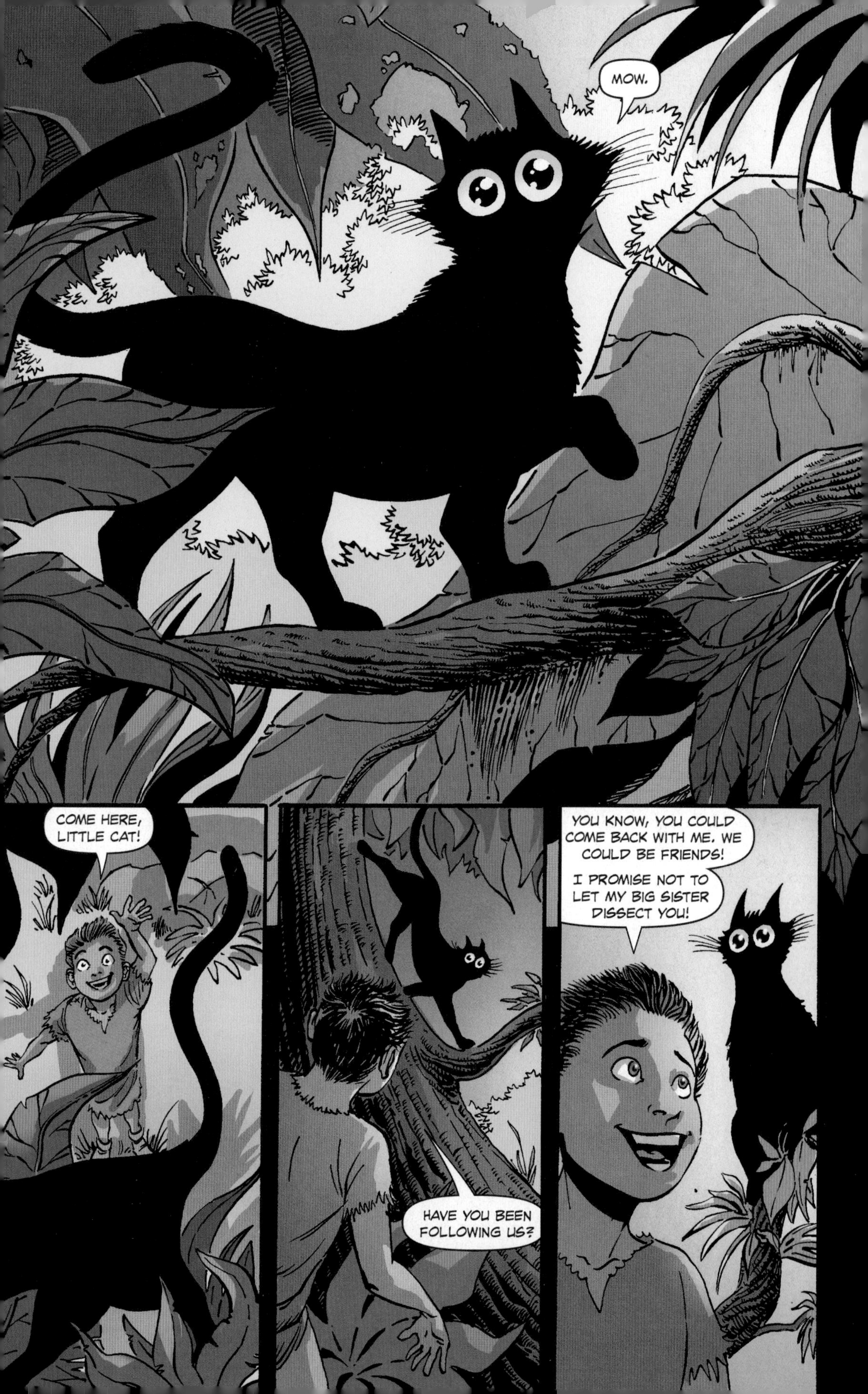
MOW.
COME HERE, LITTLE CAT!
HAVE YOU BEEN FOLLOWING US?
YOU KNOW, YOU COULD COME BACK WITH ME. WE COULD BE FRIENDS!
I PROMISE NOT TO LET MY BIG SISTER DISSECT YOU!

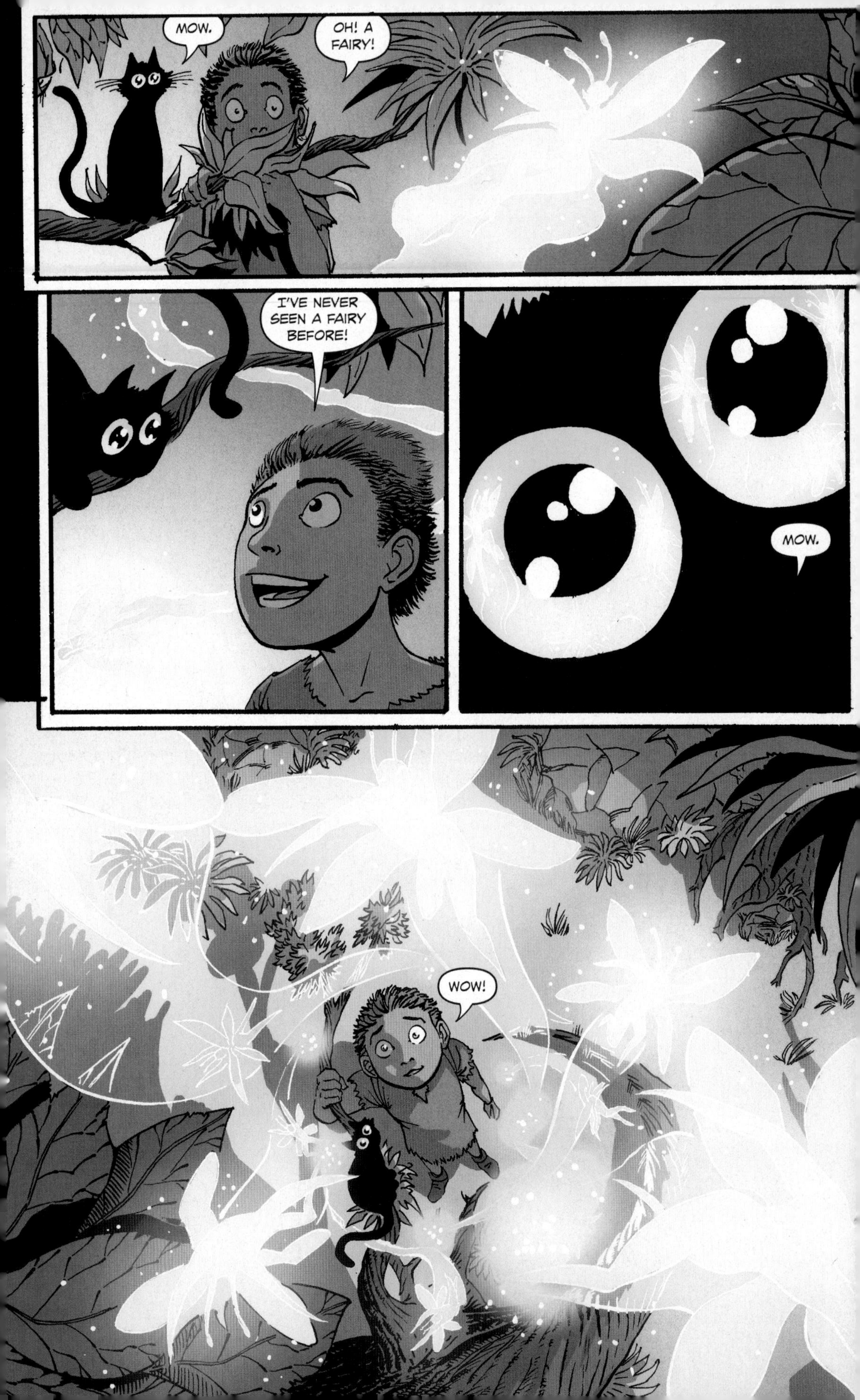
MOW.
OH! A FAIRY!
I'VE NEVER SEEN A FAIRY BEFORE!
MOW.
WOW!

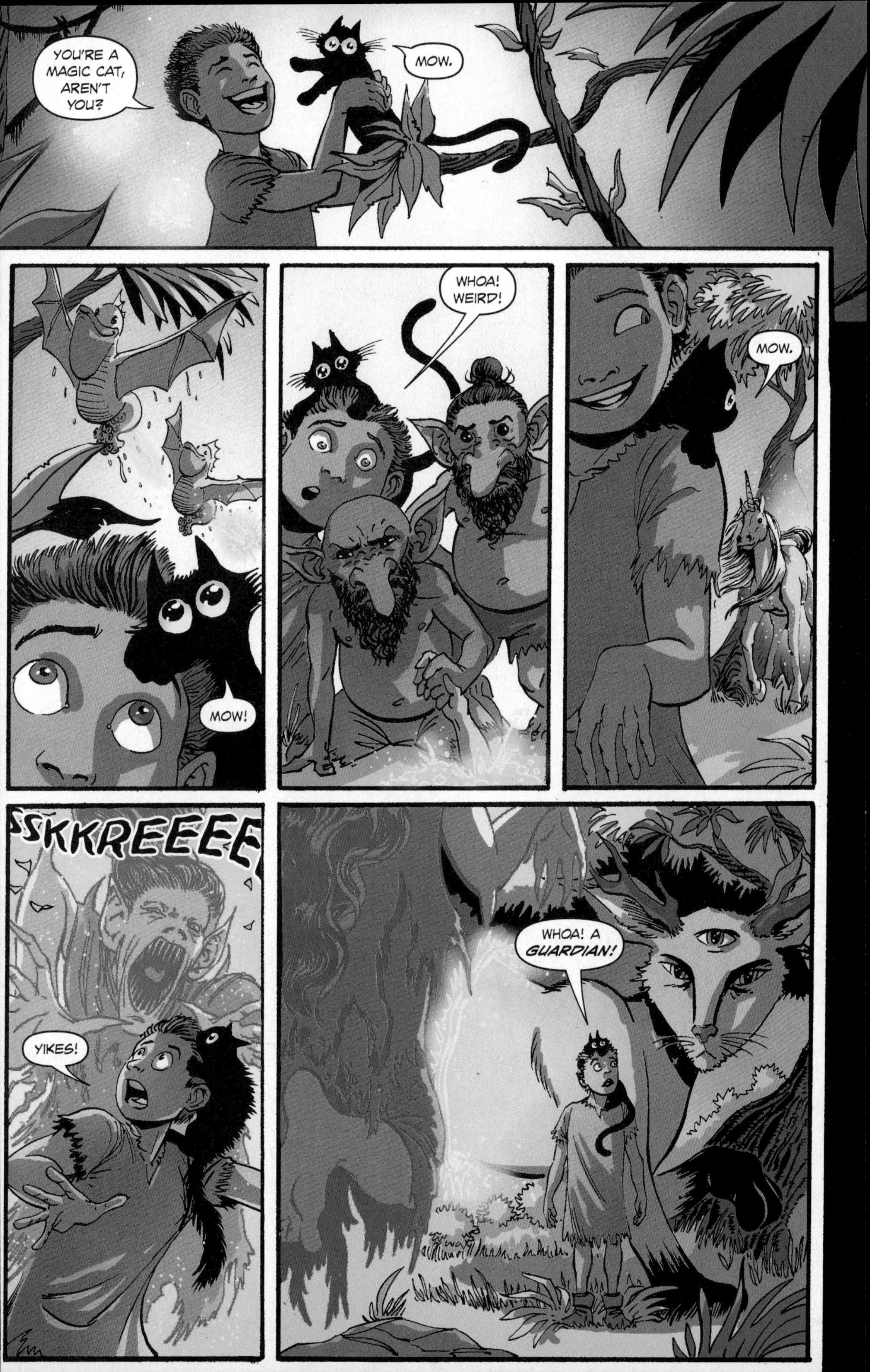
YOU'RE A MAGIC CAT, AREN'T YOU?
MOW.
MOW!
WHOA! WEIRD!
MOW.
SKKREEEEE
YIKES!
WHOA! A *GUARDIAN!*

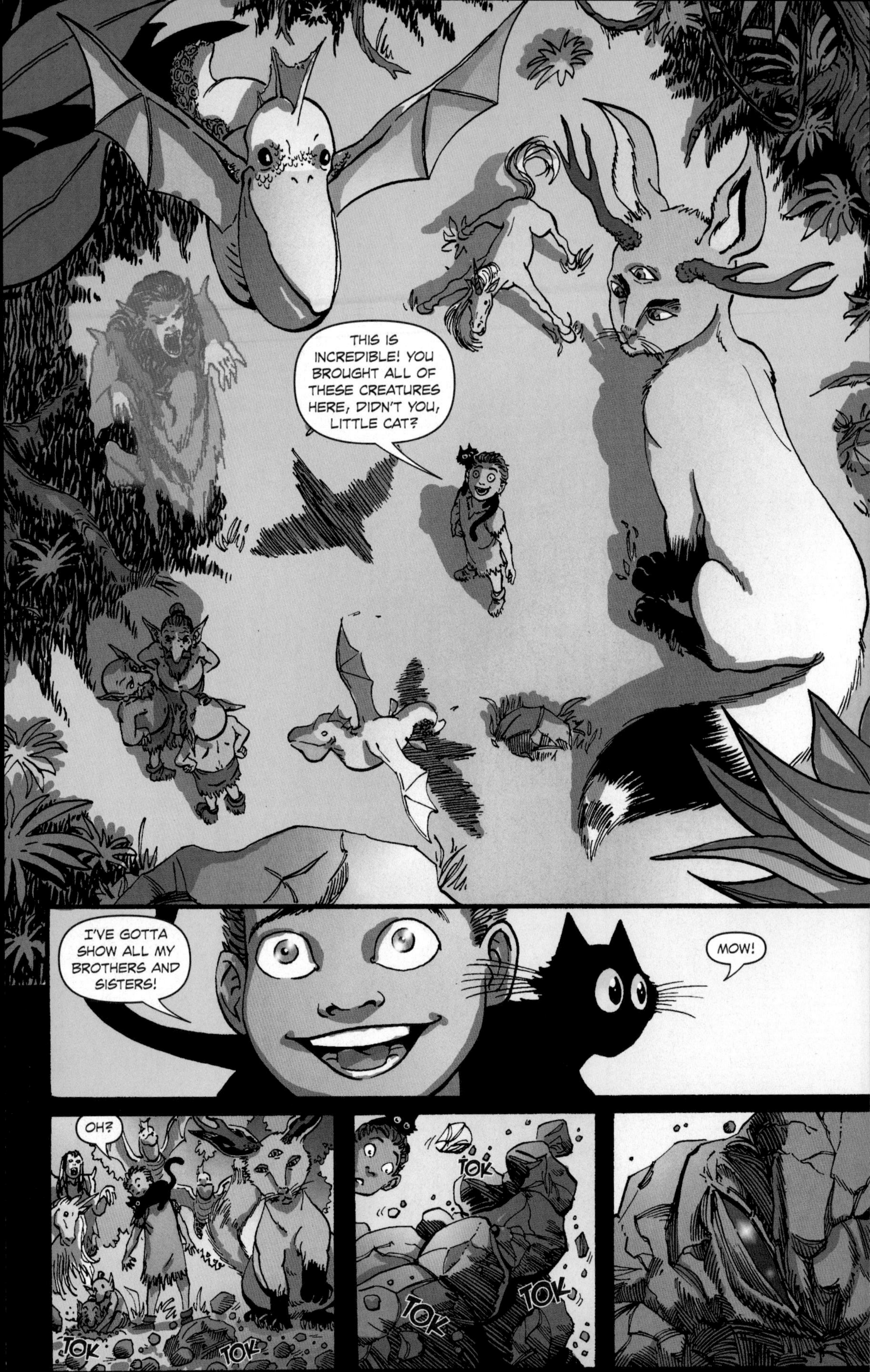
THIS IS INCREDIBLE! YOU BROUGHT ALL OF THESE CREATURES HERE, DIDN'T YOU, LITTLE CAT?
I'VE GOTTA SHOW ALL MY BROTHERS AND SISTERS!
MOW!
OH?
TOK
TOK
TOK
TOK
TOK

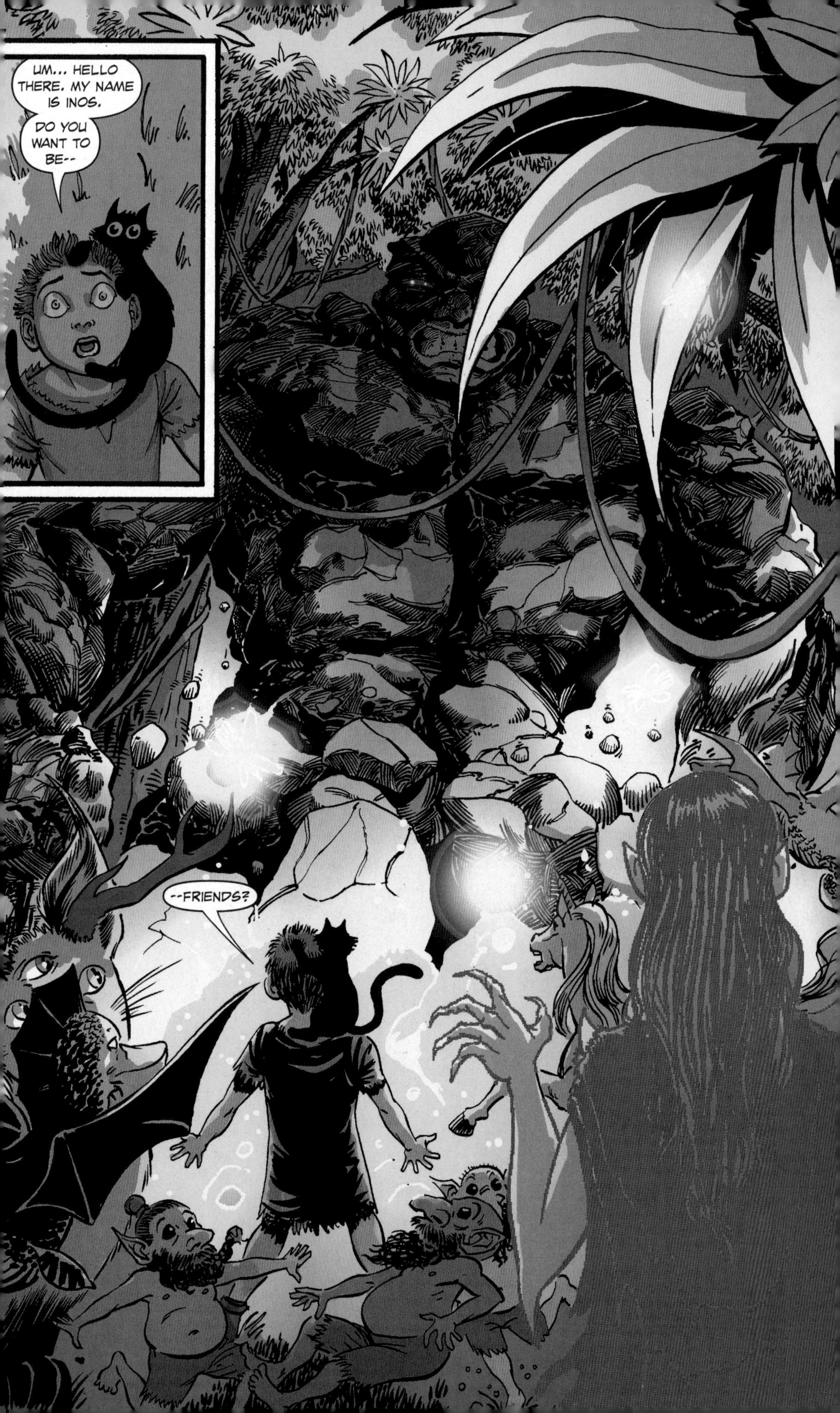
UM... HELLO THERE. MY NAME IS INOS.
DO YOU WANT TO BE--
--FRIENDS?

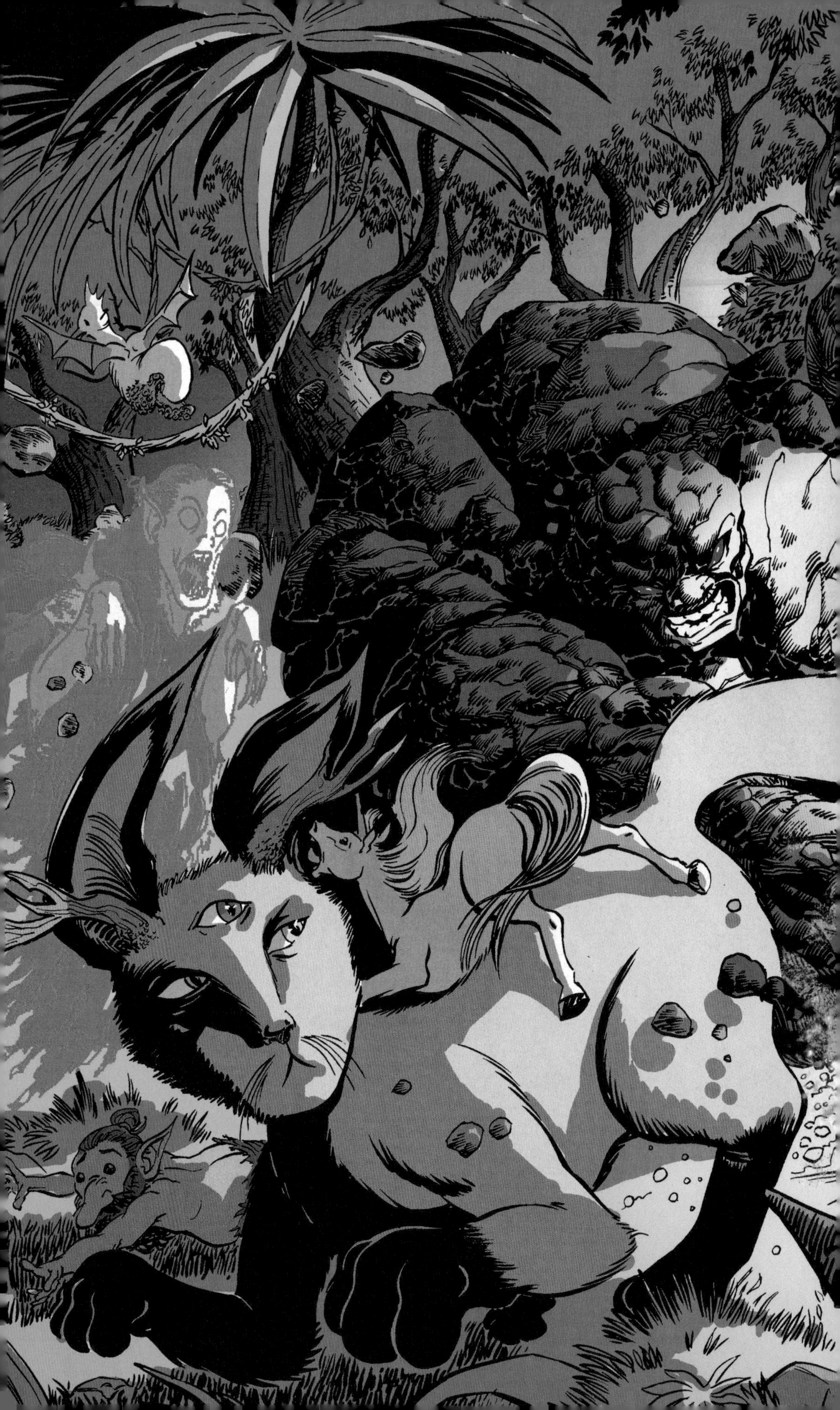

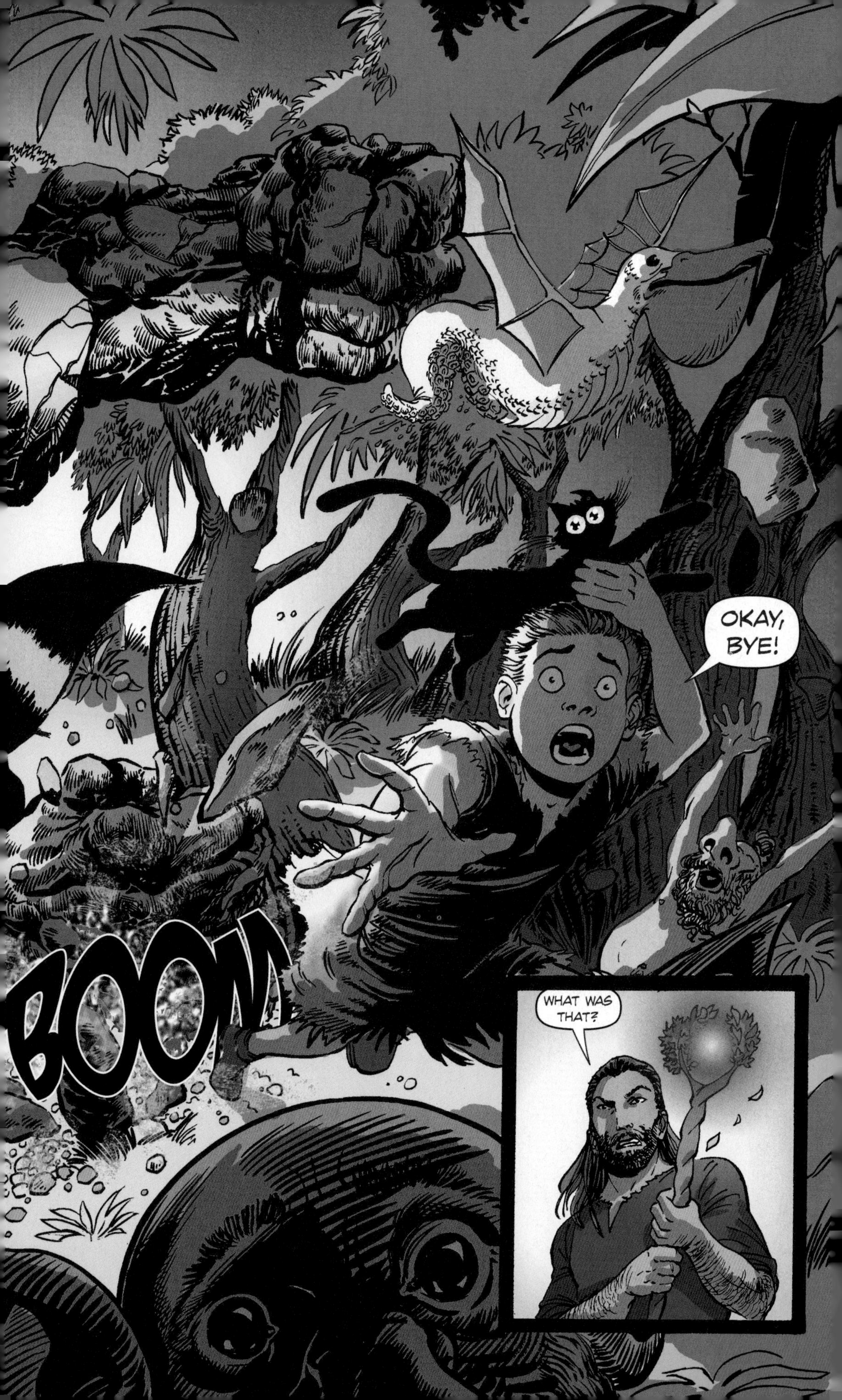
OKAY, BYE!
BOOM
WHAT WAS THAT?

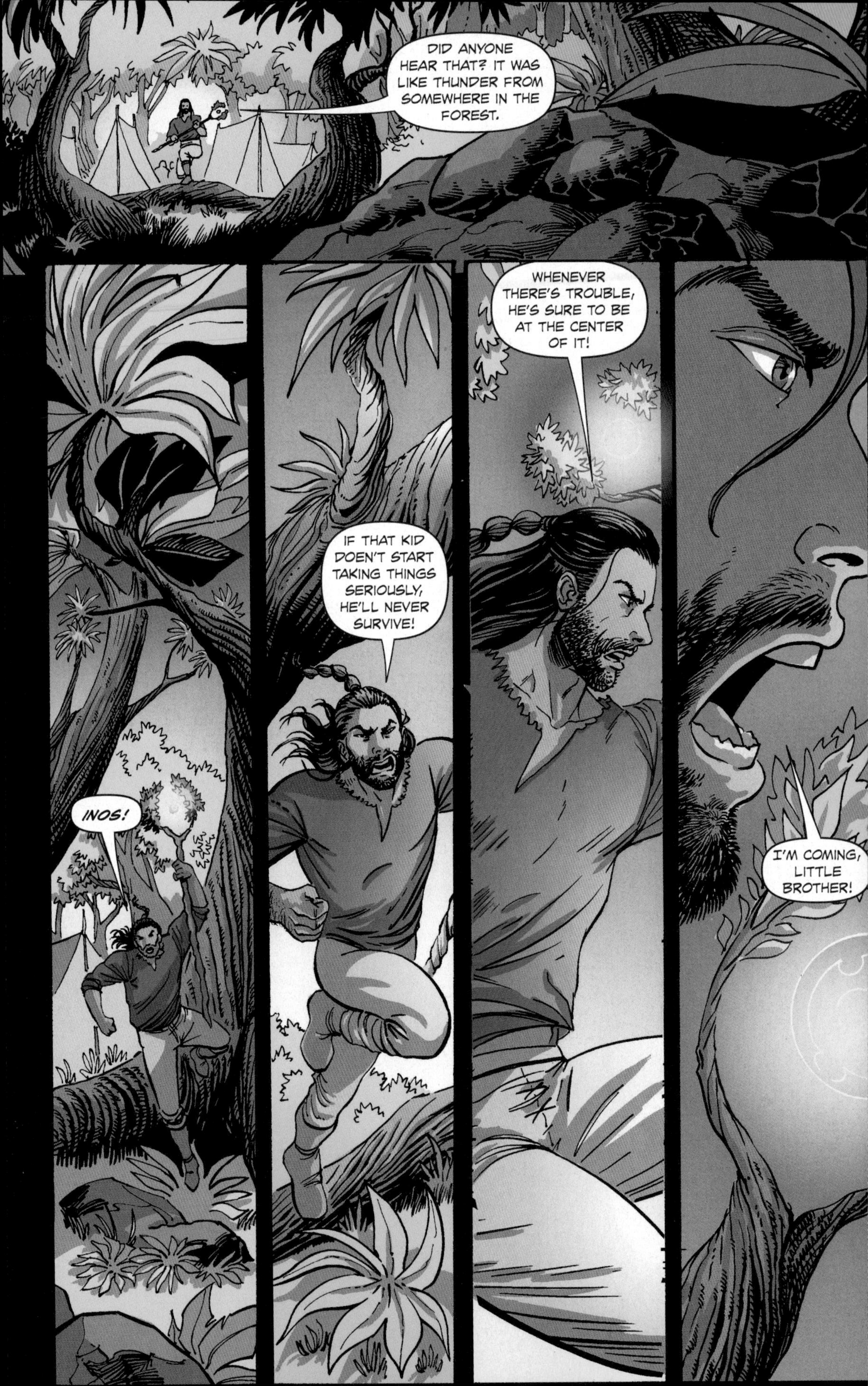
DID ANYONE HEAR THAT? IT WAS LIKE THUNDER FROM SOMEWHERE IN THE FOREST.
INOS!
IF THAT KID DOESN'T START TAKING THINGS SERIOUSLY, HE'LL NEVER SURVIVE!
WHENEVER THERE'S TROUBLE, HE'S SURE TO BE AT THE CENTER OF IT!
I'M COMING, LITTLE BROTHER!

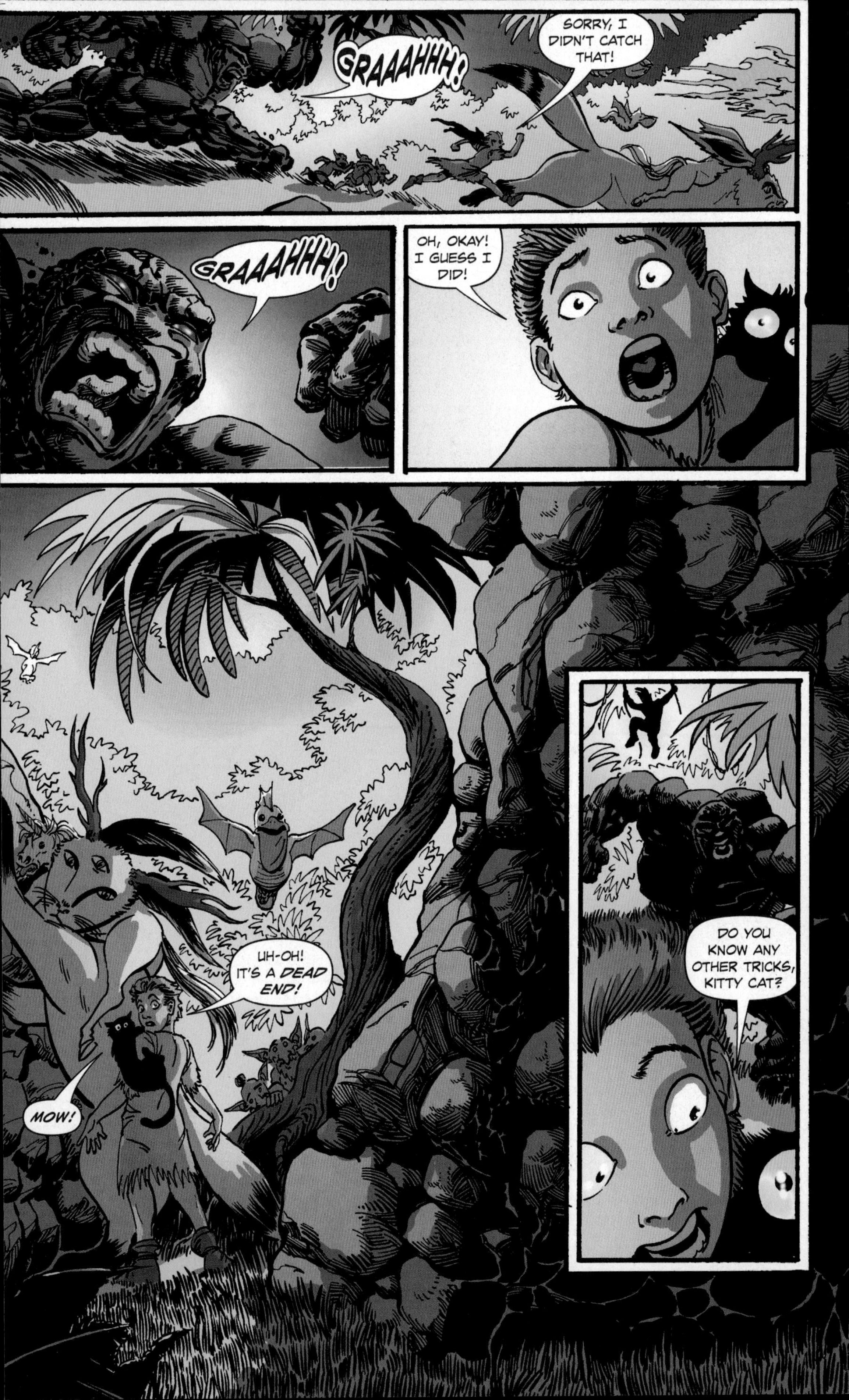
GRAAAHHH!
SORRY, I DIDN'T CATCH THAT!
GRAAAHHH!
OH, OKAY! I GUESS I DID!
UH-OH! IT'S A DEAD END!
MOW!
DO YOU KNOW ANY OTHER TRICKS, KITTY CAT?

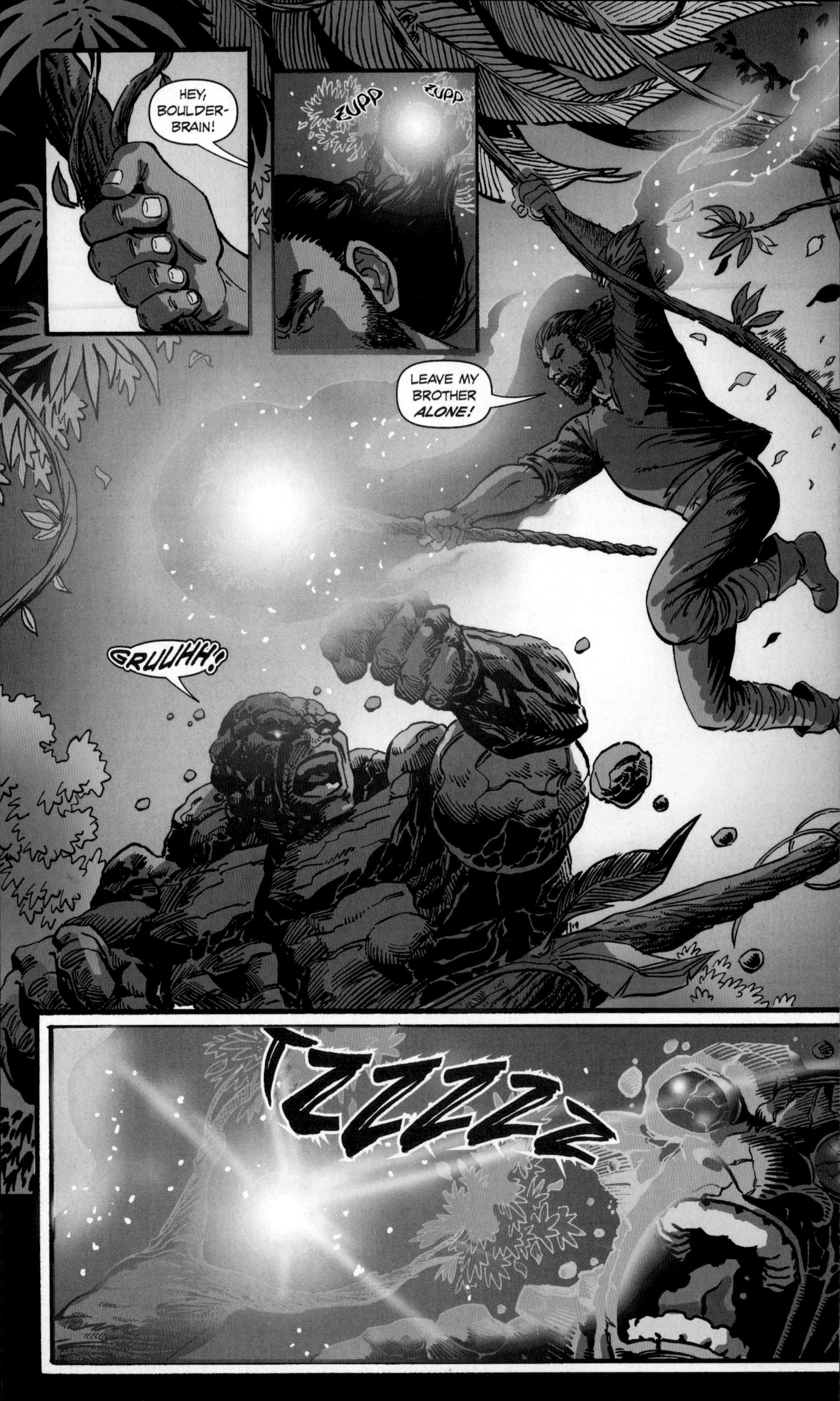
HEY, BOULDER-BRAIN!
ZUPP
ZUPP
LEAVE MY BROTHER ALONE!
GRUUHH!
TZZZZZ

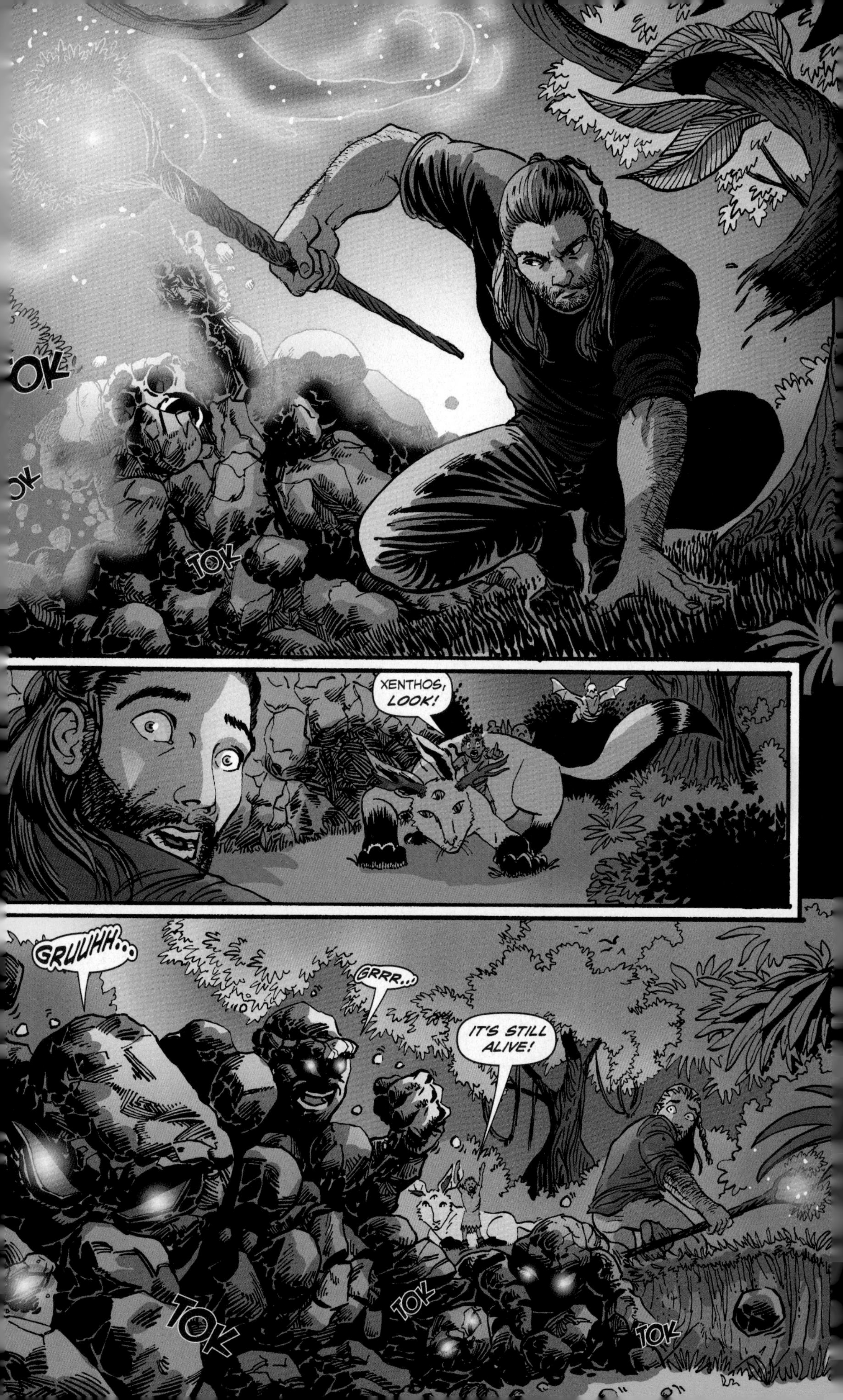
TOK
TOK
TOK
XENTHOS, LOOK!
GRUUHH...
GRRR...
IT'S STILL ALIVE!
TOK
TOK
TOK

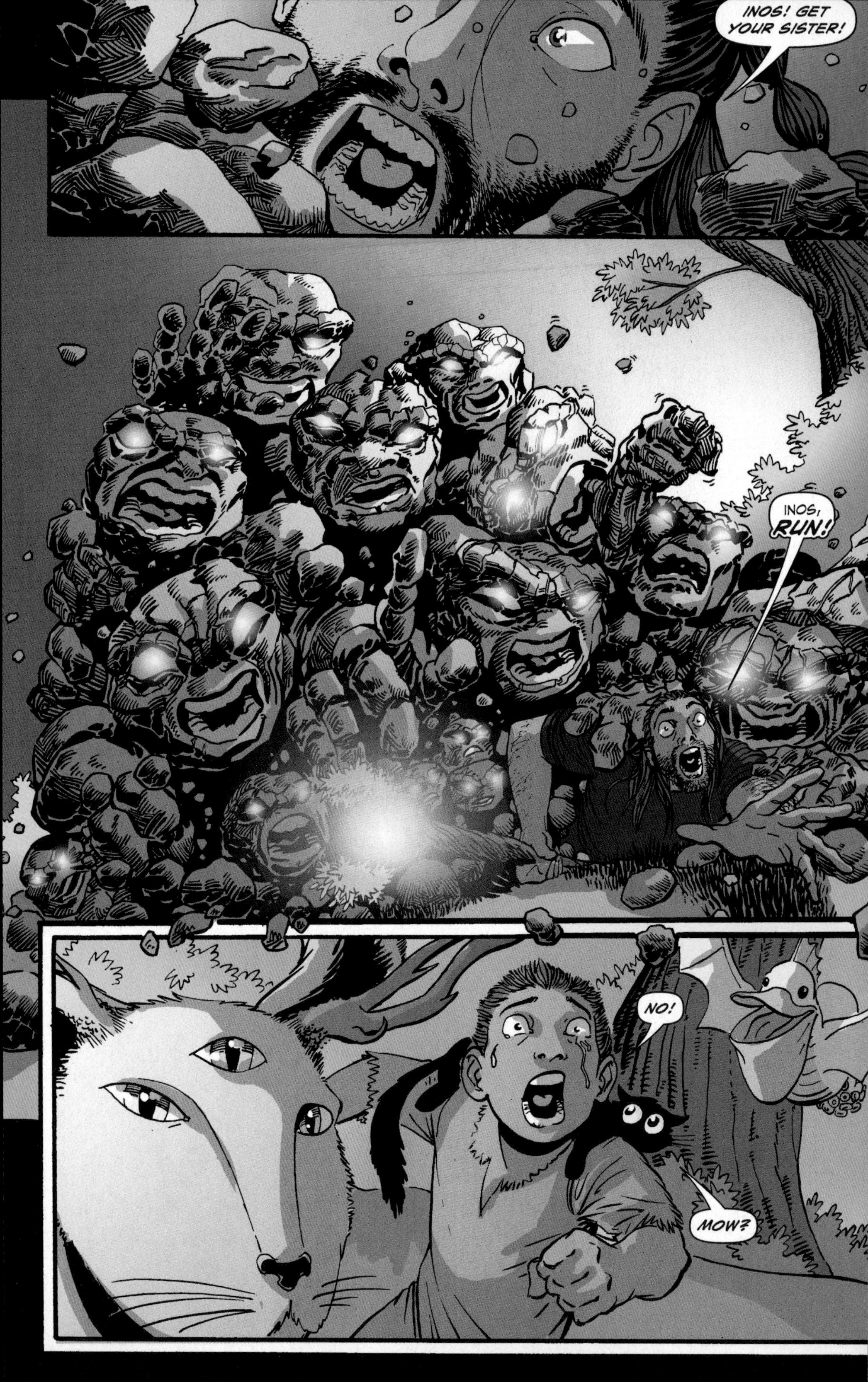
INOS! GET YOUR SISTER!
INOS, RUN!
NO!
MOW?

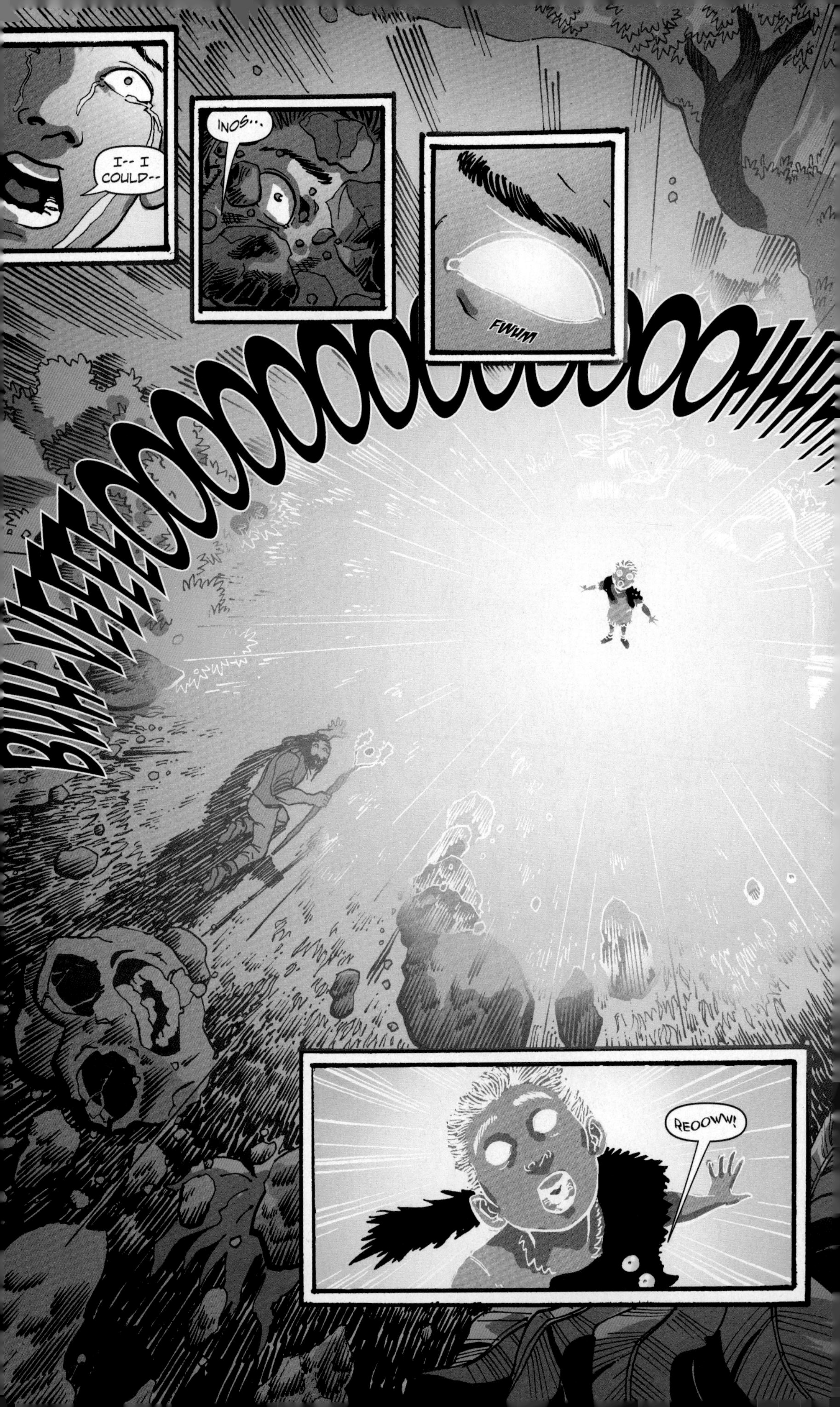
I-- I COULD--
INOS...
FWUM
BWHA-AAAHHOOOOOOOOOOOOOHHH
REOOWW!

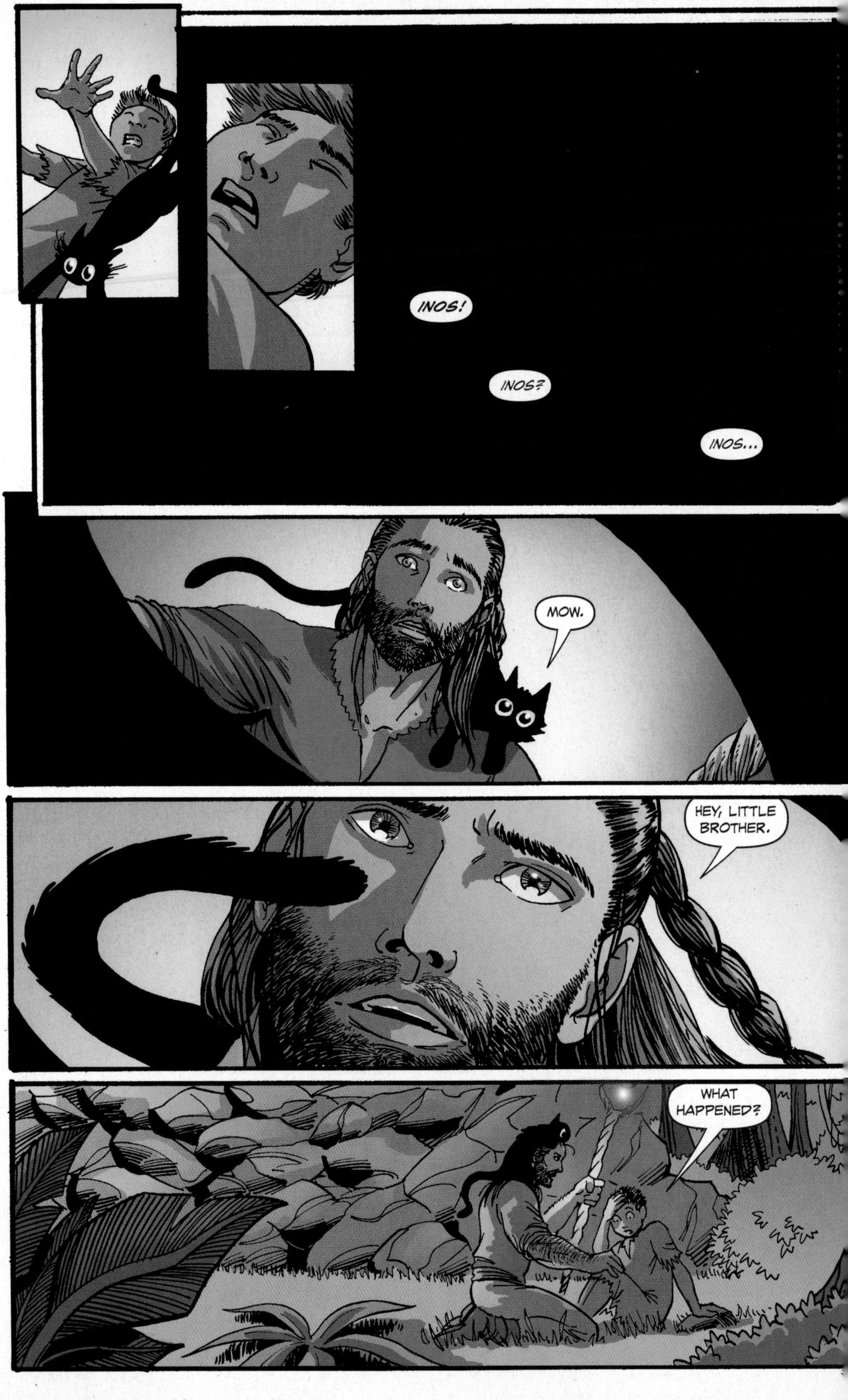
INOS!
INOS?
INOS...
MOW.
HEY, LITTLE BROTHER.
WHAT HAPPENED?

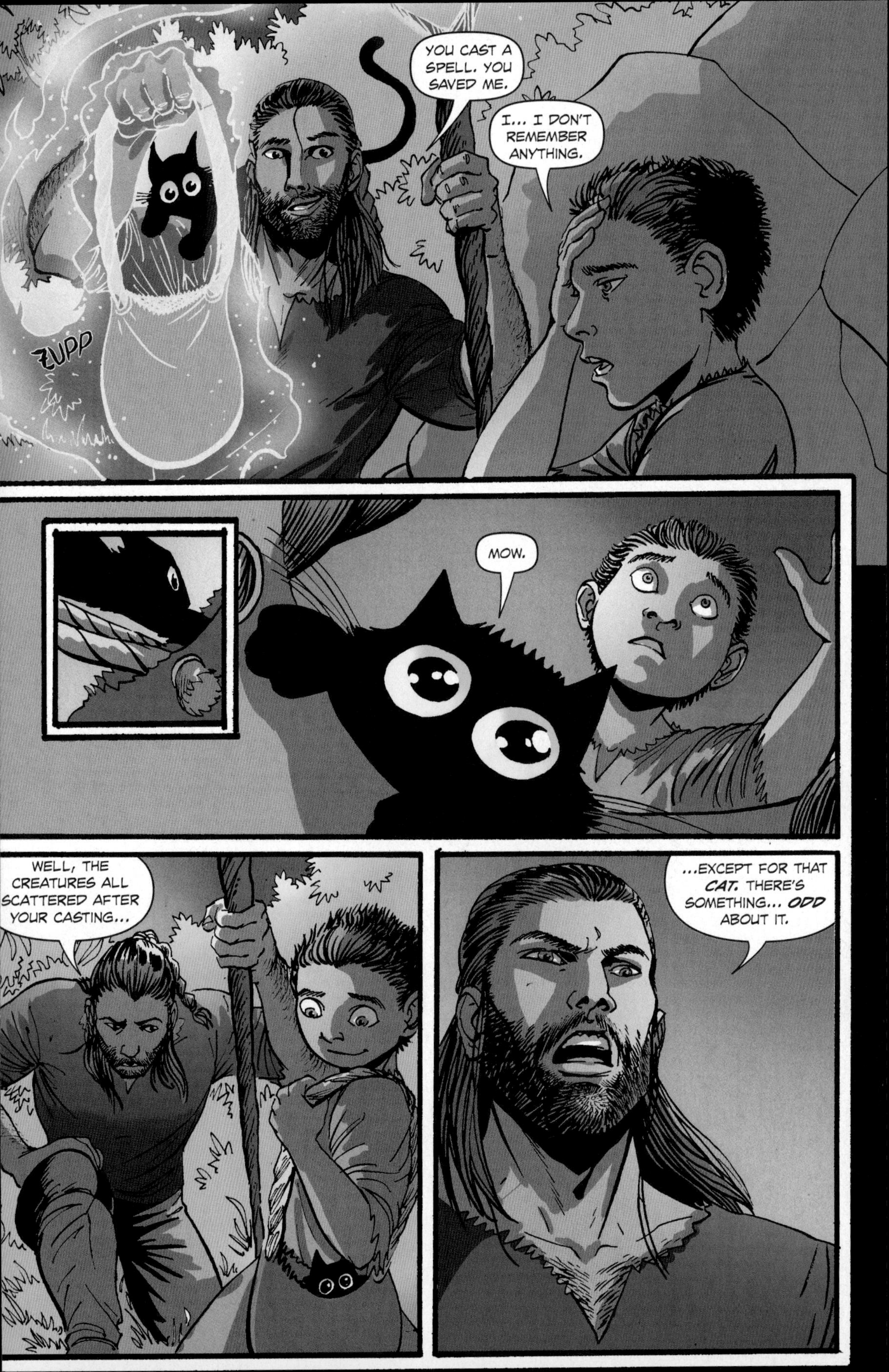
YOU CAST A SPELL. YOU SAVED ME.
I... I DON'T REMEMBER ANYTHING.
ZUPP
MOW.
WELL, THE CREATURES ALL SCATTERED AFTER YOUR CASTING...
...EXCEPT FOR THAT CAT. THERE'S SOMETHING... ODD ABOUT IT.

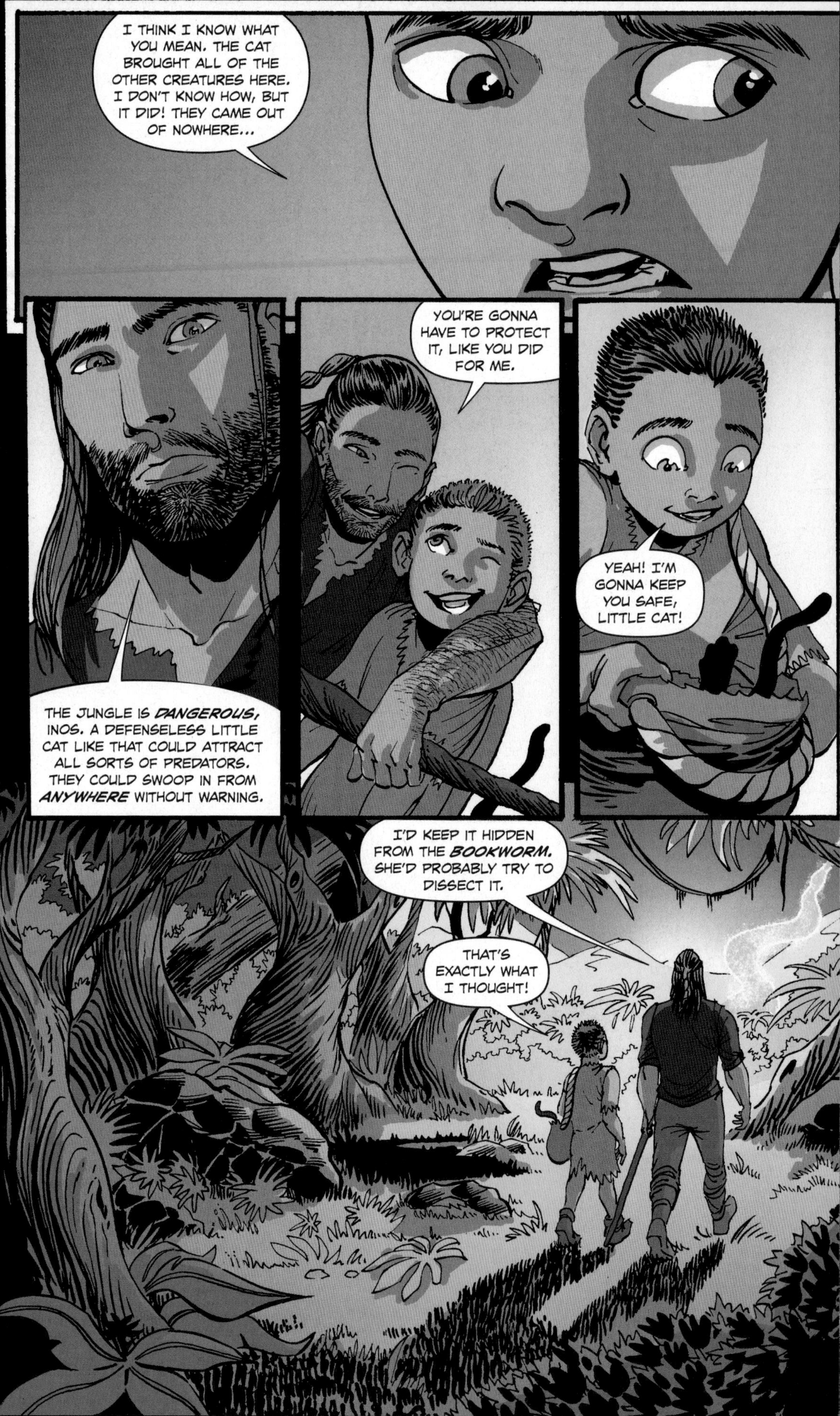
I THINK I KNOW WHAT YOU MEAN. THE CAT BROUGHT ALL OF THE OTHER CREATURES HERE. I DON'T KNOW HOW, BUT IT DID! THEY CAME OUT OF NOWHERE...
THE JUNGLE IS *DANGEROUS*, INOS. A DEFENSELESS LITTLE CAT LIKE THAT COULD ATTRACT ALL SORTS OF PREDATORS. THEY COULD SWOOP IN FROM *ANYWHERE* WITHOUT WARNING.
YOU'RE GONNA HAVE TO PROTECT IT, LIKE YOU DID FOR ME.
YEAH! I'M GONNA KEEP YOU SAFE, LITTLE CAT!
I'D KEEP IT HIDDEN FROM THE *BOOKWORM.* SHE'D PROBABLY TRY TO DISSECT IT.
THAT'S EXACTLY WHAT I THOUGHT!

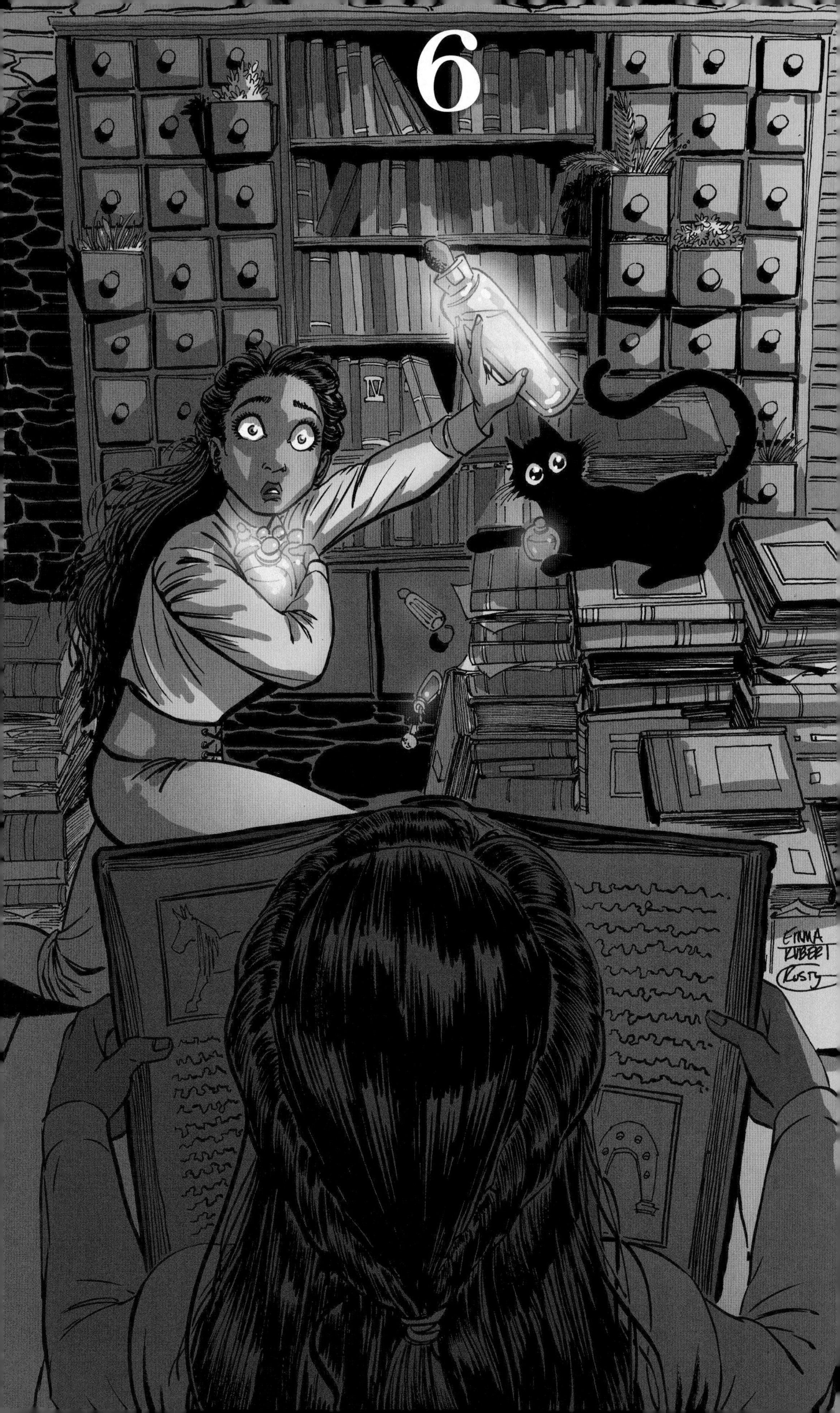
6
EMMA KUBERT
Rusty

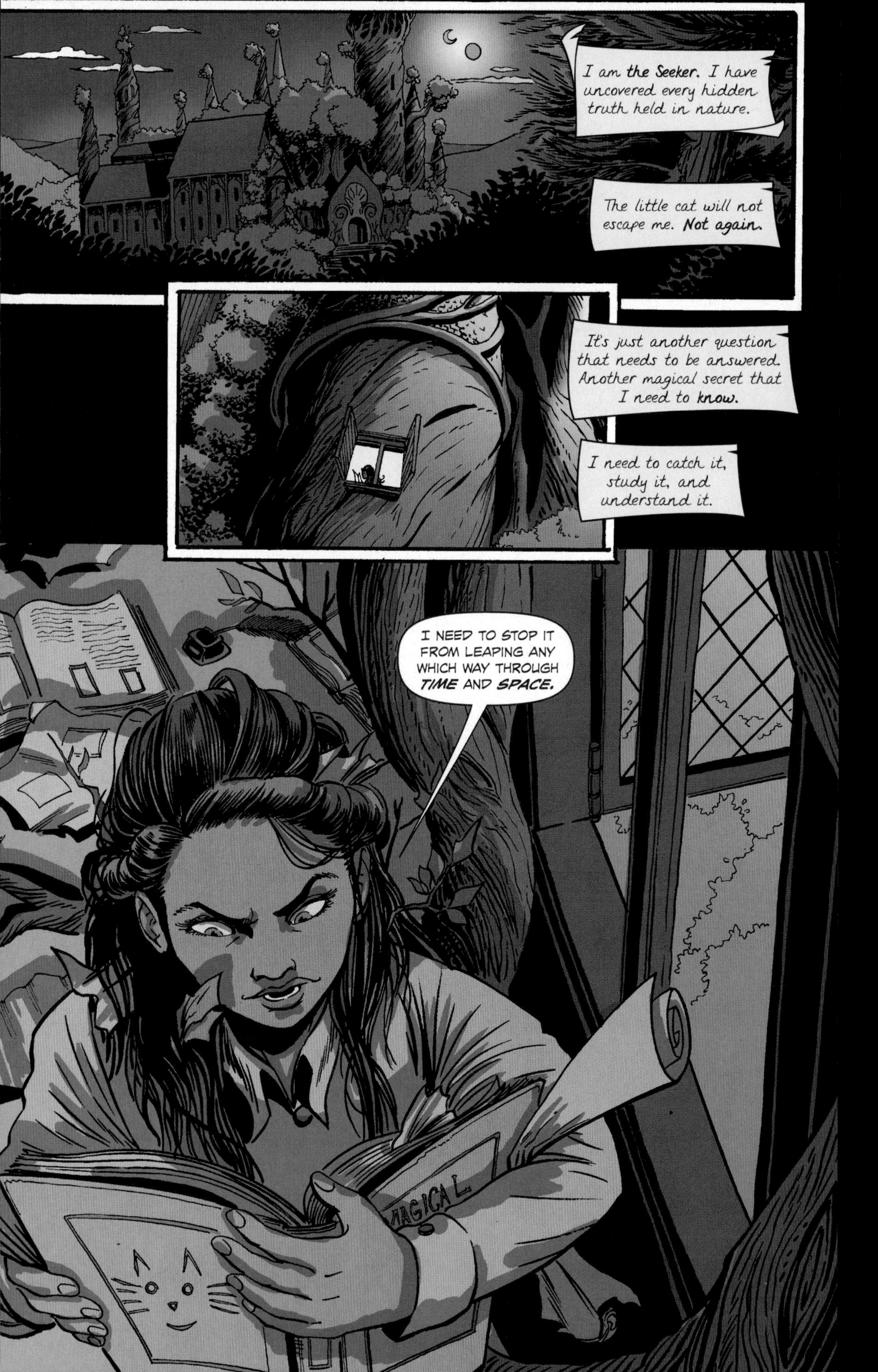

I am the Seeker. I have uncovered every hidden truth held in nature.
The little cat will not escape me. Not again.
It's just another question that needs to be answered. Another magical secret that I need to know.
I need to catch it, study it, and understand it.
I NEED TO STOP IT FROM LEAPING ANY WHICH WAY THROUGH TIME AND SPACE.
MAGICAL

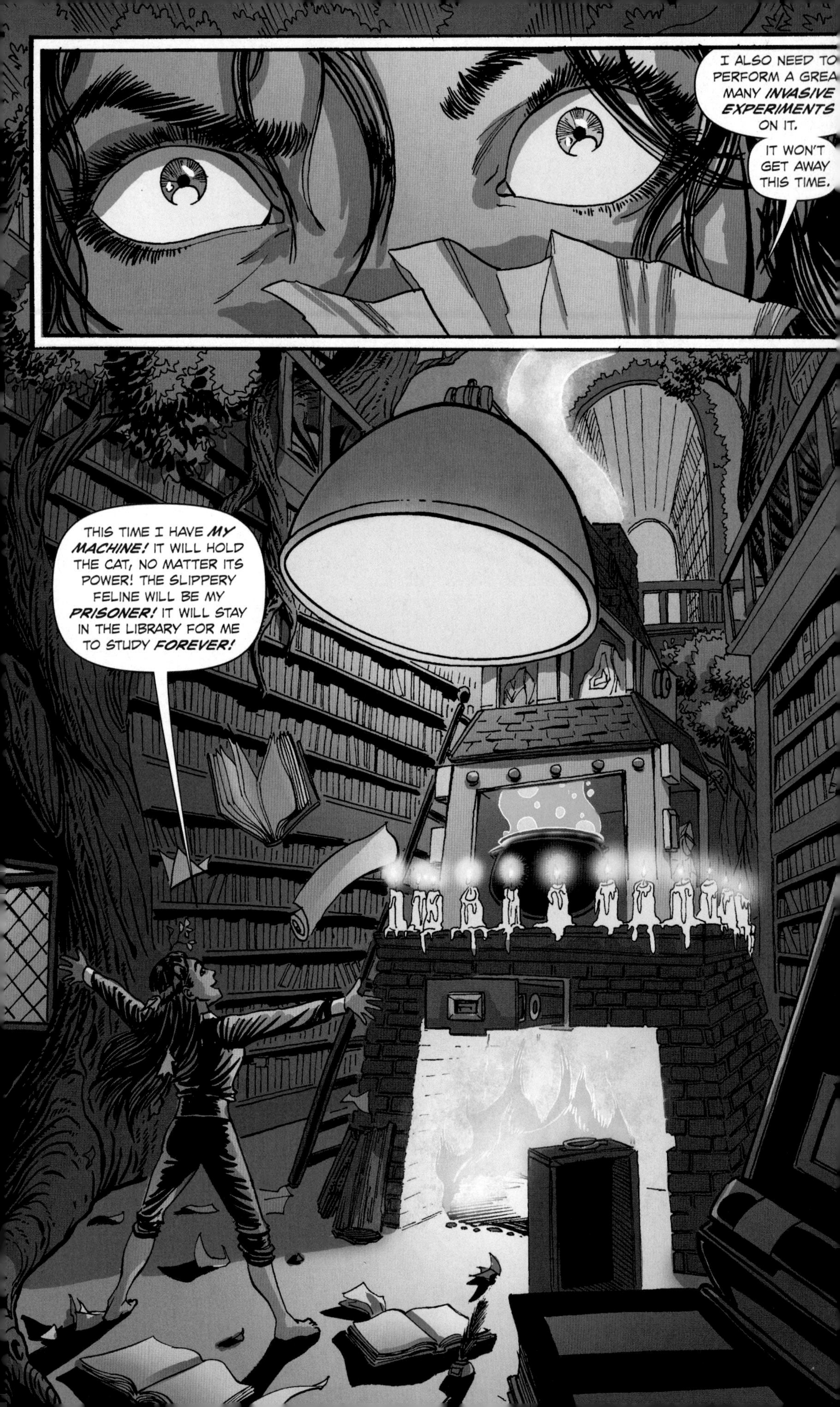
I ALSO NEED TO PERFORM A GREA MANY INVASIVE EXPERIMENTS ON IT.
IT WON'T GET AWAY THIS TIME.
THIS TIME I HAVE MY MACHINE! IT WILL HOLD THE CAT, NO MATTER ITS POWER! THE SLIPPERY FELINE WILL BE MY PRISONER! IT WILL STAY IN THE LIBRARY FOR ME TO STUDY FOREVER!

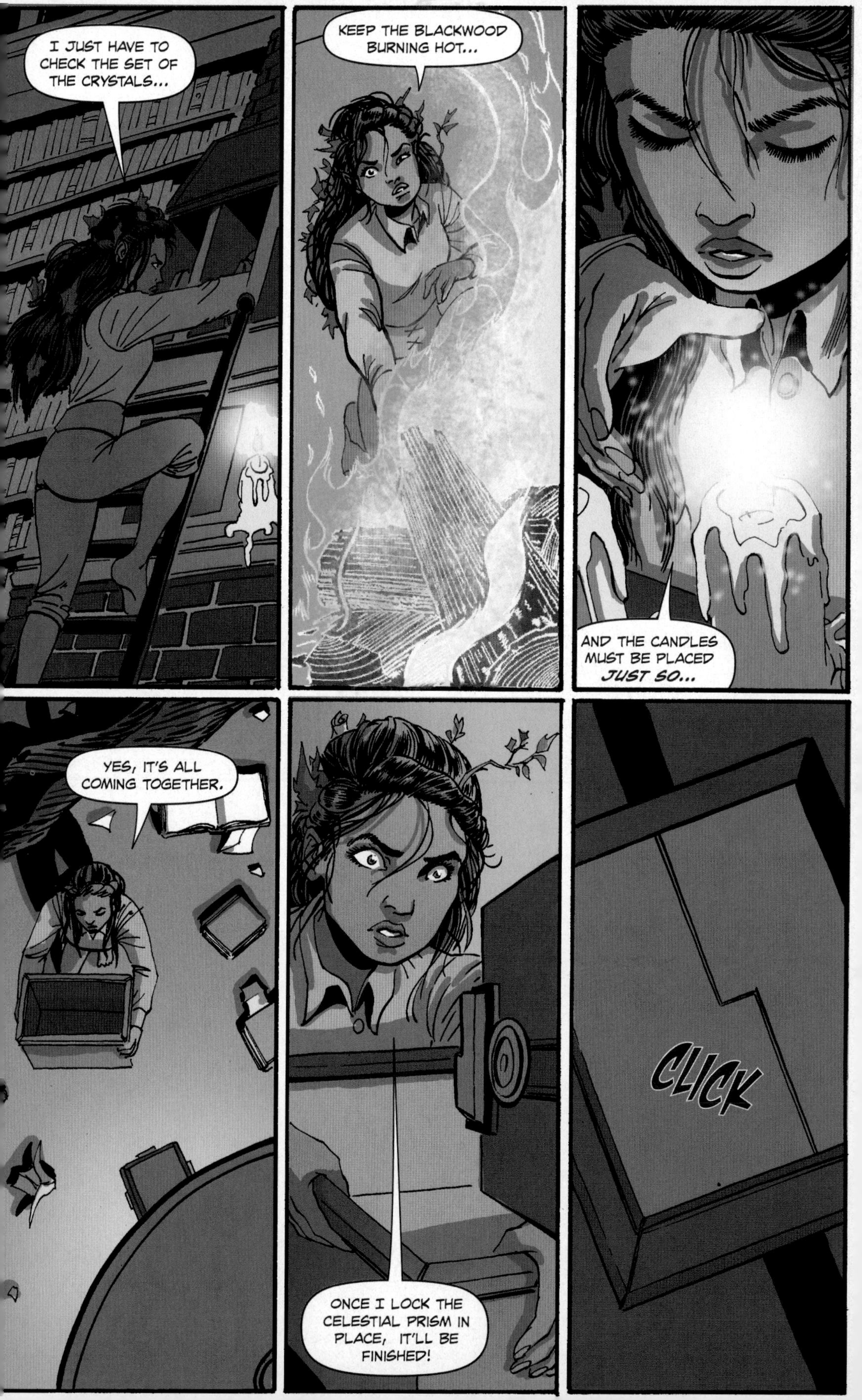
I JUST HAVE TO CHECK THE SET OF THE CRYSTALS...
KEEP THE BLACKWOOD BURNING HOT...
AND THE CANDLES MUST BE PLACED *JUST SO...*
YES, IT'S ALL COMING TOGETHER.
ONCE I LOCK THE CELESTIAL PRISM IN PLACE, IT'LL BE FINISHED!
CLICK

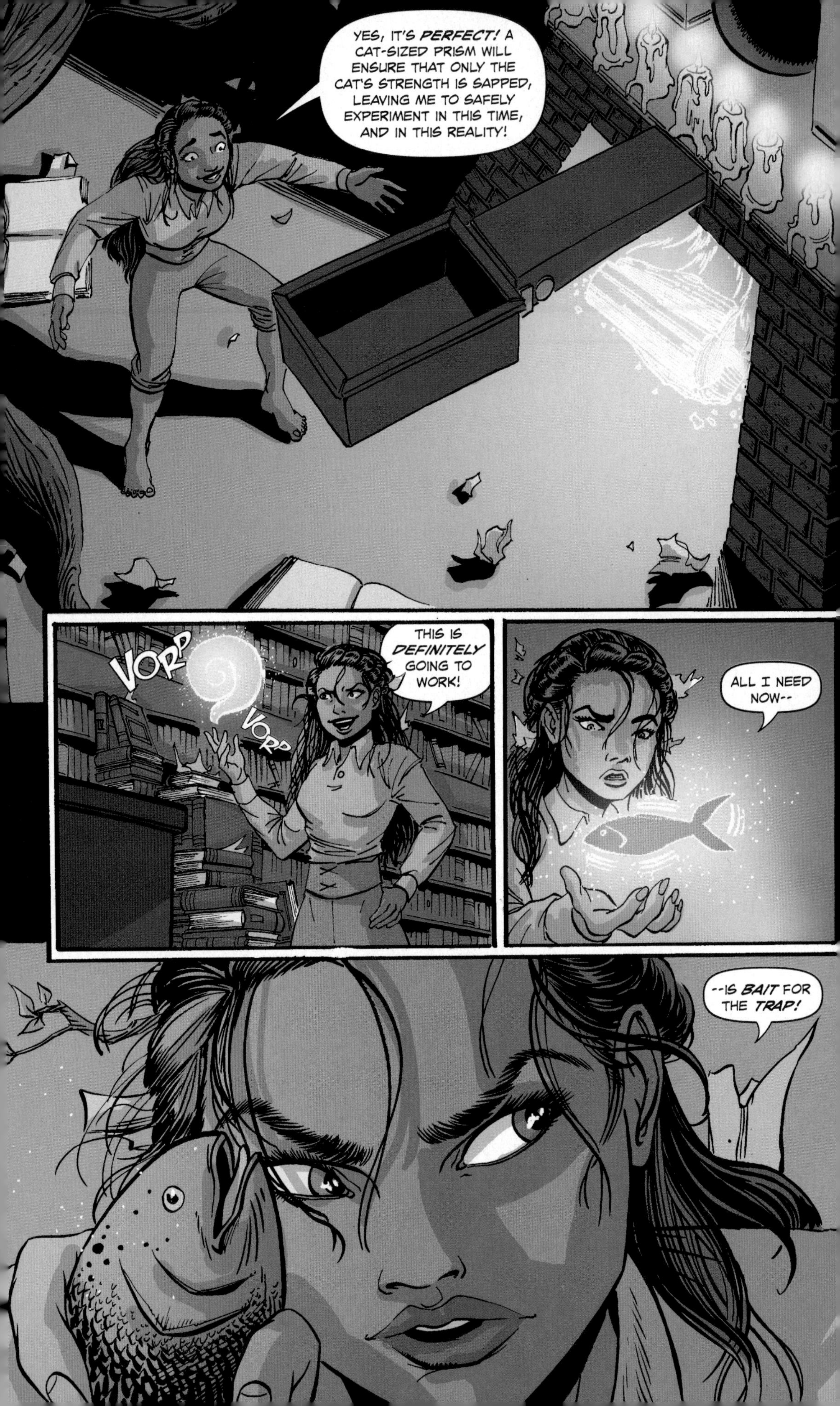
YES, IT'S *PERFECT!* A CAT-SIZED PRISM WILL ENSURE THAT ONLY THE CAT'S STRENGTH IS SAPPED, LEAVING ME TO SAFELY EXPERIMENT IN THIS TIME, AND IN THIS REALITY!
VORP
VORP
THIS IS *DEFINITELY* GOING TO WORK!
ALL I NEED NOW--
--IS *BAIT* FOR THE *TRAP!*

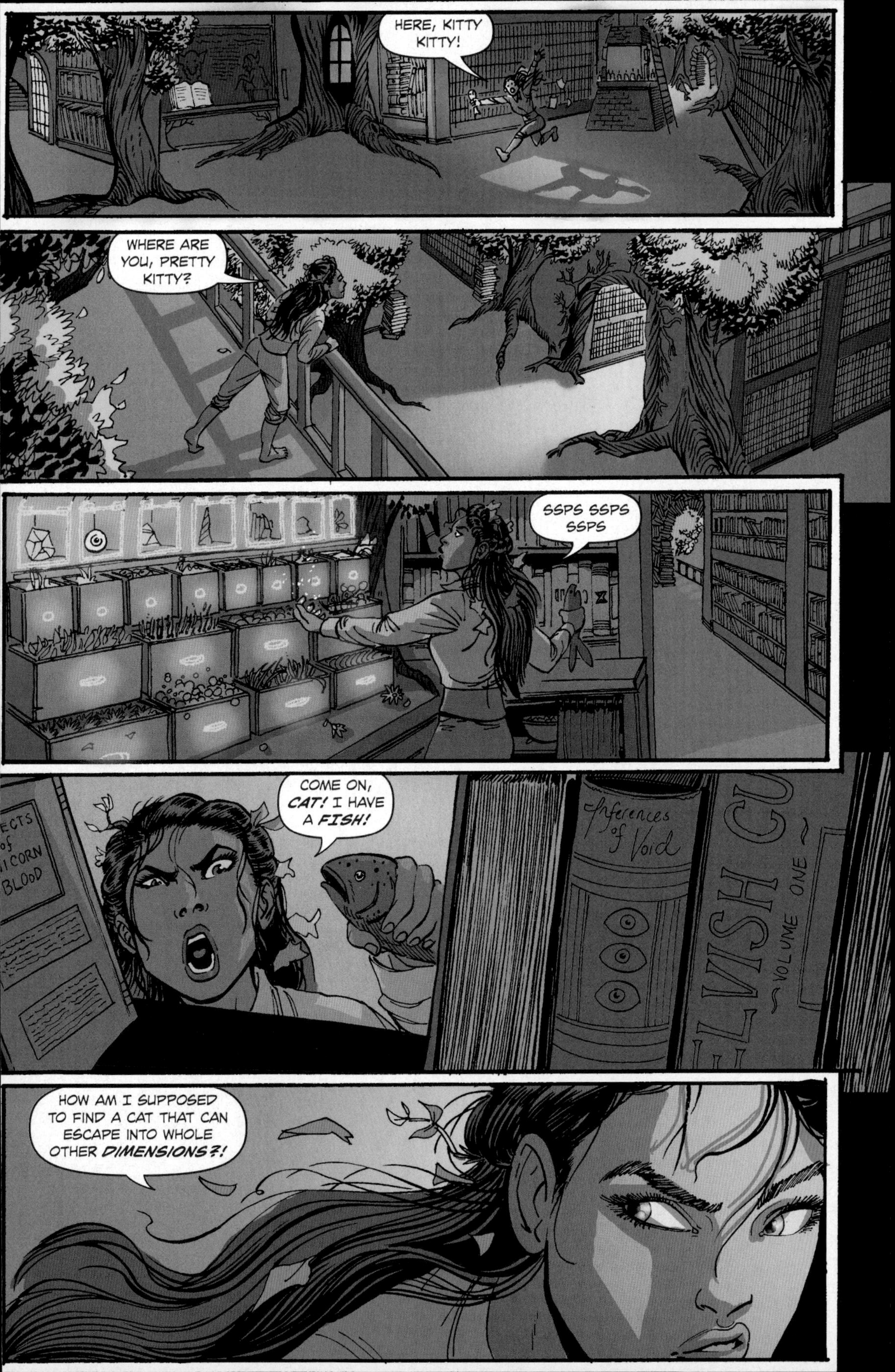
HERE, KITTY KITTY!
WHERE ARE YOU, PRETTY KITTY?
SSPS SSPS SSPS
COME ON, *CAT!* I HAVE A *FISH!*
Inferences of Void
VOLUME ONE
HOW AM I SUPPOSED TO FIND A CAT THAT CAN ESCAPE INTO WHOLE OTHER *DIMENSIONS?!*

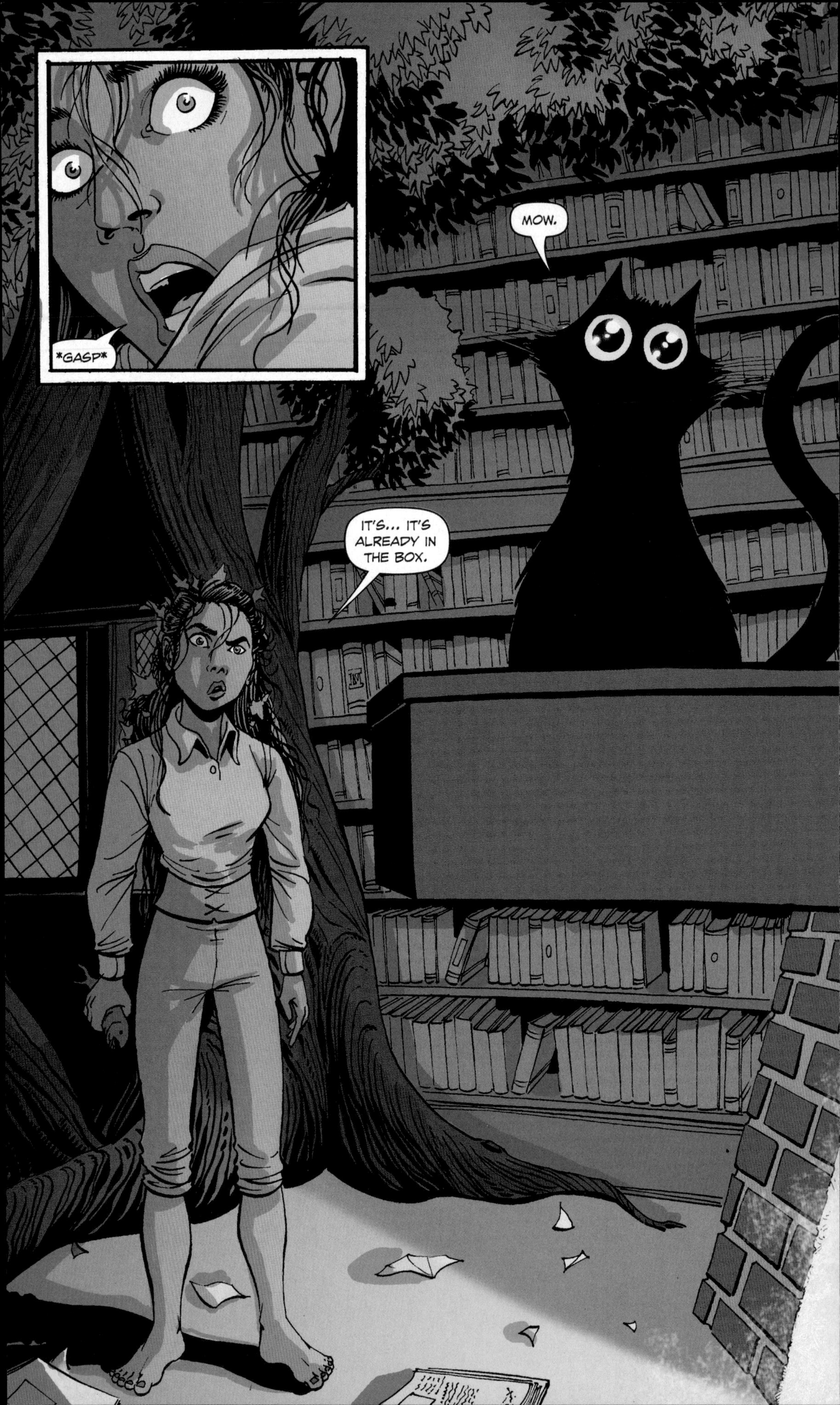
GASP
MOW.
IT'S... IT'S ALREADY IN THE BOX.

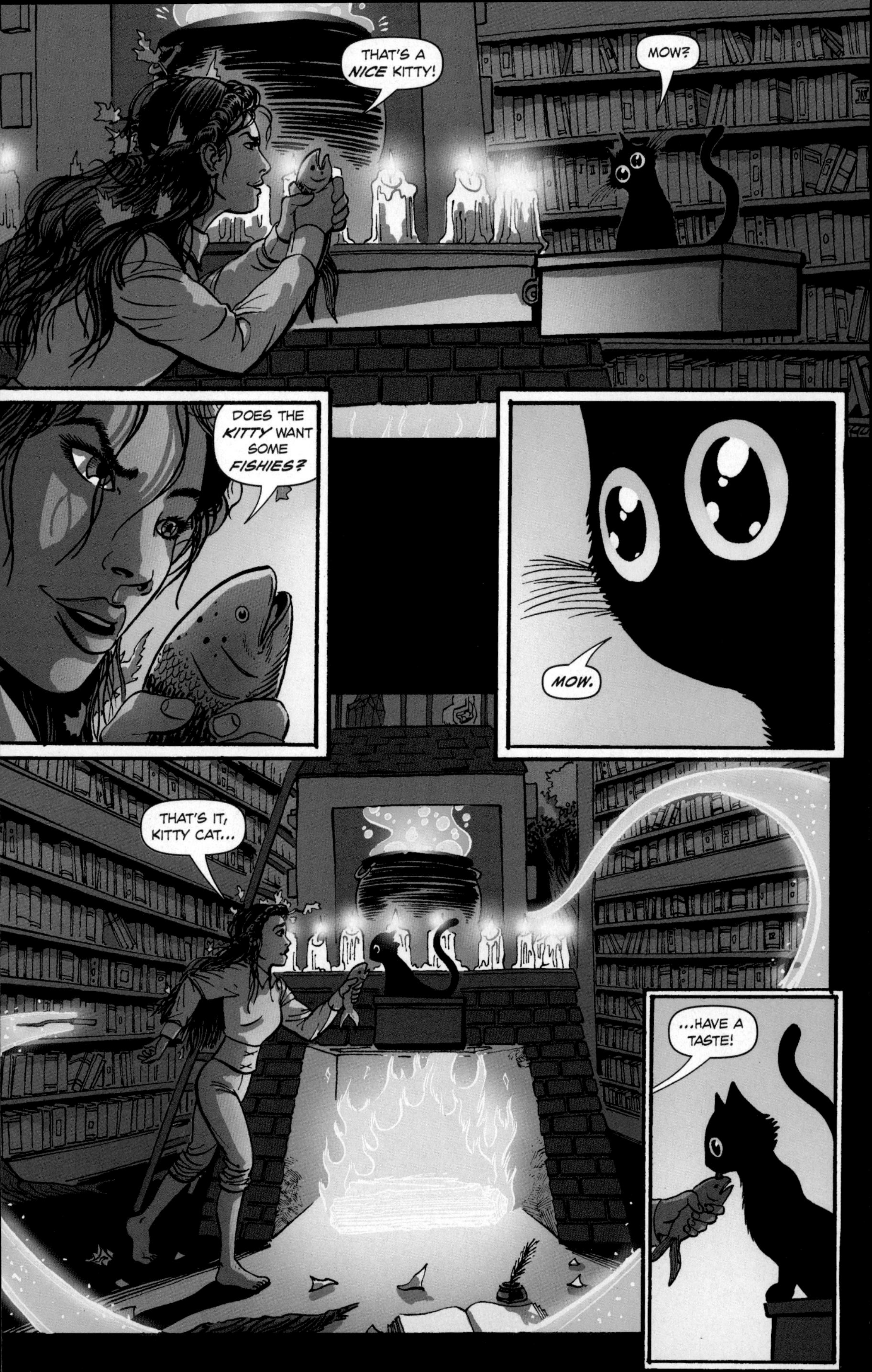
THAT'S A *NICE* KITTY!
MOW?
DOES THE *KITTY* WANT SOME *FISHIES?*
MOW.
THAT'S IT, KITTY CAT...
...HAVE A TASTE!

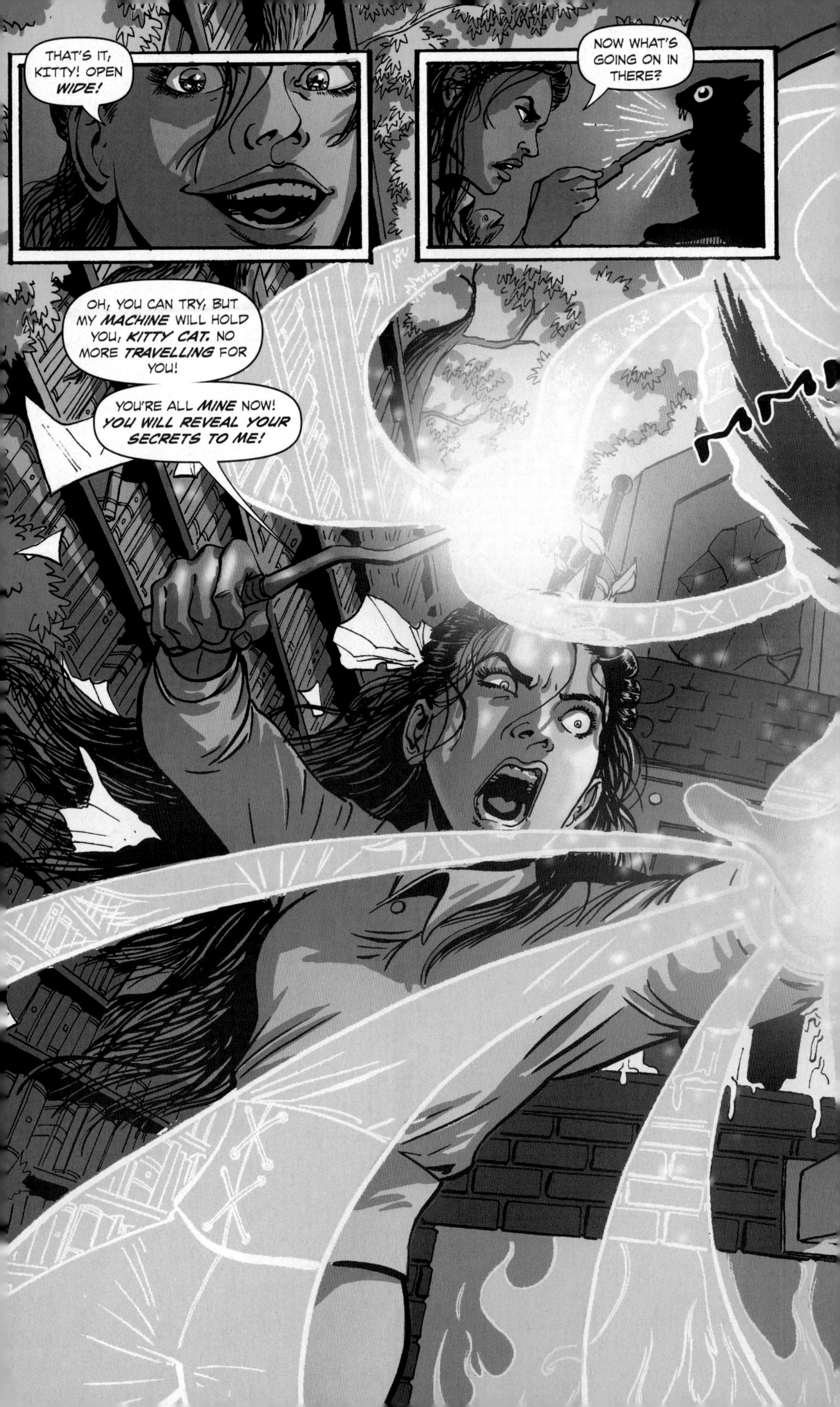

THAT'S IT, KITTY! OPEN WIDE!
NOW WHAT'S GOING ON IN THERE?
OH, YOU CAN TRY, BUT MY MACHINE WILL HOLD YOU, KITTY CAT. NO MORE TRAVELLING FOR YOU!
YOU'RE ALL MINE NOW! YOU WILL REVEAL YOUR SECRETS TO ME!

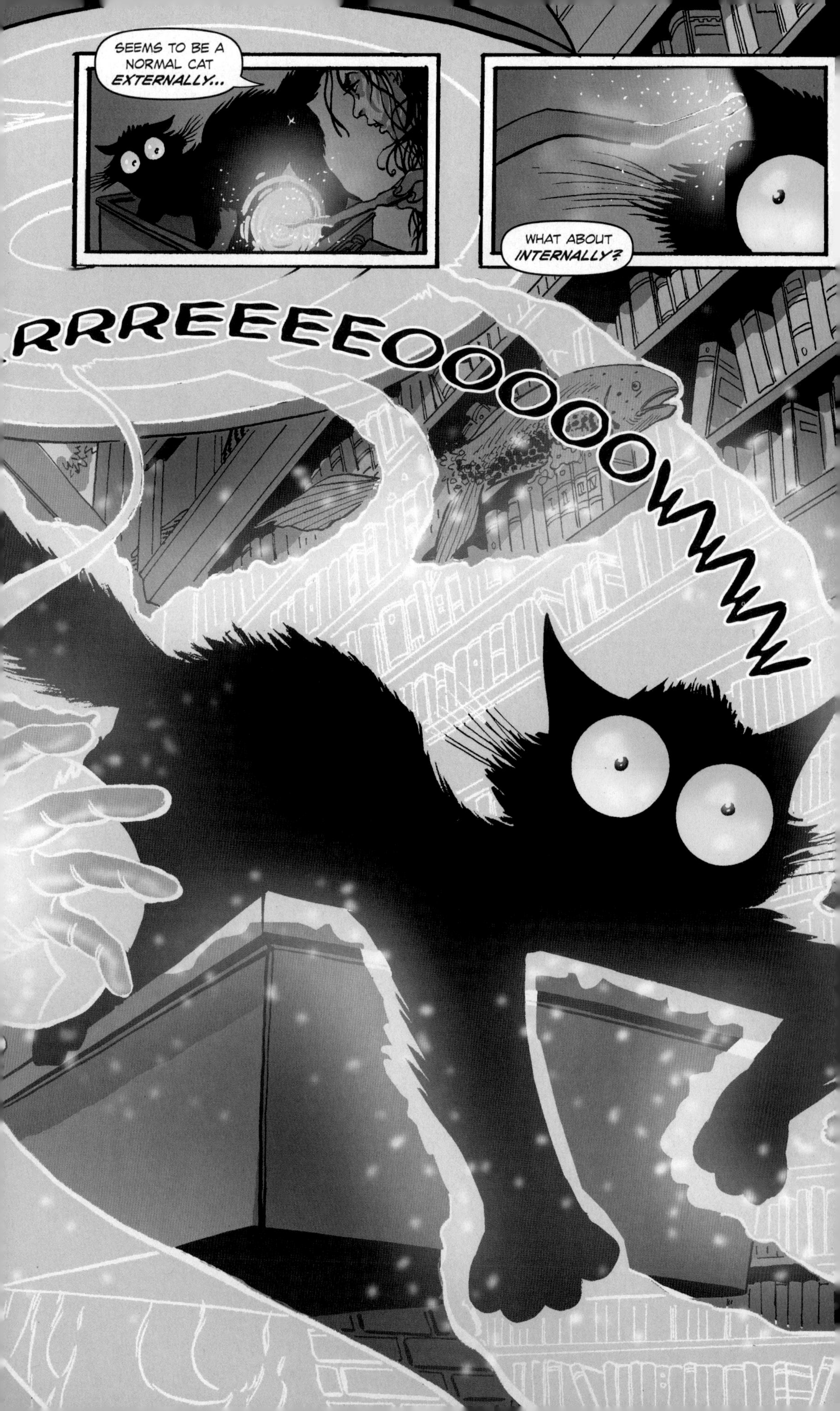
SEEMS TO BE A NORMAL CAT EXTERNALLY...
WHAT ABOUT INTERNALLY?
RRREEEEEOOOOOOWWWW

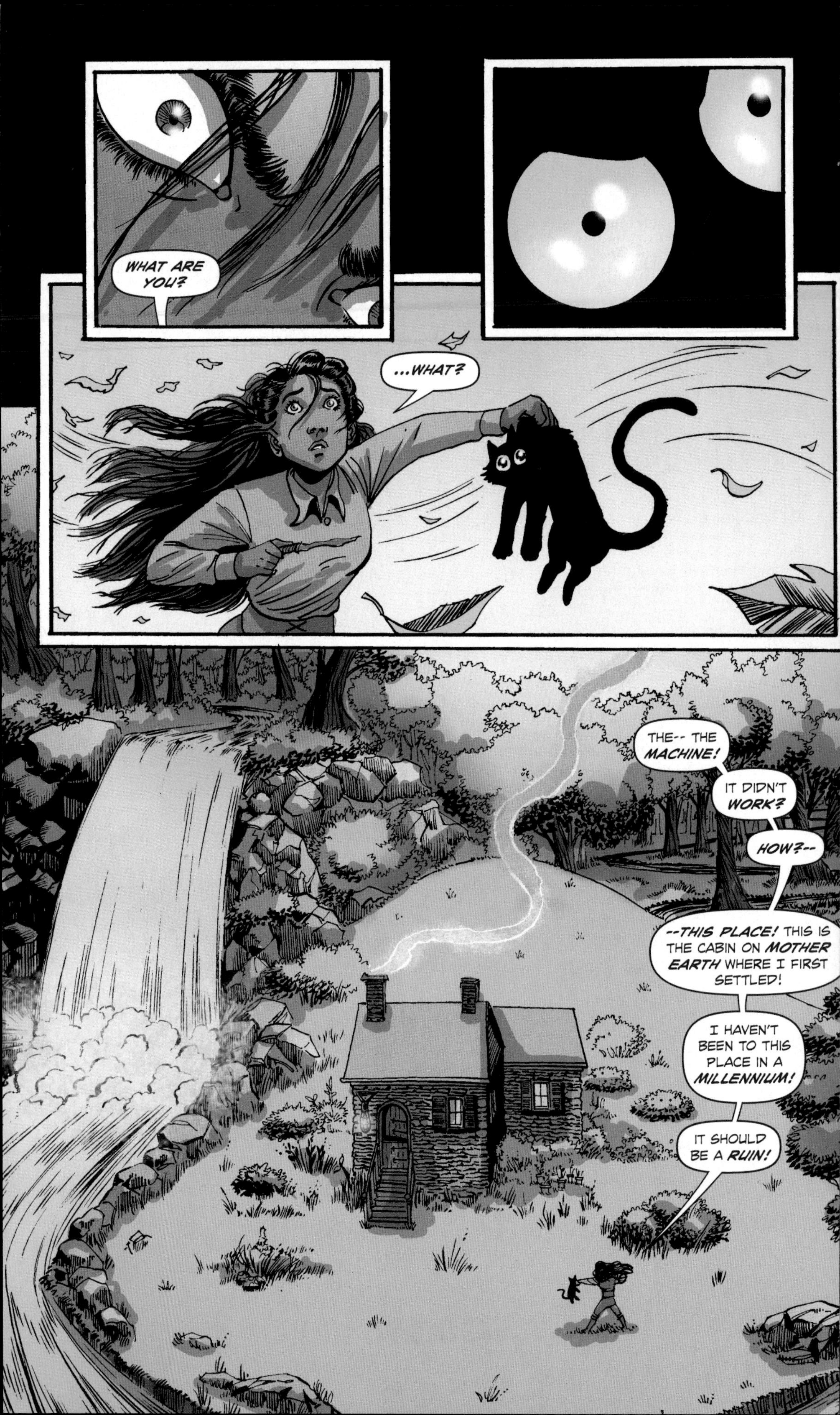
WHAT ARE YOU?
...WHAT?
THE-- THE MACHINE!
IT DIDN'T WORK?
HOW?--
--THIS PLACE! THIS IS THE CABIN ON MOTHER EARTH WHERE I FIRST SETTLED!
I HAVEN'T BEEN TO THIS PLACE IN A MILLENNIUM!
IT SHOULD BE A RUIN!

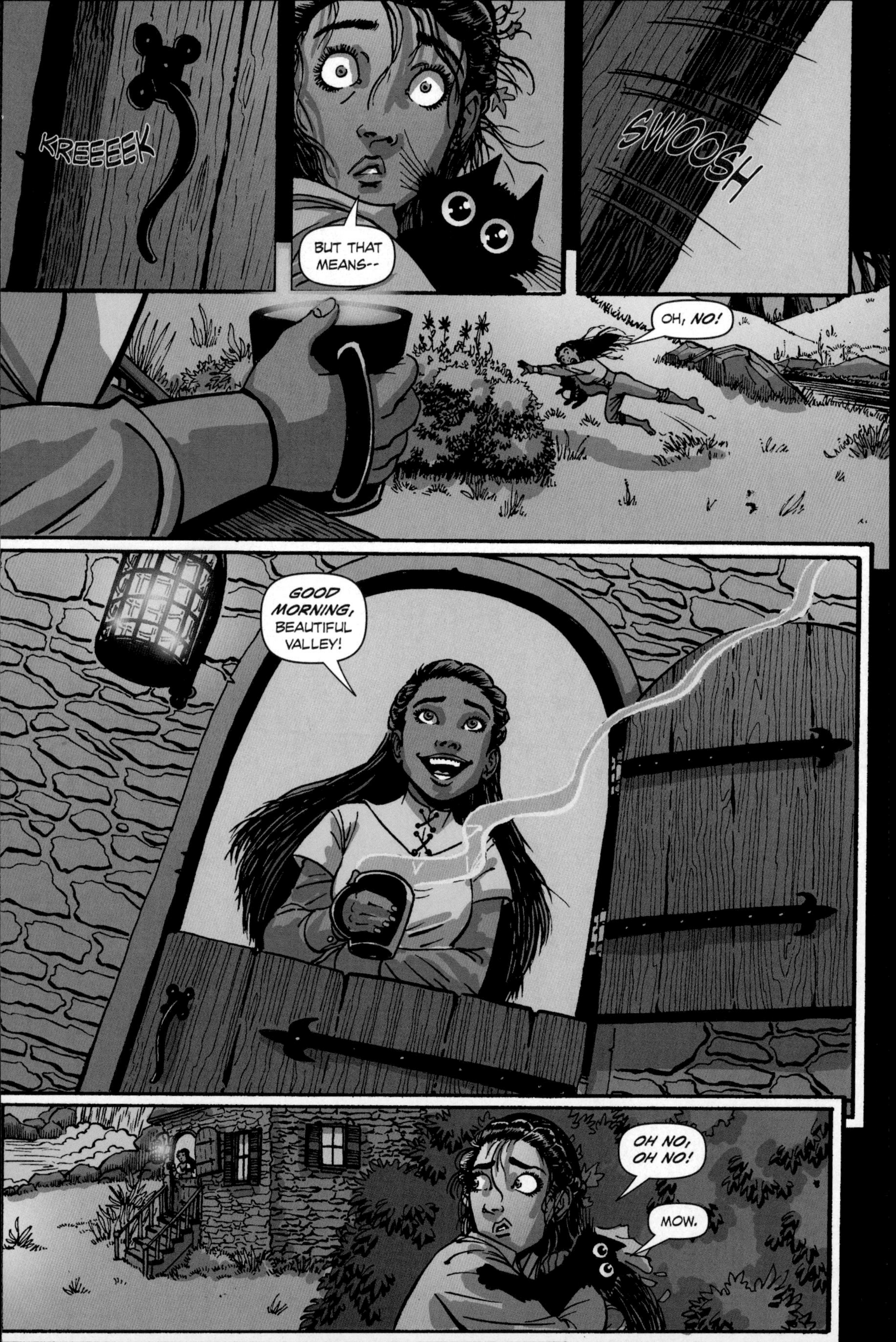
KREEEEK
BUT THAT MEANS--
SWOOSH
OH, NO!
GOOD MORNING, BEAUTIFUL VALLEY!
OH NO, OH NO!
MOW.

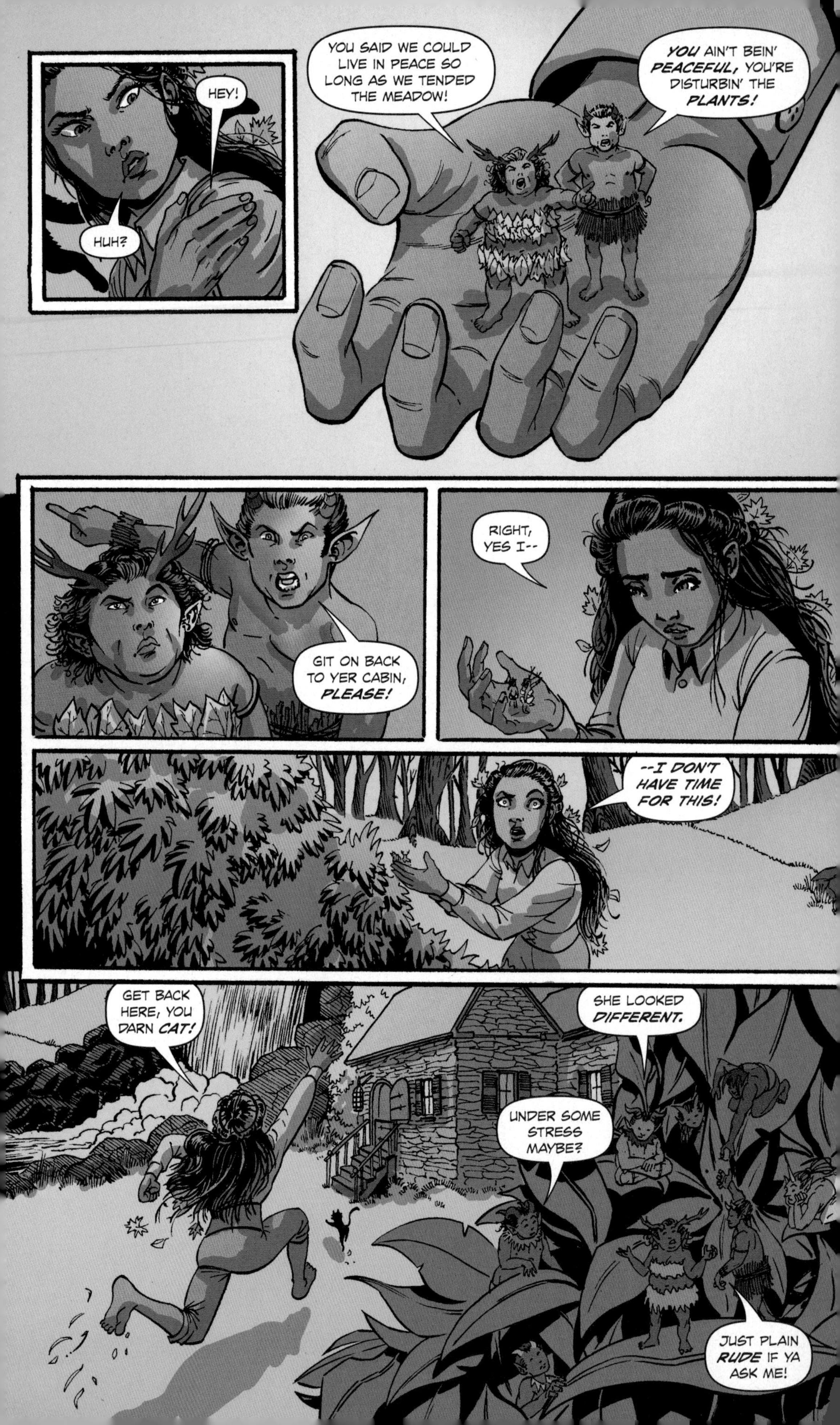
HEY!
HUH?
YOU SAID WE COULD LIVE IN PEACE SO LONG AS WE TENDED THE MEADOW!
YOU AIN'T BEIN' *PEACEFUL,* YOU'RE DISTURBIN' THE *PLANTS!*
GIT ON BACK TO YER CABIN, *PLEASE!*
RIGHT, YES I--
--I DON'T HAVE TIME FOR THIS!
GET BACK HERE, YOU DARN *CAT!*
SHE LOOKED *DIFFERENT.*
UNDER SOME STRESS MAYBE?
JUST PLAIN *RUDE* IF YA ASK ME!

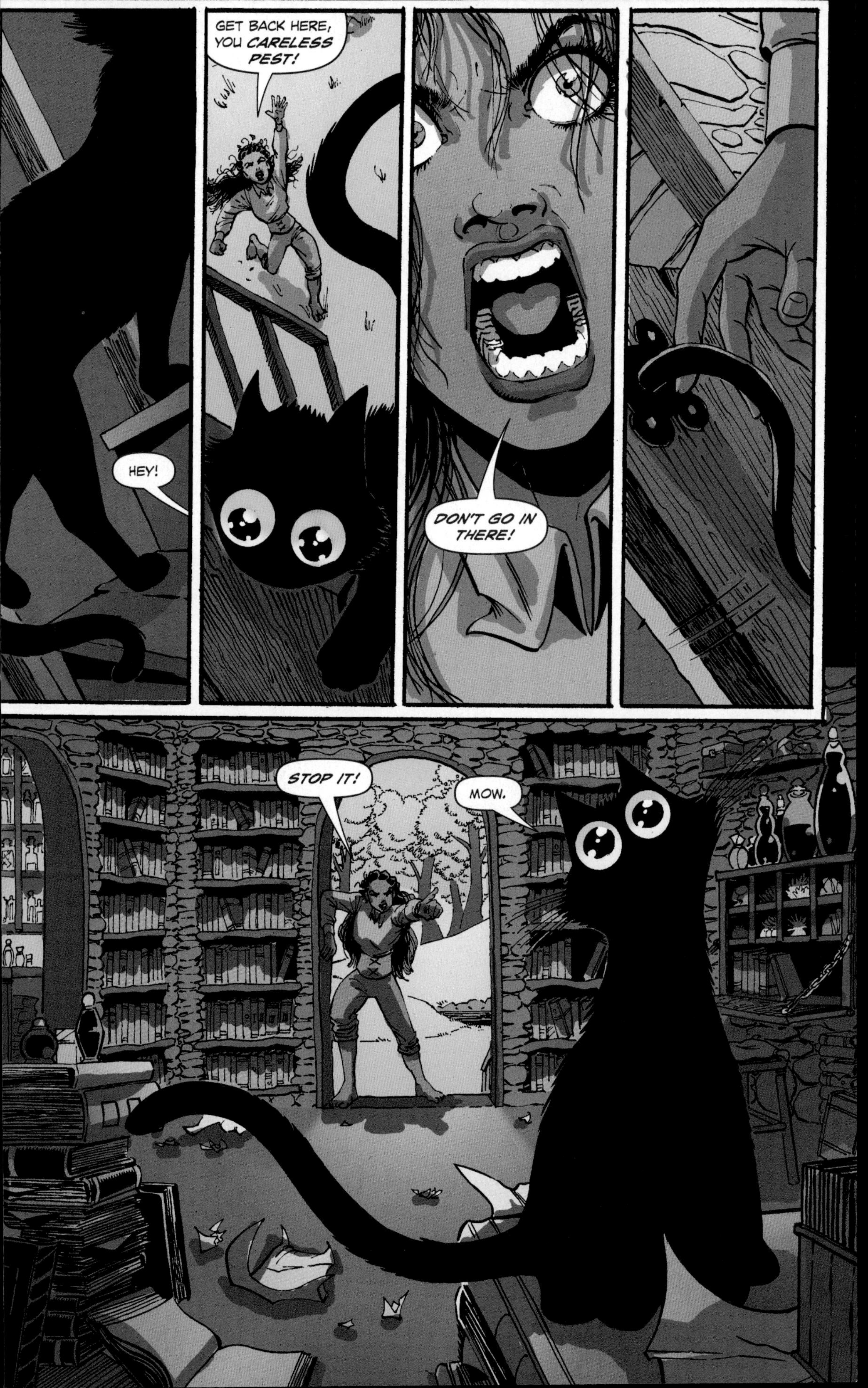
HEY!
GET BACK HERE, YOU *CARELESS PEST!*
DON'T GO IN THERE!
STOP IT!
MOW.

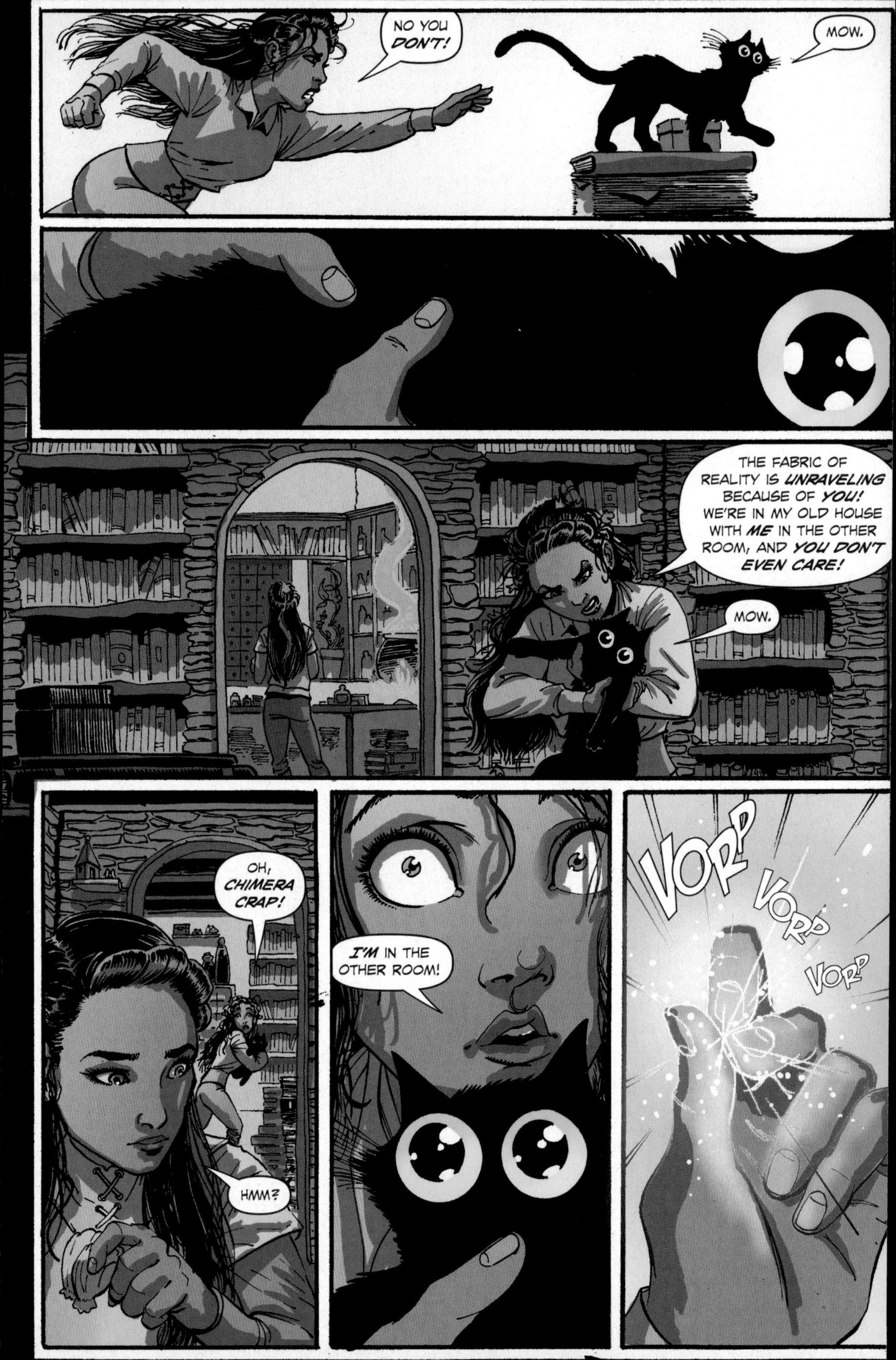
NO YOU DON'T!
MOW.
THE FABRIC OF REALITY IS UNRAVELING BECAUSE OF YOU! WE'RE IN MY OLD HOUSE WITH ME IN THE OTHER ROOM, AND YOU DON'T EVEN CARE!
MOW.
OH, CHIMERA CRAP!
HMM?
I'M IN THE OTHER ROOM!
VORP
VORP
VORP

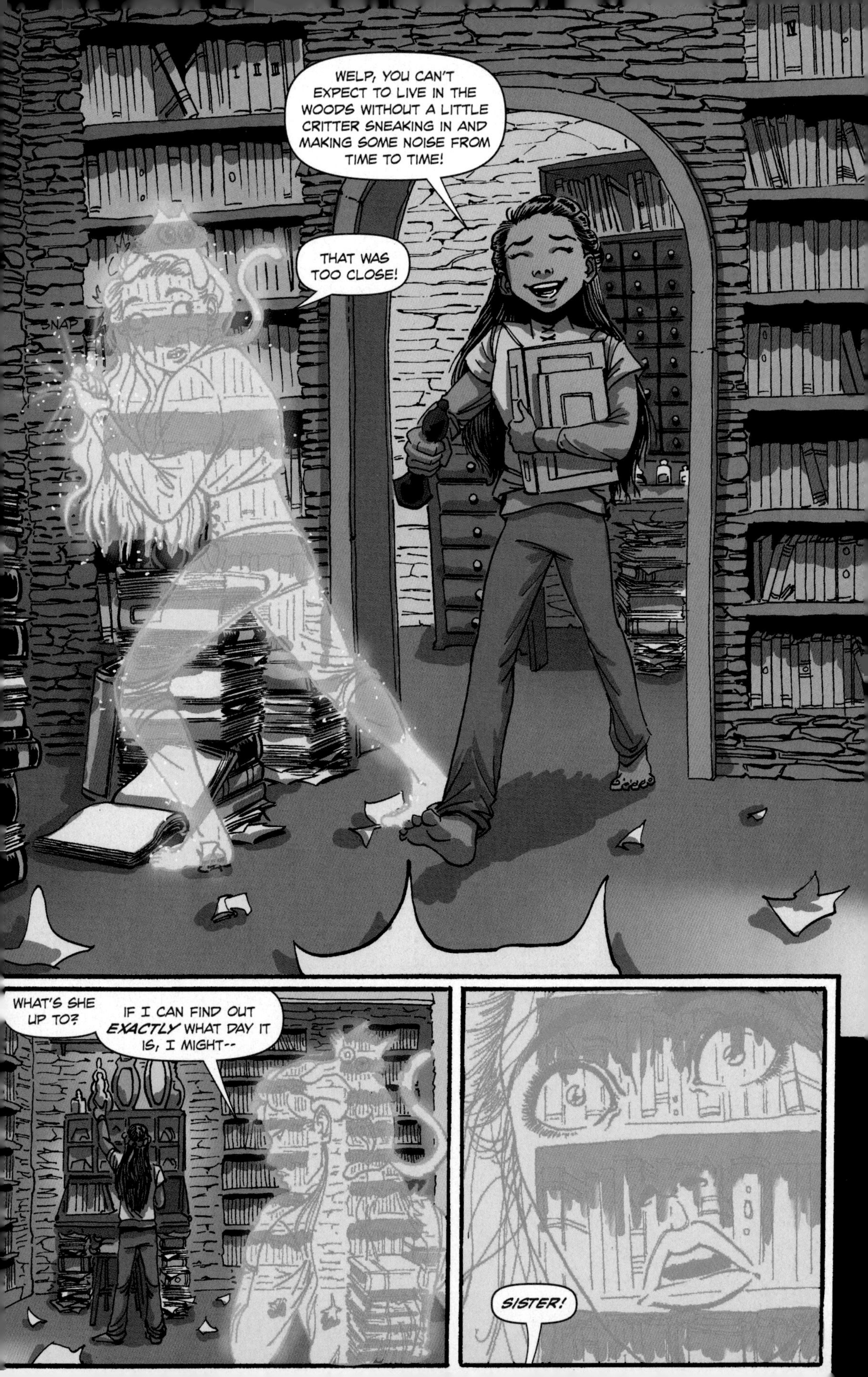
WELP, YOU CAN'T EXPECT TO LIVE IN THE WOODS WITHOUT A LITTLE CRITTER SNEAKING IN AND MAKING SOME NOISE FROM TIME TO TIME!
SNAP
THAT WAS TOO CLOSE!
WHAT'S SHE UP TO?
IF I CAN FIND OUT *EXACTLY* WHAT DAY IT IS, I MIGHT--
SISTER!

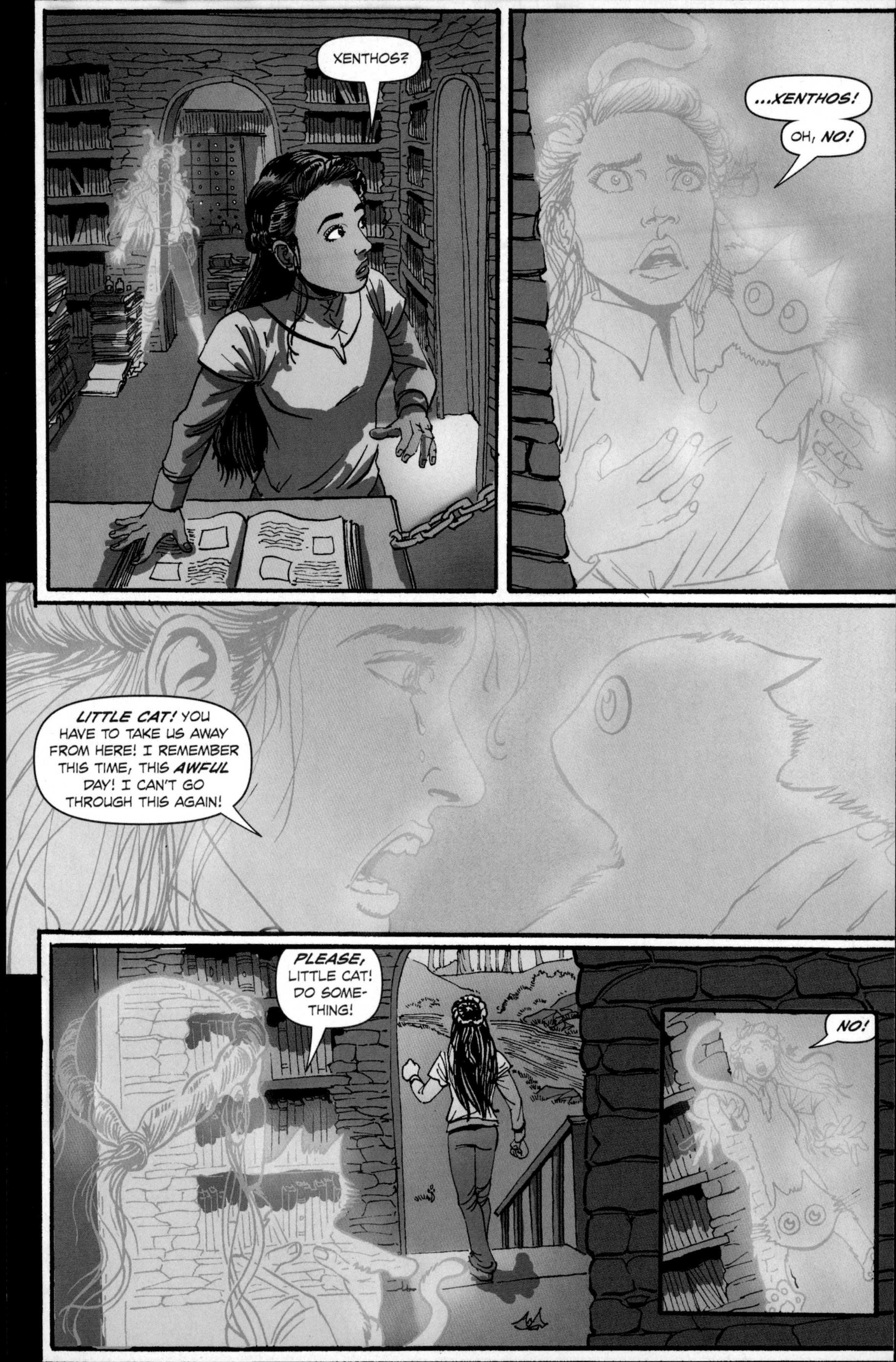
XENTHOS?
...XENTHOS!
OH, NO!
LITTLE CAT! YOU HAVE TO TAKE US AWAY FROM HERE! I REMEMBER THIS TIME, THIS AWFUL DAY! I CAN'T GO THROUGH THIS AGAIN!
PLEASE, LITTLE CAT! DO SOME-THING!
NO!

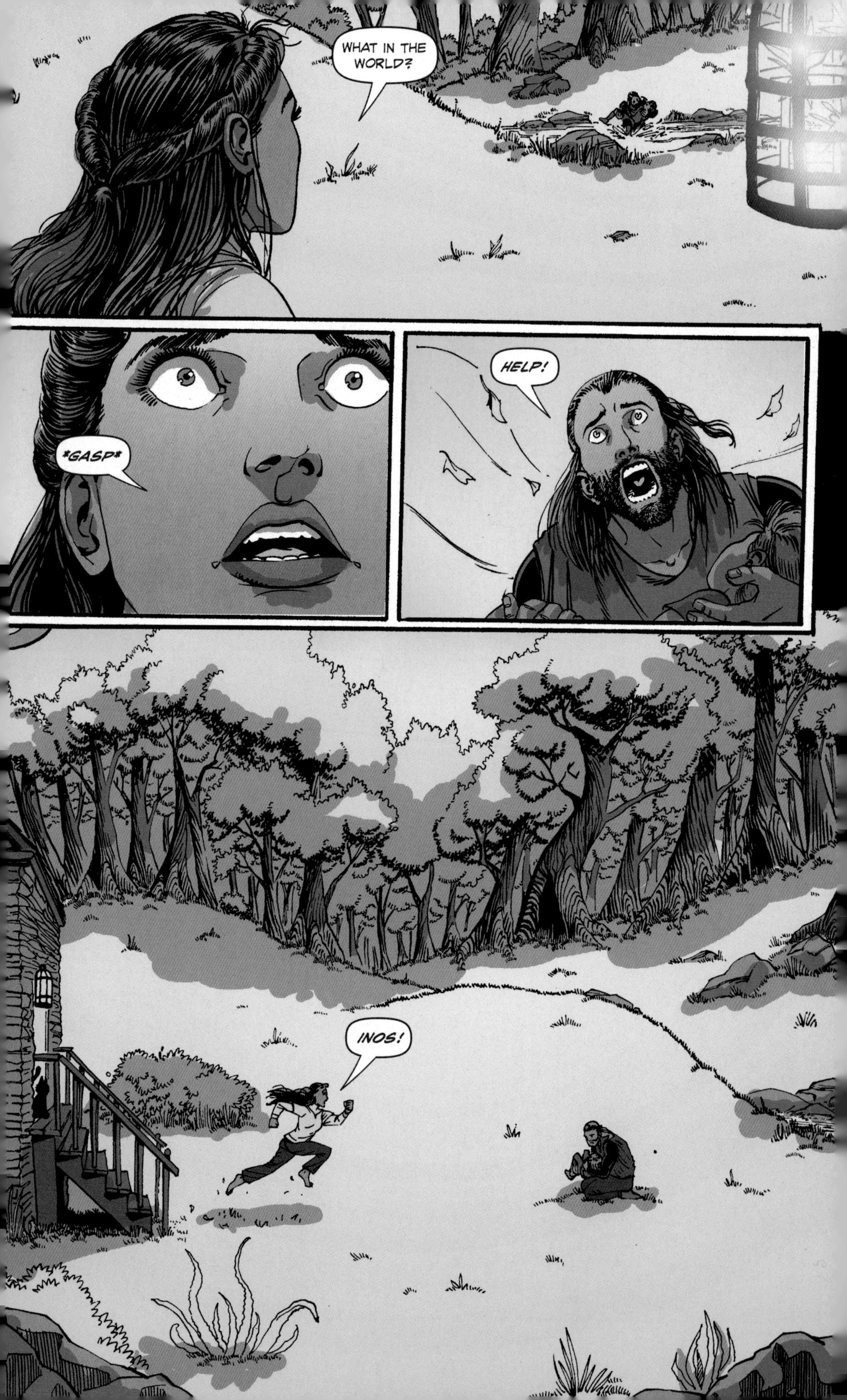
WHAT IN THE WORLD?
GASP
HELP!
INOS!

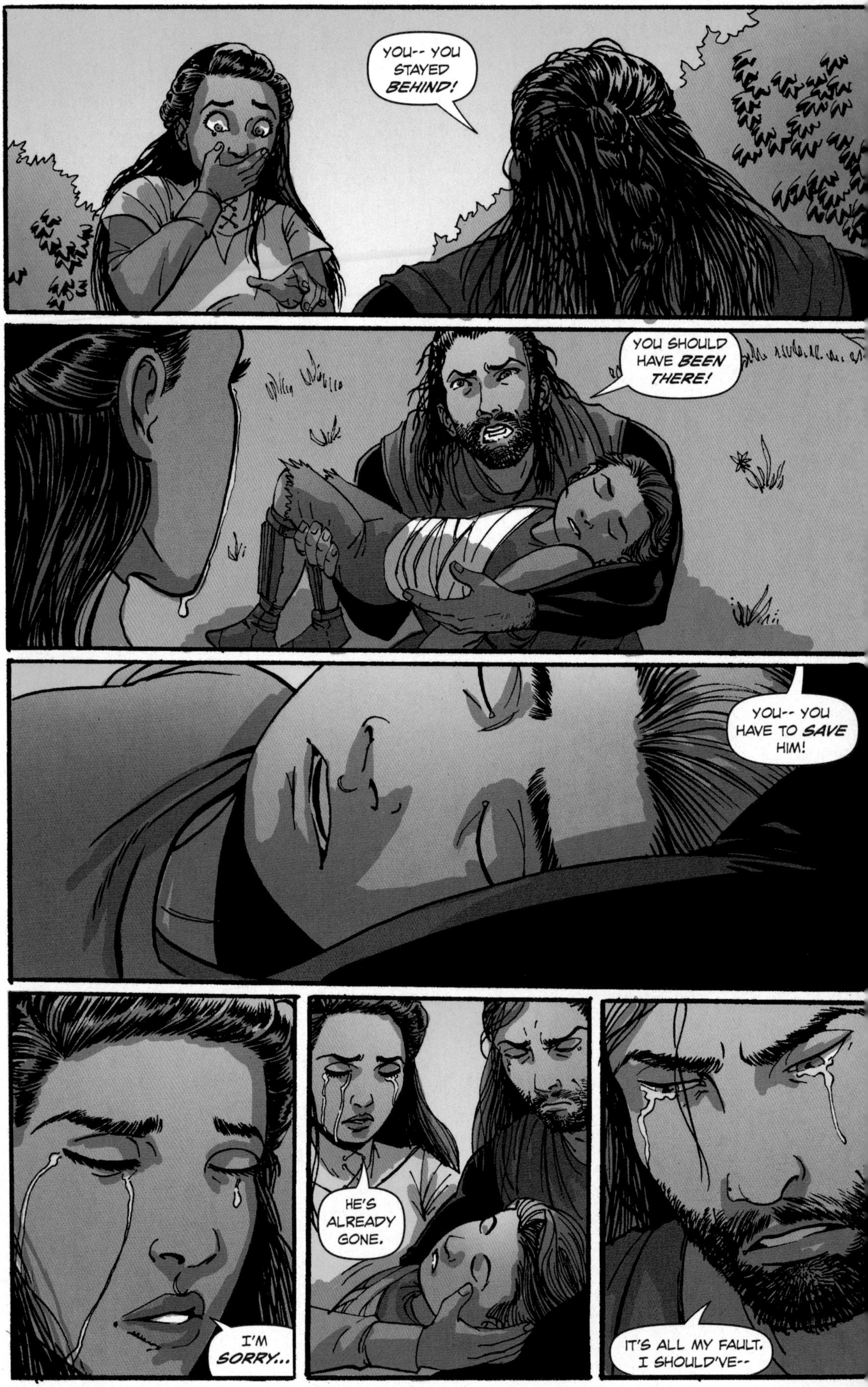
YOU-- YOU STAYED BEHIND!
YOU SHOULD HAVE BEEN THERE!
YOU-- YOU HAVE TO SAVE HIM!
I'M SORRY...
HE'S ALREADY GONE.
IT'S ALL MY FAULT. I SHOULD'VE--

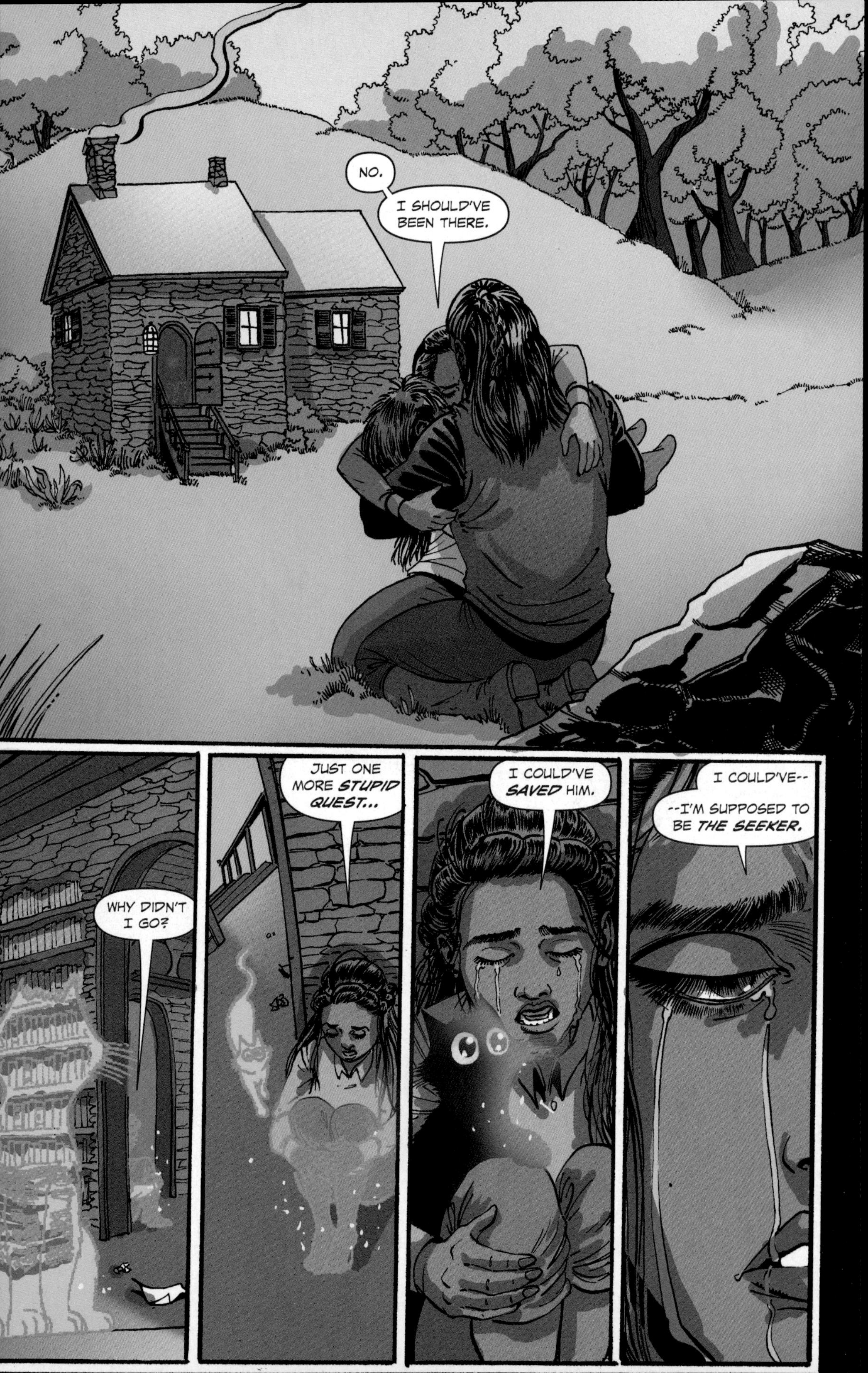
NO.
I SHOULD'VE BEEN THERE.
WHY DIDN'T I GO?
JUST ONE MORE STUPID QUEST...
I COULD'VE SAVED HIM.
I COULD'VE--
--I'M SUPPOSED TO BE THE SEEKER.

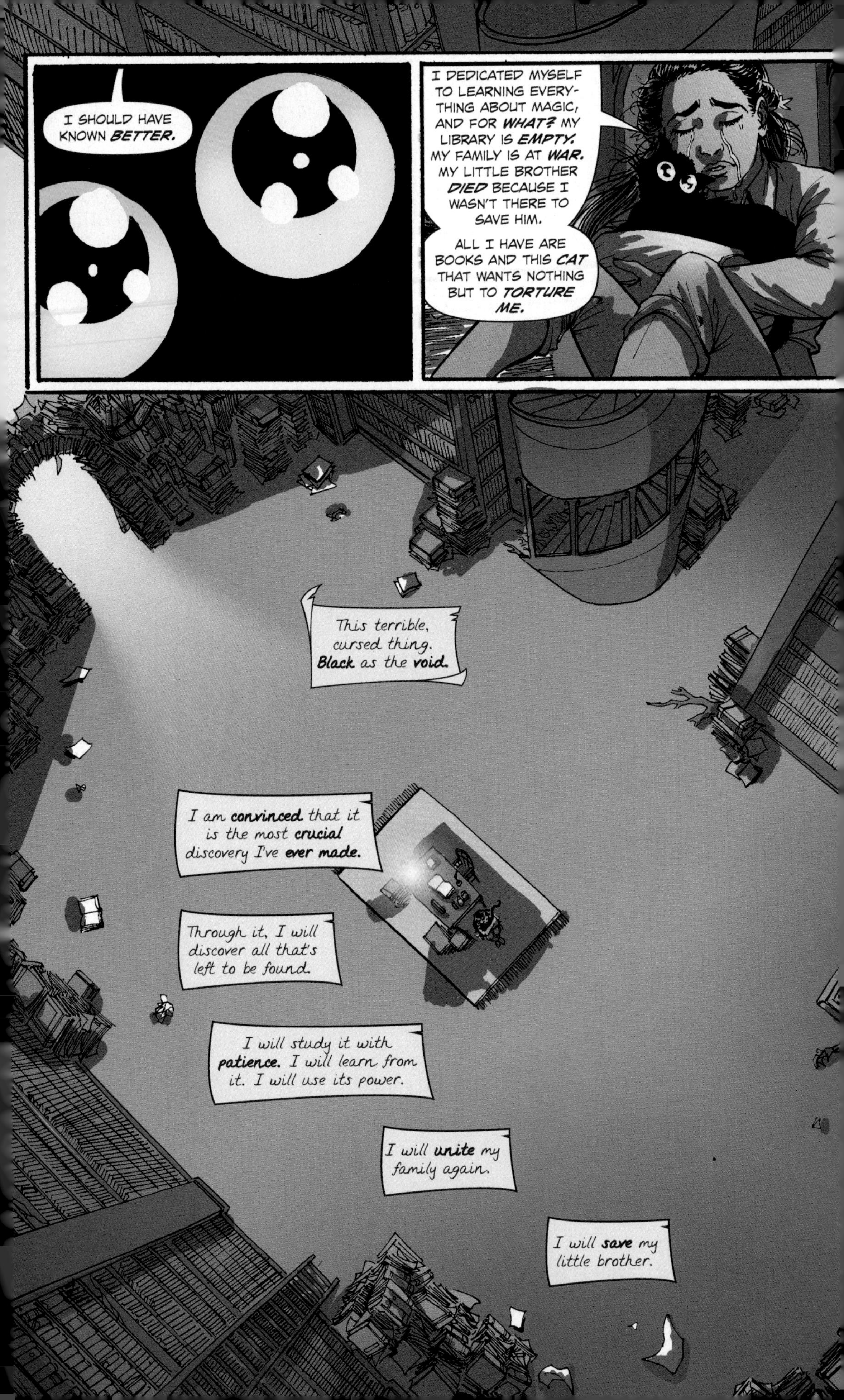
I SHOULD HAVE KNOWN BETTER.
I DEDICATED MYSELF TO LEARNING EVERYTHING ABOUT MAGIC, AND FOR WHAT? MY LIBRARY IS EMPTY. MY FAMILY IS AT WAR. MY LITTLE BROTHER DIED BECAUSE I WASN'T THERE TO SAVE HIM.
ALL I HAVE ARE BOOKS AND THIS CAT THAT WANTS NOTHING BUT TO TORTURE ME.
This terrible, cursed thing. Black as the void.
I am convinced that it is the most crucial discovery I've ever made.
Through it, I will discover all that's left to be found.
I will study it with patience. I will learn from it. I will use its power.
I will unite my family again.
I will save my little brother.

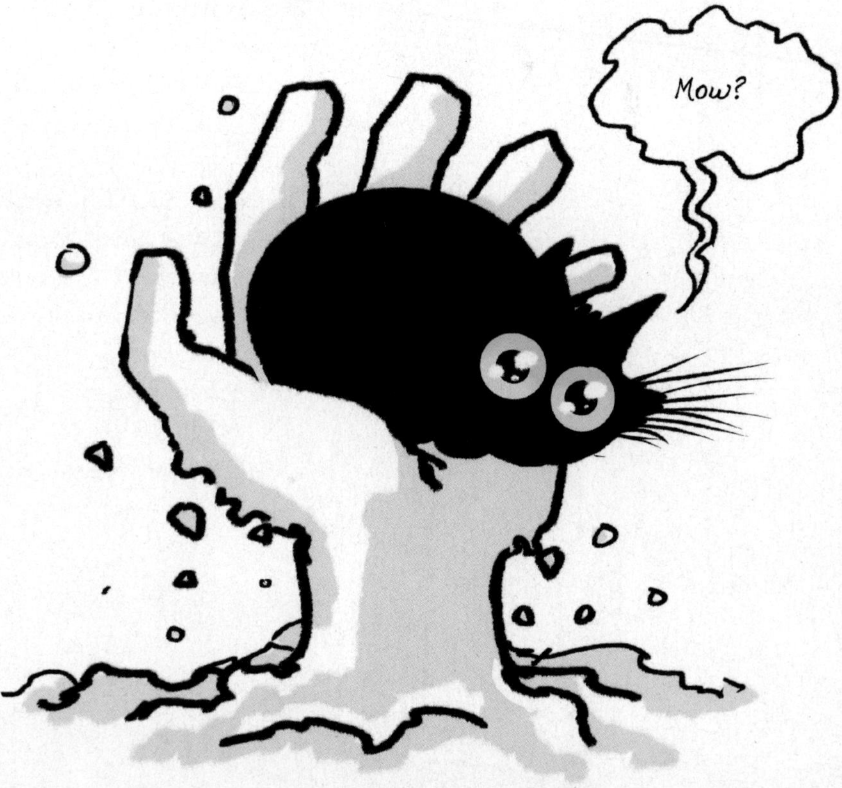
Mow?

ABOUT THE ARTISTS...

Emma Kubert is a third-generation comic book artist, and is every bit the adorable freckled dumpling that you see before you. Her dad Andy taught her narrative art, as his fathe Joe did before him. Emma's from a comic book family, and she has in her a spark of creativity that's enough to burn, blind, or utterly bewilder anyone who draws close. In short, she's special.

Emma sees stories everywhere she looks, and erupts in frantic noises of glee whenever a cat is near. It was only natural that her very being would compound with her belief in magic and love of cats to create Inkblot, a magical cat created from a spilled ink bottle. The genesis of Inkblot dates all the way back to her childhood, where a bespeckled little Emma found a partner in a friendly black cat named Busch (Boosh). It is Emma who contributes the feline whimsy, joy, and mischief to Inkblot.

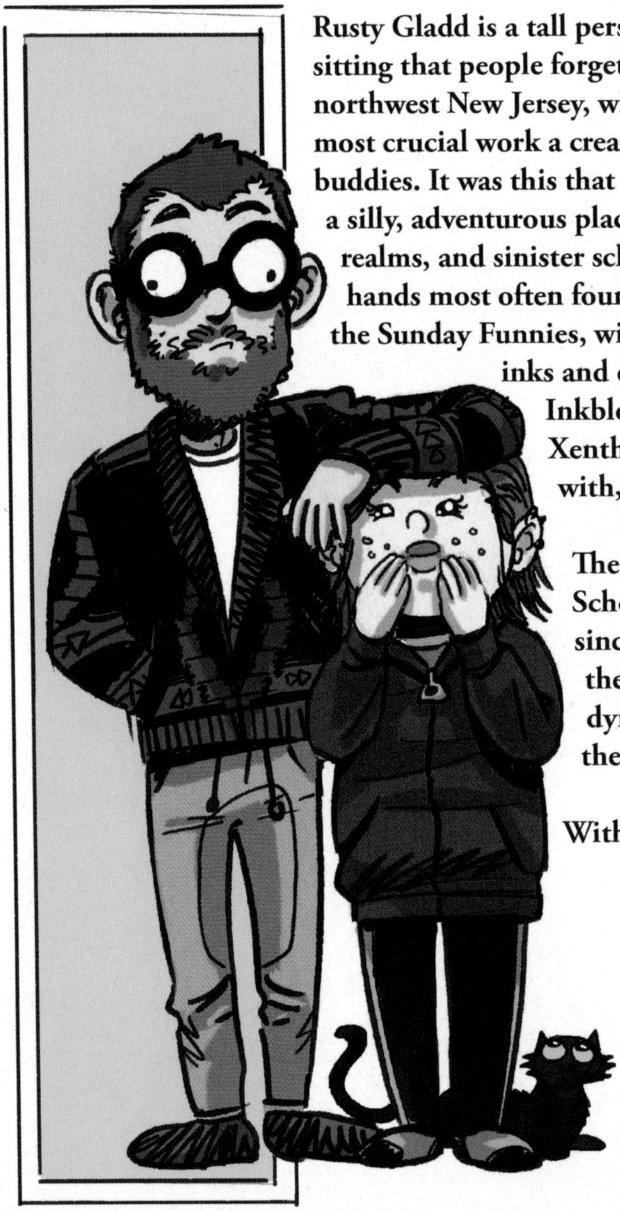

Rusty Gladd is a tall person who spends so much of his time sitting that people forget he's tall. He's from a small town in northwest New Jersey, where he gained experience doing the most crucial work a creative person can do: goofing off with his buddies. It was this that flexed the muscle of his imagination in a silly, adventurous place, full of characters, lore, fantastic realms, and sinister schemes. Growing up, Rusty's grubby hands most often found themselves handling fantasy novels o the Sunday Funnies, with not so much in between. It is he who inks and contributes the words to the story of Inkblot, from the narration to the dialogue. Xenthos Voidbreaker is a name he came up with, which is just too cool, right?

The two met while attending the Kubert School and haven't left each other alone since. It's this close partnership that presen the possibility of creating Inkblot in such dynamic way, which is described further in the coming pages.

Without further ado, Rut & Mem present…

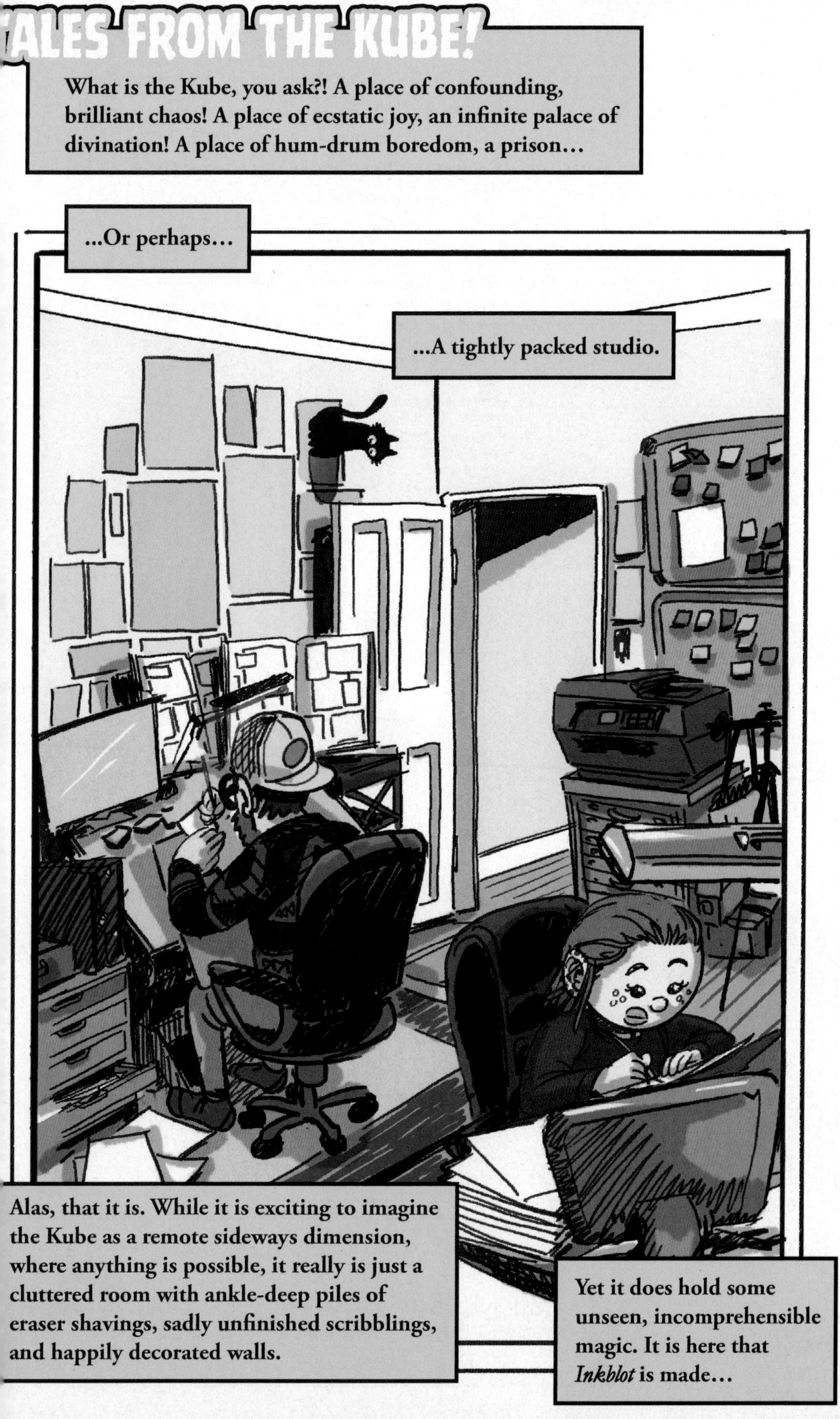
ALES FROM THE KUBE!
What is the Kube, you ask?! A place of confounding, brilliant chaos! A place of ecstatic joy, an infinite palace of divination! A place of hum-drum boredom, a prison…
…Or perhaps…
…A tightly packed studio.
Alas, that it is. While it is exciting to imagine the Kube as a remote sideways dimension, where anything is possible, it really is just a cluttered room with ankle-deep piles of eraser shavings, sadly unfinished scribblings, and happily decorated walls.
Yet it does hold some unseen, incomprehensible magic. It is here that *Inkblot* is made…

"WRITING"

The origin of any story starts with an idea. Or better, ideas. The first step of the *Inkblot* process is excessive, albeit necessary, discussion. Rut & Mem create characters and plot simultaneously. They allow characters freedom to grow in whatever direction feels natural, with an end goal forever in sight. Every character met by the cat has a story. Every story intersects with another. The timeline is a ruin, as it would be if handled by the elastic moods of a cat.

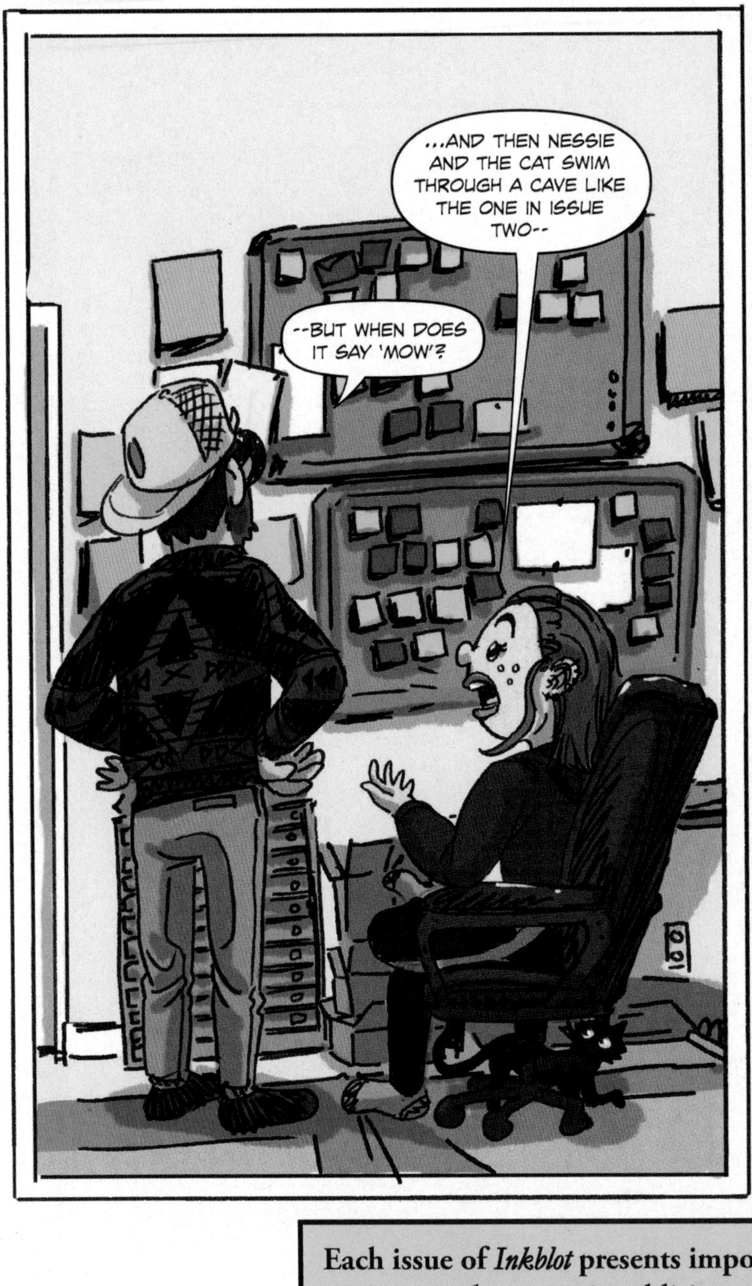

...AND THEN NESSIE AND THE CAT SWIM THROUGH A CAVE LIKE THE ONE IN ISSUE TWO--
--BUT WHEN DOES IT SAY 'MOW'?

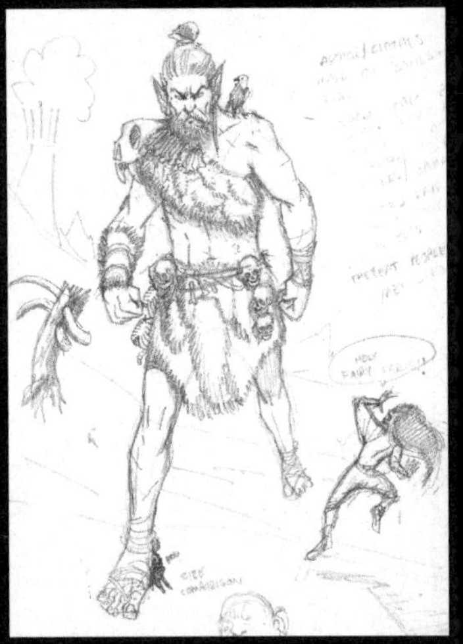

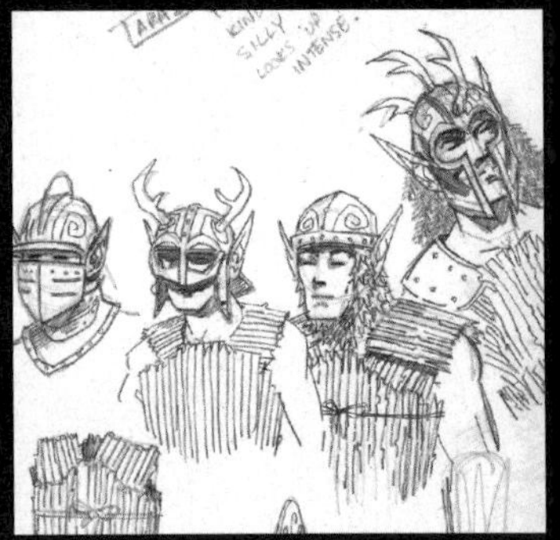

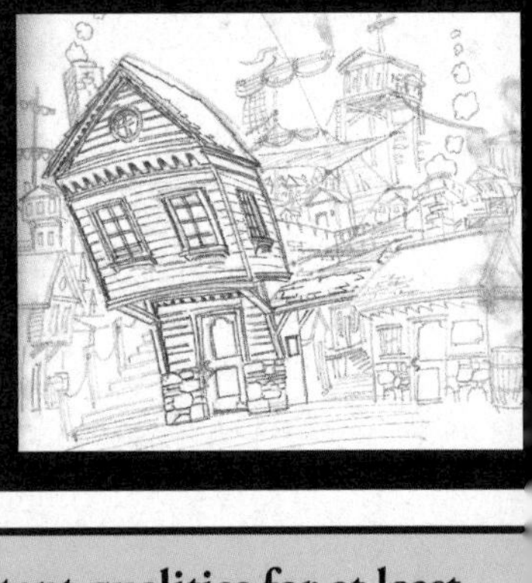

Each issue of *Inkblot* presents important qualities for at least one major character, in addition to a world-breaking event. We knew going in that our concept was ambitious, and we really wanted things to happen issue by issue, which is what led to the decision to allow the art to set the pace of the story.

PENCILS

The second step is all Emma. Once we work out the content of a chapter in our wild cat-driven fantasy, Emma gets to work. 20 thumbnails quickly become 20 layouts and 20 pencilled pages. As stated previously, the art comes first. The craft of a cartoonist is usually to decipher a script, and manifest from words images to set a pace. A beat. Many panels in sequence create the impression of things happening fast, and conversely, a big moment needs plenty of room for itself on a page. It's in the pencils that the feeling of a story is told, and we think it's best to let that come across as naturally as possible.

WORK, WORK...
Look at her go!

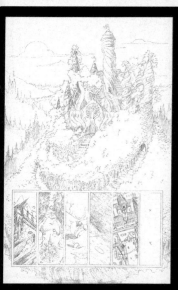

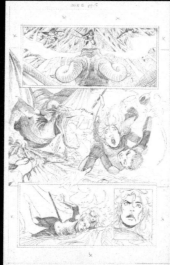

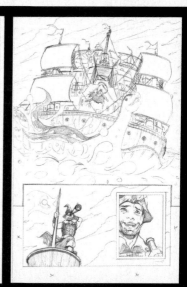

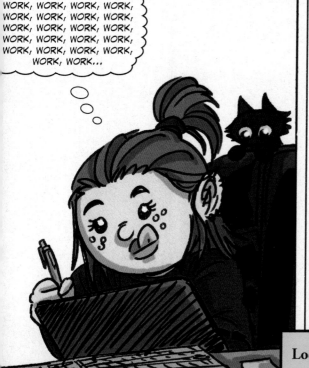

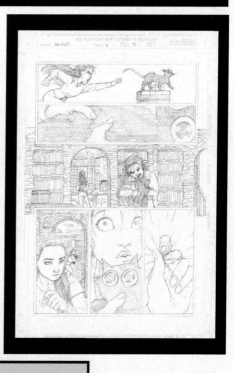

INKS

Next comes Rusty, the *Inkblot* inker. Inking can be a very fussy thing, and sometimes the comic simply refuses to be rendered with a pen or a brush without dropping messy blobs across the page. Nonetheless, the book has to get made. Both proximity and familiarity with his penciller allow Rusty to make some bold inking decisions. Adding two lines as opposed to one. Adding chunky blacks. Creating textures. He gets carried away once in a while, but that's what white-out is for.

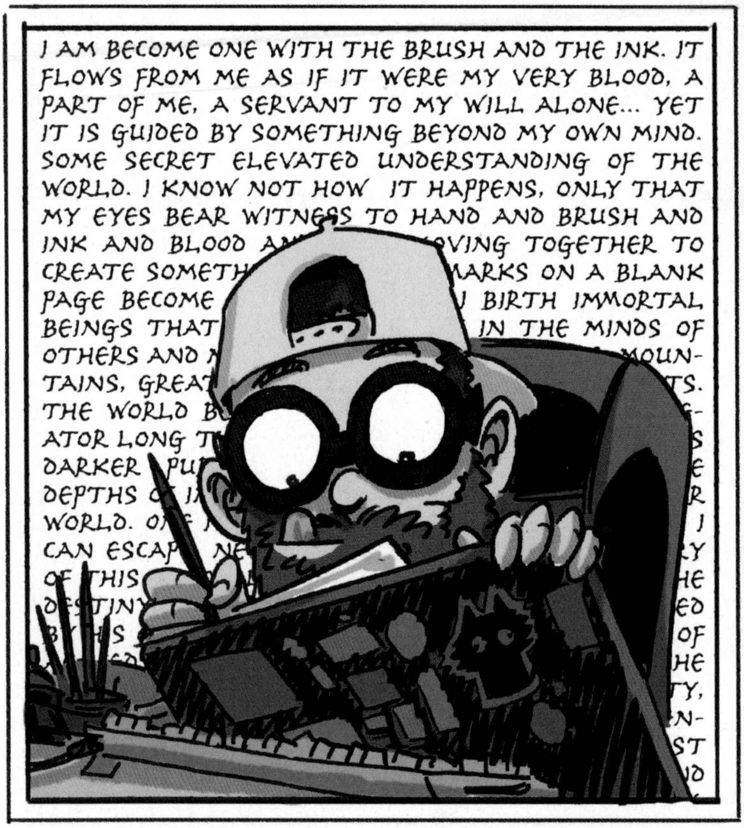
I AM BECOME ONE WITH THE BRUSH AND THE INK. IT
FLOWS FROM ME AS IF IT WERE MY VERY BLOOD, A
PART OF ME, A SERVANT TO MY WILL ALONE... YET
IT IS GUIDED BY SOMETHING BEYOND MY OWN MIND.
SOME SECRET ELEVATED UNDERSTANDING OF THE
WORLD. I KNOW NOT HOW IT HAPPENS, ONLY THAT
MY EYES BEAR WITNESS TO HAND AND BRUSH AND
INK AND BLOOD
OVING TOGETHER TO
CREATE SOMETH
ARKS ON A BLANK
PAGE BECOME
BIRTH IMMORTAL
BEINGS THAT
IN THE MINDS OF
OTHERS AND
TAINS, GREA
THE WORLD
ATOR LONG
DARKER
DEPTHS
WORLD.
CAN ESCAP

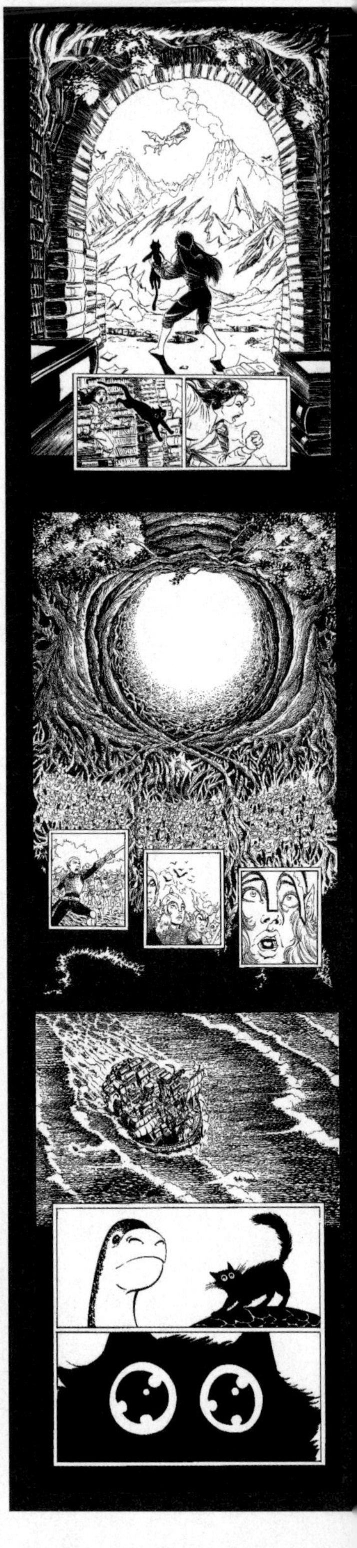

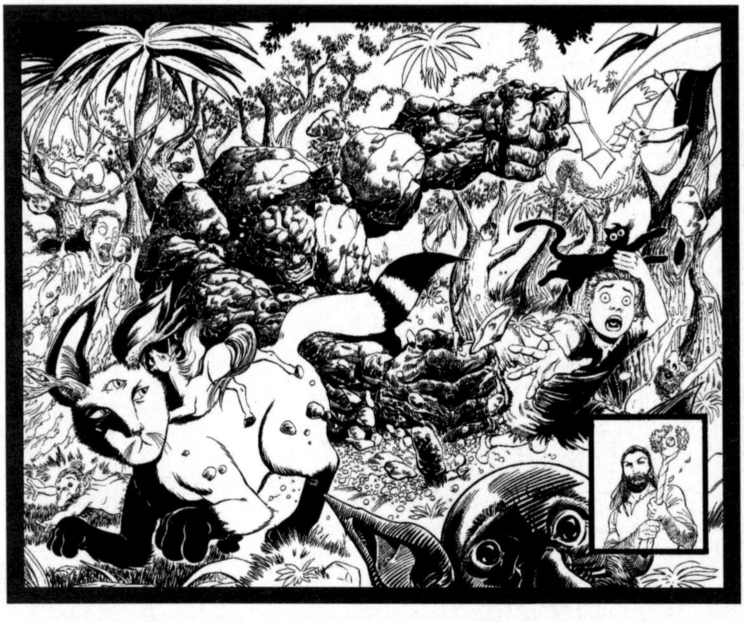

DIALOGUE/LETTERING

Once everything is defined in black and white, Rusty refers to the finished pages as he creates the dialogue. The pace of the story is already decided for him, as is the emotional context of the characters. It's his job to create voices for the characters. Each of them speaks in their own way, whether they're determined, frightened, vengeful, joyous or upset. One of them talks like a pirate. One of them has a very limited vocabulary. Once everything is written and lettered, it's reviewed by Emma and tweaked to ensure the right ideas are coming across to the reader.

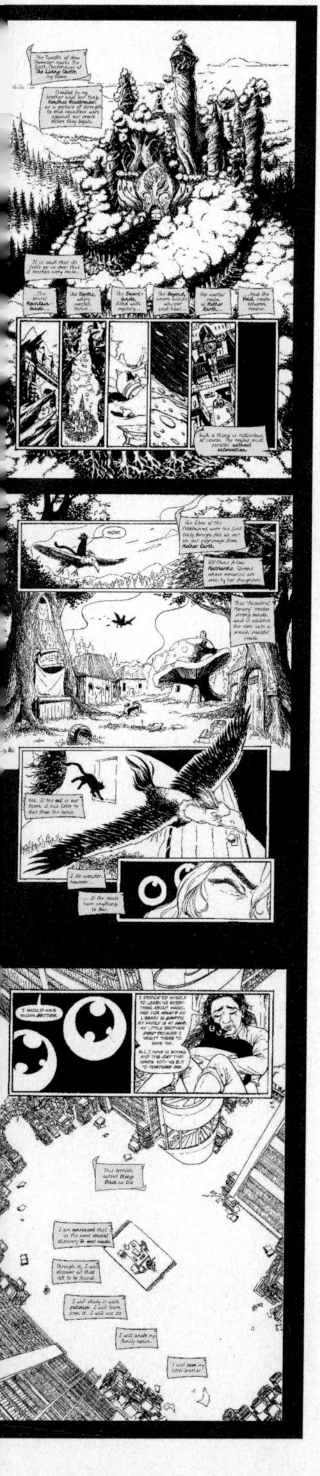

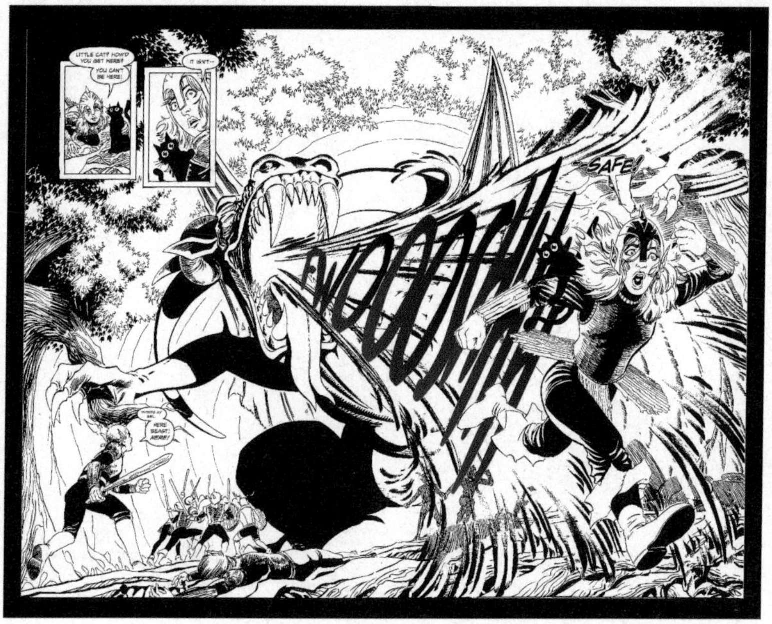
LITTLE CAT? HOW'D YOU GET HERE?
YOU CAN'T BE HERE!
IT ISN'T--
--SAFE!
HERE BEAST! HERE!

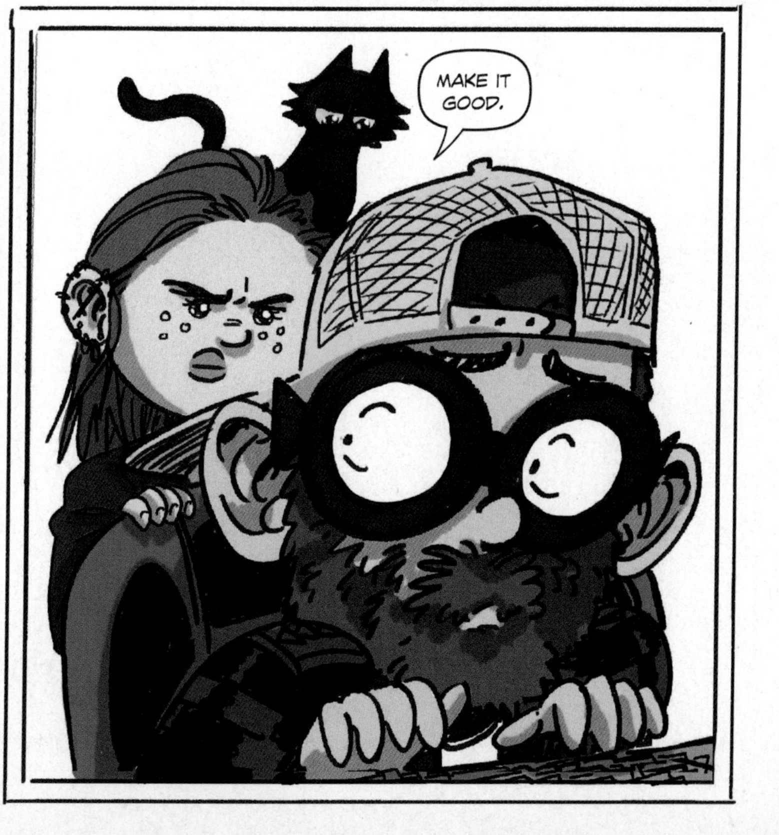
MAKE IT GOOD.

COLORS

The final step happens at the same time as the previous step, as Rusty can just ad in a replaced, colored file with the one he lettered over. Emma keeps the colors simple. Light and shade. Mood. Consistency. She also seizes this opportunity to revert Rusty's zealous over-corrections of her pencils.

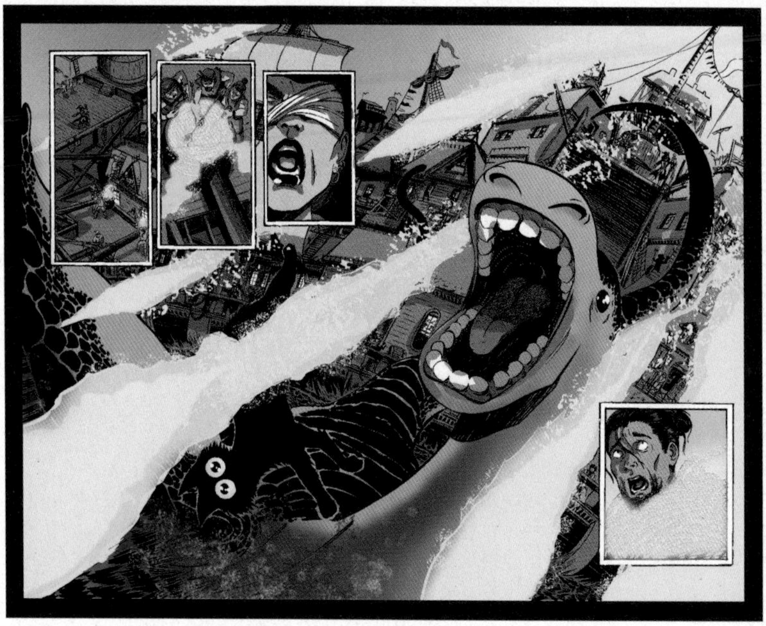

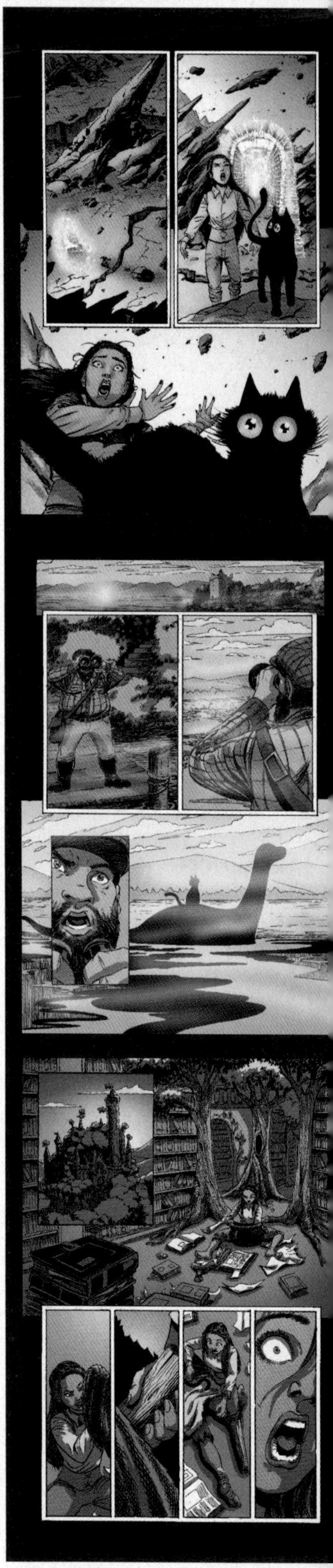

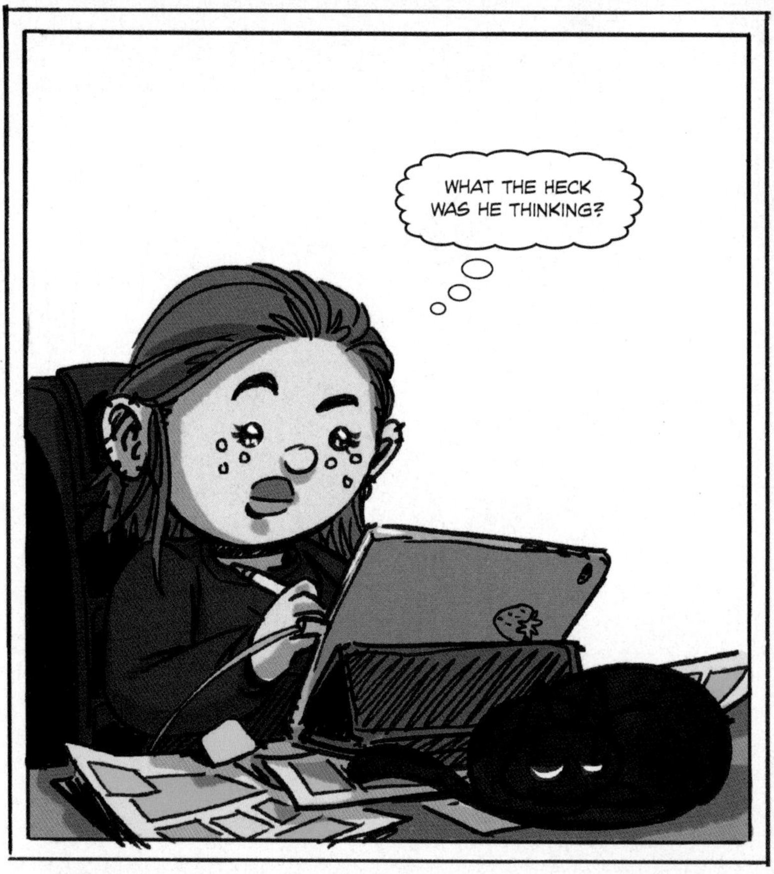
WHAT THE HECK WAS HE THINKING?

THE RESULT

The result is a whirlwind of creative dichotomy that comes to compromise on the pages of *Inkblot.* Each step along the way of creating a new issue, a story is handed back and forth and embellished by each creator. Emma can't expect what the characters will say any more than Rusty can predict what the first pages of pencils will look like. In working this way, the ideas are kept fresh, the story interesting, and the craft very, very special.

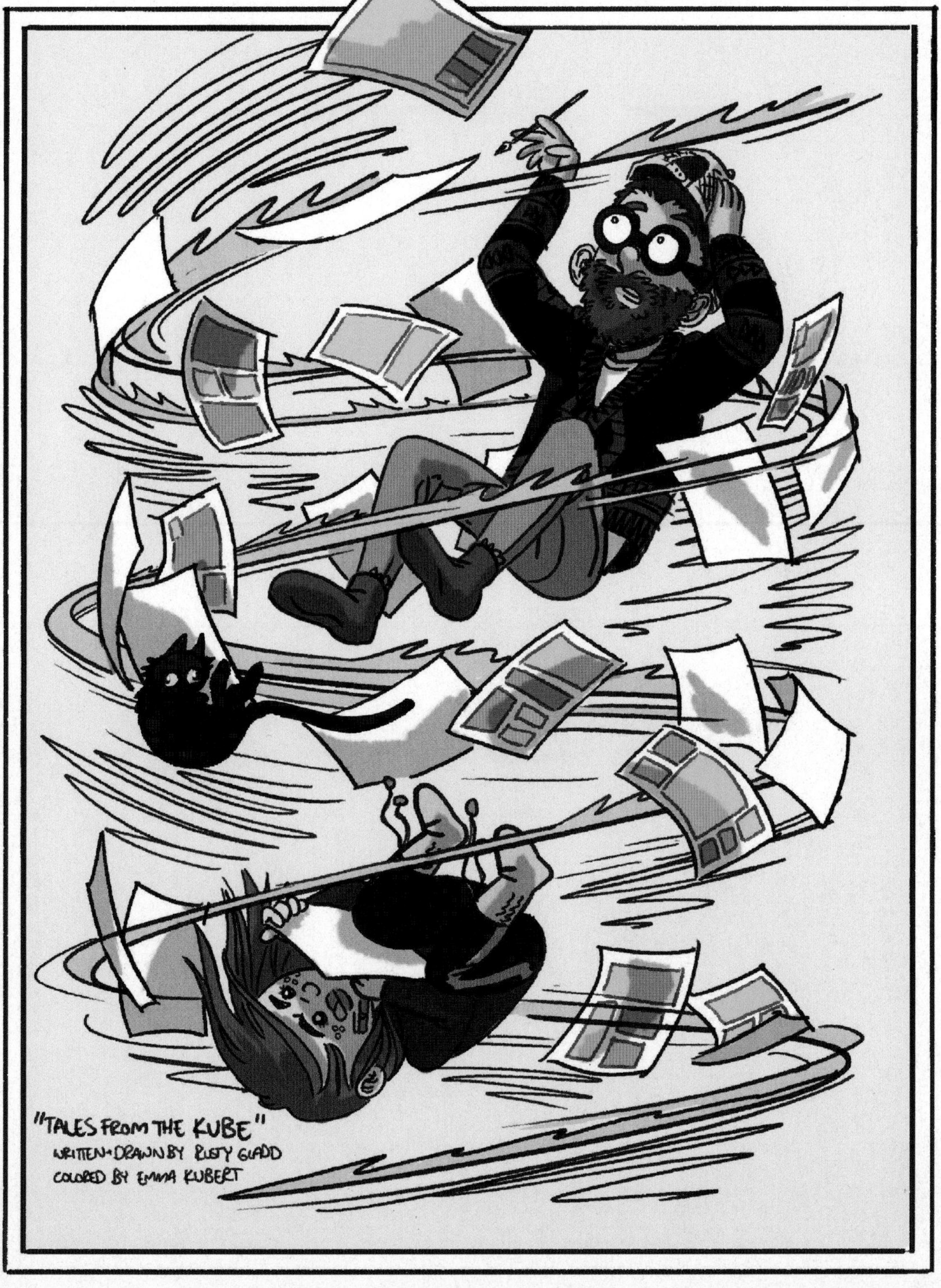
"TALES FROM THE KUBE"
WRITTEN+DRAWN BY RUSTY GLADD
COLORED BY EMMA KUBERT

IMAGE COMICS, INC.

Todd McFarlane – President
Jim Valentino – Vice President
Marc Silvestri – Chief Executive Officer
Erik Larsen – Chief Financial Officer
Robert Kirkman – Chief Operating Officer

Eric Stephenson – Publisher / Chief Creative Officer
Nicole Lapalme – Controller
Leanna Caunter – Accounting Analyst
Sue Korpela – Accounting & HR Manager
Marla Eizik – Talent Liaison
Jeff Boison – Director of Sales & Publishing Planning
Dirk Wood – Director of International Sales & Licensing
Alex Cox – Director of Direct Market Sales
Chloe Ramos – Book Market & Library Sales Manager
Emilio Bautista – Digital Sales Coordinator
Jon Schlaffman – Specialty Sales Coordinator
Kat Salazar – Director of PR & Marketing
Drew Fitzgerald – Marketing Content Associate
Heather Doornink – Production Director
Drew Gill – Art Director
Hilary DiLoreto – Print Manager
Tricia Ramos – Traffic Manager
Melissa Gifford – Content Manager
Erika Schnatz – Senior Production Artist
Ryan Brewer – Production Artist
Deanna Phelps – Production Artist
IMAGECOMICS.COM